P9-DII-811

The Gimmicks

Also by Chris McCormick

Desert Boys

The Gimmicks

A Novel

Chris McCormick

HARPER
An Imprint of HarperCollins*Publishers*

This is a work of fiction. Names, characters, places, and incidents are products of the author's imagination or are used fictitiously and are not to be construed as real. Any resemblance to actual events, locales, organizations, or persons, living or dead, is entirely coincidental.

HarperCollins books may be purchased for educational, business, or sales promotional use. For information, please email the Special Markets Department at SPsales@harpercollins.com.

FIRST EDITION

Library of Congress Cataloging-in-Publication Data
has been applied for.

ISBN 978-0-06-290856-8

20 21 22 23 24 LSC 10 9 8 7 6 5 4 3 2 1

for Mairead

It takes a lot of rehearsing for a man to get to be himself.

—WILLIAM SAROYAN

A Voice from Parts Unknown

You can't explain pain, you can only feel it—a lesson I learned from the great Irishman Dave Finlay, who, after slamming opponents with his patented Celtic Cross, strolled the anonymous cities of the world in search of a peaceful pub. Most nights, though, no peace could be found. Some big-bellied dope or another would lumber toward him, barking insults about professional wrestling. The sport was a homosexual fantasy, they claimed, or a joke, or—most commonly—the sport was fake. That word alone would stir Finlay from his barstool. He'd grab the insulter's thumb and say, *Listen. You prove to your friends that I'm hurting you. I'll just put a bit of pressure on your thumb. You prove to your friends that I'm hurting you.* And he'd press the thumb back, stretching it far enough so that the thumb flopped pink as a tongue, and the thumb's owner would mewl and beg to be released. But Finlay would hold on, and he'd start to whistle the happiest little song. Onlookers gathered and filled the bar with uncomfortable laughter. Even the crying man's friends were confused by the collision of pain and good fun, and they surrendered in their confusion to disbelief, suspecting the entire ordeal to be pre-orchestrated. A gag. Fake. Only then would Finlay stop whistling and snap the man's thumb—quick as a pulled tooth. And every time, in pubs from Cologne to Osaka, from Kansas City to Perth, the man who'd called wrestling fake would try to stuff his broken hand into his pocket. Maybe that'll be Mr. Finlay's greatest legacy: hundreds of dislocated thumbs slumped over denim, spindly bits of proof that his profession was legitimate, that he was nobody's fool, that his life and his pain were real.

One

1

Kirovakan, Soviet Armenia, 1973

A greasy lane of mud cut into the hills, splitting the pasture in two. The livestock, off to find dry bedding, had left the brothers entirely to themselves. Halfway to the village above the city, boots all sludge and muck, one of the brothers stopped to swallow a gulp of rain, letting the other catch up. One big, one small—it was impossible in the heavy staves of weather to say which brother was which. They were cousins of cousins, really, not brothers at all, but they were seventeen years old and the distinction seemed theirs to make. It was as if, in the two years since the big one had arrived to join the smaller one, they had spent all their multivariate powers soldering together their separate histories. Saying brother this, brother that. Making it so.

In the village, an old woman shouted and waved them over. Even in the rain the brothers could see it was Siranoush, on account of her being the only redhead they'd ever known. When they joined her underneath her scrap-metal awning, one of the brothers said, "How is he?"

"He's still talking," she said, meaning her husband, Yergat. The old man was eighty-eight and planted beside her under the awning in an armchair with worn brass buttons at the thumbs.

One of the brothers—the big one—had dragged the armchair out of the house three days earlier, and since then, Siranoush had draped a scratchy-looking wool blanket over her husband's legs and an ashy coat over his shoulders. One by one the brothers bent to kiss his cheeks. Yergat, ignoring them, started in on a story from his younger life, another story about the genocide. The *jart*, he called it.

The shattering. Almost sixty years had passed, and Siranoush had heard these stories a thousand times, but she'd recently stopped telling him to shut up. He'd started telling the stories differently, she thought, more completely, because he was dying and, in his dying, remembered nothing so clearly as the time he'd bested death.

Above them, the rain beat against the makeshift awning. Springtime in Kirovakan was loud with those beatings. The entire season was spent leaning in close to hear what the person nearest to you was saying. More preferable to the brothers was the winter, when the snow fell so silent and heavy you could almost climb the sky, when Party officials operated a ski resort nearby and the villagers gathered a dozen to a blanket to watch the distant adventurers pulleyed to the mountaintops like angels. Winter—when a group of Russian or Georgian skiers would file into the village after a day on the slopes and let the local children take turns sitting on the fronts of their skis. Now, though, it was spring, and the hills had turned green as a graveyard. Tall grass swelled where the skiers once fell. Webbed, hairlike moss rimmed the northern faces of outhouses and stumps. Long rows of mold blossomed in the mortar between the bricks of chimney stacks and henhouses, and little islands of algae frothed at the surface of puddles. Rain, every day. Springtime in Kirovakan.

"The smell," Yergat was saying, and the brothers leaned in to hear him. He wanted to die outdoors, he said, with his nose full of the smell of rain. He wanted to live his last days in a place where he could tell the stories of his life, where passersby could catch bits of him like seeds in the wind.

"Now he's a poet," muttered his wife.

Over her husband she swayed, impatient as a flame. She looked like one, too. Orange hair and freckles—no one could believe she was a real Armenian. She'd once been a typical Armenian girl, went the story, hair as black as birds' eyes, skin as plain as cream. Then one day in her youth, after her father—a mean man, a tyrant—cursed her for some petty crime and wished aloud that she'd never been born, little Siranoush disappeared. Three days she was gone, and even she couldn't tell you exactly where she'd been. She could, however, remember who she was with. Angels, she maintained, who stole her in the night to punish her ungrateful father. The angels were teenagers, disappointed by the adults of the human race. Petty and vengeful. Who could blame them? Still, even her most faithful listeners had to admit the story was somewhat fishy. Impossible to prove. But the only person whose opinion mattered had already believed Siranoush, and that was her father. When she returned after three days, he cried and cried and held her and studied her. She told him the story and he believed her. She was the same girl she'd always been, but different. Freckled and red and irreversibly missed. From then on, her father worked hard to love her better.

Enough. She'd leave the past to her husband, who was relishing his new role as the village historian. Everyone should hear, at least once, an old Armenian man lecture in his language. Operatic and stoic all at once—less a man talking than a vessel, delivering.

"First," Yergat told the brothers, "the Turks came for the guns." Back then he'd been living with his first family—a wife and a little daughter—in a village near Van. It was 1915, when Yergat was thirty years old. That's when the Turks came, he said, and why, at first. For the guns.

The brothers—one big, one small, both the age of disappointed angels—leaned forward to hear him. Like all Armenians, they knew the genocide backward and forward. They felt that their own lives were only tendrils climbing the gate of it. Each unearthed memory from a survivor was a new bar in that gate.

Yergat said he'd never owned a gun. Only cowards needed weapons, he thought, so while the other men in his old village hurried to deliver their weapons by the imposed deadline, Yergat—nothing to turn in, nothing to be confiscated—had stayed at home, smug, drinking coffee. He even asked his daughter, who was only ten years old, to pour his customary splash of cognac.

The Turks, however, hadn't believed him. They said they knew the truth, that Yergat had hidden a gun somewhere in the village and was refusing to turn it in. A gun he meant to use against them in the future. The Turks suspected Yergat to be one of those treacherous Armenians who preferred the Russians to the Ottomans. Yergat laughed. "I said, Fuck the Russians, and fuck you, too." The Turks, however, did not laugh. They waited until the middle of the night, when the whole village was asleep, and knocked down his front door.

Now Yergat was using a Turkish word that broke through their language like three gunshots: *falaka*. Foot-whipping. The Turks arrested Yergat and then tortured him that way, threatening his wife and daughter until he admitted that he had, in fact, stowed a gun someplace in the village. Under torture, Yergat promised to return the hidden gun—which he knew did not exist—to the authorities by noon the next day. He invented a gun to save his life. Temporarily satisfied, the Turks allowed him to return home. He crawled across the entire village. When he finally arrived, he was so tattered that his wife and daughter had to lift him to the armchair. "Just like this one," he said now, to the brothers. He propped up his feet on an imaginary cushion. "Just like this." He'd begged his wife for a mirror. The bottoms of his feet, she told him, looked like the feet of dogs—"Pouches, here and there, of padding, black with blood and blisters."

Instinct sent both sets of the brothers' eyes to check the bottoms of Yergat's shoes. As if almost sixty years and a pair of loafers hadn't obscured the old man's wounds. In Kirovakan there was a rumor that Yergat used to have a beautiful singing voice. He used to sing while Siranoush played the duduk, that ancient double-reed instrument. Now that he was dying, the only song Yergat wanted to share was the endlessly harrowing song of deportations, of forced marches through the Syrian desert, of rapes and tortures and beheadings, the discordant anthem of drowned and bloated bodies skimming along the Euphrates like flowers, like trash, like—depending on how much Yergat had had to drink—the wretched souls beneath the boat of Charon, wailing in the River Styx. These last few weeks of his life, the notes could change, but the song never did. Mothers around the village were hoping—and it was a sin, they knew—that the old man would give up the ghost sooner rather than later.

"The hidden gun was fiction," he told the boys. "The wounds on my feet had immobilized me, but I'd promised to return that fictional gun by noon. I needed a real gun to turn in. So at dawn I sent my daughter to purchase one. If God loved me, I would've had a son to send on that errand. My wife was packing our belongings, hiding our silver. Meaningless, I know now. I instructed my daughter to go to an old Turkish friend who lived in the next village. He would help us. I put money in her hands, and off she went. I imagine she held the coins so firmly that their imprint was on her skin the day she died. For many years, I dreamed of checking the palms of little corpses, hoping to find her by the marks in her hands."

A chicken wandered under the awning. Earlier that day, Siranoush had picked up another chicken by the neck and twisted it like a wet rag until the head lolled. She'd plucked it and then cooked it while Yergat made himself comfortable on the armchair. Now she disappeared inside the house and returned with a broiled chicken leg for her husband. His favorite. He chewed what little meat there was, and then savored the bone. He jostled the thing with his tongue against his cheek, making a broth in his mouth.

Siranoush asked if the boys were hungry.

"Tell the brothers about my teeth," Yergat said. "Age eighty-eight. Never a cavity, never so much as a toothache. Perfect, perfect teeth."

The smaller brother cleaned his glasses on his shirt and asked Siranoush, "What do his teeth have to do with the Turks?"

"I'm sure he'll explain," Siranoush said with a shrug. "He doesn't tell stories, he explains them."

"Armenian stories require explaining," Yergat said, chicken bone tucked into his cheek.

"Even to other Armenians?"

"These boys aren't Armenians, they're Soviets."

"We're Armenian first," said the smaller brother, the one in glasses.

"Maybe," Yergat said, taking the chicken bone out of his mouth and then waving it like a conductor's baton. "Maybe not. Either way, here's a lesson for you: Don't throw out your bones. Eat them! Chicken, pork, beef—every stew my mother made, I begged her to toss me the bones. I ate more bones as a child than a cemetery. I taught my daughter to do the same. When the Turks imprisoned me, when they forced her and her mother on that death march into the desert, the only food my girl had to eat must have been the bones of dead animals. Maybe a grain or two from horse dung, I've heard, if she was lucky. But I hope I trained her teeth to be strong. Other children probably starved immediately, but because I had already trained her teeth, she probably gobbled those desert bones like a princess at a feast. Dogs, vultures, rodents—my daughter probably gnawed each bone to dough."

"If I can ask," the larger brother said, "do you know what happened to her? Your daughter."

Yergat didn't know. If she survived, she might have converted to Islam, might believe herself to be a Turk. Who knows? He could only guess the most likely story.

"What was her name?"

The old man breathed loudly through his nose, bringing the rain closer. Finally, he shook his head and said, "I don't remember." Then he sucked the bone dry.

"And you survived how?" the smaller brother said. "I thought the Turks wiped men your age out of the picture."

Siranoush swung an open palm at him, barely missing. She said it was time for her husband to nap. "We'll save the rest for tomorrow."

Did she know her husband wouldn't live that long? Maybe. She ended his story anyway. He was tired, and she knew better than he did. They'd met in a refugee camp in 1917. She'd wound her red hair in a head scarf to avoid strange looks, and he'd covered his head, too, had dressed like a woman to save himself. Shameful, he knew, but she didn't see it that way. It was his life. She knew it and no one else did. Now that he was dying, he was telling everyone everything. She wouldn't allow him to arrive again at that shame. Plus, he was tired. She knew better than he did. See? Already he was beginning to snore, the chicken bone dangling in his fingers just above a puddle. Nearby, a stray and patient dog paid close attention, licking his chops.

The smaller brother sulked. He wanted to hear how Yergat had escaped the Turks.

Siranoush whispered, "Tomorrow he'll tell you." And then, as a penance, she offered something better than history. She would tell the brothers—cousins of cousins, really—a story about the future. "Let him sleep," she said. "I'll be right back." Then she disappeared again into the house and returned with a bowl of milk. She peered longingly into the bowl. She crossed herself. She blew little ripples onto the milk's marble surface.

"I see a couple things—I'm very good at this, one of the best still doing it, it's a dying skill, shame. First I see that you both will love the same woman—good luck to her!—but when I picture who she'll love in return, I see only one of your names. Ofe, that sounds messy—glad I won't be around to see that! What else. Ah, this one's big. I see that only one of you—only one!—is a real Armenian. The other will prove to be a phony."

"Says the woman with red hair," snapped the smaller brother.

The old woman laughed. She set down the bowl for the cats who'd come sniffing. Feeling bad for that old patient dog in the rain, Siranoush plucked the chicken bone from her snoozing husband's hand and tossed it in the mutt's direction. The dog caught it in the air and seemed to do a slight curtsy before trotting off to enjoy the one thing he'd been waiting for all this time.

The brothers studied each other. They were the same as they'd always been, but different, as if they'd been stolen and replaced, as if the milk and the bone had been wrenched from inside their own bodies. On the walk back to the city, the larger one joked about how the angels should have dumped the old red lady off in Ireland or

America, where she might have fit in better. But as they approached the city square in Kirovakan, the smaller one took off his glasses, cleaned them with the hem of his shirt, and said, "I wouldn't have let them arrest *me*, I wouldn't have let them whip *my* feet, I wouldn't have let them take *my* daughter." When he put the glasses back on, his eyes turned enormous behind the lenses. A stray eyelash languished beside his nose. His brother, the larger one, noticed. He reached out to swipe it away.

2

King County, Washington, 1989

It's a marvel how memory works on the road, how it holds its shape like smoke in the cold. I bet there are people in the world who appreciate that, who find the power of a long drive to undo the process of forgetting a divine gift. But most of my best forgetting is done on purpose, after many years of dedicated work, so as far as I'm concerned, the power of the road is a danger. A threat. That's why I retired all those years ago, I think, and why I'm dreading so gravely the trip I'm embarking on now.

Clearly, the journey was not my idea. After a lifetime on the road for the wrestling business, driving across the country from territory to territory, I've chosen to lead a steady life with my cats out where my brother and I grew up, just on the verge of Seattle. Aside from a meet-and-greet convention here and there, when old-timers from the territory days—Buddy Rose and Dutch Savage and all us lesser gods—are corralled into high school gymnasiums for fifteen dollars a photograph, or aside from a biennial phone call from folks I used to manage or manage against—Mickey "Makeshift" Starr, for instance, or the vulgarian Johnny Trumpet—my life in wrestling hardly ever enters my mind. Those years feel waxen to me, that part of my history, decades and decades of a life

I hardly recognize as my own. Waxen and contained, road stories told so many times they might as well be myths.

No, nowadays for me it's the cats. Breeding, selling. Just the other day, I sold a litter of golden-eyed Persian mixes—Maine coon blood for the size and fur, Siamese for the flatter nose and the temperament—and made more money than I used to make in six weeks on the road. I'm never lonely, not even out on the coast, near the docks where my little brother shipped off to Korea a lifetime ago. Between my cats and my customers, between the barn house and the ocean, that purple skim over the world, I'm happy. That's rare, you know, after all those years in a business like the one I survived, to be living a happy old life.

So this trip I'm taking isn't an attempt to relive my glory days in wrestling. And I'm not trying to exploit any of the wrestlers I outlasted, either, the ones who strangled their pain with drinks or drugs or worse. Those terrors might be real, but sometimes a real story wears so thin it no longer rings true. Besides, I couldn't explain all that dying and killing, when all we were taught to do was to protect ourselves, to protect one another, and to protect the business.

No, this trip didn't begin with wrestling. And it didn't begin with a breed of cats. This trip began with something I never knew much about at all. It began with a woman.

She called last December—on Christmas Day 1988, in fact—and I only mention the date because I'd gone out, as I usually do on the holidays, to the docks, where a bright white cruise ship had taken the place of the USS *Juneau*. The pier that morning was gray and emptied of folks, and the windblown whitecaps in the glassy water sprouted like threads from worn buttonholes. Nearly frozen but lifted, I returned to the barn house, where I was surprised to find the answering machine flashing its auburn light. It was peculiar to receive a business message on a holiday, but just as strange was the voice belonging to the woman on the tape. She spoke with an accent I couldn't immediately place, and I pegged her for an Arab, or an Israeli, or—as soon as I heard the name of the breed she was calling for—a Persian. Her little daughter, she explained, badly wanted a pet but suffered from severe allergies. Through the testimony of some previous customer, she'd discovered that Angel Hair Kittens—even my longhairs—were bred hypoallergenic, and she was interested in making a visit. She lived all the way down in Los Angeles but was willing to travel up the coast. She left a return number, a home address—700 Orange Grove Avenue, as if I were supposed to respond by mail—and her name, which was Mina.

At the docks that morning, I'd been entirely alone except for Gil, the one I'd gone out there to remember, and a Salvation Army Santa Claus who, upon seeing another soul for the first time since daybreak, slung his hands out of his coat pockets and started rattling his bell. I put all the money I had into that bucket of his. It wasn't much, but the man said, "God bless." I'm not a believer myself, but the truth is I did feel, for a moment, anyway, as I sometimes do whenever kindness springs a bridge between two strangers, a little bit holy.

So maybe I was after that feeling again when I picked up the phone to return Mina's call. When she answered, I could hear a celebration in the background, laughter and other mysterious music. She said, "When are you letting me to come see the cats?" I told her I appreciated her business, but that if she was looking for a last-minute gift, I could refer her to the names of some fellow breeders located nearer to her, in Los Angeles. Seattle, I explained, was a long way off.

She made a spiteful sound with her teeth that made me feel stupid for explaining the size of America. She said, "I am coming in three days, you will be there?" And what could I say except "Sorry, thank you, yes ma'am, travel safe."

When the lime-green taxi stalled on the muddy path up to the barn house three days later, I slushed out to the car with an umbrella to welcome her. Despite almost reinjuring my neck cleaning the place before her arrival, I hadn't anticipated the rain unearthing so much of what the cats had buried. I knew as soon as I saw her pretending not to notice, pretending not to be pinching her nostrils but only scratching them instead, that she hadn't really come for a pet. Still, I went on talking about the specific kitten I'd set aside for her, a nameless black American Curl. "And look," I said once we got to the stables, plopping the kitten into her open palms like soup into a bowl, "she's even got some of your features." I meant that the kitten's fluffed ears reminded me of the woman's hair, which was dark and teased to enormity in a way I remembered being stylish some years earlier. Instead of being flattered, she let the kitten down and said, "Are you drinking coffee?"

Sometimes her English had english on it, and it spun out in strange directions before I could pocket the message. In this case, she meant to ask if I generally enjoyed coffee and if I'd like some now. In other words, she wanted to leave the stables. I said right this way, and before she followed me into the kitchen, she walked down to the cabdriver and tipped him for his patience.

While the coffee brewed, the charade went on a while longer in the living room. Mina asked vague questions about the American Curl's feeding habits, potential size, and temperament, and I went on and on, offering answers and the occasional suggestion for a name. "The right name's vital," I said. "The right name allows a personality to vessel forth."

She'd glided over to the fireplace to look over a forty-year-old picture of my ex-wife and my brother, Gil, arm in arm on the docks. Its frame anchored an old championship belt whose sweat-bloomed leather strap draped from the mantel. Mina touched the leather softly, once and then twice. Then she asked again if the coffee was ready. By the time I came back from the kitchen, my guest had pulled a pillow onto her lap to keep the cats at bay. Three of them peered judgmentally from the armrest. I set a mug of Folgers in the center of the table, safe from the cats but slightly out of Mina's reach.

"Nice of you to be getting a kitten for your kid," I said, "when you so clearly don't like cats."

"I used to love them," she said. "But—Mr. Krill, I'm having to tell the truth now."

"The truth?" I said. I could feel the rust flaking away from my acting chops.

"I'm not coming here for the cat."

"Now, hold on a minute," I said. I stood. I put my hands on my hips for the back rows to see. "Then how come you've been asking all those questions about the American Curl?"

"You are Terry Krill, yes? Angel Hair?"

Here she reached into her coat pocket and unfolded a large flyer in black and white, staple holes in the corners like rips in the fabric of time. I took it from her and examined my waxen life. The flyer promoted a card at the Grand Olympic Auditorium in downtown Los Angeles in 1979, main-evented by Rowdy Roddy Piper and Playboy Buddy Rose. Underneath their enormous names and faces, in smaller print and unphotographed, were the midcard matches between guys like Thunderbolt Patterson and the Mongolian Stomper. And even farther down, in a typeface so miniature I had to hold the page up to the light to read it, I found: THE BROW BEATER, accompanied to the ring by his manager, TERRY "ANGEL HAIR" KRILL.

At that point, I straightened my ponytail like the cats with their tails and considered, for the first time in many years, rebleaching my hair. "What do you think," I said. "I still fit the bill?"

A long time had passed since a fan had come searching for me. This woman didn't come off as your typical mark—she wasn't wearing a T-shirt with a catchphrase of mine, for instance—but nonetheless I was enlivened by her recognition of me, and was just on the verge of retrieving a quality pen so I could sign her old poster, when she disrupted my delusion.

"The Brow Beater," she said. For the first time, I noticed her wedding band. "You were being his manager, yes? What was his name? His real name."

In many ways, I'm not so old-school anymore, but one tradition I try my best to keep is my allegiance to kayfabe, the illusion of pro wrestling's reality. Nowadays, guys expose the business all the time, but too many of my brothers killed themselves protecting it for me to go around revealing industry secrets to every housewife-turned-detective in America. I said, "Brow Beater was who he was, in and out of the ring, ugly and mean, the baddest foreign monster I ever had the privilege to manage."

Her mug of coffee, untouched, still waited on the table out of reach.

"I keep milk around for the cats," I said after a minute, "if that's too dark for your liking."

"No," she said, taking back and folding the poster into her coat pocket. "Actually, it's the opposite. In my culture, we're making the coffee in small, strong amount. Dark. Thick."

I want to say that was when I placed her accent, but that's not true. I'd known as soon as she asked about The Brow Beater. But now I knew for certain where she was coming from. More important, she knew I knew what she was really after. I said, "You'd better go tip that cabdriver again."

She did. And when she returned, she took off her coat for the first time since arriving and said, "He moved to my town as a boy. We were growing up together."

We were growing up together, too, I wanted to say, but I was afraid she'd mistake me for making fun of her English. It was the precise truth, though: we really *were* growing up together, Brow and I, even though he was younger than half my age when I knew him. I was one man when I discovered him and another when he left me. In that way, we'd been growing up together.

"You were in—the USSR?" I said, trying to remember.

"Yes," she said. "Armenia."

At the corner of the couch, Fuji, my oldest cat, had taken the little black-haired American Curl into his paws and was licking clean the kitten's ears. Seeing this, Mina smiled. She was wearing a turtleneck sweater and kept tugging at the collar, pulling it up to her bottom lip. I figured she was the same age as The Brow Beater, which would've made her thirty-two. She had a bright, striking face—all nose, like a Hershey's Kiss—and big, heavily lashed eyes. I might've fallen for her, too, if I'd been a young Soviet and not an old American carnie. "You still in touch with him?" I asked, as casually as I could.

"I'm not speaking to him since 1983," she said. "I'm hoping, actually, you are the one knowing where he is."

But the truth was she'd been in contact with The Brow Beater more recently than I had. I told her so, that in 1980, after we'd spent two years on the road together, in a town just outside Greensboro, North Carolina, he up and disappeared. I didn't tell her the full story. I've never told anyone the full story.

Mina looked around the living room. Several towers of carpeted cat trees lined the eastern wall, and between them, oak shelves bowed with the weight of several dozens of my brother's old records. Their spines were cracked and colorful and thin. I finally took a seat on the other end of the couch.

"No wife?" Mina asked. "Children?"

"I was married once. But it was unconventional, let's say."

"Because always you're traveling?"

"That and—well, the business we were in, it's a tough business."

"He was telling me he was coming back to work with you. That's why I'm coming here. I'm thinking he's here, maybe, with you."

"He said that? In '83? Coming back here? For me?"

"He was saying a few possible places."

"Oh," I said. "Well, he clearly didn't mean it. Look, you should take him—the kitten, I mean."

"Were you knowing also a man named Ruben?"

I'd honestly never heard the name. "Who?"

"Ruben. He was the other one of us. Three of us, growing up together in Armenia."

"Look, I'm sorry the kitten's all I can give you. I told you not to make such a long trip for a cat, but it's all I've got, I'm afraid."

I'd placed the coffee out of her reach, but she'd reached it. I'd thought I was sitting out of her reach, but now she reached me, a hand on mine.

"I'm knowing him his whole life," she said, "except two parts: his time in America with you, and where he is now. I'm thinking if I learn the first part, I learn the second. Like you are one half, I am one half, and together we are finding him."

I left the couch and got as far from her as I could without leaving the room, off near the fireplace. I said, "All that time on the road kind of bleeds together. I don't remember anything that'd be useful to you. I just wouldn't be able to tell you what you need to hear."

Finally, she wrapped herself back into her coat and, coming to say goodbye, threw out a hand for a shake. She pumped my hand twice and then bent to pick up the American Curl. "Okay," she said. "What name am I giving him?"

I could tell she'd imagined all the possible outcomes of our old friend's whereabouts. Lost by design, his or someone else's. I said, "Give that kitten a strong name. Something real." And then I spoke it out loud, the name I hadn't said in almost a decade. The name behind The Brow Beater, the man behind the gimmick. "Call the kitten Avo," I said. "As in *Bravo*."

I'd thought it might be a moment of profound connection, as if speaking the man's name would lace this strange woman and me together in some final and intricate way. But Mina only tilted her head and narrowed her eyes. She said, "You're wanting that I give Avo's name to a cat?"

Soon I was left to do my work, profound or not. But in the months following her visit, Angel Hair Kittens came under a fresh and ugly scrutiny from the local chapter of the National Audubon Society, concerned—so they said—for the safety of migratory birds. I spent the better part of the first quarter of the new year constructing measures to ensure the health and happiness of both the cedar waxwing *and* Angel Hair Kittens, LLC. It was all very tedious and personality-blunting work, and whenever my mind drifted to the conversation Mina had traveled so far to begin, I blamed the monotony of installing plate-glass walls on either side of the chain-link fences in the stables, or else stitching miniature bells into every collar on the premises. Of course, every solution led to a new problem. Suddenly, the plate-glass wall—which successfully stopped the cats from scaling into the woods—became itself a culprit, smashing unsuspecting warblers in midflight. I should've learned by then what is always the case with self-righteous people: every measure I took to appease them became a piece of evidence that they'd been right in the first place (why else would I agree to appease them?), and as they drifted deeper into the sea of their own indignation, every sincere effort I made to build a raft of compromise seemed increasingly futile, and my frustrations turned to bitterness, and I sat cross-legged and mean on the shores of my own resentment. I tried to explain myself, but I could only come up with the sea metaphor, which many people said felt forced.

One day in May, I was called into town over a petition of three hundred names, many of which I recognized and, to my surprise, hurt me to see listed. The paperwork aimed to limit the number of cats I could keep. In order to show how unprofessional such a low number would appear to my clients, I showed up to my city council hearing with the allotted twenty-two cats in tow, packed in my camper-covered truck. Admittedly, it was a confusing publicity stunt that ended with not only a failed appeal against the petition but also a citation from the regional branch of the Humane Society, not to mention an expensive detailing of my Ford Ranger.

All of which is to say, during the summer after Mina's visit, I found myself in need of money.

At those wrestling conventions I used to go to, behind the booths where we splayed out collectibles like the scavenged debris from a catastrophe, I was almost always approached by this one well-meaning and well-traveling mark. He was middle-aged and soft, gluttonous for nostalgia, and he enjoyed telling me his opinion that, during the height of my mouthpiece work for Mickey "Makeshift" Starr's two IC runs in the mid-'70s and then again in the early 1980s, there was no manager more scandalously underappreciated in the history of the sport than me. The first time he said it, I was profoundly moved and grateful, going so far as to climb out from behind my booth to give the mark a hug. I'd harbored the idea of my unappreciated greatness myself, secretly, and to hear an outsider give voice to a belief I'd dreaded was unfounded not only shined my ego but seemed—momentarily, anyway—to release me entirely from fear. Maybe I'd expressed my gratitude in too strong a language because, from then on, every few months when I participated in those meet-and-greets, the same mark would find me, pin me behind the evidence of my bygone life, and recite to me the exact same speech. Needless to say, the more often he duplicated his compliment, the more threadbare I found the texture of his respect, and his looming, certain presence at almost any event within a hundred-mile radius played an overwhelming part in my decision, a year or so prior to Mina's visit, to stop attending those conferences once and for all.

This past summer, however, after practically liquidating Angel Hair Kittens, I called an old contact and arranged to sell photographs and signatures in an overheated community center in downtown Kent. Of course I expected to see the mark in question, and so when he lumbered toward my booth, starting in on his practiced remarks before he'd even reached handshake distance, I changed the topic immediately. "Forget Mickey Starr," I said. "Do you remember the guy I managed *between* my two stints with Makeshift? From 1978 to 1980?"

Under one arm, the mark was carrying a small stack of signed photographs he'd purchased before finding his way to my corner of the room. He nearly dropped the stack several times, moving them from one armpit to the other, as he searched his memory. He said, "You'da been managing a few of the boys, yeah?"

"No," I said. "Just the one."

"Huh," the mark said. "Couldn'ta been a Don Owen guy. Musta been someone you corralled outside the territory."

"Met in Los Angeles, matter of fact."

"No hints, no hints. Wasn't a tag team, was it? Wasn't, maybe, Psyche and Fathom?"

"Look," I said, "there's no shame in not remembering," though of course that was a lie. What greater shame was there in the world?

"Los Angeles, huh? Musta been Chavo, or Tolos, or, hell, I wouldn't be struggling if the guy'da been a star like that, I suppose. Go on and tell me," he said. "It'll drive me crazy now if I don't hear you say the guy's name."

That was when I agreed to relieve his pain if he bought one hundred dollars' worth of merchandise.

"The Brow Beater," I said, counting the money and then studying the mark's eyes for what wasn't there, the shine of recognition. I tried all the gimmicks Avo Gregoryan ever wrestled under, but the mark didn't know those, either. He didn't know The Ugliest of God's Creations, or The Biggest of God's Creations, or The Meanest of God's Creations. He didn't know The Unique Unibrow, or The Brow Bruiser, or, simply, The Brow. He didn't know Harry Knuckles, Harry Krishna, or Hairy Harry, and he didn't know The Shah, The Ra, or The Beast from the Middle East. He didn't know Gregor the Ogre, Killer Kebob, or Bravo Avo. He didn't even blink at King Kong of the Caucasus. He didn't remember Avo at all.

"What happened to him?" the mark finally asked.

"No one knows," I said. "We were just about to make real money, and he—poof, straightaway—disappeared."

And so it was in this state of mind—beleaguered and involuntarily reflective—that I received, just last weekend, a phone call from my old associate, the vulgarian Johnny Trumpet, asking me to go back on the road.

"I hear you've been poking around about the old days," he said, "and it got me reminiscing, too, especially about that favor I never called in."

If he'd phoned at any other time in my life, I would've hung up and ignored him forever. I said, "What do you want from me, Trumpet?"

"Your cheeriness continues to dazzle. You do know that the business is booming, right? Hogan and Warrior up in New York, trickling down the golden age of our sport? Even the yokels I'm working for—who sing fuckin' homilies about the territory days—even they have to admit the new monopoly's been good for wrestling. What I'm saying is I'm calling in a favor that's actually going to end up costing me money. I'm calling in a favor that'll actually get you paid, you understand, because I know you, I trust you, I don't want to rub your dick under a bridge or anything, but I like you, and I'm financially unwise and exceedingly generous, and besides, I'm willing to buy anecdotes like these to be used by my future biographers, all right?"

"Get on with the favor itself," I said.

"So I've got a bunch of tongue-tied motherfuckers down here in the California desert who could use you as a mouthpiece. I thought California would be smarter than Kentucky, but I find myself in confederado territory, all cowboys and Indians, both of which have to formulate and remember what the English fuckin' language sounds like before saying a goddamn word. You can practically see them diagramming sentences in their heads as they speak. Right now I told 'em all just to grunt—at least that has feeling. I still got athletes to book, though, and if you can get 'em talking all right, they might be able to draw real money. I need you here Thursday."

"This Thursday? You'll send me a plane ticket?"

"That's the favor part of it, motherfucker. The territories are dead. Our travel budget is zero. All our work's done in-studio, straight to VHS. That old Catalina still running?"

"Traded it in for a truck years ago."

"Good, so you'll make it. What I *can* offer is a place to sleep when you get here. I got a bungalow out in the desert with a mustard-colored veranda. Brand-new cedar decking, really a beautiful job."

"Thursday? You know tomorrow morning is Tuesday, yeah? From where I stand, I've got about a twenty-hour drive, no stopping."

"Don't stop, then, and you'll be here a whole day early. Besides, you miss the road, I bet."

"I really don't," I said.

"I'm sure it misses you."

And so here I am, steeling myself against the undoing of all my best forgetting. Tuesday morning, I left about as early as a man my age can leave a place he calls home, just before the light flared up in the east. A hard rain had started in the night, and I swaddled Fuji, the only cat I hadn't sold or given away, out to the Ranger under my coat. The truck rumbled. The wipers waved goodbye to the barn house. We backed up and turned our wheels and drove.

Almost immediately on the slick Washington lanes, I remembered an afternoon downpour in Alabama. The deluge was so biblical we had to pull over to wait it out. This was in 1979, a full decade ago. I was surprised to see The Brow Beater get out of the car, all six feet six of him, bald-headed and unibrowed, wearing nothing but a Gold's Gym tank top and a pair of track shorts that, on him, looked like a napkin auditioning for the role of a tablecloth. I watched from the dry safety of the car as it thundered in Tuskegee. When he crunched back in beside me, drenched, The Brow Beater said the storm reminded him of home, of the green hills of Armenia, where the rain fell so thick it felt feathered.

In the two years I spent with him, that was about as much as he ever said about home. Much more interesting to him was the question of America, of Americans. Again and again I told him he was in luck: there was no better way to get to know his new country than through professional wrestling. People would claim baseball or football, I explained, but *our* sport was the true American pastime.

He winked his Soviet eye and said, "Why, bro? Because it's an elaborate fiction staged as honest competition?"

"Don't be cynical," I said. I put it to him this way: What was the American Dream if not the ability to trade gimmick after gimmick until you got one over? Life as a citizen of this country was an "I Quit" match, I said. The only way to lose was to give up.

He pawed his heart and belted the national anthem.

"Go ahead and laugh," I said, "but I'm going to turn you into a patriot yet, big fella."

The truth was I hadn't talked that way about my country since before my brother had set sail for Korea. But that was one of the effects The Brow Beater had on me. His company somehow got me excavating versions of myself I'd forgotten I once believed in. The question of whether or not he found my refurbished patriotism convincing, I don't know. But he laughed a lot, more and more often the longer we spent on the road, which boded well. Maybe it was different in the Soviet Union, but in America it was easier to believe someone if you found him entertaining. That could be dangerous in the wrong hands, but it's a lesson I've been glad to know. With The Brow Beater, I could tell when he believed me because he had this wheezing glee about him, and sometimes he'd cap my skull with his enormous mitts and befoul my trademark hair. I was his manager, already past fifty, and he was just this big foreign boy, twenty-three, I guess, greener than the hills where he came from, stashing all the money we made together in a cheap red fanny pack manufactured for tourists. He never let that fanny pack out of sight (it became a trademark of mine, wearing it at ringside as he wrestled). There in the squared circle—brow down, arms outstretched and wide as history—he'd look down at me to make sure I hadn't lost the damn thing from around my waist. When he disappeared, he'd spent the money but left that red fanny pack in my truck, where it still remains, cash replaced with knickknacks and little nothings he must've collected from around the country.

There it is, nestled beside my cat on our trip south to Johnny Trumpet's bungalow, where I'll finally repay the favor I owe. In the meantime, I ask Fuji to help me keep my focus on the task at hand, but he rolls onto his side, facing the other way. He's not ignoring me but paying attention to something else, already under the spell of the road.

3

Kirovakan, Soviet Armenia, 1971

Despite what she sometimes remembered, Mina didn't grow up with Avo, not at first. At first she lived with her family on the ground floor of the tallest building in the city, while Ruben, the only other backgammon student invited to the grandmaster's home after practice, lived with his parents in a rain-soaked village in the surrounding hills. For a long time that was it, despite what she sometimes remembered. Mina in the city, and her rival, rain-soaked, in the nearby hills.

It wasn't until Mina and Ruben were fifteen—already grown, really—that Avo arrived, bigger already than every man in the train station. That was in the winter of 1971. Earlier that morning Avo had shaken his uncle's hand and boarded a train in Leninakan heading east. The uncle, Avo told Mina later, smelled so strongly of bulgur that the train carried his wheaty scent at least through Spitak. He was the same uncle who'd told Avo at the citywide dedication service a few months earlier that Avo should be proud of the way his parents had died. "You know our people," the uncle had said, laughing. "We have a long tradition of dying in big group catastrophes. A factory fire? Take pride in that, son—at least your folks died like real Armenians."

"Sure," Avo had said, watching but not hearing the chairperson of the Executive Committee of Leninakan deliver his speech at the podium. The freezing wind screeched louder than the microphone, and it carried the smoke of a hundred cigarettes into Avo's nose. When he sneezed, his uncle raised a handkerchief to his towering nephew like a flag up a pole. He was right to make a joke of the whole ordeal—Avo's parents were only two of fifty-nine casualties, after all. It was selfish to focus on individual grief in circumstances like those, to confuse a national tragedy for a personal one. In Avo's defense, it was almost impossible to tell the difference sometimes, especially if he stayed in Leninakan and moved in with his uncle, as was the plan. It would be easier to split the two, he hoped, in a place where no one knew his past, in a city of strangers.

"How far away is far enough?" his uncle asked a few nights later, after finding Avo skipping sleep to study a map.

To his amazement, Avo learned he had family in places as far-flung as Lebanon and Syria and Iran. He even had a third cousin once removed living in a place called Fresno, USA. Any of those places would work, he told his uncle, but could they first try the family in Fresno, USA?

His uncle spent long weeks writing letters and making long-distance phone calls with a lurching operator acting as a third rail on the line. But the results were dim. Most families couldn't afford to bring Avo in, and others never even responded. Finally, a cousin of a cousin, the mother of a boy of fifteen—same as Avo—offered her home enthusiastically. It was as if, Avo's uncle said, "she'd always wanted another son."

"Where is she?" Avo asked. "Beirut? Paris? Fresno, USA?"

"A little closer than that," his uncle said, beating the dust out of his hat.

And so Avo boarded the train in Leninakan swathed in the pearly scent of bulgur, leaving home on a meager one-hour ride to a smaller, neighboring city. To him, Kirovakan was known only for its green hills and its overly sensitive and gullible people. "Here," his uncle had told him in Leninakan, "every joke has a punchline. There, an explanation." Still, technically speaking, Kirovakan was somewhere else, and Avo was grateful to the men who'd laid down these tracks. He'd shaken his uncle's hand and boarded the train as if he were one of them—a grown man—as if he were leaving not only a place but a time in his life.

As soon as the train slowed into the station, extended families of clouds gathered in the sky and burst forth into rain. A skinny ticket officer threaded down the aisles, announcing the fact of their arrival—"Kirovakan!"—without the sweet pretense of a welcome.

"Let me help," Avo told the small woman who'd come to get him at the station, and he took the umbrella from her and lifted it high above them both. "Cover him, too," she said, and pointed to a little bespectacled boy tagging along behind her. Avo had been told she had a son his age, but this couldn't be him. Avo had reached his father's height at age twelve, and was used to being larger than his classmates, but this boy—a relative, no less, however distant—was barely the size of a girl. And he looked bitter about it—the scowl he wore beneath the large frames of his glasses gave him the look of an old man cursed to live in a child's body, and Avo felt a sudden need to turn back toward the train and ask his uncle to forget his plan about leaving. Instead, the little bitter kid stuck up his hand for a gentleman's shake, and Avo took it gingerly. This was the boy his age he'd been promised. This was Ruben.

It was some time before Mina met Avo herself, but she heard about this first meeting at backgammon practice. Along with Mina,

Ruben was the top student of a beloved grandmaster named Tigran. In addition to their daily morning lessons before school, the two students spent time at Tigran's home for dinner and practice three nights a week. They were the only two students invited to his home, and for many years Mina never saw Ruben without Tigran's supervision, never heard a word from Ruben that wasn't spoken over the painted fangs of a backgammon board. But when Avo arrived, things changed.

Early that first year in Kirovakan, Avo's new life at home in the village above the city was peaceful and easy. School hadn't started, and the other families were kind and welcoming, and the rain fell constantly, turning the glass in the windows fogged as a dream, and the sound of the rain pelting the roof calmed and comforted him at night, and he slept as well as he'd ever slept. Ruben's father went around the house calling Avo a specimen, applauding him for his past junior wrestling achievements, and gawking at him while he ate. More than once Avo noticed the man comparing him to his own son, whose meat had been pulled from the bone by his mother before serving, and whose fingernails she clipped with a tender precision. Avo enjoyed the surrogate father's pride, even as it came at Ruben's expense, and he relished his seeming inability to do any wrong in the house. He was even free to browse the collection of books Ruben's father kept on a high lacquered shelf. Ruben had taken the large history textbooks to bed, so Avo was left with only the slimmest volumes. He stretched on a blanket on the floor beside Ruben's bed and stayed up listening to the rain, reading those impossibly skinny books. They were all filled with poems. Pushkin, Nekrasov, Mandelstam—all in Russian, with handwritten Armenian translations in the margins. Avo was glad not to find Tumanyan among them, as if finding the one poet his parents could name would have turned him away from the bookshelf altogether. These other poets wrote in another language, and Avo had to turn the books this way and that so he could read every slanting line of translation. He took pride in decoding and understanding each word individually. Still, he never came away with a whole, and he feared the possibility that Ruben might look down at him from the bed one night over the spine of one of his giant histories and ask, out of the blue, what those little books of his were about.

In fact, Ruben hardly ever asked Avo a question at all, which was fine by Avo because it meant they naturally avoided talking about the death of his parents. The boiler explosion and the resulting fire—the 1971 Leninakan Textile Meltdown—must have made the news in Kirovakan, and so, in a way, his angle on the story would've felt redundant. Instead, whatever stilted conversations they had in those early days consisted mainly of Avo asking questions of Ruben, and Ruben bringing those questions back to one of his three main interests: backgammon, history, or the possibilities of an afterlife. Of the three, backgammon seemed to Avo the least grim, so he tried as often as possible to steer the conversation in its direction.

"It's the greatest sport there is," Ruben once told him, adjusting his glasses over the board he'd pulled out from under his bed. "Unlike chess, which is strictly strategy, and unlike dice, which is pure luck, backgammon combines both skill and circumstance, and in this way it's the sport that most resembles life."

"You come up with that yourself?" Avo asked, and just from Ruben's hesitation he could tell the answer was no. The grandmaster, Tigran, had come up with it.

"But I agree wholeheartedly," Ruben added, as if the ability to recognize genius were genius itself.

For fear of switching topics to Ruben's other two interests, Avo didn't press the issue. He didn't even contest the idea that backgammon was a sport. He just kept listening to his cousin's cousin explain the rules, dice as big as walnuts in his tiny, boyish hands.

Exactly in the middle of his first summer in Kirovakan, Avo woke to the sound of a plate shattering in the next room, followed by a terrible yell. Ruben's parents were fighting. Avo sat up and checked the bed above him, but Ruben went on sleeping. Or pretending to sleep.

Once the first fight broke out, it became unusual to go two nights in a row with peace.

Ruben's father, who once called Avo his son, now grumbled between meals, between drinks. How could his wife have agreed to this arrangement? Taking in another boy, especially one who occupied so much space, who gobbled up more food than the rest of the family combined? Ruben's mother would hush and then scold and then beg him to keep his voice down, warning that Avo might hear. But of course Avo had already heard, and after a few weeks during which Ruben's father practically drew a family tree to litigate how Avo was his wife's burden and not his, Avo reached up to nudge Ruben awake and said, "It's good news, in a way. I don't know what I did, but I got your father to stop liking me more than he likes you."

Ruben turned on his side to face him. "You have nothing to do with it," he said. He didn't get up, but he reached for his glasses and held them to his face. "They stopped sending him work. Textbooks to translate. He thinks it's because of a sentence his editor cut from one of his histories, a line about American aid after the genocide. But he drinks, he misses deadlines. Everyone knows it."

In the next room, a door slammed. An unbreakable thing—a pot? a hammer?—was thrown to the floor.

"You sleep through this?" Avo asked.

And that's when Ruben told him about his midnight walks into the city.

Ruben had spent a lot of his time alone, those years before Avo arrived, avoiding school whenever he could, and leaving the house whenever his parents fought. Those were the days of long walks past the village into the forests in the daylight, the long walks into the city at night when it seemed he was the only person awake in Kirovakan. Those were the days of imagining the pain that awaits the damned, the nights when he sat alone at the foot of the city's namesake, Sergey Kirov, and spoke to the statue as if he were real. As if he were a friend.

His mother had caught him once, talking to the statue. She'd left the house in a flurry, having been driven out by her husband, who'd thrown a book at her and was threatening to burn himself with his cigarette. Enough, she thought, and though she'd never tell anyone, it really did feel as though she'd made up her mind, that she would take her son and move back to Yerevan to live with her brothers and parents. It was late, and she was tired. But she would go. Pick up and go.

But Ruben was not in his bed, and even as a flit of panic rose in her, even as she ran through the rain and mud down to the city where Ruben's backgammon teacher lived—where else but to Tigran could Ruben have gone?—she knew she would return home, that the window had closed, that the one time in her life she could have left her husband had come and gone, and that Ruben—his absence, his not being present and ready—was to blame.

Still, having found him sitting alone under an umbrella, conversing with a statue like the loneliest little boy she'd ever seen, she pitied him. Growing up with a father like his in a country like this, in a body as fragile and small as that. Alone. Two generations ago, the strongest of her people had been slaughtered, and her son was the proof. Later, she thought she should have confronted him at the statue and ordered him to cheer up. Ordered him to laugh at himself, the way people in Leninakan did. Talking to a statue—it could be funny if it weren't so sad. But she didn't tell him that. She didn't tell him anything. Instead, she hid behind a tree, hoping he hadn't seen her.

He hadn't. And she never—not once—spoke of it.

Now Avo had arrived, and Ruben took to bringing him to the statue in the city square at night. This late, when the streets were vacant, Avo found the unlit stone buildings against the backdrop of dark hills eerily archaic, as if he'd sprung to life inside a historian's memory. And as Ruben went on and on about his different backgammon strategies—priming and holding and blitzing and all the rest—Avo wondered if that feeling of his had ever been written down in a slim volume of poems, and he wondered what those words in those poems might look like, if he'd even be able to identify them.

It was after one of those long walks into the city that Avo and Mina met for the first time. The boys had stayed at the statue later than usual, well after the sun had come up over the hills to the east.

People on their way to work crossed the city square in droves, and from the crowd came a girl with a black ribbon in her hair and a lacquered backgammon set tucked under her arm. She was waving awkwardly as she stomped past them down the street.

"Who's that?" Avo asked.

"Nobody," Ruben said, packing up his board.

"She waved at you. She has a board, too. You didn't think it was worth mentioning a real-life friend you could introduce me to?"

"She's not a friend. She's a fellow practitioner. A competitor."

"You like her?"

"I don't have feelings one way or the other."

"For you, that's liking. What's her name?"

"Aren't you hungry? Don't you need to eat all the time? Haven't you missed a meal?"

"Everyone in this city's so sensitive," Avo said, deciding that friendship with this little naysayer wasn't in the cards, that he'd tried as well as he could, but they were incompatible as friends. They walked the whole way back to the village in silence, sleepless and irritated and—yes, Ruben was right—ready for food.

The previous year, a Yerevan-based recruiter at the Ministry of Education had invited Ruben on a visit to the Armenian capital and a tour of the university there. The recruiter had sent the note to his school based on test scores, and his teacher, Mr. V, had been asked to deliver the note in person.

The problem, Ruben told Avo, was that Mr. V had cheated in a game of backgammon with Ruben's father some twenty years earlier, and had turned his shame into petty vengefulness. On the day Mr. V was supposed to deliver that letter to Ruben—stamped "From the Department of the Mobilization of Scientific Forces"—he instead kept it himself, unfurled the note from its envelope at the head of the class, and read the invitation aloud. He put on an ostentatious voice, so that any joy or pride Ruben might have experienced at the honor was washed out with irony.

When Ruben told him the story, Avo tried to make a sound like understanding. But the truth was he'd met kids like Ruben back in Leninakan—strange, humorless kids who seemed born to the wrong place or time—and he'd felt very little sympathy, had done very little to help. It was impossible, if you were relatively well liked among your peers, to suggest ways a disliked kid could improve his standing, because essentially, the only advice worth giving was impossible to give: be less like *you*.

The truth was, Avo looked forward to the start of school, a chance to meet new people. It hurt to admit it—even to himself at home, lying on the floor under the sound of bickering rainfall—but when he imagined his forthcoming social life in Kirovakan, it did not include the strange and gloomy fifteen-year-old in the bed above him. Just the thought of abandoning Ruben struck guilt into his heart and shrank his conscience like plastic over a flame. But the split seemed inevitable. Avo would find a group to join, and he would leave Ruben behind, send him back to whatever peculiar existence he'd been surviving so far without him, and in their old age they would hardly remember each other.

At first, he was right. When the other students heard he came from Leninakan, they asked Avo to tell his best jokes. He told the ones he could remember overhearing at the Poloz Mukuch restaurant and beerhouse, where his coaches would take the wrestling team to celebrate after practice, regional jokes about the idiocy of people from Aparan, about the drunks of Kamo, about the naïveté of the people from Kirovakan.

"A farmer asked a doctor in Aparan if it was possible to give his sick cow an abortion, and the doctor said, 'I didn't realize you'd grown so lonely.' "

In Leninakan he'd been a middling joke-teller, but in Kirovakan he found himself surrounded by a crowd of his peers after school, all of them laughing and asking for more.

Except for Ruben, who folded his backgammon board under his arm and disappeared after class into the city.

They saw less of each other, even at home. Ruben would miss dinner, and his mother would blame Avo, and Avo would make a joke, and Ruben's father would watch him eat as if tallying every grain of pilaf his family was sacrificing.

New friends invited Avo to their homes for dinner, and he slept many nights in the new condominiums in the city, and returned to the village in the hills less and less often.

Once in a while Avo caught glimpses of Ruben in far corners of the village, up near the home where the survivors lived, where the old woman with red hair would play her duduk like a grass harp, where even the sheep and the chickens seemed to stop and listen.

And there was Ruben, sitting on a tree stump with one of those big history books in his lap, pages as thick as the stump he was sitting on.

Mina continued seeing Ruben at Tigran's place. One night, after one game turned into four, the grandmaster looked at his watch, blanched, and asked if Ruben would do the gentlemanly thing by walking his rival home. "It's a short walk to her building," Tigran said, helping the girl into her coat.

On the street, Ruben walked beside her in silence. Her legs were longer than his, and he kept having to jog a little to catch up. They didn't speak. When they arrived at her building, the tallest in all of Kirovakan, he was in the middle of remembering the day she noticed that he'd parted his hair in the opposite direction of how his mother used to comb it. "Your face looks brighter," Mina had said, and he hoped she'd say something now, parting at the door of her building, that would go humming on similarly in his heart. Instead, she only mumbled a quick thank-you and then left.

All those Soviet buildings, the slate upshot of progress. The city had its charms, but it was the surrounding villages and mossy hills that felt most like home to Ruben, that came closest to the authentic Armenian life he'd been reading about in his father's books. The Kingdom of Cilicia—chivalry and knighthood and Armenian independence. He wished he could make it so again, and with this wish in mind he strutted through the city square, tipping his glasses to the statue of Kirov, a passing nobleman on the road.

From Kirov's shadow came the sound of laughter. A group of three young men Ruben recognized as classmates emerged and then surrounded him. They'd seen him saluting the statue. One member of the little mob pushed him, knocking his backgammon board to the pavement and spilling its checkers and dice across the city square. Another grabbed him by the shirt collar, calling him the drunkard's son and mocking the recruiter's note from Moscow. The third stole and wore his glasses and cavorted around, twittering, "I am *important*, I am *significant*." He ripped off the glasses and threw them to the ground. Crunched them under his boot. "Maybe the Ministry will take him to Yerevan," he said, "and maybe they'll even take him to Moscow. But wherever he goes, he'll always smell like rain."

Finally, he was left alone to find and collect his things, the empty frames of his glasses, blind as a statue.

The next morning, he stayed in bed.

"Don't you have school?" his mother said, but he pretended to sleep. She made him breakfast, eggs with tomatoes and cheese, and left it on the table next to his pillow. He ate the food, adding salt, and then fell asleep for real.

He woke again to the sound of his parents yelling.

"Then stop drinking, idiot," his mother shouted from the doorway as his father stormed in and out of the house. Ruben followed him to the smoking tonir next door. His father was throwing all his books into the burning well where the bread was baked.

"They don't appreciate my work, they've cut off their funds, they're giving all the work to those cock-sucking bums in Yerevan," he said, carrying pile after pile of books to the fire.

Ruben checked the nearly empty bookshelf. All that was left was the big textbook he loved—an Armenian national history published during the brief window of independence after the Ottomans and before the Soviets—and a stack of two or three slim volumes of poetry.

In one of the genocide stories Ruben had heard from the survivors, the Turks torched Armenian villages to the ground. For the survivors, there was enough time only to save some of what was being destroyed, and some chose to save historical records rather than the children being burned alive inside. Life could begin again, went the thinking, but the history, once lost, would be lost forever.

His father's shouting was growing louder. He was coming back for the last of the books. The history he loved and the poetry, which his cousin's cousin seemed to enjoy. If Avo were home, they could have saved all the books from the fire without having to choose, but Avo was nowhere to be found.

When his father returned, he burned the last of what Ruben had left on the shelf.

When Avo got home that night for dinner, Ruben ate silently beside him. His father had gone to sleep already, and his mother went on apologizing for him. "He's worked so hard all his life, and he's a good man, he's got a good heart . . ."

When Avo asked what had happened, Ruben's mother explained the terminated translation work, the tonir, the book burning.

"All the books?" Avo asked.

"Except for some of the poems in Ruben's bed."

Avo looked to Ruben from under that big eyebrow of his. Studied the wire holding the broken glasses together at the nose.

"I was using them to swat flies," Ruben said, looking down at his food.

"His father has got such a good heart," his mother said, returning again to what she wanted to believe was true. "Never in Armenia has there been a bigger heart."

And with all the history burned up deep inside the tonir, no one could check whether or not that claim was true.

"Look who's joined us," said Mr. V the next morning, tapping his watch. Little crack-ups filled the classroom. "And would you leave the mud *outside*, please? Everyone else brings in rain, and you bring in mud."

Ruben stomped as much of the black gunk from his boots as he could before making his way to his desk. Every step a slosh, a squeak. Every squeak another chuckle from the group.

"As I was saying," said Mr. V, as though accessing some deep well of valor within him to continue despite the interruption, "it's impossible to have a hypotenuse shorter in length than one of the other legs. Go on—try to imagine it. Try to picture in your mind a triangle with a shorter hypotenuse than leg. In order to do it, you must swivel the dangling hypotenuse to one side, thus turning the longest leg into the new hypotenuse. In other words, you have to *cheat*."

Ruben braced himself. The word *cheat* was a Pavlovian beckon to the story Mr. V loved to tell of that old backgammon match he'd played against Ruben's father.

"And I didn't even need to cheat!" shouted Mr. V at the end of his story. "I was the better player, I only let the fear of losing distract me from playing my game, and there's a lesson there for all of us, isn't there? I mean, I should have won. Look at my opponent now! He can't even get his tiny little son to school on time!"

Laughs again, only now transformed into a great roar. Ruben pricked the tip of his pencil into his palm, and suddenly, the racket stopped. The classroom got so quiet he could hear the rain dripping from his clothes onto the floor beneath his desk. Everybody, including Mr. V, had turned to look toward the back of the room.

One classmate who'd been laughing a moment ago, who'd broken Ruben's glasses a few nights earlier, was bent into a strange and impossible shape. Avo was holding him. He had the boy horizontally across his waist like a belt. The outstretched boy looked like he wanted to shout, but there wasn't any air in his lungs to do it.

"Put him down!" said Mr. V. "Put him down right now!"

But Avo was bigger than the teacher and kept the boy entangled. Mr. V could only yell from a safe distance, pacing back and forth, sweating so much he looked like he'd been caught in the rain himself. The boy gurgled out a cry, accompanied by a foamy spittle at the mouth. The other students backed away, marveling at the big jokester's strength.

"Put him down! Put him down! You'll break him! You'll break him!"

Avo said, "I'll let him go as soon as Ruben tells me to."

"Ruben?" said Mr. V. "To hell with Ruben! *I'm* the teacher! *I'm* telling you to put the boy down!"

Avo tightened his hold on his victim, whose tears fell sideways from his eyes.

"Okay!" Mr. V said, surrendering. "Ruben, for the love of peace, order him to stop!"

Ruben looked up at his cousin's cousin, big as a statue come to life. "That's enough, Avo." And Avo dropped the crying boy.

"What is the matter with this generation?" said Mr. V, moving carefully past Avo to attend to the kid on the floor. But the matter seemed to be with him, and he seemed to know so, because from then on he never brought up the old backgammon story, and never made a show of Ruben's coming to class late. In fact, he never said another disparaging word to Ruben ever again.

After that, Ruben and Avo were no longer cousins of cousins but brothers. That was how almost everyone in Kirovakan talked about them. Brothers: one big, one small. One doing push-ups between meals, the other carrying a backgammon set under his arm like a toolbox. They'd be seen rolling dice together after class and on the weekends at the city square like a pair of old men. Sometimes, in lieu of the game, they'd walk up the muddy path through the village and listen to the survivors tell stories. Siranoush would play her music, and the duduk in her lips made the unimaginably old woman seem somehow even more ancient, as if she were a castle wall, as if every strange freckle were a year she'd burned into her skin. On torrential days, Ruben and Avo had to follow the sound of the duduk over the plunking rain just to find the house. She played the duduk longer and louder, helping the boys find her. When the boys arrived, they peeled off their wet socks—one big pair, one small—and laid them out to dry against the hot clay of the tonir. Then they'd spread flat on their bellies to drink tea and eat salted cheese and listen to the old woman play. Every now and then Siranoush dumped the collected spit from her mouthpiece onto the sizzling clay.

Whenever one of the other old survivors died, Siranoush would play the duduk at the funeral. She finished a song and pointed the instrument at the other mourners. "They call the duduk a double-reed," she said, "because two canes vibrate against each other inside. Not one cane but two. Without both, no music."

When her husband died, the body was dressed in a fine suit and lowered into the ground. Avo followed Ruben's lead and dropped a handful of mud into the grave. Ruben crossed himself. He leaned to Avo and said, so softly Avo had to bend to hear him, "We can be like that. A double-reed."

The village had arranged for a priest to arrive, swinging his thurible and sweeping incense over the grave. Ruben fidgeted with the wire holding his glasses together. A double-reed—how easily Avo could have punished him, half his size, for saying something so tender as that. And he didn't.

4

Kirovakan, Soviet Armenia, 1973

By now they were spending every night in the city square. On Ruben's seventeenth birthday, Avo stole a bottle of vodka from the house and uncorked it at the foot of Kirov's statue. The bulbs in the lamps above them glowed feebly, and the two brothers passed the bottle back and forth in the stuttering dark. From a distance, they must have appeared in fits and starts, one hunched low to hear the smaller other.

"Look at this," Ruben said, fumbling something in his hands. "Can you see this book?"

In the dark, Avo couldn't, but he traded the vodka for it anyway. The book was soft and leather-bound with extremely thin pages that, when he thumbed their edges, felt sliced with metallic flakes.

"It's an old journal," Ruben said. "A priceless artifact."

"Whose is it?"

"You won't believe me."

Avo promised he would, and Ruben took another swig of vodka before beginning to explain.

The journal, Ruben said, was over three hundred years old. An imperial cleric had copied, by hand, rare proofs and algorithms from no longer extant papers belonging to a fifth-century

Armenian mathematician and philosopher named Shirakatsi. The journal, dated 1669, went on to become one of the few Armenian artifacts saved from the Ottomans in Diyarbakir in 1915. When Ruben said priceless, he meant it—not only for the journal's historical significance or monetary value but for the potential application of the mathematics inside: some of the algorithms laid out winning strategies for different board arrangements in backgammon. Seeing as how the game had been invented only a hundred years or so before Shirakatsi's time, the algorithms must have been among the first backgammon strategies ever recorded. And on top of all that? The proofs had been passed down from grandmaster to chosen pupil, and then on to his chosen pupil, and so on, never translated from the Armenian. And now it belonged to Ruben.

Avo thumbed the pages again, this time feeling a new delicacy he couldn't believe he'd missed. "Tigran chose *you*."

Ruben drank from the bottle. "Tigran didn't give me the book," he finally said. "I stole it. Three days ago."

It was easy to lose track of time in the dark, but Avo knew it wouldn't be long until someone noticed that a three-hundred-year-old record of a lost manuscript by a legendary fifth-century figure had gone missing. He said, "Tigran's probably dying right now."

"He doesn't know it's missing," Ruben said. "I didn't steal it from him. I stole it from the student Tigran actually chose to give it to."

"Which student? What's his name?"

Ruben drank again. "*Her* name. He gave it to Mina."

The girl who covered her chin when she spoke, the girl Ruben seemed to dislike less than he disliked other people.

"Your girlfriend." Avo laughed.

"This isn't funny," Ruben said.

"She might drown herself in a lake, thinking she lost this thing."

But Ruben said she'd get the journal back soon. He'd spent the last three nights copying the proofs into his own papers, and he'd be finished tonight.

"The trick is we'll have to give the book back to her without her noticing we had it," he said. "We should let her think she's misplaced it and found it again, all on her own."

"We?" Avo said.

Early the next morning, before class, Avo joined Ruben in the small room where the backgammon club met daily before school. Of the seven students there, the one named Mina was easy to spot.

Even if she hadn't been the only girl in attendance, she was also the only one sitting restlessly in her chair, her knee bobbing violently, her bottom lip in her teeth. When Tigran—a round, white-haired ornament of a man dressed in a heavy overcoat and a floppy blue hat—entered the room, Mina cleared her throat. She was on the verge, Avo could tell, of announcing that she'd misplaced the irreplaceable, and then she would probably climb to the roof of the tallest building in Kirovakan and jump.

But before she could do that, Tigran grabbed his chest in mock heart attack, bulged his eyes, and gasped at the newcomer in the back, "Good God, man! How tall are you?"

Two weeks earlier, Ruben had stood on a chair to mark the wall above Avo's head with a pencil. This week, he was just shy of two meters tall.

"Two meters! And how old are you?"

"Seventeen, sir."

"Good God, you look thirty! Maybe you'll be the first man to hit three meters."

"Tigran," trembled the voice of the only girl in the room. "I have something very, very important to say."

"I'll probably stop growing after another ten centimeters," Avo boomed over her. "That's what the doctors tell me. In order to grow more than that, there has to be a problem with your glands. People who grow to become freaks? They have glands like faucets you can't turn off. Hormones flowing forever, which causes many problems, as you can imagine. I'm lucky, the doctors say. I'm big, but not broken."

"Tigran?" came Mina's voice again. "I'm sorry to interrupt, but I have to tell you—"

"And when I heard *that*," Avo shouted, "I asked myself where else I could try my luck. Maybe I can roll the dice on a backgammon board and see if my luck works here, too."

"Ah," Tigran said. "If only backgammon were a game of luck. Unlike chess, which is a game strictly of skill, and unlike craps, which is a game purely of chance—"

"Tigran!" Mina shot to her feet, hammering her hip against the table along the way, which would leave a bruise for six weeks. She held it and covered her chin with her other hand. Even in a yell, her voice sounded on the verge of tears. It had the blurry quality of something seen through heat or rain. "I have something to tell you and I can't wait another minute and I won't let this overgrown idiot keep interrupting me."

Avo said, "I don't know if you missed the part about my glands, but I'm not overgrown."

"Go on, then," Tigran said. "Tell me what's so important, Mina-jan."

But just as she was about to confess, she saw it, the ancient book, its pages with their golden edges. Ruben had sneaked it into her bag—with the help, Mina realized, of Avo's distraction.

"Yes?" Tigran said.

Mina looked around the room as if trying to think of something else that might have warranted her growing bruise. She looked to Avo, relieved, and there was his heart, climbing. His overgrown, idiotic heart.

"What she wants to say," Avo said to Tigran, "is that she can't concentrate on backgammon when I'm in the room." The other students laughed. "And it's not just my height, sir. It's my mysterious hazel eyes, and my one strong eyebrow, and these bear claws you mortals call hands. I should leave, sir. Look at her looking at me—she's obsessed!"

The students laughed, and even Tigran pulled his hat over his eyes and shook his head, muttering funnily. Mina, embarrassed and relieved all at once, gave Avo a look of hatred mixed with appreciation. As for Ruben, he'd taken his seat at the front of the room, dutifully waiting for class to begin.

"It's okay, it's okay, I'll leave," Avo said, ducking under the doorway. "I won't come back! You can concentrate on your game, Mina-jan. Luck and strategy, all at once, remember. Goodbye. Goodbye!"

Once in a while, the rain held off. On one of those rare bright days in the spring, a white bus with a pale blue roof came to a hiss near the fountain in the square. From the shadow of the statue of Kirov, Avo saw Mina in the bus window, chin in her hands. Then she got off the bus and shuffled down Moskovyan Street, carrying a shellacked backgammon set under her arm. Outside the school, she stopped and spoke with a friend who made her laugh. The laughing sent Mina folded over on herself, and the backgammon board under her arm reflected the sun's white glare this way and that, rays of light that flew across the square and into Avo's eyes, so bright they made him sneeze. When he regained his sight, he saw that Mina had spotted him. He waved. She waved back.

"I wonder," Ruben said, reminding Avo he wasn't alone. "I wonder if there's something funny going on between her and Tigran. Would explain why he gave her the journal and not me."

Avo said, "Or maybe it's possible she's the better backgammon player?"

"That's not it," Ruben said. "It's strange—she's the luckiest player I've ever seen."

Ruben returned to his book, a Russian history of the genocide he couldn't stop talking about, extolling the empire's humanitarian response to the refugee crisis. He'd read the book so many times, he could hold long conversations while he read it again. "I don't know how, but the dice seem to do whatever she wants them to do." He turned the page. "And someone *that* lucky can only bring bad luck to others."

Avo returned to his own reading. Tumanyan, the son of a priest, was too religious for his taste, but every once in a while in his poems, a line would emerge from the preaching—"Sweet comrade, when you come someday to gaze upon my tomb"—to stand stark and true as a friend.

When Ruben left to use the toilet in the nearby census directory building, a voice shot out over the square.

"I don't know if I've ever seen you alone," Mina said, and Avo looked across the way to find the small figure of Ruben climbing the steps of the directory in the distance, walking away with that little bounce of his, checking his glasses against the sky for smudges as he moved.

"Won't last long." Avo laughed. "I'm surprised our leash stretches this far."

"Who's the dog and who's the master?" Mina asked, switching her backgammon set under her other arm.

"We take turns," Avo said.

She didn't sit down beside him, but she seemed to consider doing so. "It's not that I don't like Ruben. It's just I see him all the time at practice. I don't see you very much at all."

"Really? I'm hard to miss."

Mina plucked a die from her backgammon set and threw it, plunking Avo right in the forehead. "Hey, you *are* hard to miss."

"Here I've been trying to make you laugh, and you're funnier than I am. Are you sure you're from Kirovakan?"

"We're not all as dour as Ruben," Mina said.

"He's strange, but I like that. He's my brother, what can I say?"

"It's not that he's strange," Mina said, a bit annoyed at herself for continuing to talk about the one person whose absence allowed this conversation. "If anything, he reminds me of a few of my uncles and their friends, stern old Armenians who never talk about anything except the Turks. It's so—"

"Boring?"

"I was going to say male, but boring works, too. Don't laugh—it's true! It's boring and male, all that talk about the past. It's a repetitive, endless waste. Have you seen the lemon trees by the ski lift? Imagine if they never dropped the dead lemons from last year, or the year before that. Just went on carrying all their old shriveled lemons until the branches sagged so low that no new fruit could grow."

"You're a poet," Avo said, and as soon as Mina covered her chin, he knew she'd misunderstood him, had thought he was making fun of her. The truth was he wished he'd had the imagination to come up with something like that, those dead lemons hanging on, or the courage to say it. Instead, he pressed on with his argument.

"If you talk to Ruben," he said, "he says we have to keep remembering what the Turks did to us because they deny it ever happened."

"See? See how boring that gets? Of course it's true, but—I saw your eyes glaze over, and you were the one talking!"

Avo laughed. "Duties aren't hobbies, you know."

"Well, let's talk about hobbies once in a while. Or movies, or music—my sister has a record player but listens to the worst Russian music, so I found this guy who sells records underground and bought this British album called *Pink Moon*, and it's the most beautiful music I've ever heard, and it's only from last year, it's something new, and that's what people are doing in the spinning world, they're *making* things, not just remembering them—they're making beautiful new things. Do you have a portable record player?"

"I—"

"No, it's okay—I'll just borrow my sister's. Where can we go where Ruben won't find us?" She was supposed to be luck-graced, he knew, and now he could feel it whisking around her, this girl with big eyes and a small chin standing over him in all her endless fortune, asking him for a place where, together, they could hide.

His shoelace had come undone, he noticed, and he bent and reached and then pulled at the strings, hiking them so tight and quick that his boot let out a leathery yelp. He said, "I'd love to listen to that record with you, but I want to invite Ruben, too. We're a package deal, I'm proud to say."

Once again Mina switched the backgammon set to her other arm. "Ah yes," she said, "the leash," and then she looked down the street. "I should go before he gets back and sees us talking without his permission. If you change your mind, you can meet me at those lemon trees by the ski lift tonight. I'll have the record player, and the record."

"Tonight?"

"It'll rain tomorrow, it'll rain for weeks."

She left briskly down the street, carrying that lacquered board under her arm, casting back the flashing light of the sun every now and then until, behind the traffic, she disappeared.

"I looked through that history book of yours," Avo said when Ruben got back.

"Oh yeah?"

"Yeah, and it got me thinking. We Armenians, you know, we're so obsessed with the past. It's like, if a lemon tree just kept growing new lemons, but the new lemons were old, then you couldn't get any fresh new lemons off the tree, you know?"

"What? What are you talking about?"

"I mean, well, let me start over. You know those lemon trees over by the ski lift?"

"Is this a joke?"

"No, no. I'm just thinking, we should do something different today, since it's not raining for once, since it's, you know, beautiful outside."

"You think today is beautiful? You know what day will be *really* beautiful? The day we do something about the fact that the Turks still deny the massacre of our people." Ruben returned to reading. "Or maybe the day we do something about the fact that no one but us seems to care about the international cover-up of two million dead Armenians? *That* day will be beautiful."

Avo said, "Mina invited us out tonight."

Ruben looked up from the page. "Us?"

"Yes. Both of us. She happened to walk by when you were gone. Said she had a new album she wanted us to listen to."

"Armenian?"

"British."

"Forget it."

"Maybe some Armenian stuff, too, I don't know."

Ruben seemed to consider it. "The only non-Armenians who can help us now are Lenin and Jesus."

"How am I supposed to keep a straight face when you say something like that?"

"Lenin and Jesus kept a straight face, didn't they? Were they funny? Did they find a joke to make in the absence of justice? Did they convince themselves that life was nothing but a joke, that they were the butts of it, and that there was nothing to be done but join in on the laughs? Did Jesus laugh, huh, or did he weep? In the Psalms, God says to the kings who have taken counsel against Him, 'He who sits in Heaven shall laugh.' So laughter, you understand, is the *prize* of living a significant life, not the means."

"The album is supposed to be very good, I hear."

"Admit it," Ruben said. "You didn't joke to distract Tigran. You did it because you want her to like you."

"And you don't?"

Ruben closed his book. "You don't need my permission to spend time with Mina," he said. "You're a man, aren't you? Make your own choices."

"I choose both," Avo said, palming Ruben's head, but Ruben said, "Both's not a choice."

Meanwhile, the doubly smuggled album—first from England, then from the underground seller in Kirovakan—spun along with the spinning world. Mina didn't understand a single lyric, but she hummed along with every sad and hopeful song. The new lemons in the tree above her, small as candle flames, glowed green in the dusk. The music, the perfectly clear evening—she convinced herself she was grateful to have them both to herself. She played the record four times, start to finish, before returning home.

5

Los Angeles, California, 1989

The drive from King County to Johnny Trumpet's bungalow in the Mojave Desert can be done in one of two ways: southeast across Idaho and Nevada, or south through Oregon and California. To save myself the mountainous rifts, I chose the latter, and Fuji and I funneled our way between the valley walls of the western states as if sucked through a pneumatic tube. Aside from a few stops to refuel, we sped through the skunky redwoods of Humboldt County and the roiling vineyards of the Central Valley without rest. At that pace, we should've been able to shake ourselves off in the dusty gold pan of the California desert with an extra day to spare. Instead, sixteen hours into the drive, sleepless and dazed, I missed the junction east toward the desert and found myself in the wrong place. I found myself in Los Angeles.

By the time I got off the freeway and realized my mistake, it was past ten o'clock at night and the streetlights were beginning to confuse themselves with the taillights ahead of me, and I could hardly keep my eyes open long enough to find parking, let alone merge back onto the freeway and continue east. On a side street off the main drag, my luck changed: I found a meter abandoned with almost a full hour remaining on the clock. There, I followed Fuji into the camper shell of my truck and set up my sleeping bag.

The hour of sleep whipped by as quick as the windburn I used to get on my face as a lookout in the navy, high up in the crow's nest, but I woke up clear-eyed enough to hit the road again. By then it was almost midnight, and I figured I could make it to the mustard-colored bungalow by two or three in the morning, crash there for free, and get on to the business of repaying my favor. But just as I was leaning out of my window to check for oncoming traffic and pull away from the curb, I realized where, exactly, I'd been parked.

All of life is an accident, or it isn't, I'll never know.

I was parked one block away from the dive bar where, in 1978, I'd discovered The Brow Beater. I was one block away from The Gutshot.

Back in the spring of 1978, my top guy, Mickey "Makeshift" Starr, and I—for reasons I won't get into here—ended our working relationship. For several weeks I floundered where he left me, in a barbarous neighborhood of North Hollywood, plotting my next move. Getting old and nursing a half-healed neck that had turned me from wrestler to manager a decade and more earlier, I was left with two choices: retire from the wrestling business altogether, or find a replacement for Makeshift who could lead me back to money. I gave myself until the end of the month to decide.

By the final week of my self-imposed deadline, I'd given up on finding a new top wrestler and started searching instead for the city's most generous bartender. That's how I found The Gutshot and the bartender there, named Longtin. Although he'd gone gray early in life, he was my junior by many years and had just become a father for the first time. He'd quit drinking since the birth of his baby daughter, and seemed to pour his would-be share of bourbon into my cup, right on top of mine.

On the last night of my deadline to choose between the wrestling business and home, Longtin opened himself a can of pineapple juice and clinked my bourbon to salute the decision I'd made: I was moving to Tucson, I said, to be near my ex-wife. All of Longtin's talk about his baby daughter had inspired me. There I could forget about the mess I'd made by marrying my ex-wife in the first place, and remember that she was the closest thing I had left to family. Already she and I were past fifty, and maybe she'd started a family of her own, I didn't know, but I remember thinking: It's not too late to be kind to her.

So it happened that I'd just made my declaration to quit the wrestling business and was hoisting my glass to Longtin's can of pineapple juice like some gesture of numinous fortune when I first laid eyes on him, The Brow Beater. I won't deny that what initially caught my eye was his size, and I won't deny, either, that my reconciliatory spirit must've affected what I saw when I looked.

Two enormous shoulders had established themselves like kingly epaulettes on either side of his wide neck. Even the dishwashing apron knotted stringently around his waist couldn't disguise the strength in his body, which didn't appear collected so much as kinetic. When he yawned, he seemed to do so from his innermost core; he probably sneezed and farted, I thought, with a firm efficiency. Finally, he turned just so, and I recognized what would become his signature feature: one solitary eyebrow, black and dense, which signaled to me almost immediately the names of several auspicious gimmicks. It was impossible to say if the two eyes flashing underneath that unibrow brought to mind a pair of snakes coiling in the weeds or a pair of gems concealed in the rough, but that confusion only worked to further enthrall me. Whether they were the eyes of terror or the eyes of grace, they were money eyes, theater eyes, eyes with the power and range to sell.

His size and look caught my attention, to be sure, but what kept me staring was something altogether else: the strange work he was at, and the almost loving focus with which he was doing the job. He was reaching up with a piece of chalk to the chalkboard set high behind the bar, up near where the expensive bottles lived, and he was drawing little wayward shapes. The bar was closing—I was among the last at the rail—and I could hear him, this giant on his toes, humming a tune while he looped together whatever lines he was making. Finally, I said to Longtin, who had his back to me as he balanced the register, "Are you aware of the large, ugly fellow tagging your beer list?"

"He's kind of like a foreign-exchange worker," Longtin said. "We call him Bravo."

I looked back to the chalkboard, but the big man was gone. Where he'd been drawing, I saw a string of shapes that must've been letters in his alphabet, must've been words. Later, when I told The Brow Beater the story, he said he didn't remember what he'd been writing. We'd been on the road for a few months by then, and I think he trusted me enough to tell me the truth. "Maybe I was translating the names of the beers," he said, and laughed. I said, "The words looked more meaningful than that," and he said, "That's Armenian, bro. Every curse looks like a prayer."

That night at The Gutshot, I knew right away that he was my ticket back to the wrestling business. So as soon as he bulldozed back through the service doors, wielding a mop, I sprang off my barstool and tied back my hair.

"Hey there," I said as he rolled the bucket past me.

"We're closing, bro," he said without stopping.

"I've been told I should introduce myself to you," I said, shadowing him, and only then did I take the time to consider who it was I might appear to be introducing. To him, I probably looked—

middle-aged and tanned, wearing my bleached-blond hair down to my busted C7 vertebra, a bowling shirt unbuttoned to my heart—something like a Hollywood phony. I adjusted my tone to seem realer than that. "Usually I introduce myself as Angel Hair," I said, feathering the evidence, "but I'm also just, you know, a regular fellow." I couldn't tell if he understood a word I'd said. I threw out a hand for a shake. "Terry Krill."

One of his monstrous hands flew off the mop to shake mine, and then he went back to work.

From behind the bar, Longtin called out, "Just about time to go, Terry."

I ignored him and got to asking Avo a hundred questions. Nothing stopped his mopping until I asked if he'd ever considered wrestling before. He said he'd been a Junior Olympic wrestler once, and I beckoned him low so I could whisper into his ear, "That's great, kid, but I don't mean *shoot* wrestling. What I mean is professional wrestling. You know the difference?"

He didn't, and so, in what amounted to one of my most blatant betrayals of kayfabe, I described it to him this way: it was entertainment, the kind of wrestling I was recruiting him to do, and the only two things that were real in pro wrestling were the money and the miles. Leaping Lou Albano had taught me that, I said, but the name meant nothing to Avo.

I asked him how much Longtin was paying him, and went on to paint extravagant dreamscapes involving the money we might be able to make together. But he just kept repeating that the bar was closing, and kept on mopping, right up to the toes of my loafers.

A long time passed before I realized how little the money weighed into his decision. Back then I kept harping on it, the money. Maybe I would've dug up other promises—fame, girls, or the singularly heady phenomenon of manipulating a crowd of strangers to adore or despise you—but before I could, Longtin interjected again from behind the bar: "What happened to driving off to Tucson?"

And that's what did it. That's what got Avo interested. "You're leaving Los Angeles?" he asked.

There were those eyes of bothness, shining different.

"The job I'm recruiting you to do," I said, "would have you living out of hotel rooms and cars for years on end."

He wanted to know how soon we'd hit the road, and that's when I knew I had him.

"First thing in the morning," I said, rattling my car keys in my pocket, and when he said he'd need until noon, I pretended it was a real burden before agreeing. Sure enough, right at noon the next day, he walked up to my Pontiac Catalina with that red fanny pack around his waist. A fresh welt bled out on his forehead, and I said, "Did Longtin punch you on the way out?" I didn't blame Longtin, me taking his big barback out from under him like that. But I'm glad I did. I was, anyway, for a good while, glad I did.

To return to The Gutshot after so many years felt like a trespass, but at least I was the one trespassing into the memory rather than the other way around. Since I expected never to be in the neighborhood again, I figured I'd go inside and see if Longtin remembered me as well as I remembered him. His daughter, Harper, would be twelve now. Who knows why certain names stick. The Gutshot, and Longtin, and Longtin's baby girl—her name was Harper.

Having left Fuji in the truck with a window cracked open and a can of tuna I'd pocketed at a gas station in Buttonwillow, I followed the familiar alleyway to the five steps descending into the yellow door of The Gutshot.

The bar—portraits of the Tombstone Gunmen hanging at odd angles on every wall—hadn't changed much in the years since my last visit, but right away I noticed the major difference: the young man behind the bar—pink-haired and pierced—was certainly not my old friend Longtin.

I took a stool at one end of the rail, opposite a group of four kids who were clearly—metal in their skin—friends of the bartender's. I asked for a minute to consider my order and a cup of coffee creamer in the meantime, which I knew Fuji would enjoy.

"Longtin?" said the punk before I was even through asking. "Never heard of him. You gonna order a drink?"

I'm old, but I'd like to think I still intimidate people. I tie my hair back to showcase the main feature of my face, the glossy vertical runs of scar tissue on my forehead, which I got blading myself year after year in the wrestling ring. The art on my forearm—a pair of crossing cannons stamped onto me in the navy in 1946, when I crossed the equator for the first time—has been misconstrued as a prison tattoo, though I've never been locked up, not in that sense, anyway. What I'm saying is, for the past thirty years, shoppers in the supermarket have leaped out of their way to avoid the aisle I'm in, but this new generation, these punks, they aren't intimidated in the least. They seem to recognize me as one of their own.

I said, "My ex-wife once told me, if you don't have enough money to tip, you don't have enough money to drink. So, no, I was just passing through. Good night."

The punk filled a mug under the tap and told me to sit down a minute. He was a good kid, and I told him so. I could hear in his voice that all those piercings and dyes, all that traveling in gaggles and packs, were balms for some great fear in him. In that way, I suppose, we were of the same ilk. I thanked him and pulled the beer to my lips.

The punk left me to drink alone. I was halfway through when he returned from his pack of friends at the end of the rail and asked me, "You said his name was what, now?" Then he called to the back, "Raul—come out here!"

From the kitchen came a man wearing what might have been the same beige apron The Brow Beater was wearing when I'd first seen him eleven years ago. This new donner of the apron, Raul, wore the strings more loosely around his waist and neck and hardly lifted his feet when he walked. "Huh?"

"This old ponytail is looking for someone who used to work here."

"Longtin," I said.

Raul scratched at his goatee and said, "Damn, I haven't heard that name in a minute. I worked with him a long time back."

"When did he leave?" I asked.

"Shit, like ten or eleven years ago?" Raul untied his apron, coming over to the bar. "Our girls used to play together with the jukebox." He draped his apron over the stool next to mine and told the bartender to pour a beer for him and another for me.

"I can't tip," I said, but Raul waved that away like smoke.

"So there's a story with Longtin," he said after a gulp, mustache all foam and drip. "He was opening the bar one afternoon, and this guy knocks at the door."

"Oh," the bartender said. "This is the guy who got held up at gunpoint and quit the next day?"

"Kind of," Raul said. "Only it wasn't a holdup. The dude with the gun didn't take any money, nothing like that. In fact, the dude looked rich. He was a small guy but dressed real nice. Suited and booted, the whole nine."

"Like a gangster," one of the other punks said.

"So what did the gangster want?" I asked.

"He was here for the same reason you're here. He came looking for someone. Don't ask me who—I think it must've been someone who worked here before I did. Maybe another hermano, I don't know, because Longtin said the guy had been directed here by this woman who used to teach English around here."

That's when I remembered Longtin telling me how he'd hired The Brow Beater in the first place. A regular of his, an older woman, taught English to immigrants. In her Southern California youth, she'd studied Spanish, the language of almost all her students, but she'd also worked with a select group of immigrants from Soviet Armenia, the country her own parents had come from. These students were personal projects, she said, and in addition to helping them learn English, she tried whenever possible to arrange for them some semblance of an American social life. Hobbies, sporting clubs, volunteer work. Her most recent Armenian student—"An enormous but entirely sweet-hearted boy"—might make for a strong bouncer or handyman, she said, at The Gutshot. When Longtin agreed to hire her student, she brought him a warm dish of homemade honey-dripped baklava.

"You remember the name of this woman," I asked, "the English teacher?"

Raul nodded while he finished his beer. "Val-an-teen," he said. "She used to come in for a drink every other night. Had a rat-sized dog with her that Longtin always let in. She used to give me an ESL business card every time she talked to me, and I'd be like, Bitch, first of all, we've already met, like, a hundred times, and second, we've *been* talking in English."

"Racism," chimed in one of the punks, the only white one.

When the door came open, signaling the arrival of new customers, our impromptu symposium broke gently apart, and we each returned to our rightful spot. I watched Raul head back to the service doors, knotting his apron behind his back. Out of curiosity I called after him, "You don't happen to have one of those business cards of hers still lying around, do you?"

Only the money and the miles were real, I'd told The Brow Beater the night I'd discovered him, but of course time was real, too. In our sport, there was no off-season, no sick day, no union regulating the hours we worked or the pay we received. No insurance, no pension. As contractors, we were freelancers in almost the medieval sense of the word, fighters and jesters for hire, traveling from territory to territory so that our gimmicks stayed fresh to the rotating audiences. It wasn't unusual to fight nine matches a week in five different cities, doubles on the weekends, gyms in the mornings, and highways between them.

Time was too real, too fleeting, to train The Brow Beater in any real sense of the word. He learned on the job, in the ring, and we'd practice promos on the road. His English was pretty good, but he couldn't speak without thinking, so I did most of his promos for him. On top of that, I'd give him a few basic pointers—how to take bumps without busting his spine, for instance—and then we'd go over his matches in detail in the car to the next city. His Greco-Roman background helped with his footwork and his endurance, but otherwise I told him to forget all that grappling.

"You're a giant," I told him. He had to fight like one—lumbering but strong, invulnerable to punches and kicks, almost impossible to take down to the mat. It was all psychology, I told him. Who are you in that ring? Who's your opponent? What's the story we're telling? I told him he was too big to show pain unless he was gouged in those buried eyes of his. "That's your only downfall," I said, "those eyes under that big brow. Nothing else, you understand?"

He understood—for a while, he understood. But soon he discovered that pain was real, too. Trying not to hurt each other, we hurt ourselves instead. The Brow Beater was still green, after all, and nothing wreaked havoc on a body like being big and green at the same time. I watched him pay his dues, just like we all did, wrestling through a broken thumb, a dislocated shoulder, a torn meniscus, at least two concussions, and enough mat rashes and bruises to make the hairs on his chest hurt. There was a time, about four months after I'd discovered him at The Gutshot, when I was absolutely sure he would quit. And that's why I started telling him so much about my brother.

For those first few months, as we traveled from Los Angeles to Vancouver, I'd be rambling on and on about psychology, about the business, and I'd look over and find The Brow Beater staring out the passenger window of my Catalina, half-listening at best. Eventually, I chalked up his distracted nature to a lack of interest. One day in the car, after a particularly long stretch of silence on the road, I said, "No shame in getting out of this business, big fella. I would've done the same a long time ago, I bet, if it weren't for Gil. He's the only reason I got into wrestling in the first place. Gil's my brother."

I swear—The Brow Beater turned so fast in his seat, the Catalina changed lanes without my steering.

"Bro," The Brow Beater said, focusing on me for the first time. "You have a brother?"

"Had," I said, and pretty soon I was telling The Brow Beater the story of the Sportsmen's Club in Bremerton, Washington. It was the venue where I'd seen my very first wrestling match, back in September 1945 (The Brow Beater—"The hair, bro"—couldn't believe how old I was). Back in 1945, I told him, just after my eighteenth birthday and while most people were celebrating the end of the war, I was getting ready to leave home for the navy. Back then,

Gil was only twelve, and he'd embarrassed himself a few weeks earlier by begging me not to leave. I'd struck him with an open palm—lovingly, half-jokingly, I thought—but he cried and embarrassed himself even further. After that he saw a poster for a professional wrestling event at the Sportsmen's Club, and I decided I'd take him to see it. I was feeling pretty guilty over the way I'd ribbed him into tears, and I guess now I can say I was probably feeling, too, a kind of longing for our time together as boys. So I bought two tickets and surprised him after school.

What did I remember of the event now? Not much—nearly naked men, small as mice from the nosebleeds, throwing their shining bodies into each other with abandon. There was that noble childish vision of clear good triumphing over clear evil. One of the wrestlers, the winner of the main event, was a man by the name of Lou Thesz. All these years later, I still remembered his name. I'd taken Gil to the arena knowing full well that the matches were staged. But on the bus ride back, when Gil lifted his cap in mock modesty and said, "See, I told you it was real," I, Terrence J. Krill—Seaman Recruit Krill, for God's sake—said, "Well, maybe Lou Thesz is legit. I'll give you that. Maybe his match was real."

When I told the story to The Brow Beater, I didn't mean it as a window into my biography but as a demonstration of what a great wrestler could accomplish, what he ought to send a fan out into the world feeling. A kind of magic trick, I said, and all that's needed for the magic is one person in the ring who believes in the story he's telling so completely as to create doubt among the doubters. One person with enough talent and charisma and conviction to make fiction more convincing than life.

Only later—after the navy, after my years on the fishing boat—did I learn the specific techniques to get the magic trick to work. I couldn't explain pain, but I learned to get mine across. I learned what to pay attention to in other matches: not the blood—which is where the average fan looks—but the eyes. In them I saw presence, real presence. Not the presence we talk about when we talk about star power, but that other, more elusive presence, that unwavering attention to being alive. I'd gone all over this country and told The Brow Beater what I'd found: the wrestling ring was the only place where two men could be present in that way together, where two men used their presence to take real care of each other. Real care. Out there we had each other's literal breathing lives in our hands, and if we watched a wrestling match closely enough, we could spot a devoted focus in every slam, a tenderness in every hold. It's like one of those modern paintings, I told him. From a distance you see violence. Up close you find love.

The Brow Beater stopped me there. He said, "Had? You had a brother?"

"I'm getting to that part," I said, because I wasn't telling only the story of my brother's death but also the story of how my guilt over his death led me to my life in wrestling, and a story about guilt is a confession, and a confession can't be rushed. So I told The Brow Beater how, after four years in the navy, I'd taken a job onboard a fishing vessel. The war was done—I'd come of age the day after the second bomb dropped in Japan—and my time in the service felt merely decorative. I'd come home from the navy with all the markings of a sailor except the ones that counted, the ones I might've gotten had I been born a little earlier or a little later. I came home in 1949 with nothing to do but drink and show off my tattoos, so I jumped back onto a boat as soon as I could, leaving Seattle one morning for the Alaskan coast. I was called a "seafood processor," a fancy term for a deckhand. I lifted nets as big as trailers to identify and sort the different species. I ran the processing machinery, cleaning the guts and blood and slime from its rollers.

I packed the pans, labeled and stacked product in the freezer hold. I backloaded supplies onto the vessel, I repaired nets, I scrubbed the head, I scraped the frozen blisters off my hands while taking the coldest shits I ever took, I watched the steam rise up between my thighs like the eight vaporous minutes of rest in my sixteen-hour workdays. For three months at a time, with no days off, I was out on that vessel with fish guts in my hair, all shine and silver scales, and the bosun took to calling me "Angel Hair."

Between contracts, I spent a miserable week onshore. I resented those breaks, staying with my parents and my kid brother as if I were a child, and if the law hadn't forced a break between contracts, I'd have stayed on the ocean the rest of my life.

Spending twelve out of every thirteen weeks on the water, I missed most of the major life events in my family. I was on the boat during the burglary that stole my mother's favorite heirloom, a Saint Christopher medallion she'd planned to give her first grandson. I was on the boat during my father's second heart scare. I was on the boat during Gil's graduation from high school. When I got back on land, he told me he'd joined the army. This was in February 1950. "Anything I should know?" he asked, and I told him, "War's over. We were born too late to matter."

Back on the boat, I couldn't accompany my family to the docks in June, when the conflict started, when Gil shipped off to Korea. By December, he'd been killed, but because I was on the boat when it happened, I wouldn't know until my contract was up in February 1951. His remains had already been sent back. I'd missed the funeral. My parents had been grieving for months by the time I heard the news, and Gil's girlfriend, Joyce—who was like family to us—had already begun to digest the news in her own absurd and disturbing way. That left me alone to speed up my grief so that I could catch up with the rest of them, a process I figured might be easier on the road.

"How I joined the wrestling business is a whole other story," I told The Brow Beater. "But now you've got the why."

He palmed the top of my head, and we drove quietly like that for a while. From that point on, I knew he wouldn't quit.

Back in the camper shell of the truck, Fuji and I slept until the meters started running again. It was early Wednesday morning in Hollywood, but I was on pace to arrive at Johnny Trumpet's bungalow a whole day early. In my shirt pocket, I found an old business card, thin as lace with age and yellow with grease. Raul had untacked it from a bulletin board in the kitchen at The Gutshot. *English Language Lessons from Valantin*, it read. When he handed it to me, Raul had said, "If you find Longtin, tell him I said what's up." Of course, I'd said, but already I knew I was searching for someone else.

6

Batumi, Soviet Georgia, 1974

Mina herself admitted it: the dice really did roll differently when hers was the hand that threw them. They rolled her way more often than not—more often, certainly, than they did for Ruben. The two of them had spent the entire smack of their youth competing with each other in tournaments regional and national, and Mina almost always won. It came as no surprise, then, when Tigran—tasked with choosing a student to represent Soviet Armenia for the world tournament in Paris—announced that he would be taking, for the first time in the tournament's history, a girl.

Leading up to the trip to Paris, Tigran appointed her old rival to be Mina's sparring partner. The gig had been sold to Ruben as iron sharpening iron, but ten daily hours lurched over the losing side of a backgammon board had him feeling aggrieved and blunted. Several sessions in, he escaped one night to the city square and complained to Avo.

Just earlier, as the sun was setting, Avo had overheard a group of girls making plans to see the new Russian film showing in the theater, *The Duel*. Avo didn't particularly want to watch the movie—he'd never even heard of the book it was adapted from—but one of the girls involved in the plan was Mina. When Ruben found him,

Avo was hiding from the rain under the lip of the bureau building, peering around its corner to keep an eye on the theater at the other side of the square. The night had just begun, and so had the movie. Maybe, Avo thought, a seat near Mina was still available.

Ruben clapped his hands together without a break in his venting. He had seemed larger in Avo's split attention, but now that Avo was looking at him against the long wall of the bureau office, Ruben appeared much smaller. On the wall beside him stretched an enormous poster, mostly washed out in the rain. It used to say: "We Grow Under the Sun of Our Country," but now cried, "row Under . . . try."

"Then again," Ruben continued, "maybe I'll surprise myself. Maybe when she wins in Paris, I'll feel proud, like I really helped, like I genuinely am part owner of the trophy."

A pause in the rain lured pigeons from their hideouts. Soon they were everywhere, one enormous and indistinguishable flapping about the square, and the statue of Sergey Kirov was drenched with creamy shit. His bronze helmet of hair had gone white, as if aging in an instant, just like that, under a feathered flash of bird flight. Now the moon broke free from the clouds, and the rain seemed to be finished for the night, and a crew of men arrived with a hose to blast the statue clean. Across the square, the cinema doors opened, and Avo pictured Mina inside, chewing a string of dates and walnuts.

"I suppose I'll know soon enough," Ruben said. "They leave for Paris in just a few weeks. Maybe if she wins, it won't be all that bad. Maybe she'll stay in Paris and never come back."

They'd abandoned the bureau office for the fountain, where Avo threw one boot onto the ledge. He hadn't considered the possibility that Mina might stay abroad. "I hope not," he said. "I'm just starting to get to know her." When Ruben chose not to respond, Avo lifted the conversation back to its feet. "Tigran and Mina—just the two of them are going?"

"Just the two of them," Ruben said, and he explained how each country, including each republic in the Soviet Union, got two representatives: a teacher and a junior player.

Avo looked again to the theater, but he could hear the injury in Ruben's self-esteem. He reminded Ruben how the Ministry of Education had courted him, how he was set to do great things, regardless of one stupid backgammon tournament.

"This isn't about backgammon," Ruben said, and then pointed at the men hosing down the statue of Kirov. "You see them? That's us. That's Armenia. Empire after empire after empire, and who are we? What do we do? We blast shit off Russian heroes."

"I agree. Pigeons should have Armenian heroes to shit on."

"Joke all you want, but I have news. You know that man I've been in touch with in Beirut?"

"What?" Avo said.

"This man—he saw the letter from the Ministry, my scores, and one of Mina's uncles knows him through this international Armenian association they both belong to. They're basically a group of history buffs. Her uncle put him in touch with me last year."

"Last year? When were you going to tell me about this?"

"I thought I did. Maybe you were looking around, distracted, while I was telling you."

Avo wiped his brow. He said, "So who is this guy?"

"In the letters he's written to me, he calls himself Hagop Hagopian. I've read about him in newspapers, and they say he goes by other names, too. He's only twenty-three, apparently, even though I feel there's a much wider gap than five years between us. He's as worldly and knowledgeable as anyone Old Yergat's age, because he's been a soldier and a revolutionary in Iraq and in Lebanon, and now he's leading a new organization. Reparations. He says he's impressed by me and wants to meet me. He wants to meet *us*."

"Us?"

"I told him about you, too, about your skills."

"How big and strong I am, right, so I can be a bodyguard?"

"I told him how easy people feel around you, how impossible it is to dislike you."

Avo palmed Ruben's head and pushed him gently away. "Ah, yes. That's what the Turks have been waiting for: charm."

"Joke, joke, joke, but here's my real news. Hagopian can't travel here—the Soviets would detain him. So he asked if we could meet outside the USSR."

"Which we can't."

"Unless we're in Paris in a few weeks," Ruben said, "which is where I told him to find us."

"But we're not going to Paris," Avo said. "Tigran and Mina are going to Paris."

This time Ruben was the one to check the theater. "Now," he said, "you understand our problem."

The next day, after long hours of losing to Mina, Ruben was packing his backgammon set, getting ready to walk home. Tigran followed him outside, chasing him down with his lapels up and a hand on his cap. They stopped in the shadow of a tall, sickly shrub. "Serious boy," Tigran said, breathing hard, "grave boy. You've been humble, you've been good." A man in his sixties, Tigran smelled like dried figs and Russian cigarettes. He lit one now and pulled Ruben close. As he spoke, he held the smoke inside. "Tomorrow I'm taking my wife and kids and grandchildren on a vacation. There's a beautiful beach I know of on the Black Sea. We'll eat, talk, have a little taste of arak—you're old enough now, yeah?—and swim. I take my family every year. Tomorrow you and Mina will join us, and we'll have a celebration for what you've done for her talents and what she'll do for our country in Paris. Any other decade, serious boy, and you would have easily been my pupil at the games. She's simply a wonder, and you've helped harness her gift. Better than even I could. *Bravo*, Ruben-jan. *Bravo*."

That last word sounded to Ruben like the name of his brother, and before he realized he was speaking, he heard himself ask Tigran if Avo could join them at the Black Sea, too.

"The big one?" Tigran laughed. "We'll have to strap him to the roof of one of the cars."

"If there's no room for him," Ruben said, "there's no room for me."

"All right, serious boy, all right," Tigran said, offering a cigarette to Ruben. "We'll make room."

How many cigarettes did Ruben smoke on the drive to the Black Sea, folded onto Avo's lap beside four young children in the backseat of a boxy Trabant? "Like a ventriloquist and his dummy," said Avo, making the kids laugh, and Ruben ashed his cigarette on top of a little boy's head.

For four hundred kilometers to the coastal town outside Batumi—nine hours for the three-car cavalcade—Avo wished he had Mina in his lap rather than Ruben. Ruben was about the same size as Mina, but Avo couldn't get himself to pretend. She was traveling comfortably in the front seat of one of the other cars, the one driven by Tigran. Once in a while, whenever Ruben rolled the window down for air, Avo threw his hand out and made a stupid finger-stretching motion as far from the car as he could reach. Fingers stretching and waving like crab legs leaving their shell. Maybe Mina would notice.

At a bend in the road, a sign in multiple languages welcomed them to the SSR of Georgia. Ruben patted the back of Avo's hand as if they'd accomplished something grand. And maybe, Avo thought, they had. Technically, they were still in the Soviet Union, but the wind stealing their ash out the window seemed to move differently. For the first time, they'd left their country, and the strange wind swirled.

The Black Sea was a peaceful teal stripe along the horizon, but by the time they unpacked the cars and set up camp at the lake, there was no stopping the mosquitoes. They seemed to lurch from the endless water like spores. Ruben swatted the back of his neck, cursing, and within an hour, Avo's swollen ankles looked like kneecaps. The children cried and batted one another, running around the campsite as Tigran took a seat in front of the fire his adult son, Dev, was building. All anyone could talk about was the odd conflation of the twilight beauty of the sea and the brutal ubiquity of the bloodsuckers.

Then Mina came out from her tent in a yellow one-piece bathing suit to rest her feet. She was sitting on a flipped bucket, stretching her legs along the tips of the tall grass between her and the fire. The bottoms of her feet were glowing. She said, "What are you all complaining about? I haven't been bitten a single time."

"Her luck continues," Tigran said, lifting his cup. "Let the Parisians hear the mosquitoes buzzing: We are not worthy of Mina's blood!"

Later, after they'd gone to their tent, Ruben fumed. He and Avo were sharing the tent with three little boys, Tigran's grandsons, who had either fallen fast asleep or mastered the art of pretending. "The bugs aren't worthy of her *blood*?" Ruben whisper-screamed. "Maybe they've smartened up to the poison in it, I should've said. Or maybe, like I've been saying all this time, she's just the luckiest person who ever lived. I swear, Avo. The way everyone lavishes her with praise for something she has no control over. Nothing real—not skill, not intelligence—but luck. Luck! I really can't take this anymore."

Avo whispered back, "It's not only luck, though, is it? She's skilled, too. She had to understand and learn those proofs. I couldn't have done that."

"Well, I could, and I did. I memorized them, too. But she wins. She has luck on her side, and I don't."

Avo pictured Mina's feet hanging over the campfire, the way her toes glowed orange, how the veins in the top of her feet bulged when she rolled her ankles this way and that to crack them. All those little veins threading her together. Avo had never been a great student. He'd taken anatomy and, aside from an athlete's fixation on the names of muscles and tendons, remembered very little. But he did recall that the blood in the brain was somehow different than the blood circulating through the rest of the body. This was why infections of the brain were so rare. But Mina's feet over the fire seemed to burn the edges of that fact away, and he began to imagine that the blood flowing in her feet was the same that pumped through her brain, which was to say her self, and everything that made her *Mina* lived in that blood: the way she cradled her chin with the cup of her thumb, the curious squish of her eyes when she waved to him from across the city square, the heavy stomp to her walk, the made-up word *dakalash*, meaning *adorable*, which she'd used to describe everything from the way the dice fell to the way Avo's eyebrow had breached the gap he'd been born with to become one. Everything that made her Mina was a product of the blood in her brain. And for a moment, annoyed with Ruben and unburdened by the strict facts he'd learned in school, Avo let himself attribute Mina's personhood to those feet over that fire, and he wanted to touch them so badly that he almost whimpered.

Ruben was asleep. Avo parted the opening of the tent and crawled out to the dark shore like evolution in reverse. Including his, four tents lined the beach. Not tents, really, but cotton sheets strung up on poles and wires. Which was hers? He couldn't risk waking the others. Couldn't go rip apart the sheets of every tent looking for her. Maybe he should've watched Mina go to bed instead of following Ruben to their tent. He glided across the sand to the tent nearest to his. On his toes, he was just tall enough to crane over the top of the cotton walls and peer down through the gaps in the makeshift ceiling. The first tent belonged to Tigran and his wife, who were lying on a dark blanket. They were sleeping peacefully, but there was something inherently menacing about the sight of an old couple asleep on the ground. A pair of bodies in the sand—the image felt familiar, even though Avo had never seen it. In fact, the image haunted him badly enough that he made a promise to himself: if he didn't find Mina in the next tent he checked, he would end his quest and crawl back to bed.

But there she was, in the very next tent. She lay surrounded by Tigran's four small granddaughters, a blanket drawn to her chin. He had to stop himself from laughing at how cherubic a scene she'd fallen into, a shrouded Madonna enshrined by angels. How could he bring himself to wake her? Oh, but he had to, had to find a quiet way to signal to her to meet him at the shore.

The shore. He went to the lake, removed his shirt, and dipped it into the lapping water. He brought the dripping shirt back to Mina's tent, tiptoed over the top again, and wrung a bit—just a drop, and another—of cold seawater onto her face. He imagined her coming to angelically, each long-lashed blink a further grasping of where she was and who was waking her and what she would be doing next.

Less angelically, she screamed.

A scream in the dark was an unearthly thing. It spread quickly, not only to the granddaughters sprawled around her but to the parents and grandparents in the other tents in the camp. In a haze of adrenaline and fear, everyone rushed to the source of the scream. Tigran's middle-aged son, Dev, came wielding a sturdy plank of wood that must have washed ashore, who knows how long ago.

By the time Mina calmed down enough to explain that she'd felt something wet before waking to a shadowy figure looming over her against the night sky, Avo had successfully scampered back to his tent and out again, pretending to be as confused as everyone else. Tigran's wife had taken Mina's head in her lap beside the newly relit fire, stroking her hair. Mina was crying, Avo could see. She wasn't some Madonna but a seventeen-year-old girl. Between fits of tears, she was telling Tigran's wife all about the stories her grandmother had relayed to her growing up, of being marched from home in the night by Turks, of being raped by Kurdish mercenaries in the desert, of being split open by gendarme bayonets, of all the horrors that began with an unexpected face in the night.

Jesus, Avo thought. All he'd wanted was to rub her feet. Somehow that now seemed worse. He could hardly look at her. She was sobbing and pawing her face because of him.

Of course the children started wailing, too, and so they were all corralled into one of the tents with their parents for the night. Avo returned to find Ruben lying alone in theirs, his skinny, pale back reflecting whatever starlight Avo had let in. Avo hauled his bedding to the newly vacant space as far from his brother as he could get, and said luxuriously, "So I got us a bigger tent."

"I knew it was you," Ruben said into the wool blanket coiled under his head. "It was a mistake to bring you. Especially with that woman here."

"You mean Mina?"

"Who else?"

"I don't think of her as a woman, is all. She's our age. She's a girl."

"That's an act," Ruben said. "You can't see it because she has power over you. But she's not a girl. She's a woman. Or at least she's woman*ly*."

He knew Ruben wasn't joking, was never joking, but Avo couldn't control himself. *Womanly*. Might as well have been *evil-ish*. Avo was shaking, laughing through an apology for laughing.

Ruben, still facing the other way, seemed to be trembling a bit himself, but not from laughter. He sniffed. He sucked in air. He said, "I wish I had a crumb-sized piece of her luck."

What a miserable way to be, Avo thought, outraged on one hand and sentimental on the other. No boy half Ruben's age could say something like that without a slap upside the head, and Avo was just about ready to deliver it when Ruben surprised him by saying more.

"I don't blame you," he said. "It's just that this trip was supposed to be about showing her that I don't need Paris. That I have something she doesn't. I have you. I'm loyal to you. I've been nothing but loyal to you, and now I feel very stupid. I feel very alone."

"You're not," Avo said. He rolled, side over side, until he was there at Ruben's back. "Brother, you're not."

This close, Avo could see an enormous mosquito bite, swollen to the size of a knuckle, rising from the skin between Ruben's shoulder blades. A compulsion came over him to scratch at his own bites on his ankles and his wrists. Outside, the last of the fire was crackling, and the final concerned campers had returned to their tents. One scratch led to another, and soon both brothers were sitting up, spinning every now and then to claw at the other's unreachable bites in the dark and spacious tent, where neither of them could fall asleep again if they tried.

"There are lots of Armenians in Paris," Ruben whispered over the scratching. "I'm not sure if you knew that."

"You should be one of them," Avo said. "Can't we figure out how to get you on that trip?"

"There are two tickets. One is Tigran's. The other belongs to the player of his choice."

"I'm sure Mina would give you her spot if you asked."

"It's my spot. No one gets the kind of luck she has. She must be cheating. I'm not asking her for my own spot."

"We could plant a loaded die in her pocket to prove she's a cheater," Avo said jokingly.

"When we get home, we'll find one, or you will—it'll have to be you, since I have too much to gain to be involved. It has to be you."

"Easy," Avo said, "I was kidding." He said he'd never stamp someone a fraud for the rest of her life, reminding Ruben about how petty Mr. V had become, consumed by self-righteousness over a twenty-year-old game. "Imagine Mina spending the rest of her life trying to defend herself," he said. "Telling the truth but nobody believing her, the truth about something nobody will ever care about as much as she does. I'll help you get Mina's spot, but not like that. Not something permanent like that."

"There's another way," Ruben said. "If she can't travel."

The mosquitoes hadn't been much of a problem since sundown, but now every itchy bite on Avo's ankles and elbows seemed to birth a new bug, and he felt swarmed by them, waving at his face to avoid being eaten alive.

"You want to hurt her," he managed to say.

"Not seriously," Ruben said. "Just enough to require a reserve."

"Come on," Avo said. "The mosquitoes must've sucked the blood out of your brain."

"If she goes to Paris, Avo-jan, she'll have a nice vacation. If I go, both of our lives will change forever. We're better than hurting a girl, yes, but we're also better than spending our lives in a drunken village in the corner of a dying empire, aren't we?"

Gratitude could be selfish and genuine all at once. Who else had made room for Avo in an imagined future? No one. Certainly not Mina, who wasn't bored of the past, as she'd claimed, but terrified of it. So terrified, apparently, that she couldn't recognize him standing over her tent.

"I couldn't do it," Avo said.

"It's so easy to slip and fall on those slimy rocks near the shoreline, you know. I bet there are two or three pairs of sprained wrists every summer here. I bet—"

"Maybe when Tigran passes," Avo said. "I hate to say it, but maybe it won't be so long from now, and maybe then you can take over for him, and then you can take a student to the next tournament. Every ten years, right? Ten years isn't so long. Ten years is nothing, your mosquito bites are bigger than ten years."

"You're lying to yourself. Everything can change overnight, and who knows it better than we do? Everybody else in this stupid country is a Soviet first. Soviet first, Russian second. Soviet first, Ukrainian second. Not us. We're Armenian first, and always have been, and we've seen the world's greatest empires come and go, whole governments overturned, whole civilizations burned—overnight. Overnight, and you know it. Remember Yergat? How old was his daughter, with the coins pressed in her hand? Ten years old. Ten years was her lifetime. Ten years is *a* lifetime, Avo—you know that. In Paris, with those wider-minded Armenians, we can shape our life. This is our only opportunity to do this. Our opportunity. You and me. I have a plan for us, a real plan. We can either stay home and trade the rest of our lives and livelihoods for rejected travel visas, or we can try this. Now. Without you, I won't go, either. I'll work in the factory right beside you. I'll learn a trade and die fixing buttons to shirts or blasting shit off statues. For you, I'll do that. But we can do something greater together, if only you'll do this for me."

The fire had stopped crackling, and their scratching had stopped, but of course other sounds came to fill the silence. A wave lapped at the rocks along the shore, and another, the same but for the smallest shifts in rhythm.

One of the brothers suggested they try to sleep, and they spent the rest of the night on their backs with their eyes shut, pretending.

Fog, early. Dim but warm, like a bulb under a sock. The children collected stones at the shore. Hunted for, more like. They crouched low to study their discoveries, turned them in their hands the way they'd seen their fathers roll cigarettes, looking to see if the stones passed whatever mysterious test was being administered. They slipped the good ones into the knit bags strapped over their shoulders. As for the stones that failed, those they hurled out over the dull glass of the sea.

Soon the adults joined, Mina among them in her yellow bathing suit, scratching at the dimple in her collarbone. She'd folded her hair under a beige swimming cap, but two hooks of shiny black hair escaped in front of her ears. At the shoreline she said good morning to the children, who opened their bags to show her the best of their collections. Then she walked farther into the water, toward the approaching swells, until she was swimming, diving into one of the swells, a moving ridge of sea that swallowed her headfirst, burped her out from behind, and broke gently into a foam over the children's toes at the shore.

While Avo watched her swim, Ruben joined the adults for a fireside breakfast. Tigran's wife and daughter-in-law had made and packed a stack of lamajun as tall as a tree stump, each thin circle of beef-spread bread separated by a greasy sheet of parchment, and now the campers who weren't planning on getting in the water were at the fireside, peeling the lamajun apart. Ruben and his teacher heated their slices over the fire, spritzed them with lemon, rolled them into tubes, and ate them in no more than a few bites. Over the fire, the wheat and the spiced meat sent their grilled smells into the world, cut with the scent of lemon juice, and suddenly, the fishy coast of Georgia smelled exactly like an Armenian kitchen.

"Hungry?" Tigran asked, catching Avo loitering between the fire and the shore. "I probably shouldn't invite you to eat. I had an uncle like you—big. Had a real appetite. My aunt used to hide food in the house."

Everyone laughed but Ruben, eating silently beside his teacher, looking out over the sea.

Avo knew he was watching Mina, all alone out there in the dangerous water. Almost asking for a fall. "Eat while you can," Avo tried to joke, but the tone came out menacing. "I'd like to swim first, I think."

After a quick change into his shorts in the tent, Avo ambled past the little treasure hunters on his way to the shore. The children, afraid of or awed by his size, had successfully avoided him the whole trip. But now one of the boys, maybe seven, tugged at his shorts and said, "Guess how many I found."

Mina had gone farther out, past where the water swelled and rolled. She was floating on her back, with her hands crossed over her chest at her shoulders. One streak of sunlight broke through the cloud cover, a white scar on the water near her feet.

"How many?" Avo said, thinking, Feet, feet, feet.

"Guess!" said the boy.

Was Mina floating back to shore? The sky was opening up, and she would leave soon to get some shade.

"Six," Avo said.

"Nope. Guess again."

Now Mina did seem to stir. She was still floating, but her arms had come uncrossed. "Let me go swim and think about it, and I'll come back with an answer."

"No! You have to guess correctly or else you cannot pass."

"Seven?"

"You're big," said the boy, "but you're a bad guesser."

"I have to go," Avo said, but the boy kept tugging at his shorts. "Guess!"

The sky was breaking open now, and Mina—he'd missed his chance—was swimming back to shore.

"You have to guess!"

"Ten?"

"Nope! Guess again."

"Just tell me dammit just tell me," Avo said in a single hoarse breath. He hadn't shouted, nobody had heard him but the little boy. Still, the boy broke into tears.

"Man," Avo said, kneeling down to look the kid in the face. "I'm sorry."

Mina emerged from the foam. "What happened?" she said, coming to them. "Is he okay?" She knelt to embrace the crying boy. "Are you okay?" Beads of seawater shivered on Mina's skin.

"We got frustrated," Avo said. "I couldn't guess how many stones he had in his pouch."

"He cursed me," the boy cried.

"Well," Avo said, "I cursed the *situation*."

"How about this," Mina said, taking the boy by his shoulders. "How about if I can guess the right number of stones you have, then we can forgive Avo? Does that sound fair?"

The boy sniffled. "Maybe."

"And if I'm wrong," she said, "we can go tattle on him to your grandpa."

"Yeah!" said the boy, immediately dry-eyed. "Okay, guess!"

Mina rested her chin on her fist, making a display of a deep, long rumination.

"Good thing you have your thinking hat on," Avo said, snapping her swim cap gently. A bad joke, but a joke. The first he'd made to her in a while.

"You only get one guess!"

"One guess, huh? Okay. Here goes. How about . . . seventeen? Do you have seventeen stones?"

The boy's face dropped. His eyes peered into Mina's, studying her like one of his rocks.

"Well?" asked Mina.

The boy emptied his bag onto the sand. He counted the rocks, and then began to count again.

"Yep," Mina said. "Seventeen!"

"Wow!" said the boy. "You're way better than he was."

As the boy happily re-collected his rocks, Mina and Avo started toward the fire.

"How'd you do it?" Avo asked, a little overwhelmed by the magic of her. He could really use a rational answer. Maybe, afloat on the sea, she'd watched the boy pick each rock up?

"Honestly," Mina said, "I just guessed."

* * *

Maybe she really was the luckiest person in the world. Somewhat grandiosely, it occurred to him that if Mina consistently drew good things to herself, he would need to be a good man to end up in her life. They walked to the fire together. The smell of lamajun roasted in the thinning fog, and Mina's attention became the new litmus test in Avo's mind for his own capacity to be good.

Breakfast was delicious but lonely. Ruben had already returned to his tent, having squeezed the last of a lemon into the fire. Tigran was having a post-breakfast smoke as Mina ate and they went over opening strategies for the tournament. The flirtation just a few minutes earlier—the way Avo slid his fingers beneath her swim cap to snap it, the playfully pestered look she gave him—seemed absurd to him now, seeing her in her professional mode. She'd wrapped herself in a large green towel that brought the green flecks in her eyes to life, but her focus was on her mentor. Unlike Avo, she had a reason to be here. She *was* the reason to be here.

Ruben was the reason Avo had been invited. How had it not occurred to him until just now, watching the green specks in a pair of eyes ignore him? Ruben must have insisted that Tigran invite Avo along on this trip, must have given the old man an ultimatum: Both of us or neither. The only way a double-reed worked. That Ruben hadn't extolled his act of loyalty to Avo—that he had not, in fact, mentioned it—made it an even holier act of kindness. Ruben's allegiance was pure. He didn't perform loyalty, hoping someone would notice. He simply *was* loyal.

Back in the tent, Ruben was reading the pocket-size Bible he'd apparently packed and brought along. The first half of the book was more dog-eared and worn than the second.

"Brought you some cantaloupe," Avo said, offering the plate. "Tigran's wife just cut a bunch. I know you're probably full already, but it's a good snack."

Ruben looked up from the book and pinched a cube of the orange melon into his mouth.

"Look," Avo said, "I missed my chance out there in the water, but I don't want you to think I've given up on the plan. I hate to say I think you're right. It's a small, necessary evil to get Mina out of the tournament so you can take her place. And it's my job to help you do that."

"When?" Ruben said, and when Avo said later tonight, after the children were asleep, Ruben stood and hugged him as high as he could reach, right around the ribs.

Outside, Tigran announced that the men were hiking to a secret fishing spot on the other side of the cove. Only the men and the older boys—Tigran, Dev, Ruben, and Avo—would be going. They would return after sundown, bearing dinner.

The hike took almost two hours. Tigran's son, Dev, led the way. He carried the poles and a belt equipped with hooks and bait, and Avo and Ruben each held a handle of the icebox they hoped to fill with fish. Every now and then Dev would stop to point out a large boulder jutting from the cliff to their right, or a strange patch of blue rocks on the beach to their left, to recount a story from his youth. "Dad spanked me over there, where those gulls are hanging out," he'd say about the time he'd thrown a rock at a bird. "I never was cruel to a bird again." Tigran himself was quiet, harnessing all his energy for the walk, which, flat though it was, was littered with loose and slippery rocks. The master with his cane moved slowly. An hour into the hike, he took a seat at the rock where his son had once blown a whistle made of grass. He apologized for being old.

"If it weren't for me," Tigran said, "you all would have caught some fish by now. Maybe I should have stayed back with the women and the children. Next year, that's what I'll do."

“You said that last year,” Dev said, and laughed. “And it was just as stupid a thing to say back then as it is now. Come on! You’re still young!”

“Last year I said it as a joke,” Tigran said, throwing his elbows over his cane, which he’d rested on the back of his neck.

By the time they arrived at the inlet, it was late afternoon. The mosquitoes wouldn’t attack for another hour. In the meantime, there was plenty of shade, and some pilchard to hunt. The inlet worked as a kind of funnel from the sea, collecting unusually large numbers of typically deeper-dwelling fish. The men stood on the rocks surrounding the inlet, throwing their lines into the water one by one. Tigran fished from his seat on the icebox and had to stand every now and then for the caught fish to be stored. When twilight arrived, and when the mosquitoes searched their skin for space between day-old bites, the group put away their rods and followed Dev to a farther piece of shore.

“The lobsters live in hollowed rocks along the submerged cliffs,” Dev said. “You can hand-fish for them any time of day, if you don’t mind diving down there and putting your hand into a dark hole under the sea. Otherwise, you can wait until sundown, when they come out of their caves and cling to the rocks here. Look—I see one already!”

Soon the rocks were crawling.

“How many can we take?” Avo asked.

“As many as we can carry,” Dev called from the water. He and his father were already on the hunt.

Avo moved to join them on the rocks, but Ruben stopped him. “Who do you think’s carrying the icebox back to camp?”

Avo remembered who had carried it on the walk out. “Us.”

“So let’s not get carried away,” Ruben said. “A few lobsters, not to mention all this fish we have already, will be enough for everyone for a week."

Already Dev and Tigran were bringing back two lobsters apiece, one in each hand, hollering about how many more they could fit in the cooler.

"We've never been able to carry more than a few," Tigran said. "But with this big beast of a boy here, we can probably take twenty!"

They dropped off their catches and went back out for more.

"Greedy," Ruben said. "Have you noticed how they're the only ones who seem to know about this place? This place where fish catch themselves? You'd think we'd be among a swarm of lazy bastards."

Avo watched the men out in the water take large, careful steps from rock to slimy rock. "Tigran told me he found this place by accident on his honeymoon," Avo said, keeping his eyes on the men. The sky was going orange behind the clumsy, crouching bodies. "Forty years, and no one else has found it. No one knows it's here."

"We should get back, then," Ruben said. "That means no one knows *we're* here."

Tigran slipped on one of the rocks. He caught himself before falling, though, and bellowed a laugh into the great clouds. "There it is again—my youth! Never mind what I said back there, Dev-jan! I can do this every year for another decade, at least!"

"What did you say?" Avo asked Ruben.

"We should go back to camp before it gets dark, if no one knows we're here. Imagine if the old man had actually fallen just now. What would we do, with no one around to find us?"

Avo believed he understood what was being said to him. He rolled up his pants. Almost ran to the old man on the rocks. The idea wasn't his, and it wasn't Ruben's—it seemed to belong to nobody. Seemed to have existed before people could think it up. Or maybe it had been transmuted to him by a mosquito bite, some other man's blood carrying the idea, mingling with his own.

"Oh, good," Tigran said, seeing Avo approaching. "Dev is around the bend there, and I needed some help picking this monster up. Come, give me a hand."

"Okay," Avo said, his heart swelling. "I'm on my way."

He imagined looking back to the shore to see Ruben, but the truth was he didn't. Dev was around the bend, out of sight. Only the mosquitoes and the lobsters were watching. Avo pretended to slip on the rocks. Reaching out for balance, he knocked Tigran down. The old man fell more violently than he'd expected. He fell as fast as a young man.

"Jesus," Avo said, getting low to offer a hand. "Tigran-jan, I slipped, I'm sorry!" It was surprising how convincing he found his own act. Only after admiring his own ability to act clumsy and sound sincere did he realize he was, in fact, both. "I'm sorry," he said, waiting for Tigran to respond. But Tigran didn't get up. A wisp of color—which Avo thought at first to be a bit of reflecting sunset—floated at the surface of the water near the head.

Then came the splashing. Ruben was running into the shallow water toward them, avoiding the rocks. Hollering for Dev. "He's had a fall," Ruben shouted, bending to pick the head up from the rocks. He seemed to understand that Avo would not be of any help getting the body to the shore. When Dev arrived, he started crying immediately. Avo had never seen a grown man sob before. "To the shore," Ruben said, and he and Dev lugged the body slowly through the water.

Bloody seawater fell into the corners of the dead man's lips. Little twigs clung to his beard. Somehow Avo found himself on the shore beside Dev, who was crouched over his father's body, pressing his shirt to the gash in the skull. The blood looked too thin to be real, which somehow proved it was real. Ruben brought a hunk of ice from the cooler to apply to the wound. Useless.

Dev knew it, too. He dropped the bloody shirt and laid his face on his father's chest. The sun had dropped below the horizon. Some stubborn bit of light lingered a while longer. Then Dev sat up and asked what happened.

I killed him, Avo wanted to say, but didn't. He wanted to tell the truth—that's the truth. If he'd been able to weigh his options and *decide* that lying would be the smarter choice, that lying would protect him, he would've walked into the darkening sea and kept going until he drowned. But his lying didn't appear to be a decision. He felt physically incapable of telling Dev the truth. He could conjure in his mind the simple sentence—*I killed him*—and envision himself saying it aloud. He could do that much. He could imagine the words and the sounds of them, imagine what would happen next, a lunge from Dev, maybe, a fight. Avo would be able to handle that. Could kill Dev, too, put him in a wrestling hold he hadn't used since childhood and send him to the grave alongside his father. And would Ruben intervene? If he did, would Avo kill him, too? Three bodies on the shore, and Avo climbing the cliffs into the Georgian wilderness, running toward roads and towns, hopping a train to Russia, assuming a new identity, living as anonymous a life as possible for a man as big and guilty as he was. That ridiculous melodrama, he could imagine. But Dev had asked a simple question: what happened? And suddenly, the simplest of sentences—*this happened*—was impossible for Avo to say. How easy it was, once he decided the truth was impossible, to go on living his real life.

The stars were perfectly scattered. Under them, Ruben and Dev carried the body back to the camp. One at the arms, one at the legs. Avo brought up the rear, dragging the icebox. Inside, the lobsters crawled over the dead and dying fish.

7

Kirovakan, Soviet Armenia, 1974

What was called a caravan on the way *to* the Black Sea—the same group of cars, the same set of bodies—was called, on the way home, a procession. The corpse lay in one of the Volgas like a vacationer who'd had too much to drink, driven alone by Dev at the front of the line. He kept a wild pace all the way from Batumi to Kirovakan, taking cliffside turns so recklessly that, on one particularly thin stretch of the road, the passenger door seemed almost to unlatch, threatening to unload Tigran's body over the edge of the world. But the door held, and the road straightened, and Dev kept at his headstrong pace, as if home were a place that could disappear if not returned to quickly enough, as if the speed of a return could undo the having left.

The body had come from the sea. Unearthly, the matted foaming beard and the gloss of the skin. Remembering it, Ruben chewed on the temple tips of his glasses. The body had been wet and full of sea things, little twigs, and Ruben told Mina he would pray for the courage to remember it.

There had been a moment, just after Tigran had overlooked him to choose Mina for the tournament, when Ruben had imagined his teacher's death. In the imagined version, Ruben had felt little more than a sense of justice being served. Now that the real thing had happened, all Ruben could remember—aside from the twigs in the beard—was the gift Tigran had given him. Not his old collection of dice—though he'd given those to Ruben, too—but the way Tigran had always seen Ruben's seriousness as a sign not of humorlessness but of promise. He was the only one, besides Avo, who'd given Ruben that.

So it wasn't that Ruben—as Avo seemed to believe—felt nothing, but actually, that he felt so much that the surprise at his own pain confounded him, contorted him inward. His silence, his refusal to cry out loud or otherwise perform his pain, might have been mistaken for an incapacity to feel, but Ruben began to think of it as a kind of reverence. An attempt to record the physical memory of the disaster, to remember the precise dullness in his arms as he helped haul the corpse from the cove to the camp. To recall exactly the arrangement of twigs in the matted beard, the scraping of the icebox dragged along the sand. The number of rests he and Dev had to take—twenty-four—setting down the body. The way the wet corpse picked up granules of sand. The way Dev tied the cane to the body's chest with fishing line. The way the body looked nothing at all like a flower skimming along the Euphrates.

As for Avo, he could hardly remember a single detail. He'd dragged that icebox back to camp, knowing he wouldn't be able to speak to Mina. After seeing her reaction to the news, he couldn't even look her in the face, let alone reach out to comfort her. He couldn't imagine holding her while she cried, knowing that he would never tell her the truth of what he'd done. And so, for the first few days back home, Avo avoided walking past the tallest building in Kirovakan. He avoided the ski lift and the nearby lemon trees. He stayed in the village in the hills with Ruben's parents, who asked why he wasn't out in town with their son.

"I'm tired," Avo said, but the truth was he couldn't be with Ruben because Ruben was with Mina. What they were doing together, Avo couldn't say. Surely Mina's participation in Paris had been canceled, so if they were playing backgammon, they were doing it in the memory of Tigran, not to practice for the tournament. Fine, Avo thought. They were the only two people in the world who shared Tigran in that way, and it made sense to Avo that they would look to each other in the wake of his death.

He wouldn't bother them, he decided. He would let them do their grieving. He would wait for them to return to him.

But as he waited, the same nagging thought kept occurring to him, that they would never finish their game.

As for Mina, she decided to put her grief to use. She continued training for the tournament and begged Ruben to stay on for their practice sessions. Ruben, in what she believed was an act of respect for Tigran, agreed to help. They tried to concentrate, but no matter how many times they set up the board, no matter how many times they rolled the dice and moved the checkers slot by slot, their focus drifted, and they traded stories about Tigran. She was in the middle of the story of the day he'd given her an old journal as a gift when she stopped herself. She said, "I want to win the tournament for him, but I don't think I can go to Paris alone."

She spoke with her eyes on the board, but afterward she crossed the two cascading sides of her black hair along her nose and looked up at him.

Ruben said, "I want you to win for him, too."

They played the next few moves in the longest silence between them since Tigran's death.

"I haven't seen Avo in days," she said. "I think he feels responsible for what happened, and I'd really appreciate it if you could tell him how wrong I think he'd be to feel that way. Or for you to feel that way." Across the board, she touched his hand. Ruben looked at her hand on his hand.

"You've always been kinder to me than most," Ruben said. "I'm not as good with people as Avo is, but I want you to know I appreciate you. You're a good person."

Mina said, "You're my friend. So is Avo. I'd like to see him again."

Ruben dropped the dice. He fixed the glasses on his nose. "I'll let him know," he said.

She thanked him and played her turn, rolling exactly what she needed to win. Clearing the board, she said, "What if you took Tigran's place? In Paris, I mean. Wouldn't he have liked that?"

Ruben put his hand over his heart. "I'd be honored," he said.

And then came the paperwork.

A leak tore through the roof, and of course the dripping fell directly over Ruben's father's pillow. He was the kind of man who could never be woken gently, who took every birdcall or creaking plank as a blight or a warning, who woke shouting "Who's there!" or "What!" no matter how sweetly he'd been nudged awake. The leak began in the middle of the night, and the entire village rumbled.

"What is it!" Ruben's father shouted. "Who now!"

In the morning, Avo was sent up to fix it. He dragged an old crate to the outer wall of the house, tossed the tools from there to the roof, and climbed up to join them in one long step. The rain held off just long enough for him to pry up the faulty shingles, to remove the nails underneath, and to affix the new shingles he'd asked the carpenter to spare.

Below, Siranoush was lighting the tonir, singing. No one else was around, and she didn't notice Avo watching her from the roof. She sang for herself: "White dough, white dough, what do you know, where is the fire, down below."

Then came the smell of the coals burning deep in the well. "Where is the fire, down below."

She knelt at the edge of the well, which was really nothing more than a meter-wide hole in the ground. Beside her was a large wooden cutting board, covered in white flour like paint on a palette. While the coals heated, she rolled and separated the dough, and when the well grew hot enough, she slapped the dough piece by piece between her hands, flattening it. She dressed the flattened dough over an oven mitt the size of a pillow, and spread the dough to the corners as if making a bed. Then she slapped the pillow against the walls of the well and started flattening another piece of the dough. By the time she finished covering the pillow with a new sheet of flattened dough, the baking dough was finished, bubbled black, and she peeled it from the wall of the tonir and laid it at her side. Soon she was sitting beside a tall stack of these flat black-bubbled loaves of bread, with no sign of slowing down. She must have been ninety years old, and Avo—legs dangling from the edge of the roof—marveled at her work. Roll, flatten, spread, and slap. Roll, flatten, spread, and slap.

"Black bubbles, black bubbles, what do you see. Where is the fire, inside me."

Avo meant to stay on the roof and watch her longer, but when his pry bar slipped and landed on the crate below with a thud, Siranoush looked up and saw him.

"Tall boy, tall boy, what do you want. Where has your brother, Ruben, gone. Hey—that wasn't bad, right? For something off the top of my head."

"Very impressive," Avo said.

"Come down here," she said.

Avo leaped down and came to sit with her at the tonir. He sat on the other side of the oven and saw her as a blur through the heat of the well. She continued her work as they spoke.

"You'll see him again," Siranoush said.

She meant Ruben—of course she'd noticed his absence from the village. Almost two weeks had gone by since Avo had met him, uninvited, at the train station, to wish him luck. Ruben was there with his mother and with Mina's parents. After a night of rain, the morning had turned unusually clear, and pools of rainwater between the tracks gleamed white and nearly blinding. Mina had already taken her seat aboard the train, ready for departure to Yerevan and the flight from there to Paris. Her parents seemed to be keeping Ruben, whispering words of advice, maybe, on how to keep their daughter safe. Ruben's mother was the one, loitering several steps away from the group, who noticed Avo watching. But when she waved him over to join, Ruben spun so quickly toward the train that his glasses fell from his face. Avo expected them to fall and shatter on the wet cement, but Ruben—surprising even himself, it seemed, by the way he examined the frames before lodging them back on his nose—caught them deftly in midair.

"You'll see him again," Siranoush said, but there was a little loftiness in her tone, hued red and mysterious as her hair, and Avo let himself believe she meant someone else, perhaps the supernatural, that he would see his father again, or Tigran, or the Almighty Himself at the day of judgment. So it was with all the solemnity of a guilt-ridden eighteen-year-old boy that Avo said, "I don't believe in God, Siranoush, if that's what you mean. And I don't want to disrespect you, but I don't believe in those angels in your story, either. I don't think there's any justice in this world except the justice we make."

Siranoush yawned. "You've spent too much time with that brother of yours," she said. "You used to have a sense of humor, if I remember correctly. Besides, you should at least have the decency not to pretend you've had an original thought."

Roll, flatten, spread, and slap.

"Well," Avo said, "that story of yours. Do you believe it yourself?"

She never looked up from working the dough. "Look," she said, "those angels are no less believable than the hell I saw as a girl. You understand? You see murder and torture with your own eyes in the open streets, and you get a choice. You get to react in one of two ways. Either you spend your life worshipping a God who allowed it to happen, wondering what mysterious good might come out of that evil, or you decide that people are alone, and basically animals. Still new, I mean, to civilized life. I was saved by a Turk—the biggest, ugliest fez-donning Turk you could imagine. He saved my life, and I was grateful. And yet when I asked him what had happened to my family, to my friends, he said I never had any. They were all a dream I'd had, he said. *He* was my brother, he explained. My family was *his* family. There was no past but his. I said he saved my life, but really, all he did was keep me living. My life, he tried to erase. I escaped before that happened. When I think of God, I think of him. Thanks for the air in my lungs, you know, but also, go to hell."

Through the blur of the heat, she winked. Roll, flatten, spread, and slap.

"I still have a sense of humor," Avo said, though he wanted to punch himself for the syrup of self-pity the sentence came out dripping with. He hadn't meant to sound so alone; then again, he hadn't meant to kill Tigran, either. If he could wreak lasting damage without meaning to, then the value of his intentions seemed increasingly hollow, and that line of thinking could lead only to the nearest deadly height from which to jump. Avo peered up at the roof he'd just leaped painlessly down from, and then he asked if Siranoush needed help with the lavash.

"My way might seem like a sad way to view the world," Siranoush said, shooing his help away, "but I promise you, it's not any sadder than trying to justify what happened to us. I always kept up appearances while Yergat was alive, because he was a believer. But I watched a man beheaded in the street with a dull blade. Six whacks and a final sawing. I watched four men hold my neighbor down and light her hair on fire. For what? So that some mysterious good may come of it in the end? No. No, thank you."

Roll, flatten, spread, and slap.

"But above all that, I hate when people tell other people how to live. I'm not doing that, Avo-jan. I'm not telling you how to live. Just that you should continue living for as long as you can. You are one of the better trained animals, it seems to me. Go on living, and help others live as long as they can, too."

He would tell her about Tigran, he thought. He could never tell Mina, who loved Tigran like a father, and so Avo would have to tell this woman instead, a surrogate Mina, with the heat between them turning her just invisible enough to mistake, a curtain of rippled air as heavy as the truth itself. But the truth wasn't simply a weight to bear. It felt more like a small room he was locked inside, alone, while a party went on in the rest of the house. He couldn't tell the whole truth to Siranoush—that would be like ruining the party by crying out—but maybe if he hinted at the story of his crime, a little hint at what he'd done, maybe that would relieve some of the pain of being alone in that room all night. It would feel like a visit during the party, a prying open of the door just enough so that she could bring him a piece of cake and let him know she was thinking of him.

"Siranoush," he said through the heat. "I hurt someone, accidentally."

She didn't look up. "I've always thought you're too tall. Your brain is so far away from your hands that miscommunications are to be expected."

"It wasn't an accident, actually."

She said, "Did you know, we used to make lavash like this for money. My mother did, anyway, and I helped. We used to bring it to the market in Kars every week. I never made it myself, but the steps came back to me after Yergat died. I thought about selling it myself. I'd hire you to take it down to the city for me. Give you something to do—you look like you need something to do."

"I have a job lined up at the textile factory," Avo said, which was true. "An old friend of my parents works there."

"Well, my job would've been better for you. More sociable. You're sociable, I think, or you can fake it, anyway, which is all you need. Plus, this job would've put fewer chemicals in your lungs. Fewer accidents. Less chance of an early— Well, you know what can happen in those factories."

Avo said, "I do."

"In any case, I'm giving these away for free. I've been supplying the whole village for about a month now. You've been eating my bread, probably, and not even knowing it. I thought about selling it, but the truth is, I only make them because it reminds me of my mother. I play the duduk because my father taught me, and I do this because my mother taught me. I think every person should practice one thing he learned from each of his parents. It— I was going to say it keeps your parents alive, but nothing does that. No, it does something more peculiar than that. It keeps *you* alive. Not just surviving but alive. Do you know the difference? Besides, I enjoy slapping that dough against the side of the tonir too much to profit any further from it. The dough just sticks there, like a big thumbprint, which is fun. And the loaves never crisp exactly the same way twice, so there's something unique about each one. Nobody should profit more than that, I think."

"Do you eat it yourself?"

Siranoush scrunched her face so severely that her bottom lip almost kissed the wrinkles in her forehead. It was like her skin was made of rubber.

"My stomach," she said. "I haven't been able to keep anything down recently but dried fruit. Here," she said, peeling a fresh loaf off the side of the tonir. "Tell me how it tastes right off the wall."

Avo took the lavash, hot as coals, and juggled it between his hands. He managed to rip a piece off from the whole, letting out steam, and stuffed it in his mouth without blowing on it first. He had to chew with his mouth open to keep from burning himself.

"He put you up to it," Siranoush said while his mouth was full. "Your brother told you to hurt that person, didn't he?"

Avo couldn't speak. He couldn't lie or equivocate. The look on his face must've told the truth.

"What am I saying?" she said, turning back to her work. "He's not really your brother, is he."

For the next few days, Siranoush's stomach problems seemed, almost miraculously, to resolve themselves. She started eating full meals again, kufte and pilaf and tabouli—foods she'd loved all her life and hadn't been able to enjoy in years. She kept regular and had none of the trouble she'd grown resigned to bearing at night, the panicked waddles to the toilet or the sharp paralyzing pains. It was as though the conversation with Avo had cleared her entirely out. And then one afternoon she fell asleep on the sofa she'd had dragged outside for her husband to die on, and died on it herself.

After Tigran's, it was the second memorial service Avo had gone to in a short span, and he had to laugh. The laughter not only drew strange looks from faces in the crowd of mourners, it also served to tighten the screws of his guilt so that he almost broke down, right there and then, and cried. He supposed the crying might be more explicable at an event like this than laughing, but as soon as he was aware of his desire to cry, he felt entirely incapable of tears. Instead he looked over the heads of the other, shorter mourners, wishing he would find his friends. As the service began to wind down, and as families began to huddle into the line of black and beige cars awaiting them, a familiar voice spoke up at him.

"I used to shovel the path to the old woman's door," said Mr. V, his old teacher. "Today I shoveled her grave. How's that for symmetry, huh? Seems almost designed."

"Almost?" Avo said. "You took the shovel out of the gravedigger's hands. I heard him telling people all about it near the back of the procession."

"Dammit," Mr. V said. "You and your buddy, Levon's little son, won't let me tell one story in my life, will you? Where is that little friend of yours, anyway? Isn't he usually holding your tail with his trunk?"

"You're getting funnier as you get older," Avo said. "And braver."

"Oh, that's right, he's off in Paris. Sophisticated, right? Probably eating fine cheese."

It was the first time Avo had heard Mr. V mock Ruben since the incident in the classroom all those years ago, but this time Avo didn't come to Ruben's defense.

"I only feel worried for the young lady who's gone with him," said Mr. V. "How her parents allowed her to go to France with that strange little boy, I'll never know. I've had four sons, but if I ever have a daughter, she'll live like a train on whatever tracks I lay out for her. School, home—where else does a girl need to go? Not France, that's for sure. In fact, if I had a daughter, I'd probably name her Train, just to remind everybody that she's on a track not to be diverted."

"I can't imagine any jokes about a girl named Train."

"Agh—say no more. At an old woman's funeral, you'll say filth like that? You Leninakan folks will find the dirt in everything. A perfectly good name, and you'll find the dirt in it. It's a funeral, you don't have to be funny."

But after the service, when the last of the living souls abandoned the graveyard for the village in the hills, Avo went to the state-paid headstone at the freshly turned plot, bent to his hands and knees, and whispered a long and loving joke.

8

Glendale, California, 1989

Wednesday morning, after merging from one freeway to the next, Fuji and I reached the Glendale address listed on the business card of The Brow Beater's old English teacher. Expecting a school or a home, I double-checked the address three times before heading upstairs to a little jewelry store on the second floor of a strip mall called Hi Plaza.

The stucco building, studded with seven or eight small businesses, glowed like a church in the morning light. I didn't want to make Fuji wait in the truck again, so I carried him in the crook of my arm up the steps to the jeweler's door. Before I could even read the hours listed in the front window, the door came open with the sound of bells, and an old woman started shooing me away with a broom. She was old and round, a walnut with teeth, and her short gray hair fell in two clean swoops from the top of her head to the crown of her jowls. She muttered at me in her own language.

"Valantin," I said, "are you Valantin?" And the old woman's face shifted. She gestured for me to stay put outside, and locked the door behind her as she disappeared again into the store.

From the second floor of the strip mall, I turned and showed Fuji the view. Between the parked or passing cars on the palm-lined avenue, I counted three tailors, four bakeries, a liquor store, five restaurants with outdoor furniture, a church, a gallery, two markets, and another church. Outside one of the restaurants, a group of white-haired men sat at a table with their faces hung over wide, steaming bowls.

"My aunt thought you were homeless," a new voice said, and I turned to see a tall woman of about my age framed in the jeweler's doorway. Valantin was wearing a series of golden bangles on either wrist and rings of different colors stacked on many of her fingers. Her hair, dyed burgundy, rested in a knot at the top of her head, and she spoke from between two flat lines of lipstick the color of wine.

"You've got a cat," she said.

"I do," I said, swaddling Fuji.

"And you asked for me? You want something for your cat? A jeweled collar?"

"No, no, nothing for the cat."

"Oh, thank God. I can't stand jewelry on an animal."

I looked around her to the door she was blocking. "Well, I'm sure this guy would love the opportunity to change your mind about that, but I'm here to pick your brain about someone we both used to know, if you've got a few minutes."

"My aunt's waiting for me inside, actually, because—I don't know if you've noticed—we're a business, we sell things, and we've got to set up shop for the day, you understand."

"Can we come in with you?"

"We?"

"Fuji here is hypoallergenic, doesn't shed or stink. He's cleaner than I am."

Valantin adjusted her rings and said, "You've set me up for some easy jokes."

I smoothed the wild hairs out of my ponytail. "How's this," I said. "You can make an exception for my cat, just like Longtin used to let your dog into The Gutshot. He was the one who introduced me to an old student of yours. Avo Gregoryan?"

At that, Valantin seemed to see me differently. No longer was my hair the sign of a sixty-two-year-old's desperate grip on his youth, but the proof of persistence, a record of growth. The scars in my forehead, the tattoos on my skin—they weren't the results of a story but the beginnings. I explained how I'd found her address, and how I was in town for a few hours by accident and curious to see if she knew where Avo was located nowadays. I missed the kid, I said, and she invited me in.

After I told The Brow Beater about my brother, he started to see Gil everywhere. I'd described Gil the way I remembered him in early 1950. Soon The Brow Beater was nudging me to check out fans in the audience, young men at the gas pumps, porters at the hotels, and college kids at the bars after shows. Everywhere he looked, The Brow Beater could find a young man who looked to be the identical clone of my brother. Same square jaw, same blond waves glued back with Brylcreem, same knit shirts and rolled-up cuffs at the boot. These coincidences may not have been miraculous in 1950, when the styles were in fashion, but in 1979 and 1980, the resemblance sent my heart jumping. The strangers even had cowlicks in the back-left corners of their heads, just like Gil's, but whenever I approached to gain a closer look, the stranger—backing away, asking me if there was a problem, telling his girlfriend or his friends to keep back, as if I were some sort of menace—proved to be nothing at all like my brother. It was amazing, how much these boys could've passed for Gil until the moment they began to move and speak. It was the exact opposite of The Brow Beater, whose appearance bore no resemblance at all to Gil's, but whose movements—the way he blinked in twos, the funny way he chewed, back to front—seemed to channel my brother completely.

Even some of The Brow Beater's behaviors—carrying that red fanny pack of his, for example, full of all his cash—brought Gil to mind, and I told The Brow Beater so. "Just because you're checking that bag every two minutes doesn't make it a checking account," I said. "You don't trust banks, is that it? You know, Gil used to do the same damn thing. Hid all his money in an old record player. Speakers full of cash, turntable covered in coins like the bottom of a wishing well. You would've liked Gil, I think. I think Gil would've liked you."

You'd think by the way the strangers backed away from me that I was some sort of creep, an obsessive, but you should've seen the way The Brow Beater lit up anytime we talked about my brother. For a long time, it was the only conversation we could sustain.

After a volleyed argument with her aunt in a language I didn't understand, Valantin led me inside the jewelry store. The display cases surrounding us were filled with yellow and white gold, platinum and pearls, emeralds and topaz and lapis lazuli, which reminded me of a pair of earrings my ex-wife always used to wear. Through a plated door, we passed the register and the vaultlike walk-in safe, outside of which her aunt kept guard, eyeing me, and on to a little back room with a Victorian-era chaise longue and a coffee table lined with plates of sweets and cups of coffee with steam drifting forth. I said, "Tell me she didn't make all of this right now, just for me."

"We keep the sweets and coffee on hand."

Her old aunt stayed at the safe, tipped at an angle so as to keep an eye on both the front door and us. "Tell her I feel like a teenager at my girlfriend's house," I said, and Valantin translated. The old walnut said something back, and Valantin, keeping the translation for herself, laughed.

When I asked why she gave up teaching English for a career in the jewelry business, Valantin explained that the store had belonged to her husband, who died in 1976. She'd been running the jewelry store as her day job ever since, teaching English in what she called "the margins" of her day. Eventually, she said, her grown sons would inherit the store. In the meantime, she enjoyed the challenge of owning a small business in the age of shopping malls. She said it was a new obstacle for her but an old one for Armenians, who'd kept a small nation alive in the face of several empires. "A national identity is a kind of small business," she said, and I confessed I didn't know much about national identities that weren't my own. She did me the kindness of pretending to be surprised.

"So you're a jeweler and a teacher," I said. "Busy lady."

"It's not so bad," she said, "since all my work is here. Before my husband died, I used to teach in a classroom at the Glendale Community College. But something was off—absences were high, and, well, something essential was missing. After some trial and error, I figured out what it was. Trust. So I started bringing them here. I like using this space for my students, especially the young ones, the teenagers, who come from across the border. They come here after the store is closed, and we're the only people here, surrounded by very expensive objects and a safe full of—who knows how much money, how many priceless diamonds, are in there. My students come, I make coffee, they bring food. I want them to feel, right away, trusted. Not only do they learn better, but it's good for their self-esteem, too, when they're new to this country, which doesn't, generally speaking, you know, trust anyone except people who look and speak like you."

"Trust me," I said, "no one trusts a guy who looks like me."

Fuji wandered off to the safe, where I thought maybe he smelled a dog's trail. He rested against the aunt's shoes, and the aunt bent to scratch him gently on the head.

I said, "You still have that dog of yours that drank at The Gutshot?"

"No," Valantin said mournfully. "Daria. I couldn't imagine replacing her."

I went on talking about how a new pet doesn't have to replace an old one, but Valantin didn't seem to be listening anymore. When I finished talking, she said, "I'm surprised you worked with Avo and yet you didn't learn Armenian history. It was a central concern of his. For his language project with me, he was translating eyewitness accounts by survivors of the genocide. You know the genocide, at least—1915, yes? Over a million Armenians dead? My own grandparents included. Hitler's blueprint, he wrote in journals. You didn't know?"

When my mother used to tell me and Gil to finish our food, she'd tell us to think of the starving Armenians. That's what I knew of them before The Brow Beater. Still, he only ever told me a few stories from home. Once, drunk after a match, he told me about the celebrity he'd earned as a junior wrestler back in Armenia. The way he told it, he'd been a spry future Olympian with a grown man's strength in his abnormally large hands, able to apply holds even the coaches couldn't escape. A Soviet hero in the making, and the athletics committee in Moscow had taken notice: they'd sent a gift to Avo's parents after a successful tournament, a rare vinyl recording of Tchaikovsky's voice, recorded on an Edison phonograph cylinder in 1890. The record was one of maybe a dozen copies, priceless, and his parents—who apparently adored Tchaikovsky's music above all other art—could say they owned it.

Because of him. Because Avo had earned it for them. He was proud, telling me this story. It was the proudest I ever saw him.

He went on to say his size—what had caught my attention in Los Angeles—was what had ruined him back home. With his growth spurt came new vulnerabilities on the wrestling mat. His enormous legs became practice dummies for beginners to wrap up, and his new girth turned his speed into an erratic exercise in losing balance. In order to maintain any control at all over his new body, he had to lumber this way and that as though underwater. By the time he was thirteen, his coaches had stopped sending him to tournaments. The committee sent an officer to retrieve the ghostly recording of Tchaikovsky's voice.

Now I asked if Valantin kept in touch with Avo, but she said no. Apparently, he'd stopped meeting with her for English lessons in 1978, which was when I'd stolen him away from The Gutshot, a piece of information I decided not to share.

"I like to think he's out there someplace translating poems," she said.

"Poems?"

"That language project—those eyewitness accounts from the genocide?—that was his second choice. Originally, he wanted to translate the poems of Tumanyan—our national poet, who survived the genocide himself—into English. I told him it was an honorable goal but that poetry was a different language altogether. We'd better start with something simpler, I told him. He agreed, but only grudgingly."

"Poems," I said. "How long were you his teacher, anyway?"

"Oh, a few years. I got him in '75, it must've been, not long after he landed in this country. Some of his neighbors were students of mine, and soon he was my student, too. We made a lot of progress. He knew zero English when we began. A funny story—the Armenian word for *Armenian* is *hay*, like *hello*. So one of our first meetings, he had this look of concern and paranoia on his face. He asked me, 'How does everyone in this country know I'm Armenian?' I had to explain to him that people were just saying hello to him on the street. He was taking every greeting from a stranger as an accusation." She laughed. "By the time I got him that job at the bar, he was pretty advanced, except for a few bad habits he picked up here and there."

I knew she meant his use of the word *bro*. He'd picked it up, I later learned, from another regular of Longtin's, the son of a Pentecostal minister who'd called everyone Brother this and Sister that. Somehow or other, the word had been chopped and delivered to him, The Brow Beater, and that little half-word metastasized into his own English. Soon thereafter and forevermore, he was using it like punctuation: Where's the next show, bro? Or: I like this part of your country, bro, up here with more horses than people. Or: Tell me more, bro, about your brother, bro. It was funny at first, and then functionally undetectable, until finally, looking back, I now find it kind of touching. There's no way to quantify these things, but I'd bet no paperwork, no meal, no music or film or manner of dress, no number of miles on this country's split-foot roads—nothing, nothing in The Brow Beater's time here, helped him feel like an American more than those three letters: *B. R. O.*

Valantin sighed. "The Gutshot—God, I miss it. I'd drive Daria all the way there for a walk so I could stop in. A quirk of mine I miss, having a secret bar."

"It's changed a lot," I said. "Pink hair, all that."

"It's all changing," she said, "because we're old. It's funny, I spent too many afternoons in that place. When Longtin left, no one would let Daria into the bar, so I had to stop going."

"Valantin," I said, "the guys at The Gutshot mentioned a short man in a suit. Was he a student of yours, too?"

A platter of cookies shaped like seashells rested between us. She pinched one and lifted it to her mouth. "Are you a cop or what?"

I laughed. "Do I look like one?"

"I figured you'd ask me about him, because he came here looking for Avo in the exact opposite direction you're coming from. I pointed him *to* The Gutshot." She swallowed a bite of the cookie. "But I told him I had no idea if Avo was still working there, because by then I hadn't seen him in over a year, maybe two. My guess is Avo went back to Armenia. Not everyone is suited for this country, especially coming from the Soviet Union during the age of the shopping mall. And his cousin—that's who the man was, the man in the suit—was very kind, not too concerned-seeming, as if he was just trying to reunite with family he hadn't seen in a while. He was sitting where you're sitting now, wearing a chambray suit, orange in color, with a silken blue vest and tie, and he politely asked that I keep Daria from jumping on his lap. Indeed, the suit was impeccably cut, which was particularly vital on a man of his smaller stature. Otherwise he could have looked like a boy lost in his father's wardrobe. It was funny to think of him and Avo coming from the same genetic pool. He came and sat exactly where you're sitting now, and we talked for a little while. His English was fine, if not a little mannered. When I told him about Avo's hopes to translate Tumanyan, he agreed it was probably what Avo was doing, wherever he went. Something gentle like that. Avo was a big young man, but he was gentle. Once, when he was translating the eyewitness accounts, he brought in a passage from a boy who'd watched in terror from a tree as a Turk cut off his father's head in the streets. I would've translated the verb just like that—cut off, or chopped, or sliced—but Avo had brought in the word *plucked*. I told him, pluck is what we do with flowers and fruits. But he knew that. He was just gentle, is what I'm saying. Even down to his language.

I talk about that with my students all the time. Out there in our cheaper display cases, the labels say *cubic zirconium*, not *diamond-like*, you understand? When I talk with you, I say *genocide*, which feels, to me, academic. But when I talk to my aunt, we say *jart*. The shattering. Different, right? They change everything, the words we use."

I was thinking of the language I taught Avo to speak, the language of wrestling. I showed him how to tell a story with his body, to home in on every sinew he could imagine: his facial expressions, the way he spread his fingers and his lips when he was taunting or grandstanding, the way he chose a specific member of the audience to privilege with his attention. Even the number of straps he wore on his singlet—one, over the left shoulder, until his finishing move, when he stripped free of the strap altogether. I wanted him to enter the ring differently, to avoid the way everyone steps *between* the ropes. He was big enough to scale over the *top* rope to emphasize his size. I showed him ways to pin an opponent he respected, and how to pin a jabroni using nothing but the bottom of his boot. I told him to no-sell a chop, to let the smaller guy oversell, deflecting off him like a bike in a collision with a semi. I taught him to take not one, not two, but *three* double ax handles before falling to a knee, to catch a cross-body in the middle of the ring to end the babyface's momentum, to taunt the crowd after slamming the babyface down. I taught him tempo, how to draw out the feeling of hopelessness in the fans, the way to make it seem absolutely impossible that the babyface could come back to win over him, the heel. I taught him to cheat, and to cheat better—to rake his opponent's eyes in clear sight of the crowd while keeping the referee oblivious, to lie and to bask in the glory of indignation when accused of wrongdoing. I taught him—when the babyface finally did make his comeback, when he took The Brow Beater down to the mat in a submission hold—to store all of his strength in that one outstretched, quivering hand he'd use to reach for the bottom rope, reaching and reaching for a break in the hold, for relief. I said his thumb should twitch with every closing centimeter like a dying but dangerous snake, so that when he finally submitted, when the good guy won, the audience didn't feel only satisfied, they felt *safe*. "You're a storyteller in that ring," I told him, "and your body's your language. Those people paying to see you, they don't want stories of real life. They want justice. We're in the business of delaying and delivering justice, for maximum effect. You understand?"

"Sure," he said. "Sure."

I'd only ever heard the word *sure* used sarcastically, or to show indifference, but The Brow Beater used it only when he believed something with a real and urgent charge. Once, outside a diner in Manchester, New Hampshire, we stood before a stone archway where he spent an hour examining the stones. He was convinced the stonemason who'd done the work was an Armenian like him. "Sure," he said, low and long, fingering the cornice only he could reach.

"Looks like any old cookie-cutter archway to me," I said. "You really think you can tell the difference?"

"Sure, sure," he said, almost indignant. He was using the word, I realized, the way *sure* could mean *certain*. It didn't work that way, I wanted to say, but I couldn't explain why.

Now Valantin took another seashell cookie. "She only lets me eat these when we have guests," she said, "but your cat seems to be warming her up." Her aunt had taken Fuji into her arms and was walking him through the store like a baby on an airplane.

"Avo's cousin," I said. "You remember his name?"

Valantin had taken an enormous bite and bobbed her head this way and that as she chewed, to let me know that, as soon as she could speak again, she'd have an answer for me. In the meantime, I pocketed a few cookies myself.

"He had the same first name as my husband," she said, finishing her cookie. "Ruben. But my husband went by Rob his whole life. Not this Ruben. I think his last name was—Petrosian?"

Fuji darted into the back room, almost knocking our coffees off the table. For the first time since I'd come inside, the old lady was speaking, and this time I could actually understand what she was saying.

"Ruben Petrosian?" she said. "Ruben Petrosian?"

9

Les notes du tournoi de backgammon international

Chantilly, France, 23 au 25 août 1974

Ce journal appartient á: Mina Bagossian
Équipe: Soviet Armenia
Jour un

My mother always told me the West was free, but I never expected the complimentary meal on the flight, or this complimentary notebook from the organizers of the tournament to keep track of the matches. To be honest, I don't care very much about remembering every detail of the tournament. When Tigran died, my interest in backgammon died, too. I wouldn't be writing any of this down if I had someone to talk to about it, but I don't speak French, my Russian is elementary, and the only other Armenian around is the dourest boy in the world. Do you know how many questions Ruben asked me on the flight? Zero. Not one. Neither one of us had been on a plane before. I'd always hoped the tops of clouds looked different than the bottoms, radically different, but they look more or less the same. Really the magic of flying is that you can see the subtle curve of the horizon. Of course I knew the world was round, but seeing its roundness for the first time got me thinking. That the world is round makes me hope that time is round, too, and that maybe I'll loop to the start one day, and I'll be able to see Tigran again.

Zero questions—otherwise I wouldn't write a word of this down.

The flyers for this tournament said we'd be in Paris. They even featured a drawing of the Eiffel Tower. But we're in Chantilly, almost an hour's train ride from Paris, and although the town is beautiful, I'm slightly disappointed that we won't be seeing the "city of love." If Tigran were here with me, I would have insisted that we go. I always told people that I loved Tigran like an uncle, but that's not completely true. It wasn't a physical attraction but a kind of partnership I fell into with him. I used to dream that his wife would pull me aside one day and say, "I'm old, I have no energy, and he needs someone who can keep up with him. I don't like it, but it's the truth, and you're the only young woman I approve to take my place." It was a shameful daydream when I was younger, but now, full of missing him, I remember it sweetly. Who knows how I'll remember it in the future?

And who knows where I'll be remembering it from? Moscow, maybe? Or Paris—or Chantilly—though I doubt I'll find out if I belong here or not in only three days. Especially with the company I have. Can you imagine going to Paris with Ruben Petrosian? Joyless boy in a joyous place. Since the horrible accident with Tigran, we've had nothing but good luck. And yet Ruben is still a little brat. He's eighteen years old but looks ten and acts a hundred. That his papers went through at the last minute without a problem so he could replace Tigran as my guardian and coach on this trip—it was a miracle. But when the news came, Ruben hardly smiled. It's not that he's always thinking of something else—who isn't thinking of multiple things at once?—it's that he believes what's in his head is more important than what's in anyone else's. That's why he never asks questions, I think. He doesn't think there's a chance that what's going on in my mind might surprise or delight him.

But here's what's going on in my mind now, day one, as Ruben has retired to his room across the hall in this beautiful hotel, and as I keep this diary of my time in almost-Paris: I miss Tigran, and I miss home. My whole life I romanticized the West, I always wanted to leave Armenia, but now I miss Kirovakan. Who cares that new movies and music take so long to trickle into the country? That my father has to run his business in secret? Who cares that he has to travel to Yerevan three times a month to play poker and schmooze with informants, that he has to bribe them all in order to keep his business from the government? Who cares that when we have visitors, my sister and I have to hurry and hide the mannequins and measuring tapes? Paris—this hotel in Chantilly, anyway—is full of fast-moving, fast-talking people who smell like chocolate, and everything is free here, and yet I miss home. Nothing seems real here. I miss the smell of rain. I miss my cat, who never minds getting wet, seems to crave being wet, in fact. Refuses to come indoors when it's pouring, and we had to board up all the nearby wells so she wouldn't dive into them again. Nothing here is as real as that. Maybe I'm just lonely. It's been a long day with a boy who won't ask a single question of me. Maybe I just miss Tigran, who would've made this trip so lovely. He would have joked about the smell of chocolates. I don't care about backgammon anymore. I want to go home.

Jour deux

I woke up feeling just as sorry for myself as I did last night, when I wrote that entry. How embarrassing. But everything changed during breakfast this morning, before the matches began. The hotel has a large dining room with intricate crystal chandeliers overhead, and maybe forty or so large round tables for the guests of the tournament. Ruben and I were seated at a table with six other coaches and players from Russia, Georgia, and Ukraine. The Russian coach, Anton, had known Tigran in their early playing days. He told me that Tigran used to collect a die from each backgammon set on which he won a game. I said I'd love to see that collection, and Anton said he bet Tigran's widow had it lying around somewhere back at the house in Kirovakan. Just the thought of those dice safe at home connected me again to Tigran and put me finally at ease, and in this new comfort I leaned to the Russian coach and thanked him. When breakfast was over, Anton leaned back to me and said, "You know that Ruben boy is so sullen only because he's jealous of your talents." And suddenly, as if Tigran himself had returned, I cared again about winning the tournament.

My first match came shortly thereafter. It was against the player from East Germany, who happened to be the only other girl in the tournament. We played, and although I won easily, she was a good sport and shook my hand afterward. I think she understood, as I did, that they'd pitted us against each other in order to get rid of one of the girls as quickly as possible.

They're having a harder time getting rid of me, though! It took eight hours and twenty-seven minutes for me to win all five of my matches today (against East Germany, Canada, Israel, Sweden, and Czechoslovakia), setting me up for tomorrow's final three rounds, which will likely go just as long. It's amazing to meet people from all over the world. They each look so different, and yet they throw the dice exactly the same way. My first match tomorrow will be against the host country's representative, and I'm looking forward to spoiling their celebration.

Something strange happened today, too, besides all my winning. While I was playing the matches, Ruben watched from behind the Soviet Armenian table. From time to time I looked back to see if he was celebrating my march toward victory, but he looked on coldly with his usual lifelessness. No matter how unlikely a roll I'd just had, or how riled up the crowd became at my winning streak (the American fans, in particular, seem to be loudly cheering on the only girl left in the tournament), Ruben remained detached. And then the strange thing happened: I saw three men—two older men and a younger man who all looked like Armenians, wearing expensive suits, but I couldn't believe they actually were Armenians, since I'd convinced myself that Ruben and I were the only Armenians in the West. The three men approached the table with our country's flag draped from it. For the first time all day, Ruben stood. And they talked. I had to return my focus to my match, and when I had another chance to look back at the table, I saw that Ruben was gone.

Only after the day's matches were done, when I was taking the elevator back to my room, did I see Ruben again. He walked into the elevator and—I still don't believe it—asked me a question. And not only one but two. He said, "How are you feeling going into tomorrow? Are you nervous?" When I said I was nervous, a little, he said, "Oh, don't be. You're leagues above the competition here." And then—it's only just happened an hour ago, and so I'm baffled about it as I write this—he walked me from the elevator to my room, wished me a good night, and then—I really can't—he kissed me. Just once, on the cheek, as my uncle would kiss me. But coming from Ruben, it was as if he'd proposed marriage. Of course it was disgusting—the kiss came from a boy I've never felt very comfortable around. But it was also something more. Because the kiss didn't come only from that boy. The kiss seemed to be coming from someone else, too. And at first the only person I could think of who would send a kiss through Ruben to me was the man who should have been here with me all along. Tigran. But then I had another idea. I've been imagining that the kiss came from someone still in Kirovakan, and it wasn't a kiss of friendship but a beckoning home. And I'm smiling as I write this.

Jour trois

The tournament is over and has been for two months. I'm home in Kirovakan, the end of October, and it's late—nobody is awake in my building but me. This journal was confiscated, along with the rest of my possessions, upon my return to Armenia in August. My parents were taken in for questioning. So was I. I was asked about Ruben's behavior and about the men I described in my journal under the heading "Jour deux." I said I had no information, other than the facts of the morning after the tournament. How Ruben wasn't in his hotel room. How he wasn't at the train station or the airport, either. How he simply disappeared.

And now I can't sleep. I'm home, and it's late, and nobody is awake maybe in the whole city but me. This journal was returned to me a week after it was taken, and I threw it in the back of my wardrobe. Backgammon has brought me nothing but trouble. I thought forgetting this journal would be the same as clearing my mind of all that. But last week, I heard the news from Paris, and I haven't been able to sleep since. So, a moment ago, I thought: Maybe what's keeping me up at night is that I left the journal unfinished. Maybe if I fill those empty lines under "Jour trois," I'll be able to sleep again. Because the truth is I haven't told anyone—not my parents, not the officials—the whole story about Ruben's disappearance. And I'm afraid I'll never be able to fall asleep again until I tell somebody—even myself, in these pages—the truth. So just now I kicked out of my bedsheets, fished for the journal in the closet, and—here I go.

The final day of the tournament—the day before the flight home—I ate breakfast surrounded by reporters. Ruben was with me, and—continuing whatever transformation had occurred the night before—he seemed happy to speak to the reporters for me, interpreting their English and Russian, interpreting my responses, and answering many of the questions on his own. The local press, already rooting against me in the upcoming match, were additionally upset that Ruben, who seemingly spoke every other language fluently, didn't know a word of French. Ruben said something in English that made everybody but the French laugh. And then Ruben did what I'd never seen him do before: he laughed, too.

It took me two hours to beat the French player. Even some of the home crowd applauded me afterward. I suspect they wanted me to go on to win the whole tournament now, since they'd lost to me and could therefore claim a roundabout second place.

They knew I only had to win two more matches to win the whole tournament.

In the break between matches, while the player from Ireland prepared to face me, I shook off fans and reporters so I could go find Ruben, who'd left the tournament area before I could. I found him outside, near the carport of the hotel, smoking with the well-dressed men I'd seen the day before. There were the same three men—two older, one younger—and they called me over to join. I accepted a cigarette and thanked them for complimenting my winning streak. Then the younger man said, "Do you know who you'll be playing next?" "Yes," I said, "Ireland." "You haven't heard?" he said. "There's been a loaded-dice scandal. Ireland's been disqualified. And so their last opponent will take their place." "Oh," I said. "Who is it?" And the men started to laugh, except for Ruben, who stared at me seriously and said, "Turkey."

Of course I know the history. But my mother always told me that the past is the past, and that the only Armenians who obsess over what the Turks did to us are those who left Armenia and feel the need to compensate for the guilt of living abroad. I heard *Turkey*, and the only thought I had was that it would be a tougher matchup than I would've had against Ireland. But the men—and Ruben, certainly—seemed to have something larger than backgammon in mind.

I can see that now.

The other semifinal match—the USA versus Morocco, at a nearby table—finished early, with the American player advancing. Now all eyes were on my match with the Turkish player. The match was close, but in the end, I lost. We'd spent nearly four hours breathing into each other's faces, and afterward, I tried to congratulate the Turkish player, but he did not want to shake my hand. Finally, his coach forced him to do it. The Turkish coach—a gentle-faced man with a dark mustache and hair slicked back behind his ears—congratulated me on my play in the tournament and said I should be very proud. Then he and his student left to prepare for the final match, and the crowd—or most of them, anyway—followed.

I thought I was alone, and so I began to cry. I wasn't crying because I lost, though I'd hoped to win it all and was disappointed in myself. No, I was crying for Tigran. Dead for weeks, but not until my tournament was over did his death feel real to me. I lost, and then I lost him.

But I was not alone. A voice, an Armenian voice, called to me from the other side of the banquet hall: "Girl." He was one of the rich-looking Armenians, the young one. In his mid-twenties, I'd say. "You can't let them see you like this. They've made too many of our women cry already."

"I'm not crying because of them," I said.

"Do you know who I am?" he said. Just the way he asked the question made me feel as though I should, that I was an ignorant little girl for not knowing who he was. He ran his fingers through his hair, which was black and thick, as if to show me more of his face. There was a deep vertical line between his eyes, which made me think he was a man who spent most of his time in serious thought. He wore a neatly trimmed beard and a brown suit with his shirt collar hanging fashionably over the lapels. I worried that another five minutes alone with him, and I'd be his.

"No," I admitted.

"You will," he said. He winked. "I'm impressed with your little boyfriend. Small, that Ruben, but he knows his history. Politics, languages. An impressive young man."

"He's not my—"

"You can call me Hagop," he said. "I spend most of my time in Beirut. Have you been?"

"I've been to Georgia," I said, as if that were related. "The coast of the Black Sea."

"Armenian girls can be so provincial," he said. "Would you like to travel the world?"

"Yes," I said, because clearly, that was the answer he wanted. The truth was I couldn't wait to be home again, this time for good.

"Where do you want to go? I can send you there. In fact, I can make you a citizen in any nation in the world. You want to be an American?"

"No, thank you," I said.

"Good. To use a French word, that would've been a cliché. All your girlfriends back home want to be Americans, don't they, but not you. Tell me, though—how is it that you lost to the Turk? Did he cheat?"

"No."

"Are you certain? If he cheated, I can have justice carried out."

"He won fair."

"Do you care about justice? About the truth being told?"

"I try not to lie, myself."

"Provincial," he said, disappointed. "You're not like your partner. You don't think big enough."

And although he was dismissing me—scaring me a little, too—I still couldn't help feeling drawn to him. It was more than his sharp looks. He had a habit of squinting while he spoke, and each time he did it, I wanted more and more to follow him wherever he went.

But before I could, Ruben arrived and diffused the spell.

"You should go pack," Ruben said. "We've got an early morning ahead of us."

"Aren't you going to watch the final match?"

"I'm going to explore the city."

"Can I come?" I asked.

Ruben looked to Hagop for the answer. Hagop shook his head, which made me feel as though I'd just failed an exam I hadn't known I was taking.

"We'll be doing men's things," Ruben said. "You enjoy the match, though. I might be out late, but don't stay up for me. We've got an early morning, remember. Get some sleep."

And then they left. And I returned to the tournament and watched the American player win the final match. Then I went to my room and fell asleep. And in the morning, I waited in the lobby for Ruben to come down, but he never did. I took the elevator back up and went to his room, thinking he'd overslept. But the door was open, and the cleaning crew was there, and he had already checked out. So I went to the train station, and he was not there, and I went to the church where I'd arranged for us to have a little tour, but he was not there, and I took the train to the airport, and I waited as long as I could before boarding my plane. And he was not there, either.

I came home, alone, to interrogations from my family, from Ruben's parents, and from government officials. In all of them, I skipped over my encounter with Hagop out of pure embarrassment. I thought it was the story of my own girlishness, my flirting with a handsome, charismatic man, and my failure in making him see me as a worldly person. It was not a story I thought needed to be told. I had no idea where Ruben went—still the truth. Hagop's claim to be able to make me a citizen anywhere in the world? Bravado and flirtation and—I still thought, even after Ruben's disappearance—bullshit.

But then, just this week, news came in from Paris.

The final match of the tournament had been quick and anticlimactic—the American won easily. Afterward, I watched the trophy ceremony among an enormous crowd. I was escorted to the front of the pack, because I was to be given a ribbon, so I had a clear view of the ceremony. The American heaved his trophy, flanked by his coach and a man announced as the American ambassador to France. Similarly, the Turkish player, silver medalist, had his coach and ambassador at his side. The Turkish ambassador made a big show of giving his car key to the Turkish coach, the gentle-faced man who'd made his student shake my hand. The ambassador was offering the coach a job to be his official chauffeur, and the coach—to a large swell of cheering laughter—accepted the position. The French loved him, and the ambassador would expedite the paperwork to keep the Turkish coach in Paris. He would send for his family in the morning.

Last week, the news came in: Three or four men, claiming to be members of a new so-called Armenian army, assassinated the Turkish ambassador to France in front of the Turkish embassy building in Paris. It was one thirty in the afternoon, and the ambassador was in his car. His chauffeur was also killed, and it's his picture in the newspaper that's been keeping me awake at night. It's the chauffeur's face—a gentle face, with a dark mustache and hair slicked back behind his ears—that has forced me to dig this journal out of the back of my closet and finish my story.

The truth is I didn't know where Ruben went. And I don't know where Ruben is now. But last week, on October 24, 1974, on a clear afternoon, I believe I know where Ruben Petrosian was, and what he was doing.

There. I feel better. This has helped—I'll be able to sleep now. I'm going to fall asleep, and then I'm going to burn this journal. I want no trouble. I only want to be provincial, and to think the way my sister thinks. Time is not round like the earth. The past is the past is the past.

Two

10

Kirovakan, Soviet Armenia, 1974

To the factory, then, if his cousin's cousin had left him for good, which seemed impossible at first, when Mina arrived shockingly alone on the train from the airport, and then perfectly inevitable. Ruben had either gotten himself into serious trouble or chosen to abandon Avo in Kirovakan. Both scenarios were unbearable to think about, so all that was left to consider was the result: Ruben was gone.

The factory, then. Avo's parents had worked at a factory just like this, as had all his uncles, all the tall and thwarted Gregoryans, and why not Avo, then, too, the tallest and most thwarted yet. Eighteen years old and two meters tall, he couldn't find a pair of gloves that fit him. So the factory made a pair—synthetic rubber, fingers and thumbs as long as skewers, wide as champagne flutes, though there were no celebratory drinks to commemorate his first day on the job. Just the slot at the machinery, doing his part to manufacture synthetic fibers—polyester and nylon, mainly, though also spandex and rayon and styrene-butadiene, like his gloves—textiles that went on, according to the parents of young children in Kirovakan, to become toys, stockings, and boots. Maybe no one outside the factory was aware of the truth, that some two thirds of the textiles manufactured at the plant were for military use, nylon parachutes and polyester webbing and styrene-butadiene tires for vehicles engineered for Soviet combat. For a war that would never come.

His supervisor, a stout man who went by the nickname Shorty and therefore couldn't help but refer constantly to Avo's size, had a habit of standing too close and delivering lectures. "Come on, Stretch," he'd say, face at Avo's belt. "Cheer up! I can't have a morose Gregoryan in the barracks, no sir, not at my plant. You're young! Cheer up! Who cares if you don't want to be here? You're making synthetic fibers. Counterfeit silk, basically, but the counterfeit is better than the real thing! Where's your enthusiasm? You're helping fight the good fight, God forbid the good fight comes. Where's your energy? You don't have any?"

But faking enthusiasm seemed more difficult than feeling it. Avo had stolen a man's life, and the last person he'd told even a morsel of the truth to—Siranoush—had keeled over just a few days after hearing his confession. And now that Ruben was gone, Avo was left alone with his guilt, and even faking heart felt impossible. What was even more impossible to explain—not only to Shorty but to anyone at all—was the horrible irony that he himself was the one who'd made Ruben's escape possible in the first place; that if he hadn't killed Tigran, not only would he not feel any guilt, but he wouldn't be alone now, either. If anyone should have abandoned anybody, Avo thought, it should have been the other way around. And with all of that in his mind, the guilt and the resentment and the total isolation, it was extraordinarily difficult to fake enthusiasm for a job manufacturing materials of war. Avo, alone with his anger at his station in the plant except for the occasional needling from his supervisor, was growing angrier and more imaginative in the ways he would bring Ruben to justice for leaving him, maybe with the help of some of this equipment.

"Come on, Stretch! Why don't you put a smile on your face? You're doing your part for the people! You're chipping in! You should put on a smile, and before you know it, you won't have to put it on at all—it'll already be there! Habit into virtue!"

The only habits Avo found himself developing, however, were the long walks between the factory and the city and the village, where he was still sleeping, most nights, in Ruben's old bedroom.

In an act of foresight Avo had never seen her apply with her own son, Ruben's mother often had food—a covered pot of borscht or a lidded plate of meat—waiting for him on the nightstand. Avo couldn't say whether the meals were acts of genuine kindness or material apologies for the new ritual of Avo's having to pay rent to stay there. The monthly contributions Avo made were quasi-voluntary: Ruben's father, who had proposed the idea in the first place, occasionally claimed that the arrangement signified a distasteful act of showmanship on Avo's part, but at other times grumbled loudly that the money wasn't nearly enough.

For those reasons, Avo never rushed home from the factory after work, and his habitual strolls through the city took on a leisurely, imaginative mood. Once, in late October when the nighttime rain didn't fall so much as hang in thin curtains visible here and there near the halogen lamps and in the lightly pockmarked faces of puddles, Avo kept on walking. It was impossible to say how many countless cigarettes he smoked as he wandered past the plant and Kirov Square, on through the street curving alongside the tallest building in the city, a twelve-story apartment building with bright slitted windows like the eyes of cats, and farther still through the city limits in the opposite direction of the village in the hills. Beyond there, on to Spitak, where the smell of woodsmoke steered through the rain and reminded him of his mother, who used to fry fish in beds of stripped bark. After all that walking, he thought, he'd grow accustomed to being alone, come to prefer it, and therefore feel less angry at being left behind in a place he'd never chosen for himself.

But there he was, confused and bitter two months after Ruben's disappearance, finally turning around and walking home through those thin, still curtains of rain on a late night at the end of October, when no one else in all of Kirovakan would possibly be awake.

But—a light. There, on the ground floor of the tallest building in the city, a light in the window. And in the window, a desk, and at the desk, a girl. Writing. A girl, writing in the dim light at a desk in the window, and Avo saw that it was Mina.

He hadn't seen her in months. When she returned from Paris, he knew, she'd been pestered by the authorities and by her family and by everyone else eager to know about Ruben's disappearance, and because Avo knew Mina would've had nothing to do with all that, he'd avoided being yet another person looking to her for answers. He hadn't seen her since the day she'd come back from the airport, hadn't talked with her since the Black Sea, and now, through a dim window in the middle of the night, he was afraid that she would see him and—just as in the tent—be frightened by his looking in on her. So he decided to keep walking.

But soon, maybe thirty steps past her window, Avo heard footsteps splashing behind him on the road.

"You can stop avoiding me," Mina said.

"You'll get sick," Avo said. Mina was standing there in a nightgown, no coat.

"I didn't know he was going to stay in Paris," she said. "I would've warned you. I know how close you two were."

He lifted his coat and told her to get in. "You'll get sick."

Mina stepped beneath his raised jacket. She didn't even need to duck. He said, "Take your hands off your chin."

She did. Put them around his waist. Up near her shoulders. He craned low to kiss her. They kissed. The jacket tipped. Doused them in rainwater.

"I'm sorry," he said. "About Tigran."

She pressed her forehead to him and leaned there for a while. Finally, she looked up and said, "Do you want to see the city from my roof?"

They had to be quiet. The elevator's rattle and whine would wake everybody in the building, floor by floor, so they took the stairs. Twelve flights. Mina's rain-soaked nightgown swishing up ahead of him. On the roof, their breathing was heavy from the steps. The wind made interesting shapes with the rain, and they kissed between those shapes, and they promised to stay there together, and they kissed, and she asked him to be careful, as careful as an act of spontaneity could be, and they laughed and then laughed at their laughing, and on the floor of the roof in the windswept rain they made interesting shapes.

Mosquitoes never bit her, and the dice always rolled in her favor, and as he spent increasingly prolonged stretches of his days with her, Avo began to have some luck of his own. His supervisor at the factory announced that he, Shorty, was being transferred temporarily to the headquarters in Moscow, and that, for the price of feeding and looking after his two cats, Avo was free to live in his apartment in the meantime. Then, one day on his way to work, Avo found a hundred-ruble note on the street. A fresh bill, just lying in the road, the bust of Lenin in profile, looking off into the distance as if looking everywhere and nowhere, gazing outward and reflecting deeply, all at once. Waiting for Avo to lift and pocket and spend him on—on what? On Mina, no doubt, the source of his good fortune. He added the money to his savings and used it to buy a brand-new record from a man who sold them out of his car down an alleyway called Proshyan Street. *Songs in the Key of Life*. The man selling the record said it was the greatest music since Bach. From then on, when Mina came over to Shorty's apartment with her sister's record player, they'd play with the cats—Shorty's two, and Mina's, whom she brought along—and listen to Stevie Wonder over and over again, and sometimes they'd talk over the music, and sometimes they'd lie on the floor with the cats on their chests, just listening. When they talked, they talked about everything but the past. They talked about family and marriage, about children, about the possibility that one day she would coach the backgammon club at school, and he would coach the wrestlers. The one time Mina mentioned Tigran, it was to say she'd gone to visit his widow, searching for an old collection of dice she'd learned about in Paris.

"She looked for them everywhere," Mina said, "but they'd vanished. Avo, I felt terrible. She looked for them everywhere, and I couldn't get her to stop. Watching her slowly take to her old knees to search under the bed broke my heart all over again."

She thumbed a tear from the corner of her eye and let Avo palm the crown of her hair.

When Shorty returned from Moscow, those soothing times threatened to end. Avo complained about having to move back to Ruben's old house in the village in the hills, and Mina asked why they couldn't find an apartment of their own to move into.

Avo laughed. "Are you proposing to me?"

Mina went to cover her chin but grabbed her heart instead. "I think I am."

And Avo asked her father's permission, which he gave, and he asked Ruben's mother if she had a ring she could spare.

"I have this one," she said, returning from her bedroom with a thin silver band, a triangular jewel set in the center. "It's not a real diamond, I'm afraid. It's cubic zirconium. But it's beautiful, no?"

"It really is," Avo said, and he thanked her, and he held the little ring in his palm so tight that it must have left a cut in his skin. "I'm so lucky you took me in," he told Ruben's mother, and he thanked her and thanked her and thanked her again.

Mina was holding the ring to the light when Avo found his latest piece of luck, which arrived in the form of a postcard.

The sender's address was in Beirut. The photograph showed a grand plaza by the sea, with palm trees and hotels and, in the foreground, a long white bus emblazoned with a red stripe. On the other side of the postcard, a short message had been written in a sloppy Armenian scrawl:

> *Mr. Gregoryan,*
> *How is the old man—dead still? Maybe he'll come alive in the new year, just at the stroke of twelve, as in a children's story! Impossible, I know, but what's the harm in checking?*
> *Yours,*
> *Shirakatsi*

The postcard must've been from Ruben, but Avo had no clue as to its meaning. For a minute or two, he felt the cautious relief and anger he might've felt if Ruben had appeared in the room. Then he returned to the mystery of the note's meaning and the vague familiarity of the name Shirakatsi.

Where had he heard it before?

For days, he kept the postcard in his pocket at home and at the factory and on his long walks through the city after work.

One night in December, Mina joined him. It was in the strange in-between season, after the rains but before the snow. The air felt wrung out and empty.

"The name on the postcard sounds so familiar," Avo said. "Shirakatsi."

As soon as he saw the look of recognition on Mina's face, the way she turned her head slightly but kept her eyes on him, he remembered where he'd heard the name.

"Funny," Mina said. "There's an old mathematician called Shirakatsi. He wrote proofs."

They were walking in a kind of cuddling way, with Mina buried under Avo's arm, and it was warm but also awkward. To be held by another person while you're in motion—Mina said she preferred to stop and sit. But Avo was walking faster now, thinking of Ruben. Mina told him to slow down, that she couldn't keep up with his giant strides. Then she said, "I wonder if Shirakatsi's got a living descendant. But how would he know of you? Maybe . . ."

She kept talking, but her breath became a mask in the windless cold, and Avo could see less and less of her as she spoke, and his mind returned to the postcard. What had Ruben meant?

Something about an old man? The new year? He could sort out the details of the message later, he reminded himself. For now, he should be glad that his brother was safe. His brother was safe and hadn't abandoned him after all.

While Mina recalled biographical details of Shirakatsi's life, she noticed that Avo wasn't paying much attention to her. He was preoccupied with Ruben, the sender of the postcard. Who else could it have been, she thought. It was obvious Avo had solved the mystery, too, when she mentioned the old mathematician. She rambled on about the life of the old scholar, inserting fictional details now as she went along—did Avo know that Shirakatsi had trained a pet rat who refused anything less than the finest Greek cheese?—and she felt, for the first time since their night on the roof, that she and Avo might not spend their lives together. Just like that, Avo could fall into her past. She'd imagined so many futures with him, and he'd done the same, had told her an imagined future one morning not long ago, picking lemons at dawn. She'd worn her favorite yellow scarf, knitted by her mother. She'd let Avo bend low in the tall grass between the trees. She'd climbed onto him, one leg at a time over his shoulders, and he'd lifted her. At his full height, she'd pressed her thighs around his neck. It might have been the very last hour of the lemon season, and the sun was still nothing but a low glow in the east—lower than she was, it seemed—a low glow like a hum you could see, and she was as tall as she'd ever been, plucking lemons from the tops of trees. Not thinking to cover her chin. And he'd told her a future in which they traveled the world together.

Now, walking awkwardly in the nooks of him, she kept from crying by rambling on about her fictional Shirakatsi.

"And in his will," she said, "he left all his money to that pet rat, for all the cheese in Greece."

Avo, looking everywhere but at her, said, "I didn't know that."

Maybe he felt guilty for not listening, for not being fully present. He stopped and picked her up and blew his lips into her neck, which sometimes made her laugh. He said, "I'm sorry the ring is cheap and fake," and she told him what she always told him when he promised her a real ring in the future, that her ring was perfect, that the only way to make it cheap would've been to try and pass it off as real.

"Tell me again about our travels," she said, and Avo, letting her down softly, said, "In America, we'll have horses and cows and enormous hats, and watch movies at night and listen to music all day, and you'll take high-level math at the university while I write you poems, and in exchange for them you'll—"

"I'm not doing anything for a poem. I'm sorry, I'm spoiled, but I expect free poems."

"Fine, and I expect some things for free, too."

"Idiot," she said.

"Backgammon lessons, is what I meant. I swear, your mind is so filthy for a girl from Kirovakan."

And on and on they went, believing in the story they were telling.

According to the close-up of the Spasskaya Tower on the TV in Mina's apartment, twenty minutes separated 1974 from 1975. Mina had been penned into the small kitchen with her sister and mother and several aunts and female cousins, all of whom worked elbow to elbow like cogs in a clock tower to make spreads of the desserts they'd baked. In the main room, the children had fallen asleep in the spaces between the men, who surrounded the TV in stoic furniture made of beechwood and textiles. In the corners of the windows, triangles of frost grew like mold, mirroring the pyramids of pomegranates and nectarines arranged on the table. "I've got to go out for a minute," Avo told the men, grabbing his coat. Mina's father told him there was no need to leave to smoke a cigarette, lifting his own as proof. But Avo said he enjoyed smoking in the cold, which was true. He said, "I'll be back before Mina gets out of the kitchen," and took a nectarine on the way out.

The streets of Kirovakan carved through the pinched walls of plowed snow. For the past few days, instead of going on long walks after work, Avo had gone straight to Ruben's parents' house in the village to reread the postcard. Again and again, he'd been unable to make meaning of it. He wished Ruben had been more direct, but he enjoyed the idea of Ruben's needing to use pseudonyms and riddles. It was exciting to think of him as a wanted defector, to imagine his journey from Paris to Beirut. The international travel meant he must've had the help of professional smugglers, which made the whole scenario even more thrilling. Avo did wish, however, that one of those professionals could have passed a more straightforward message through the censors. It was a pity that a spellbinding tale of escape and life on the lam was diluted into this children's story, a "dead old man" to identify before the "stroke of twelve."

What was the point, Avo thought, of asking if a dead man was *still* dead, anyway?

He thought he'd memorized the note, and recited it aloud from memory: "'How is the old man,'" he said, "'still dead?'"

The night before, though, he realized he'd mixed up the quote. It wasn't *still dead*—it was *dead still.*

How's the old man—dead still?

Dead still—the phrase was more awkward this way. Avo's brain kept fixing it the other way around. Or else putting a pause in there: *Dead, still? Dead still* without the pause seemed to mean something else altogether. *Dead still.*

"Like a statue," Avo said to himself, and he was so proud of himself for figuring out where Ruben wanted him to go that he almost told the whole story to Ruben's mother.

Instead, he made the plan to leave Mina's apartment before midnight on New Year's Eve.

Now, in the snow, he checked his watch. He arrived at the city square with fourteen minutes to spare. A crowd of people had gathered there, and city workers were preparing the night's fireworks. At the center of the crowd stood old Kirov, the city's namesake—the old man, dead still, who might come alive in the new year—bronze and snowcapped like an old survivor full of bones.

Avo took a seat at Kirov's plinth. He watched the Manukyan boys take turns being pulled along on their sled, and the Barsamyan sisters and the Mirzoyan girl shuffling messages into the snow with their boots. A hundred more just like them, tiny, bundled people playing in the snow while their parents smoked cigarettes near the steps of city hall. This was what they'd all survived for, the one night they could spend together looking ahead and not back. Avo recognized most of the people in the square, and as he waited for midnight, a few people came by to say hello, or to offer something to eat or drink. He was surprised to find how warm he kept, sitting in the cold. But his size always made him feel hotter than most, and his heart was beating quickly now, and he accepted a few walnuts from Mano Najaryan, a coworker at the factory, and he tossed the nectarine he'd taken from Mina's place to Mano's daughter, and he felt as though he could stay in this place for about as long as old Kirov could.

When the clock tower rang in the new year, the people of Kirovakan sparked the first of their fireworks. Missiles lifted greenly against the current of the falling snow. Avo didn't follow the streaks long enough to watch their inevitable explosions. Instead, he stood and turned to inspect the statue, which was supposed to "come to life" at midnight. Avo didn't believe Ruben's clue literally, but he did expect something to occur at old Kirov's feet. He checked the statue—still nothing—then returned his attention to the crowd, waiting for someone—a messenger? Ruben himself?—to emerge from it toward him. What did he see? The awed faces of children and parents glowing under the detonations. Snow gathering in eyelashes. A hazy group laughter thrumming between the pops and whistles. No one, nobody, coming to meet him.

When the celebration finished, the families packed their blankets and sleds and went home, already back to thinking of the past. The city workers cleaned up after them and packed the fireworks, and then they went home, too, leaving the square empty, save for Kirov and Avo, who was finally starting to feel cold.

The thought of Mina waiting for him, angry or hurt—or worse, the thought of her not noticing he'd disappeared—hung a catch in his throat and almost moved him from his seat. But another idea, the prospect of his brother's having arranged a spectacle for him, kept him frozen.

Still, he didn't know how much longer he could wait. Just a little while earlier, when the clock was arranged just slightly differently, the postcard in his pocket had felt like a hand reaching down a mountain to pull him up. But now it was beginning to feel more like a boot kicking snow from above. In his heart, Avo had blamed Ruben—in part, he told himself, in part—for Tigran's death, and now he worried that Ruben had known. Ruben was punishing him, Avo realized, by sending this stupid riddle, by driving a splint between him and Mina. At once, Avo was furious with Ruben for setting him up, and with himself for falling for it so readily.

His skin went numb. The catch in his throat swelled to pain. He started to leave.

"Good night, Kirov-jan," Avo muttered to the statue, tipping his cap as he walked away, and then said it again, louder, amused with his own performance. He took a few steps down the road, only to turn back dramatically. "No, brother, I can't stay. I understand, I understand—I'd love to talk all night with you, too, but I've got work in a few hours, and you're not as young as you once were. Look at your hair! White as snow!"

To his delight, Avo's silly performance was beginning to dissolve his anger for real. He was even—maybe he'd have been embarrassed if anyone had been watching—enjoying himself. "Here, brother," he said, climbing onto the statue's feet. "Let me fix you so you're young again."

Avo stepped onto a bronze fold in the statue's pant leg and reached up. It took all of his outstretched height to reach Kirov's head with his fingertips to brush away the snow.

"There you go, old comrade," Avo said. "Old age doesn't suit you. Be it pigeon shit or snow, I'll be here to keep you young. Don't pity me—I'm in love!" Avo laughed again and decided to top off his performance with a kiss on Kirov's cheek. He grabbed the bronze face with both hands, puckered up, and leaned in for his kiss good night.

Which was when he found, rolled into Kirov's nostril, a gray envelope.

When she told the story later, Mina remembered one conversation under the ski lift in particular. When he'd been at his best, Avo said, wrestling for the Junior Olympics team, he'd had visions of becoming a national hero. "I couldn't imagine anything better than to be loved by many strangers. Now I can imagine something better."

It was sweet, she said, but she was curious about his original goal, the one about the strangers. "I had that dream, too," she said. "I guess we used to be competitive."

"I still am."

"Me, too. But we don't have many places to put it to use."

Avo said, "It's embarrassing, wanting to be recognized by strangers on the street."

"No," Mina said. "It's only embarrassing to admit it."

He did that thing he did, palming her head. "You're my great love," he said, and he kissed her hair. "But embarrassing or not, I want both. I want your love and I want the love of the public. You laugh, but I'm not ashamed to say it. I want both. I don't want to choose."

Mina was laughing not because she thought it was funny but because she wanted to make sure he would listen. She said, "It seems greedy to get both, doesn't it?"

Avo laughed. "Are you threatening to leave me?"

"Kirovakan is my town," Mina said, teasing. "If I want you gone, you're the one who has to leave." As he wrapped himself around her, she laughed and sputtered through it, "You can stay, you can stay!"

Maybe it helped that the diamond wasn't real. It made leaving her—at the party, in the country—feel less like a breach of his word. Or maybe his word was the real fake, his commitment to her a semi-synthetic material made for ulterior uses. Or maybe he was lured by the idea of America, or the official typesetting on the visa to Los Angeles—curled from the tube-rolled envelope in which it came, along with a receipt for airfare—which was so declarative that it made every other fact in Avo's life appear sentimental by comparison. Or maybe he just missed his brother—his cousin's cousin, really—who didn't prioritize being well liked, who was fighting a heroic cause, who believed that getting history right was just as much an act of *making* as any invention to come in the future.

Or maybe Avo felt that it was his job as a man—an Armenian man—to shunt aside his heart for what he'd been taught to believe was the greater good. Maybe he was ashamed to know the truth about Tigran, ashamed he couldn't share it with Mina. Or maybe—he insisted on considering—he'd been pretending to love her all that time, or maybe it was puppy love—hadn't they only been serious together since October?—and leaving could be as easy and thoughtless as catching a bus.

With this story in mind, he chose to leave first thing in the morning. The one running bus left for the capital just after dawn, and he knew if he missed it, he would never leave.

When he returned to the party, Mina was barely awake, lying on the sofa in front of the blue light of the muted TV. Her nose cast a teal shadow down her face.

"You missed it," she said, and he knelt beside the couch and kissed her forehead. She complained that his nose was cold. He kissed her again anyway.

"It feels like a big year," she said, "1975."

He could hear her falling asleep, her voice drifting. "If it's not our year this year," he said, "know that we'll have our year."

"Mhm," she said, hardly at all. "We'll have it, our year."

All night it snowed. In the hills, vacationers slept in cabins, waiting for the ski lift to resume at daybreak. From the city, though, the vacationers were invisible. Avo left Mina and waited, half-frozen at the stop, for the bus to come. He remembered seeing the ski lift for the first time from Ruben's bedroom window. The chairs rising on their cables seemed to welcome him to this next part of his life, after his parents, appearing right there in the window on the other side of the hill, lifting and returning, waiting for him to step aboard and rise.

There would be no snow in Los Angeles. Half a meter here tonight, it looked like. His bus at dawn might have some trouble getting through, he thought, and the idea of getting stuck on his impulsive escape from home sent all the dinner and walnuts he'd eaten churning in his stomach.

He'd left a note for Mina to find when she woke up, but he'd had to be vague. He didn't want a Party official, having seen them on long walks late into the night, going to her with questions again. *First the little stern boy defects, and now the tall one—and what do they have in common but you, Mina Bagossian? Surely that can't be a coincidence, can it?* All he'd written was: *I love you. When it's our year, I'll explain.*

Now he had to shovel. It was still dark when he laced his boots. He found a shovel near the census bureau and returned to the bus stop. The light scattered underneath the streetlamp, speckled with miniature shadows of snowfall. If the bus got stuck, he'd never leave. So he shoveled. In that light, he spent an hour plowing the road, all the way from the bus stop to the first bend some fifty yards out—enough for the bus to gain momentum and keep it.

He was sweating so much that when he took off his jacket, his skin steamed in the cold. In the distance loomed the tallest building in Kirovakan. Through the snow and the steam of himself, he peered from under his eyebrow. Then he got back to work. All night he shoveled snow, fearing and also hoping a light would flare up in her window. But the building kept dark. It was the tallest in the city, everyone knew, but not in the world.

11

Los Angeles, California, 1975–1978

Before he became The Brow Beater, Avo spent his California days conspiring in a warehouse at the edge of Glendale. You could find it across the Los Angeles River from the Wilson and Harding municipal golf courses at Griffith Park, at the end of a warehouse-laden cul-de-sac called Sperry Street: a misshapen cement cube of a building stooped beneath a rusty billboard that read, "You Can't Spell BIG PLANS Without *L.A.*"

Before new zoning laws restricted flammable storage there, the warehouse at the end of Sperry Street had been used as a shared overstock warehouse for companies dealing in fertilizer. A group of Armenians had signed the lease in the Nixon years, when the last of the pallets and bags of shit had been hauled out. Now, six years removed, the smell had been complicated by the paunchy, vodka-pored perfume of professional *saboteurs*—a French word Ruben had used in a recent letter from Paris to describe Avo's new Los Angeles compatriots: *Saboteurs aligned with the ahistorical agenda of the Turkish regime*. Still, despite the enormous warehouse fans whirring all day, despite the patio grill used to barbecue kebob and lamb, and despite the godlessly beefed-up lemons they siphoned over their food during meetings, the faint stench of haystacks and dung refused to stop haunting the place. Every morning upon entering the warehouse, Avo smelled it and took a seat on an old leather armchair, one of a series arranged in a circle, and said good morning to the rest of the men smelling it, too.

Meds Mart, they called him. Big Man.

Like many people who chose to identify in groups, these six men always seemed to speak in unison, even when they were speaking individually. There were no leaders among them, and yet whenever an individual among them spoke, he spoke with the arrogance of a man in charge. It was disorienting, belonging to such a collective. The six other men never shared details of their personal lives—it was unwritten but understood that origin stories and family lives were strictly off-limits—and so they remained, to Avo, basically indistinguishable. This worried Avo, since he felt so distinguishable himself, what with his size, which set him apart, not to mention his access to his inner life, which reminded him every now and then that he was inconveniently different from this group he'd chosen to join. Because the group had only one purpose, they had really only one conversation, repeating it in various forms again and again, avoiding anything at all on which they might disagree, and it was the constant sense of agreement that Avo found so disorienting, as if their purpose itself were the only leader they acknowledged. Avo knew that to be untrue, however. Any question of leadership led directly to Europe or to the Middle East or to Asia—wherever it was that Hagop Hagopian had happened to station himself that year, that month, or that day.

As for the one conversation they had again and again—the ongoing denial of the Armenian Genocide by the Turks, and their strategy for global acknowledgment, apologies, and reparations—the tone was not as passionate as he'd expected. More accurately, it felt academic, like a school project Avo might have preferred to do alone. Only three months into his membership in the Armenian Secret Army for the Liberation of Armenia, Avo began zoning out during meetings, sketching invisible memories of home in his mind, of Mina. He began pretending to listen.

Except every now and then, there came the brief inclusion of a non-Armenian name, at which point Avo remembered to pay attention. A sketchy plot to kidnap a Turkish movie star, for instance, or a more straightforward plan to assassinate an ambassador. In the background, they put on records of folk singers from the old country, the same trilling clarinets Avo had heard all his life, the same hazy breaths of a duduk over the scratch of vinyl.

One day, just to change the tone of the room, Avo decided to tell a joke. He'd heard it in Leninakan, as a kid, from an old drunk who paid for his vodka by making the bartender laugh. The joke went like this: An old commander is telling war stories to his troops. The commander was once captured on the front lines, he says. His captors were notoriously ruthless, and to their prisoners, they did one of two things: they killed them or they raped them. "What did they do to you?" a young soldier asks the commander. And the old commander pauses and says, "They killed me."

Avo put his hands up to signal that his joke was finished. But the men weren't laughing. One of them began a long lecture about the brutalities inflicted upon Armenians during the forced marches to Deir ez-Zor. "Here we are trying to win justice for the victims of barbarians, of rape, of murder, and this big oaf is auditioning for Johnny Carson."

Avo sank as low as a man his size could sink into his chair. The truth was he found the joke mean and unfunny himself, always had, even as a boy. But he'd thought the men would like it and had performed it—worn the joke like a costume—hoping to connect with them. Having failed, he offered an apology, but the group had moved on already. They were back to their ongoing conversation. Avo listened for a while longer, picking up a new detail about the Turkish ambassador's home in La Crescenta. He rubbed his head, balding already at nineteen, and brushed his one eyebrow back from his eyes. He wondered where his brother was. His cousin's cousin. Ruben wouldn't have laughed at the joke, either, but he might have at least understood Avo's motives for telling it.

When he wasn't at the warehouse, Avo ducked underneath the doorways on Chevy Chase Drive, living in a studio apartment Ruben had arranged for him from overseas. To his surprise, Armenians were his neighbors on the other side of every wall. Glendale was a city with Armenian butchers, grocers, and landlords. Almost every tenant in Avo's building was an Armenian, and he spent long stretches of those early days in America never hearing a word of English. A diaspora city could feel like home the way distant traffic at night could be mistaken for the sound of rain, he thought.

Almost every night, several of the families in the building would choose an apartment to gather in and drink and eat dinner. Sometimes, when loneliness settled like a scratch in the throat, Avo would join them. He was too young to have much in common with the old folks, and besides, his size made him a hit with their children. They gawked up at him as if he were the Armenian statue of liberty, and he'd tell jokes and let them climb to his shoulders, around his neck, and he lifted them so they could look inside the light fixtures for the bodies of dead flies, and it was as if he'd given them a better view of not only the apartment but also this new sunbeat country they called theirs.

On Sundays, instead of going to church, Avo went to a jewelry store to meet the only adult with whom he spoke more than a few words outside the warehouse, an older woman with a pet dog she adored.

Valantin read to some of the children in his apartment complex and had been in attendance at one of the building's dinners. Immediately she'd taken a liking to the big man entertaining the children, and struck up a conversation. When she realized he hardly spoke English at all, she gave him a trilingual business card and spoke every sentence to him twice: first in their old language and then in English.

"*Gari daragan es?* How old are you?"

"*Tasniny.*"

"*Tasniny*. Nineteen," she said, and so on.

She'd practically ordered him to meet with her at a jewelry store in town.

"*Sa* Avo Gregoryan," she told her aunt the first Sunday at Nor Jewelry. "This is Avo Gregoryan. *Khosel anglaren e nran*. Speak English to him."

"Wow!" her aunt said. She was hardly five feet tall and reached into her dress pocket for a pair of purple glasses, which she then held over her nose. "*Shat, shat medz*," she said.

"Very, very big," Valantin echoed.

"Sure," Avo said in English. "I thank you, sure."

Sunday after Sunday, they took their coffee the Armenian way at a table in the back, near the safe. The weekly sessions might've felt like church if not for the way Avo checked over his shoulder every now and then during the conversation. Ruben had instructed him not to associate with anyone unaffiliated with ASALA, and that fact haunted every Sunday he shared with Valantin. It lingered in the steam over their cups of coffee, over their cheese-filled *boreg* and their sweets. It snaked its way through their vocabulary words and their conjugations, settling in the margins of the history textbook

Valantin brought in one day, after explaining the difficulty of translating poetry. Ruben had gone to great lengths to arrange everything for Avo so that there would be no need to talk to anyone who didn't speak Armenian. And yet, for almost three years, Avo traveled to the back of a jewelry store, secretly and in violation of his word, to learn an impossible and illogical language. For what? Any time the question came to his mind, he pushed it away as if he were back at the factory, monitoring the textile machinery for bad signals. But at night, falling asleep to the sounds of his neighbors fighting or loving, the question reemerged.

He could imagine it so well, he could make it so. A mirage of the ear. Sometimes this new life felt like his. A mirage of the heart. Month after month, he wondered if the illusion would ever be made real, as Ruben had promised him. Mina—if Avo didn't put her at risk by contacting her—would be sent for in the coming months, and this new place would become a real home. In the meantime, the way he saw it, if he protected Mina and did his job, he could spend his own free time any way he chose.

From time to time, he wished the old world could come calling, but the only taste of that other life came in the form of the occasional phone call from Ruben. The calls were brief and business-oriented, usually making sure that Avo hadn't noticed anything or anyone strange near the warehouse. In this way, his brother's singularly high-pitched voice felt less like a signal from home than a reminder of how far he'd traveled. They avoided talking about Kirovakan, about growing up together, or about Mina. And they certainly never talked about the incident at the Black Sea, for which they, secretly or not, still blamed each other. Whenever Avo tried to turn their conversations toward the personal, Ruben stopped him. All of that, he said, could be discussed later, once their job was complete. Now was the time to focus.

So he corresponded with Mina instead, if only in his mind. Already he'd written imagined letters and read imagined responses, in which Mina had accepted his apologies, promising to join him when the time was right. It was easy to invent her side of the correspondence because, when they were teenagers, he'd once seen a page of her journal, which she'd left near the ski lift they used to go to in the hills of Kirovakan. She'd forgotten the journal, and the wind had splayed it open, and he'd read a page before picking it up and returning it to her. Even in one page he could see a rambling, endearing writer, and he could hear her voice clearly when he read her words. She wrote the same way she walked—patiently, looking around this way and that—and Avo wondered if that was a coincidence, or if it was possible to tell how people think and write by the way they walk, by the way they move through the world. Remembering how he walked—lumbering and crouched and unsuited to the world—he trashed the theory quickly. Still, that was what that one page of her journal had done to him, gotten him imagining long letters written in her hand, gotten him thinking about lovely, useless things. Even in his imagination, none of her would-be letters was particularly romantic—though she did leave a lipstick kiss at the end of each note. Instead, she'd have written about her new role at the school, teaching backgammon in the same room where she'd been taught to play by the great grandmaster she loved so much. More than once, she might've called her students adorable, and the word would act like a shield that reflected itself directly back to her, and Avo thought about how much those imaginary children would have adored their teacher.

In the warehouse, the men had spent several months planning an elaborate attack on the Turkish Airlines kiosk at LAX, studying the intricacies of the international terminal and preparing homemade explosives over the interminable compositions of Komitas on vinyl. They'd organized protests, vandalized several dozen Turkish institutions, written educational pamphlets to be distributed to Armenian day cares and schools, and spent many thousands of dollars investing in weapons training and equipment, but the Turkish Airlines kiosk was to be their first major operation. Almost a full year of planning and development had come to this, details being finalized. And then—just as they were about to do what they'd all come to do—the phone rang. The caller was Hagop Hagopian, telling them a flag had been raised at the LAPD. They were to nix the whole plan.

"They're doing it in Rome instead," said the man who'd spoken to Hagop. "Apparently, our brothers in Italy get everything worth doing, no matter how long we've been working on it."

"Damn," said another of the six warehouse men. "I guarantee they don't have the smell of shit lingering in their place of business, either."

"Well, at least now we can focus on the professor."

"And there's only one of him," said another. "So unless he moves to Rome, the professor is ours."

"Right," a few of them said at once, reinvigorated.

Avo couldn't recall any mention of a professor. He considered asking for clarification but decided just to pick up the facts as they developed. He joined the men at their chalkboard, and they all seven got to work.

Everything Avo knew about Professor Marlon Tanaka came from the perfectly square text of biography found underneath his photograph in the back of a textbook. Avo had imagined an old man in a white beard, but the professor in question was only a decade older than he was.

Born in Burbank in 1945, Tanaka was conceived while his parents were detained at Manzanar. In 1961 he left Southern California for early enrollment at Berkeley, where he befriended Mario Savio and took part in the Free Speech Movement. In 1965 he returned south to begin his doctoral work at UCLA in Late Ottoman history, shirking the expectations of his advisers that he'd pursue Japanese studies. "I looked at the faculty list for each department," he said in one interview, "and it was very clear that like with like was buried there. Arabs studying Arabs, Chinese studying Chinese. I thought, Perhaps I've discovered a source of our problems. And so I declared: Let there be a student one day who learns about Turks from a man named Tanaka!"

Here is what those students learned: As the empire was falling, Armenian loyalties—already teetering between the Russians and the Ottomans—landed treasonously with the Russians at the Battle of Sarikamish. This, followed by what Tanaka called the "rebellion" in Van, led to a civil war within the even messier context of the first burgeoning world war. Many Armenians—though far fewer, Tanaka claimed, than most Western historians alleged—were killed, but there were bad people on both sides, and many virtuous Turks were also killed in the haze of war. An unfortunate—but justifiable!—wash.

Avo had never met a denier. He'd never seen their lies so clearly laid out, and he could hardly believe his eyes. How could a thirty-one-year-old wunderkind, an assistant professor at a world-renowned university, be so irresponsible with the truth? How many scholars, Avo wondered, had tried to explain how the Armenians in Turkey had already been subjected to the Hamidian massacres some twenty-five years before the genocide? How many scholars had brought to Tanaka's very corridor (the ninth floor of Bunche Hall) the private letters and public decrees of the three

Ottoman pashas, proof of Talaat Bey's orchestration of the deportations and forced marches, proof of the concealment of the exterminations? There was proof. But that's how denial worked. Every structure of truth provides a new shadow to scurry to. No evidence could matter.

Jart. The shattering—that was what Avo's parents used to call the genocide, and it made sense to him that another shattering was what it would take for the world to acknowledge it, too.

For the next two months, the warehouse men took shifts tracking the professor. They would do this—from his office to his classrooms to his home—mapping out the particulars of his routine. Avo, whose size made him too conspicuous, was relegated to watching the professor on campus. He had to take a bus to Westwood and call one of his colleagues from a pay phone whenever Tanaka left the history department building. Avo found it to be an oddly serene task, like meditation, staring at the doors for the little man to exit and scamper across the bright university. Avo had learned the layout at UCLA well enough through blueprints and books, but he couldn't have guessed its beauty. The city smog lifted miraculously there, and the gray blade of the sky buckled to reveal the white-rimmed leaves of London planes against the sun. He had killed a man once, but not on purpose, and the slow unfolding of this new crime had him craving beauty. For example, he saw the coral trees lining the walkways of campus as writhing, arthritic fingers, and he imagined complex histories for the students and families and occasional bicyclists zipping by along the curving paths near his bench.

There he sat, watching the doors of Bunche Hall, an ugly gray building pockmarked by black square windows jutting out like the buttons on a television remote. The home of the history department reminded him, fittingly, of the Communist apartment complexes of his childhood, all slate and futureless. It was the perfect kind of building from which to look back, to obsess over the past, to end a love affair, or—as seventeen students had in the past decade, according to one book—to leap to one's death.

Valantin spilled her coffee all over his week's homework. He'd summarized an American children's story and had written something of a sequel. From what Valantin could salvage of it, she was impressed. His understanding of English was coming along very nicely, she said, but sooner or later, he was going to have to get comfortable speaking it with people.

"What do you do for a job?" she asked in both languages.

Avo said, "I work in a warehouse," the answer Ruben had given him to practice.

"That won't do," Valantin said. "That's quiet, lonely work. You need to interact with people."

"He can work here," her aunt said from the safe. "Your sons are never coming by the way they used to."

But Valantin said Avo would speak only Armenian in a place like this. She thought for another minute and then asked Avo to lean in so she could whisper in English.

"Don't tell my aunt, but sometimes I enjoy going to this place in Hollywood. A bar. Anyway, I know the bartender there. He'll take one look at you and give you a job at the door."

"The Doors?" Avo said, strumming an invisible guitar.

"No, not *the* Doors. The *door*—of the bar. They call the job a *bouncer*. Check ID, break up fights. Easy for a man your size."

"I don't know, Valantin-jan. I'm busy at the warehouse."

"It'll replace your homework, and it's only Friday nights. Once a week. Good practice. I'll pick you up this Friday, seven o'clock. Yes?"

Over by the safe, her aunt was washing the pet dog's paws with a wet cloth. Avo brushed his eyebrow back with his thumb and told Valantin, in English, "I'm thanking you."

Between his taxi rides from Glendale to Westwood to Hollywood and back, Avo was beginning to feel like a real Angeleno. He could smell the difference in neighborhoods, the citrus and tobacco sting of Little Armenia or the hollow smell of spilled liquor near downtown. He imagined writing about it to Mina, and he imagined her replying, asking if, despite everything, he still smelled like rain.

Probably he smelled worse than that. He'd begun working the last-call shift at The Gutshot two nights a week, and although checking for ID was the face of the gig, Valantin hadn't detailed the full extent of the job. Most of his time was spent scrubbing the toilets and sinks, mopping the tiles of vomit and liquor, and washing the mop clean of what he'd just wiped from the floor.

So he smelled worse, probably, than rain, but at least his English was getting better. The bartender who'd hired him had quit drinking years ago and served his customers with a kind of gentle understanding that Avo found disarming. Longtin could tell when a person was drunk about three drinks before anyone else could. Avo suspected it was the relative silence placed on him by the language barrier that allowed Longtin to take a liking to him.

Sometimes a group of girls would flirt, and sometimes a curious woman would tell him exactly what she wanted to try with him. But in all his nights at The Gutshot, he always said, "I have a woman, bro. Thank you, bro, but I have a woman."

Meanwhile, the men in the warehouse were itching to act on the professor. "How long has it been since they sent us here to do a job," one of them complained, "and why don't they just let us do it already?" But the order had to come in from Paris—or Beirut, or Madrid, or Moscow, or wherever Hagop Hagopian and Ruben happened to be—and in the meantime, all the warehouse men could do was wait. "I'm getting bored following this little Japanese professor around L.A.," said one of the men, and the others agreed.

For Avo, the problem with the delay had nothing to do with boredom. It had something to do with himself, the ways in which he could feel himself changing. The vision he'd trusted on the way to America had by now been frayed by doubt. The morale in the warehouse, which had peaked early on, was gone. Nothing—no Turkish acknowledgment—had come of their work. Avo was tired of waiting in a manure facility along a dying river for the world to change, for Mina to be able to join him. He was tired of his job at The Gutshot, too, soaking up what the body rejects. He was tired of being a million kilometers away from the tallest building in Kirovakan and the woman who lived inside.

Increasingly often, Avo found his mind wandering in those warehouse meetings and on UCLA's campus, composing whole letters he would write to Mina detailing their future together.

Sometimes in the responses he imagined her writing, she would beg him to tell her the truth about Tigran. *I know you did it,* he imagined in her handwriting. *Just tell me and I'll forgive you. Just tell me, and our split will end.*

But even in make-believe, he lied and lied and lied.

In the warehouse, the men imagined what they'd do to the professor. The rumor among them was that Hagopian had hired a man somewhere in the Mediterranean who tortured Turks the way their ancestors had been tortured, using the exact instruments and techniques. They wanted to do the same to this professor, peel back his fingernails, or whip his feet, or march him out into the desert until he blistered and collapsed and split open. Just north of Los Angeles were countless acres of the untamed Mojave, the closest thing they had to the Syrian desert and the concentration camp at Deir ez-Zor. Maybe they could film the professor recanting his lies and admitting he'd been paid by the Turkish government to spread denialism in the United States. They would share the video with news outlets. They would show the world that the evil of the crime was perfected by its denial.

When they spoke, the men sounded the way people in freezing conditions might speak about summer, and afterward there fell a wide, shameful stretch of silence between them. It was as if, just by imagining it so vividly, they'd already done the torture, and Avo wondered if the real thing would only feel redundant.

Whenever Ruben called, he lovingly rambled on about his exploits in Europe and the Middle East. Despite his electrified focus on his own adventures abroad, Ruben's familiar voice came like a salve to Avo's homesickness through the telephone speaker. Without mentioning names, Ruben would extol the vision of Hagop Hagopian, the depth of loyalty he felt among the men he was stationed alongside, and the swelling sense of purpose driving him. All his life, he'd been at the mercy of his circumstances, at the mercy of history, and now history seemed as alterable as a poorly fitting suit. It was the feeling of being a man, Ruben claimed, no longer a boy, which is what most men remained forever. He assumed Avo was feeling the same way, out in Los Angeles. Like a man, wasn't he?

And for a while, Avo was—or at least he said so. Over the last few conversations, his feigned enthusiasm had begun to wear through, and he'd even asked, futilely, if he could take a break from Los

Angeles to visit home. In a patient tone, Ruben explained how dangerous it would be—not only for Avo but for everyone, *everyone* back home—to remain in touch, let alone return.

"Not too much longer from now," he said, "we'll be able to go back, and we'll be hailed as heroes when we do."

"I miss the past," Avo said before realizing that missing the past was what missing was. How could he explain to his brother that he had made a mistake in coming to Los Angeles? That he wished he was still working in the same factory he'd worked in before leaving home, was still with the girl he'd loved since fifteen? How could he tell his brother, a man of ideas who wanted to correct history, that his only ambition was to revive his?

After a silence, Ruben said, "I know who you miss." Through his ceiling, Avo could hear the neighbors laughing.

Ruben went on, "We're almost there, brother. I have a big job coming up very soon over here, but once that's done, I'll ask for a transfer. Okay? I'll join you in Los Angeles, and we'll run things out there together. And we'll send for her to join us. What, you don't believe me? I'll send you something in the mail you can hold on to until you see her again. Something that will make the wait worthwhile."

In the next days, just after the gift arrived, the men in the warehouse got the call they'd been waiting for, and Avo knew his conversation with Ruben had sped up the decision. The men in the warehouse celebrated. Finally—no more following the mundane life of the professor of denial.

Finally—the operation was set to go. Two of the men would wait for the professor at his home, wait for him to get out of the car, and smuggle him back to the warehouse. There, Avo and the others would be waiting, making sure no one had followed. The plan was set for a Thursday night, less than a week in advance. The men—including Avo—toasted. Finally, they would be doing what they had volunteered to do.

"Don't call me bro," Valantin said on Sunday. "Other than that, your English is becoming superb."

"Super?"

"Superb."

"What's the difference?"

"One has a *b* at the end of it."

"Why?"

Valantin squinted. "Mokor-jan," she called out to her aunt. "Bring us the cognac."

They spoke in both languages until Avo asked if Valantin had heard about these Armenians in Lebanon and France who were using violence to remind the world of the genocide.

"These idiots," Valantin said. "Who raised them? What kind of mothers did they have? No brains. They're just as bad as the Turks, is what I think."

"You're wrong," her aunt said from the counter. "I don't care what he does, no Armenian compares to the Turks."

"I don't know about that," Valantin said, "but these idiots are not real Armenians, in my opinion. Would you both agree? No real Armenian would kill another person, no matter what. It's not Christian, it's not in our blood. We're a peaceful people."

"But sometimes," her aunt said, "to protect the family . . ."

"Okay, yes, a man comes with a gun to your home, you can defend yourself. But a man comes to your great-grandfather's home sixty years ago, and you blow up a bomb in a market full of people? That's not protection. That's not what a real Armenian does."

"But they haven't blown up a bomb in a market full of people," her aunt said. "They've only targeted ambassadors of Turkey, political representatives."

"Still."

"Maybe."

"Well, what do you think, Avo?" Valantin asked. "*Gisht'em?* Am I right? Or are you on my mokor's side?"

"It's terrible," Avo said. "All of it is terrible, bro."

"We can all agree on that," Valantin said. "But don't call me bro."

Over the weekend, Avo broke up seven fights and a couple having sex in the bathroom. And a man—some might say middle-aged or old, others stately—this stately man with long bleached hair and tattoos on his arms, well, he struck up a conversation. And before Avo knew it, he was being offered another job. He ignored the man in the ponytail until he realized the opportunity he was being presented.

Wrestling, but for show. And the job would involve living on the road for the foreseeable future, inventing whole new identities, and living as secretly as possible. He could save money in the meantime, to return home to Mina.

"Let's say noon, bro," Avo said, because what he planned to do would take up the morning, and Angel Hair pumped his hand.

At 11:45 the next morning, Avo went to a pay phone near The Gutshot. He remembered the numbers he'd scratched into the back of a history textbook, just beneath the square of text that made up the author's biography. As he dialed, he imagined where the numbers led, down the wire into the walls of The Gutshot, up to the crucifixes lining the street, the telephone poles that connected to the roof of his apartment building, where he'd once seen a bird nesting. Two by two, he'd lifted the children of his neighbors onto his shoulders to see. Now he imagined the call traveling from the bar to the wires of that nest, around and around, until a home was made of his voice, and then up through the cables leaving the city, winding in silence along Forest Lawn Drive, past the famous cemetery where the bones of old Hollywood lay rotting, past the overlook to the Bowl, where a concert raged in electric neon streamers, past the limits of the city and up through the Valley and on into the Vasquez Rocks, those jagged slabs of sediment thrust from the earth by the grinding plates of the San Andreas Fault. The one time he'd followed the professor to his home out there, Avo had passed those rocks, had felt the unnerving effect of history flaunting itself like that, in layers and layers and out in the open, twenty-five million years of sawtoothed fact just sitting there, waiting, the disinterested teeth of time. And now he imagined his voice trundling down the wires into the house near the rocks, and the voice from the other end racing up and back to him.

"I hear you," the voice said. "Who is this?"

"Thursday night, bro. You are careful. Okay?"

"Excuse me? Who is this?"

Avo considered how to say *hapshtakum*. Person theft. "You are the professor, yeah? They are following you, bro. They're planning Thursday night."

"Is this a joke? Am I supposed to laugh or be afraid?"

A problem of fluency, Avo thought, the distance between his heart and his words. His lack of confidence in the language turned every word he said into satire. "You lie with the genocide, bro, I hate you, why you're lying I don't know, killing families again forever and forever, very evil," he said, bunching the metal cord in his fist. "But I'm calling you anyway. My thinking is like that, bro, to be killing you is wrong."

And before Tanaka could thank him or curse him, Avo placed the phone gingerly back on its receiver. He'd had to lurch and bend to fit inside that phone booth. Now he head-butted the glass once, twice, before unfurling himself to leave.

In the distance, double-parked along a curb as red as the fanny pack he'd put Ruben's gift inside, Angel Hair was waving his hand out of the driver's side window of his station wagon, and Avo walked toward the glowing curb, and didn't stop for two whole years.

12

Los Angeles, California, 1989

The old walnut had recognized Ruben's name, but she wouldn't say another word on the matter. Instead, she left the jewelry store and marched across the street to one of the churches. "She goes and prays sometimes," Valantin explained. There was no promising that her aunt would open up when she returned in an hour or two, but I was welcome to stick around and see. "Or you must be hungry for more than sweets," Valantin said. "Why don't you go get a bite to eat? My friend owns a restaurant a short drive from here, on Everett and Elk. Leave the cat here, go tell him I sent you, and when you come back, my aunt will tell us everything. I'm curious, too, now."

Because my stomach was bleating and because I didn't want to leave without hearing what the old walnut had to say, I agreed to the plan. I stayed in the office for a minute after Valantin left to help a customer, and then I went to Fuji, who'd made himself comfortable on the back of the couch. "I'll be back in a little bit," I whispered into his fur.

Outside, with their language still ringing in my ears, I realized just how thoroughly the Armenians had made a home of Glendale, California. Storefronts bore the letters of their alphabet, and as I drove to the restaurant, I saw that even some of the street signs at the intersections had an Armenian addendum. Wilson did, and Broadway did, too, but Harvard didn't, and neither did Orange Grove Avenue.

As soon as I passed it, I remembered the address Mina had left on the answering machine, as if I were supposed to respond by mail: 700 Orange Grove Avenue.

The Brow Beater never talked much about home, but a year into our travels together, he did mention a woman. This was the night we were leaving Minnesota, after the debacle in Duluth.

Along with a dozen or so other wrestlers, we'd gotten ourselves stuck in the northern territory during the worst of the weather. Every night for over two weeks, the good guys left the wrestling ring for one bar, and the bad guys left for another. By the end of the two-week residency, we practically owned the places. We'd fought with every local bigmouth, we'd taken shots from every bottle on the shelves, and all of us had slept with our fair share of the women of Duluth. All of us, that is, except The Brow Beater.

He'd laugh with us, he'd fight with us, and God knows he'd drink with us, but as soon as a girl introduced herself to him, The Brow Beater would call it a night. After a while, of course, the boys started ribbing him about it. It wasn't like it is now, with the wrestling audience made up entirely of sentient pimples with boys attached to them. No, back then there were girls, real women, in the crowd. They flocked from town to city, from bingo hall to arena, from tavern to hotel bar.

They came for the bodybuilders and the studs, the blondies and the heartbreakers, but they'd settle, out of curiosity or lonesomeness, for a masked man or a savage or a giant like The Brow Beater. They even showed a little hospitality to old managers every now and again. Regardless of their motives, we were appreciative. Except The Brow Beater, and the rest of the boys never understood that about him. It's a hard life out there on the road, in the ring, and the touch of a strange woman was more than the touch of a strange woman. We grappled with men, we trained with men, we ate with men, we shared excruciatingly small cars and motel rooms and locker rooms with men, we cut those men open, gimmicked or hard-way, we choked those men with our hands and arms and thighs, we allowed those men to brutalize us the same, we drew money from marks in the stands who happened to be, even then, mostly men, we aimed to entertain those men, to earn the respect or admonishment of those men, and so by the time the men in stripes counted their last pinfalls of the night, of the week, of the month, of the year, by the time the marks had gone and the showers had rained down on us like leaves from a shaking, it came as a kind of godly intercession to find a woman, lonesome or curious but real, to cleave to.

I knew wrestlers who married those strange women, who mistook those nights of flesh and mercy for love. But not The Brow Beater. The Brow Beater seemed to know the difference.

Well, the boys let him have it. They pissed in his boots, they pinned him down and tried to shave his signature eyebrow in two (we fought them off), they potatoed him in the ring, breaking his nose. Finally, the weather cleared, and we drove off to a new, warmer territory. It was during that car ride that The Brow Beater, eyes still ringed in yellow and green, said he was planning to marry a girl back home.

What did he tell me about her? She loved music, and cats, and something about skiing? She used to carry something reflective in her hands that would cast light out in every direction as she walked. His hope was that she'd be joining him in the States.

There was a rise in his voice when he spoke about her, a kind of climbing that his heart seemed to do up his vocal cords. It was the same quality, I realized far too late, that I'd heard on the answering machine last Christmas. The girl—The Brow Beater's girl back home—was Mina.

I skipped lunch. The clouds came on as I turned the truck around, and I was glad for the light to change. I never trusted a person who prays for cloudlessness, who prefers his days sun-stroked and harsh. Much better are those thumb-licked days when the dim light is a shroud, when no sight in the sky gets lost in a glare, when even an idea can seem matte and precise. When I found the right address, I steered into the narrow drive of an apartment complex, three stories high and square, plastered brown and flaxen as an ice cream bar.

At the gate, I could hear music. I pushed through and followed it—battling clarinets, keyboards, and vocals I remembered overhearing in Mina's phone call on Christmas—up the fire escape. On the roof, there were about two dozen people, some of them children, dancing. It occurred to me that I was crashing a lunchtime party. A grill was going at one end of the roof, and smoke drifted as thickly as the music from the speakers. Several men huddled around the grill, turning the meat every now and again with a pair of pincers. Elsewhere, a row of elderly folks watched the party stoically from wicker chairs, and the children rushed between their dancing and the staircase beside me, going up and down to the apartments below, returning every time with new bowls and platters of food. A blue tablecloth was anchored to a table by a rock the size of a skull, and some of the smallest children were setting out the silverware. I couldn't spot a woman between the ages of twelve and seventy. Finally, one of the men left the grill to approach me, pincers in his hands. The others watched him, and he put on a big smile. "I'll offer you a drink," he said to me, "if you tell me who you are."

"I'm here to see Mina," I said, and the guy turned to his compatriots at the grill, translating.

They let out a big roar of laughter. One of the men, gray-haired and dressed in an open-collared leisure suit, wasn't laughing. He started marching over to me. The other guy, the one who spoke English to me, introduced the gray-haired man. "Here comes Galust, coming to get you. He's Mina's husband."

Galust seemed too small and old to be married to Mina—half her height and twice her age—but who was I to disrespect him? I said to the English speaker, "Tell him I'm here for business. His wife bought a cat from me last year. I told her I'd come by about this time to administer the final vaccination."

Galust listened to the translation. He nodded and then planted his hand on my shoulder and guided me to the grill. "Vodka?" he asked, and I said, "No, no, thank you." He signaled for one of the other men to start pouring, and soon I was raising a glass to new friends for the second time since arriving in Los Angeles.

The English speaker drank with us, too. His name was Shen, from Apartment Six. "The whole building here is Armenian," he said with pride. "We have lunch and dinner up here almost every day and night, the families."

When I asked if I should go find the cat in one of the apartments below, he told me to wait on the roof until the women were done cooking.

"But aren't you guys cooking?" I asked, motioning to the grill.

"We're *grilling*," Shen said.

From Shen, I learned that Mina and her husband had brought their children here just before the earthquake. "Like she knew it was coming," Shen said. "People say she's always been lucky like that. Not everyone in this building has had the same luck." He poured another round. "I'm being a big drag, forget it. Let's toast to something upbeat."

Galust interrupted and drew a huge laugh, and I asked what he'd said.

"It's not as funny in translation," Shen said, "but he's basically saying, Did you come here to give the cat medicine, or did you come here to get medicine yourself?"

I raised my glass to Galust at the grill. He'd been a census worker back home, apparently, and now was doing accounting work at a restaurant owned by Shen's uncle. Mina's new American role seemed to be no different than what I imagined her old Armenian role to be, staying at home with the kids, making lunch with the other wives and mothers while the men drank liquor on the roof. But that wasn't entirely true. Based on what these men seemed to recall about Mina's purchase of the cat—they assumed I lived someplace nearby—I realized Mina hadn't been totally forthcoming about our transaction. A fuller picture of her visit to me appeared in my mind: on limited money, on a passport whose stamps hadn't yet dried, she had flown round-trip, alone and in secret, to a stranger's house a thousand miles away, equipped only with a new language and an old professional wrestling poster, hoping the stranger would be helpful. I drank another shot with the men, and—in my mind, anyway—dedicated the toast to luck, yes, but to bravery, too.

Two children arrived like angels to offer me food, a plate of barbecued lamb with a side of rice pilaf and a hunk of flatbread piled high with tabouli. The girl, maybe eight or nine, had her hair up in a ponytail not unlike mine, and she held the little boy by the hand. There was no mistaking them for anything but sister and brother. The girl said, “I’m Araksya, and this is Shaunt. We wanted to tell you thank you for Smokey. He is such a good cat.”

I looked across the roof to see who’d sent them. I lifted my plate. Mina lifted hers. Our hellos.

13

Transatlantic, 1978–1979

On the second morning of June 1978, on a quiet street in Madrid, a small band of gunmen opened fire on the car of the Turkish ambassador to Spain, Zeki Kuneralp. The ambassador escaped with his life, but the three others riding with him—his predecessor, his wife, and his chauffeur—either died instantaneously or else bled to death over the newly upholstered interior of the car. White leather, smothered red. Not unlike the Turkish flag, or like parfait with fruit, or—well, enough already. Death wasn't a simile. It actually happened.

Not even seven hours later, gunshots still humming in his skull, Ruben was unfolding a napkin over his lap at an outdoor café in Lisbon. He was with Hagop Hagopian, as he had been for four years already. The heavyset, light-footed woman serving their table came by again, placing a tray of thick little cups of espresso beside a dozen glazed and flaking pastries, none of which had been touched yet. Hagopian, smoking his fourth cigarette of the evening, slipped another folded bill into the pocket of her apron, as he'd done each time she'd brought something new. Hagopian had been described in newspapers of various languages as a monomaniacal, brutish man, but here, Ruben thought, was another side of him. If Ruben were ever asked to contribute to Hagopian's biography, he'd recall this moment, this tip money folded and tucked as precisely as a note of love. This generosity.

Just then came the news, brought over by a long-fingered man wearing several rings, a man from Moscow whom Ruben had met once before, at the backgammon tournament in Paris. The man crouched beside Hagopian and said, in Armenian, "There's been a problem in Los Angeles."

Los Angeles, and Ruben had known immediately that the news concerned his brother. His cousin's cousin. He expected to have to wait to find out what exactly had happened, expected Hagopian to call for the check, to speak with the man from Moscow in private, in the hotel upstairs or someplace altogether else. But Hagopian didn't even ash his cigarette. He only said, "Sit down, eat one of these *pastéis de nata*. My mother always said you should have a good taste in your mouth if you have to tell bad news."

The man from Moscow thanked him and dragged a chair from another table across the cobblestones. He plucked one of the pastries onto his dish and took a bite. Then he began to explain what had gone wrong on the other side of the world. "The police were waiting for them at the professor's home," he said. Hagopian asked if it was possible to know who had tipped off the police.

The man from Moscow ate more of his little cake and washed it down with an espresso. "Well, of the seven men we'd stationed in the Sperry Street warehouse, six were arrested."

"And the other?"

Ruben lit a cigarette of his own, and the sound of the match bursting into flame came exactly at the moment the man spoke his brother's name. "Avo Gregoryan," he said. "The big one, with the eyebrow. He's disappeared."

Hagopian's dimples were so sharp they carved through his

beard. He called the waitress back to the table and ordered another round of sweets. "Surprise me," he told her, and then turned again to the man from Moscow. "This means two things. First, this means we'll have to put our other operations on hold temporarily. Maybe a full year, or more, to be safe."

Ruben thought it unfortunate, after the momentum they'd built—starting with the ambassador in Paris and having just come from the successful operations in Madrid and Athens—to stop now.

When the sweets arrived—an assortment of marbled cookies and jellied doughnuts—Hagopian tipped the woman again, and the man from Moscow asked about the second meaning of the news.

"The second meaning is obvious," Hagopian said, dipping his finger into the jelly. "We have to find our missing man." He sucked the jelly from his finger and then wiped his finger dry on the end of Ruben's necktie. "He's your brother, correct?"

"Actually," Ruben said, "he's a cousin of a cousin."

One hair in Hagopian's beard, beside the right nostril, sprang free. "But when you convinced me to let him join us," he said, "you called him your brother."

"Yes, I did, but I didn't think he would, well, and a real brother wouldn't—"

"I sometimes forget how young you are, Ruben-jan."

Ruben forgot, too. He was only twenty-two.

"You don't have a family. No wife, no children."

"No," Ruben said. "Just this family, here."

"Plus your parents, who are still living in Armenia."

"Yes."

"So that makes you young. Parents but no children. And no siblings, no real family to speak of."

"Other than you."

"Other than me," Hagopian said, smoothing out Ruben's necktie, sharing a little wink with the man from Moscow. "Be my friend, then. Find him, your brother. Your cousin's cousin—excuse me. Find him. That's your new job, as we wait out the new attention we'll be getting."

"I promise, Hagop. I didn't know. I never would've—"

"Find him, and I'll believe you. The sooner you do, the sooner you can get back to the work I know you care so much about. I can see you as a leader one day. You're too bright and passionate to be running errands, so I expect you'll find him quickly." Hagopian had removed his own tie and given it to Ruben. Then he made a show of offering the plate of sweets. "Don't let these go to waste," he said. "Our grandmothers, who survived hell, would kill us."

Since Avo had been given only the one forged passport, he must have remained in the United States. Before his flight, Ruben packed a suitcase with enough clothing and shaving cream for three weeks, which seemed excessive. How hard could it be to find a tall Armenian in a single country?

For all his travels, this was the first time Ruben would be stepping foot in America. Getting off the plane in Los Angeles, he marveled at the plastic weather, but he didn't smell freedom in the taxi line, and he didn't see liberty in the makeshift village of homeless people he eyed on the overpass. His driver spoke worse English than he did.

He took a hotel room in a place called Burbank, where islets of grass separated slabs of concrete sidewalks like compromises, and where the steps leading to some of the homes were painted a candy red. From time to time, he looked down from his third-floor hotel window on to the parking lot below, and to the hills behind it. It was only then that he saw the resemblance. If the hills were greener, if the steps hadn't been painted, if his passport didn't read a false name, and if he weren't there to hunt down his brother, he might have forgotten he'd ever left home.

Ruben's first stop on his search for Avo was the Los Angeles County Men's Central Jail on Bauchet Street, where the six ASALA members—American citizens, all—were awaiting trial for conspiracy to kidnap. One by one, they met with Ruben across a grated screen and a telephone wire. One by one, they mistakenly thought he'd come to bail them out.

"Hagop can help with that," Ruben said to each one, "if you can help me."

What they knew—that the big bald unibrowed Soviet was a traitor to his people, a secret rotten Turk, a fucker and a bitch and a faggot coward shit—was less than helpful. What they didn't know—namely, where Avo had gone, or with whom he'd been in touch outside the warehouse—was frustrating in its scope. On his way out, Ruben promised each of them that they'd hear from Hagopian in the days to come, though he'd heard no such promise himself.

From the jail, Ruben took a cab to the city of Glendale, where he visited the apartment he'd arranged for Avo to live in. He stepped out on Lomita Avenue in front of a tall apartment complex pockmarked by stucco. Cheap brickwork housed a small garden in the front, and a child had drawn flowers on the driveway in chalk.

He was thin enough to slip between a gap in the gate, and he moved from the ground floor to the top, knocking on every door along the way. There were four apartments on each of the four levels, and the first-floor doors went unanswered. The next several were answered by Spanish speakers, and several others also went unanswered. It wasn't until the fourteenth door—a middle apartment on the top floor—that Ruben introduced himself to another Armenian.

"*Barev*," he said to the woman who answered. She was his mother's age, and her hands were wet. She was cooking. He could smell the kufte. "I'm looking for my friend who lives here," he said, and she told him to come inside.

As he described Avo, the woman brought him a cup of tea and a plate of bread and cheese. She recognized Avo but said she hadn't seen him in about a month. Sometimes he would talk to her grandchildren, she said, but otherwise, she didn't know much about him, other than that he was fresh from the old country. Did Ruben want anything besides the tea? The food was almost ready. Beer? Whiskey?

"Thank you," he said, "but my search continues."

"Okay," she said, "I'll ask my granddaughter if she knows anything. Your friend would talk to her outside when she was visiting. Are you sure you're not hungry?" she added. "Here, let me pack something for you."

In the end, he took a wrapped plate of dolma, kufte, and lavash back with him in the cab. The driver made a show of sniffing but didn't complain. He just said, "Spill in my car, I'll spill you."

Several days passed before the phone in his hotel room rang. He'd given the number to the woman at the apartment and had told her to contact him when the granddaughter visited next.

"You're friends with Avo," the granddaughter said. She was eight years old.

"You remember him? About a hundred feet high."

"He wasn't *that* big."

"Oh, he must have shrunk in America."

"He was still pretty big."

"Oh, good. Do you know where he is now?"

"No," said the girl. "Do you? He was nice."

"While he was here, did our dear friend Avo mention where he might go next, what he wanted to do next?"

"No," she said, and her grandmother's voice in the background said, "That's enough, let me talk to him now."

Shit, Ruben thought. There was nothing to learn here. He'd hang up and think of where else he could search. "Okay," he said, wrapping the phone's cord so tight against his forearm that his hand turned white. "*Tstesutyun*, goodbye."

The girl said, "You speak Armenian and English, too? Did you learn from Valantin, too?"

Ruben said, "Valantin?"

"She teaches English. The grandparents won't try, but everyone else here learned from her. My mom did. Avo, too. She speaks the way you just did, once in Armenian, once in English. It takes her *so long* to talk."

Her grandmother took the phone. "God be with you," she said before hanging up.

Leaving the hotel, Ruben asked the man at the front desk if he could put him in touch with an English tutor. And the man knew just the woman.

"I set him up with a job," Valantin said. They were at a little coffee table in the back of a jewelry store, and nobody but her sons had passed through in thirty minutes, but she kept looking around as if the feds might burst in. "I've gone over there to ask for any information at all, but the owner said he's lost so many undocumented workers, from Central America and Mexico and the Soviet Union, that he's grown accustomed to replacing them without asking any questions. Questions lead to a serious risk for his business, he said, and although I understand, I'm worried. I'm so worried that Avo's been detained, taken somewhere, disappeared. His English was improving well, but he wouldn't be able to understand or speak on legal issues. I'm very, very worried."

"Where did he work?"

She bent forward and whispered. "A bar. Called The Gutshot. It's classier than it sounds."

Ruben waved his hand. "No judgment here. I'm just concerned about finding my cousin," he said, and Valantin put a hand on the lightly padded shoulder of his suit.

"I've been feeling so guilty," she said. "It's my fault he was working illegally. It's my fault he's disappeared."

"He knew the risks," Ruben said. "And when I find him, he'll tell you the exact same."

"*Shnorhagalem*, Ruben-jan. Ruben, thank you."

At four o'clock in the afternoon, the door to The Gutshot was locked, and the alleyway was empty. His taxi driver had told him the bar wouldn't open for another hour, but Ruben pulled on the chrome handle anyway, and knocked at the door with the fat of his fist. When it opened, a man—young but with silver hair—said, "Please stop that."

"I'm here to talk about Avo Gregoryan."

The man was holding a white rag. He said, "Don't know him."

"I'm not the police. I'm a friend of his."

"Still don't know him," the man said, ready to close the door.

Ruben, in a flourish he'd practiced in the mirrors of Europe, opened his jacket to show his gun.

Longtin had just become a father. Not long after the birth, he'd come into the baby's room to find his wife folded impossibly inside the cradle with her tiny daughter snug in her arms, singing a melody she told him later she'd invented right on the spot. The girls in his life—that's what Longtin was thinking about when he stepped aside to let Ruben in, when he described the bleached-blond manager who'd taken Avo on the road, and the sport he'd taken him to do. Who knew where they were now, what company or part of the country they'd landed in? Not Longtin, whose life was no longer his alone to risk, and not Ruben, who thanked him and left, blinding the bar with daylight as he opened the door to the world.

Later, in the hotel room, the phone rang. Ruben muted the television. Hagopian asked how his search was going. "I'm close," Ruben said, "I'm close."

In fact, he wasn't. He hadn't even learned the difference between the kind of wrestling Avo had done as a child and the wrestling he was doing now, the distance between the sport and the spectacle. And when he finally did, thanks to a bemused trainer in a San Diego dojo, Ruben still hadn't discovered just how protective the professional wrestling industry was about its inner workings. Taking him for a reporter or a cop, no one would speak to him. It took Ruben over a year to find someone willing to talk, and even he—a vulgar carnival barker based in the negligible state of Kentucky—had no immediate answer to Ruben's question.

"I'll see if I can get ahold of his manager," the Kentuckian said, and another long wait began.

Ruben had been living out of his hotel room in Los Angeles for nine months when he was beckoned back to Paris. He was taken to a jazz club and shown to a small table near the stage where Hagop Hagopian sat, watching two saxophonists duel. When Ruben joined him at the table, Hagopian didn't acknowledge him. The band played chorus after chorus for the soloists to explore. Ruben stopped checking to see if Hagopian had noticed him and turned his attention to the musicians. A waitress bent her ear. Vodka neat, he said. He looked to Hagopian, who dashed his cigarette and ordered another cognac. According to the glasses on the table, it would be his fifth.

The band began a ballad. Brushes on the snare. Bass notes, whole measures apart. A breathy tenor over a dampened piano. Dim and smoky, the music seemed to infect the club, and the longer the band played, the dimmer went the room.

Ruben felt a touch on his elbow hanging from the edge of the table. He thought the waitress had returned. But it was a card-stock coaster, slid to him along the table, bearing scribbles in Armenian handwriting. Ruben kept his face toward the band but lowered his eyes to the note: *Your cousin's cousin is not alone. Organized coup from inside. You still with me?*

The band quieted for the bassist to take a solo over the pianist's comping. Brushes hissed and snapped, and the sounds of the audience came alive: ice rattling in glasses, matches striking, the hushed tones of secrets passing lips.

For the first time all night, Ruben's boss looked at him. Something had changed in Hagop Hagopian. He seemed decades older than the charismatic idealist Ruben had met in the same city five years earlier. The lines between his eyebrows had been troweled deep, and his nose had grown so sharp that the blue shadow it cast on one side of his face made a perfect triangle. And he hadn't said a word. Drunk and quiet was an unsettling combination that reminded Ruben of his father in the moment before he'd burned their books.

To Hagopian's scribbled question, Ruben nodded. He tried to convey his seriousness. He would be loyal until the end.

Hagopian reached for the coaster and added another line in pen. He passed it along. *Prove?*

The bassist was walking now, and the sax was trilling a high note in a long, unfurling, single breath. The musicians were drenched in sweat and seemed to come up occasionally for air.

In the end, Hagop Hagopian applauded, and so did Ruben. In order to prove his loyalty, in order to buy more time to search for Avo, he'd have to run an errand.

From the jazz club, Ruben had followed Hagopian to a hotel room with vaulted ceilings and a view of Sacré-Cœur lit up at night like paradise above the city. There they met the man from Moscow, a longtime ASALA member who looked up briefly from the money he was counting to greet them. All the furniture in that room was antique and upholstered in velvet. A dinner cart with dirty dishes and silverware was parked near the foot of the bed.

"You ate already?" Hagopian said.

"A while ago," said the man from Moscow, who was married to a woman he hadn't seen in three months. They spoke over the phone every chance he got. The calls to Moscow were expensive, and he spent most of those conversations listening to his wife complain about his job.

Their sons, five and seven, didn't need reparations, she said. They needed their father. Okay, he said. He would drop the boss off at the airport soon and be done with Paris forever. Or at least he would have a break. Of course he knew he shouldn't have told his wife about his role in ASALA, but he never could keep a secret from her. She'd once been engaged to his closest friend, and even that hadn't stopped him from telling her the truth. On recent calls, he'd started interrupting her complaints. "It's almost over, babe. Finish this assignment, and then a change of management coming soon, I promise." He'd promised her it wouldn't be another six months before the boss was replaced with Monte Melkonian, who was less—what was the word he used? Demanding.

Hagop Hagopian used the telephone cord to strangle him. He had long fingers, the man from Moscow. He was using them to pull away the helix at his throat. Before returning to Los Angeles, Ruben found a serrated blade on the dish cart and took care of them.

14

Kirovakan, Soviet Armenia, 1980

A white bus with a pale blue roof came to a hiss beside the fountain in the square. The door opened, and a line of children filed out. The old Russian church with its golden dome welcomed them as if to the great hereafter, but instead of a saint at the gate, they were welcomed by their teacher.

"This way," Mina said, and the children followed her the short distance to the train station. Mina walked backward, facing the students, counting them. Twelve. Like Jacob's sons, she thought. Like the apostles. Like the number of days she'd gone without speaking to her parents.

Now she and her students were off to Tbilisi, a six-hour train ride through the northern forests. Rumor had it that Byzantine and medieval ruins lay at the bottom of those rolling thickets, but Mina had never seen them for herself. She hardly strained to look out the window. There was too much undiscovered history at the surface of the world, she thought, to go digging for it in the woods.

Not thirty minutes into the journey, the train screamed to a stop. An attendant came though the cabins, explaining that a mudslide up ahead had blocked the tracks. The delay would last overnight, possibly two days. Apologies, he said, but the train was heading back.

The twelve students groaned. They would miss their exhibition, and their parents would not be pleased. Somehow Mina would take the blame, as if she could control the rains of Lori province. As if anyone, especially her, had control over a single droplet of her own destiny. The train began to move back in the direction it had taken her away from, and she had nothing to do but watch the world in the windows reverse.

From one of the adjoining cars came a man her age, bearded and open-collared, who took a seat facing her. He didn't seem from around here, but he said hello in Armenian, and she nodded. He had that open look in his eyes, the same look she'd noticed in the man in Paris. Handsome with ideas—that was what she'd called it in her journal. This man was handsome with ideas, too, and she knew he'd start a conversation before he'd even fallen into his seat.

"You don't look like a woman who's given birth to this many kids," he said.

"I'm their teacher."

"Yes," he said, "that was a joke."

Mina covered her chin. "Oh. I'm sorry."

"Don't be. My delivery, probably. Where were you taking them?"

"We were supposed to go to an exhibition in Tbilisi."

"In what sport?"

"Backgammon," she said.

"Ah. I always preferred chess. You have to use every string bean in your brain." His accent was strange. She couldn't place it.

"Maybe," she said. "But backgammon is more like life. Luck and skill together."

The man smiled. "What's your name?"

She told him.

"Monte Melkonian," the man said, and reached across to shake her hand.

"I can't place your accent," she said.

"I'm traveling around, picking up new accents every day. I'm from the United States originally. California."

"I've never been," Mina said. She considered stopping there but didn't. "I know someone who lives in the United States, though."

He laughed. "I was going to ask for a name, as if I'd know your friend. It's an enormous country. My state of California alone has eight times as many people as all of Armenia."

She watched his eyes. He caught her watching.

"Don't worry," he said, "I'm not coming on to you. I'm in love—her name is Seda. I haven't told her yet, but I think she knows. I've just been traveling so much—I was just in Tehran for the fall of the shah."

"I hope you're not planning a revolution on this train."

"Ha, not here. I was an archaeology student—I'm just traveling, taking notes for a book."

Mina looked out the window. The hills were as green as she'd ever seen them. She almost said something embarrassing about the future, about how she hoped the '80s would be the first good decade for Armenians in generations, but she stopped herself and kept looking at the trees.

"I really wasn't trying to come on to you," Monte said. "I'm sorry if I made you uncomfortable."

"It's okay," Mina said. "Even if you were, I would've told you I'm married. Well, I've just been engaged."

"Oh yeah? To the man of your dreams?"

"No," she said. Maybe because she'd never see this stranger again, she thought, she felt safe telling him the truth. Or maybe it was the space they were in, the shared and enclosed and moving train. "My parents have arranged a husband for me in Kirovakan."

"That's very old-fashioned," Monte said. "Is he . . . Do you at least like him?"

"I don't know him very well. He's older. His first wife died. He's just moved from Leninakan."

"Well, he should be funny. I heard they're supposed to be funny in that city, right?"

"Some of them are funny. Some of them are just as naïve and sentimental as we are in Kirovakan."

Monte bent forward and planted his elbows on his knees. He was so close to her he could whisper. "What if you don't go back?"

"Excuse me?"

"What if you just stay on this train after letting the children off at Kirovakan. Come with me to Yerevan, travel with me. You would like Seda, I think. She's easier to like than I am. She's a genius."

Mina felt the rare awareness of a certainty: she would replay this moment in her mind forever, following each tine in the fork.

"I can't," she said.

"Okay," Monte said, and fell back in his seat. "In that case, don't despair—I'm sure you'll find a happy life in that arrangement somewhere. We're Armenians, after all. We've survived worse occupiers than a funny old spouse."

At that, he gave his attention to a book, which she hadn't noticed him holding all this time.

Disappointed, she returned to counting the kids. Twelve—half the number of her years.

Back in Kirovakan, she wondered: what would she do with them?

The first few months after Avo had disappeared, one of two disturbing possibilities confronted her: either Avo had abandoned her in the middle of the night, avoidant and cowardly, stripping her of any respect she might've built for him in the past; or else something terrible had happened to drive him away. Under the second category, she wondered half sanely if she herself had done the harm, a question that could never—even after she learned the truth, many years later—be totally solved. In her more self-affirming theories, the only way Avo could've left her so suddenly was under the threat to her own safety, in which case her love had been exploited as leverage. In one way or another, she felt burglarized of her respect and her love, and because what had been stolen from her was in both cases abstract, she had no place or ritual specific enough to help her recover.

For that reason, she spent those first months alone trying to find something more concrete that had been lost, Tigran's old collection of dice. In the past, she'd watched as Tigran's widow scoured the house without any luck, but now Mina took the search upon herself. She asked the old men playing backgammon outside the café and in the city square, old chums of her coach who had no leads but wished her all the luck she was already famous for. She went to the census bureau's office to see if they had any information on possessions of Tigran's that might've been collected by the Party, but the middle-aged man behind the desk—squat and hairy, with a dinky pin clipped pseudo-professionally to his lapel—stumbled over his unhelpful words as if he'd never seen a woman with a question before. Then she even voyaged up the muddy path to the village in the hills where Ruben's parents lived, to ask his mother if she'd seen the dice.

"I'll ask the boys when they get back," she said, and her husband said, "The boys will know." Mina, turning down their offer to stay and eat, never visited them again.

Finally, her search led her to an antique shop four blocks from the statue of Kirov, and although the dice weren't there, either, she did find her next obsession: American maps.

The whole city knew that Avo had gone to America, thanks to the bus driver who'd taken him to the airport. The bus driver also insisted that Avo meant to return, shortly, to his fiancée, but Mina could see through a lie told for the sake of kindness. Now, though, in the back of the antique shop, Mina studied dozens of Armenian, Turkish, and Russian-language American maps, annotated with informative facts, wondering which place Avo had chosen to call home. She memorized the names of fifty American cities. Among her favorites: Baton Rouge, Chula Vista, Minneapolis, Chesapeake, and Chattanooga. What a country. There was a picture in her parents' home of her grandfather's cousin posing with Lenin. All her life, she'd heard about the lie of peaceful cohabitation in America, the violence and the hatred between races and classes. But when she spoke aloud the names of those cities, she felt a curious zap of hope. Whether or not the experiment was working, she couldn't say, but all the languages of the world were in those cities, and it was impossible not to admire, at least a little, the gall of America. Maybe it was propaganda, but she could really hear its ships drawing people together over oceans, its trains—never stalled by something so inconsequential as a mudslide—drawing people together over borders. *Chattanooga, chattanooga, chattanooga, chattanooga.* She imagined Avo writing her postcards from those cities, imagined him licking the stamps.

Even if he'd written her, she'd never write back. All she would've done was imagine herself transported to whatever city he was writing from, to that day in the past when he'd licked the stamp, pretending she'd been there, too, that she'd watched the ospreys dive at the Bayfront in Chula Vista, that she'd closed her eyes in Louisiana and breathed in the lovely smell of fresh petroleum from the refinery in Baton Rouge.

But her imagination only worked so far, and where she'd been or what she'd done never actually changed just because she could imagine a different past. That was for the best, she thought. Dwelling on history was a luxury reserved for people who didn't have present demands. Her mother always attributed this to the political activism of the diaspora, who obsessed themselves with setting history into place like a broken bone. Armenians at home talked about the genocide, but they didn't live in it, and they certainly never plotted—beyond drunken what-ifs—to avenge it. Mina's ancestors had been mostly out of harm's way during the genocide, too far east, and no matter how deeply she felt the injury to her people, no matter how sincerely she sympathized with her cousins from Turkey and Syria and Lebanon, she could never quite reach their hearts, never fully understand their absorption with the past. She never said it, for fear of causing further pain, but she wanted—very badly wanted—to move forward already.

And so Mina did, preparing for the wedding she did not want. Twenty-four years old, she'd waited as long as she could for Avo to return, or for him to send for her in Bismarck or Amarillo or Sault Ste. Marie. Her sister had married at seventeen, ten years earlier, and had told her, "The wedding is the easy part, don't worry. Talk to me when you have a baby. Every first child is a twin, because the husband turns into an infant, too."

With that in mind, when Mina was introduced—in her soon-to-be mother-in-law's living room—to her fiancé, she almost cried, and then almost laughed. She'd always been accused of having good luck. Now that reputation would die at last.

"*Barev*," said her fiancé, a wolf in a white leisure suit. He'd rolled his sleeves to the elbows to show that the hair on his wrists matched the thickets at his chest. Just barely she could make out the glint of a gold chain buried in that chest hair, ancient ruins at the foot of the woods. "I'm Galust."

Before they could spend the rest of their lives together, she thought, she would have to sit with this man, with her parents and his, for several hours. They would discuss their families. They would discuss their expectations. Her only job that day was to appear happy. She wondered how her sister had done it. She wondered if her mother had. Suddenly, the whole of civilization seemed to her an accident based on precedence, that if one woman long ago hadn't been forced to sit patiently through an event like this, there would be no such thing as nations.

She hated that woman, whoever she was. And now Mina was beginning to hate her soon-to-be mother-in-law, too. The old woman was the age of Mina's grandmother, and she was explaining why her son, at fifty-one, hadn't been remarried in the decade since the death of his first wife, who was never able to bear children.

"My Galust is a worker, first and foremost," his mother said. "God has graced him with sharp eyesight and an organized mind, which he has put to use for twenty-five years down at the census bureau in Leninakan's city hall. After the death of the Childless One—God rest her soul—Galust was transferred here to Kirovakan, where—speaking only factually—the women are relatively disappointing. I joined him here, and we've waited years for a beauty to materialize, but time is getting short, and Mina here is—how would you put it?—perfectly acceptable."

"More than acceptable," Galust said. "Gorgeous."

His mother patted him on the knee. "And he has that famous Leninakan sense of humor."

"No," Galust said, speaking directly to Mina. "I find you very beautiful."

Mina broke the rules to say, "Thank you, but that's enough, really." But Galust went on: "I happen to have the opposite dimensions, a very big chin and a tiny little nose, so it's like our faces were custom-made to be kissing."

"Good idea," said Mina's mother, rushing things along, and both families watched as, at the center of the room, the newly engaged couple fitted their perfectly matched face shapes together. "Bravo," someone coughed as the stubble on Galust's enormous chin scratched Mina, and as her nose rammed into his like a tractor into a kitten. From the corner where Galust's mother was seated, Mina thought she heard a short quivering sound of disgust. It took Galust's lips in her teeth not to make the same noise herself.

A city can go by many names. Long before the Soviets had graced the city with the name of its hero, for instance, Kirovakan was known as Gharakilisa. The word—a Seljuk Turk's word—meant *black church*, because when the Seljuks invaded the land, they found an ancient Armenian church made of black stones. It stood for five more centuries, until 1826, when one of history's great earthquakes destroyed the city, bringing down the black-stoned Holy Mother of God. Reconstruction began two years later, using black and orange tufa stones imported, like Galust, from Leninakan, a city once called Alexandropol and, before the tsar, Gyumri. The tufa stones at the reconstructed church in Kirovakan—in the churchyard, in the shadow of the single-domed basilica, a few surviving thirteenth-century cross-stones called *khachkars* would serve as the perfect backdrop to wedding photographs. For now, though, Mina had the churchyard to herself. Everyone else was inside, between the stone walls of a shifting and rebuilt history, waiting for the bride to enter.

How many cousins did she have? They seemed to have multiplied, sitting in the pews while they waited. She couldn't name many of the faces. They all belonged to a larger family, the one she was expected to contribute to. The one she was expected to represent. At the altar, she kept her eyes on her shoes.

The priest asked the man and wife to touch their foreheads together, and he held over them an enormous bronze cross. The weight of it came down on them as the priest read long passages from the Bible and from the city ordinance. At some point, a funny thought flitted into her head.

She imagined having to stand on a chair to touch foreheads with Avo. Or else he'd have to crouch uncomfortably low. Maybe he would've bent to a knee. She smiled so wide that Galust noticed.

Forehead to hers, he whispered, "I'm so relieved you're happy." It was, she thought, the sweetest thing anyone had ever said to her, and she began to cry. He was slightly shorter than she was, and she realized she was bearing the brunt of the priest's accessory. For the rest of her life, she would wake early in the morning with a slight headache that didn't dispel until the afternoon. It would always feel as though that bronze cross had never fully been lifted.

The reception was held outdoors, in the city square. The weather, rainless, was an act of grace. At one point, while the men danced in a circle around her, and while they whistled and dusted her feet with dinner napkins, she spotted a familiar face near the statue of Kirov. As soon as she had a chance, she lifted the hem of her dress, so as not to drag it, and walked toward it.

"Ruben," she said. "Is it you?"

"All the way in Paris, they're talking about this wedding," Ruben said. "I couldn't stay away. I had to come and congratulate you in person."

Mina didn't know what to say. She wanted to ask where he'd been, why he'd disappeared, whether or not he knew where Avo had gone. But she also wanted to run back to the wedding. She feared being seen with him.

"I'm giving you the best wishes for your marriage," he said.

She started to ask a question, but Ruben must've known what was on her mind, because he interrupted her to say, "Is Avo inside the church?"

"Oh," Mina said. "He's—no. No, he hasn't been here for a very long time. You didn't know that?"

"I haven't seen him since we left for Paris," Ruben said. "We speak on the phone, however. I thought he might've returned for your wedding."

"You talk to him?"

"All the time. He's my brother."

Mina spun her ring on her finger. This diamond was real. "Is he happy?"

"I think so," Ruben said. "He sounds happy. Every time we speak, he goes on and on about how much he's enjoying Los Angeles."

Mina said, "California."

"That's right," Ruben said. He smiled. "He's found work as a fighter, he says. He always was an athlete, a competitor. He fights for good money, I hear, but it's a dangerous life, as you can imagine. People trying to kill each other for money. I can't imagine a more American life for him. Oh, we talk about it all the time, although I haven't heard from him since arriving here. It's easier, as you can imagine, to call him when I'm outside of the USSR. When I'm in France or Israel, or when I'm in Spain, you see."

"He's a fighter?"

"I guess he's been traveling a lot, too, otherwise I'm sure he would've come for the wedding."

Again Mina said, almost to herself this time, "He's a fighter?"

"America can bring it out of a man."

"But why did he leave in the first place? Ruben, please, tell me if you know."

Ruben put his hands on the shoulders of her wedding gown. "Well," he said. "Or—no, I shouldn't guess."

"Tell me," Mina said.

"Well, I think it might have something to do with what happened with Tigran. It broke Avo, I think."

"But he hardly knew Tigran. You and I should've been broken, if anyone."

"Oh, Mina-jan. He hasn't told you?"

"What?"

"I hate to be the one to tell you. I assumed he already had, a long time ago. He told me just after he got to America."

"What is it?"

"When Tigran died," Ruben said, and then he stopped. He straightened the sleeves of her dress and stood back. "Avo told me that—well, I came here to tell you something Avo kept a secret for a very long time."

"Tell me."

Ruben seemed smaller than he'd ever appeared across a backgammon board. He adjusted his glasses and started again. "Well, when Tigran died, you see, Avo—well, he pitied you. That's the truth. Believe me, I hate to tell you, but it's the truth—I swear it. He told me he saw you crying and childish, and you reminded him—yes, that's what he said, you reminded him of himself when his parents died, and, well, Avo confused pity for love. That's how he put it to me. Pity for love. And I wanted you to know, so you can live happily with your new husband, without ever having to think back on what could have been. He confused pity for love, and he decided to leave before you both made the mistake of marrying."

Mina covered her chin. She said, "I see."

"But it's good news," Ruben said. "You're free, and happily married, and Avo, well, he'll be relieved when I tell him how perfect your life turned out now. No need to look back. You don't need his pity anymore, right? Look at you in your gown."

Soon he was gone, and Mina returned to the party. Whistles and hollers, hollers and whistles.

The married couple moved into a flat up the stairs from the bride's parents, up to the top floor of the tallest building in Kirovakan. For some years, she continued to teach backgammon after hours at the school, and she cooked and cleaned and sewed buttons on Galust's shirtsleeves, which she gently suggested he keep rolled down. She became pregnant after only a few hairy attempts. And then pregnant again. Immediately after the wedding, she'd stopped studying the map of America, but she continued for a while to recount the names of her favorite cities. At first she kept the map, right there in her drawer along with Shirakatsi's proofs and her journal from Paris. But soon, with the babies, it became a lodestone of a burdensome past, and one day she folded the map into a small, sharp triangle and flicked it into the trash.

15

Paris, France, 1983

Several stories below his balcony at the Hôtel de Crillon, horsemen in white garlands shouldered épées to the galloping shots of distant firecrackers. A marching band rolled its snares and brass into the deafening blares of aerobatic jets, whose shadows blinked now and then over the assembled crowd. There must have been fifty thousand people on this block alone, Parisians and tourists alike feeding candies to the children seated like demiurges on their shoulders, waving feverishly to the president and the visiting heads of state. It was Bastille Day 1983. Just shy of two centuries earlier, seven meager prisoners had been released during the storming of a prison, and now the entire country swaggered in its freedom. One little flashpoint had led to this, a national glistering. Ruben finished the last of his bottle of apple cider vinegar and went inside to fetch another.

His shoe hadn't hit the carpet before his partner, Varoujan, stood from the chaise longue. He tried and failed to fold the newspaper he'd been reading, and finally resorted to splaying the pages out on the oval coffee table like a map. Sticking out from underneath was a corner of the blueprints for the terminals at Orly. Varoujan rushed to pluck out the blueprints like a card from a deck, as if he'd been looking for them all morning, as if he'd been doing his job, and spoke as he reshuffled the pages. "How's the parade?" he asked. "Is it good? A good parade?"

Ruben went to the refrigerator. He'd miscounted; he'd underpacked. He'd already taken the last of his apple cider vinegar.

"One day soon," Varoujan continued, "we'll have ourselves a parade just like it."

"No," Ruben said. "We won't. And sit down already."

Varoujan sat. He smoothed out the wrinkles in his oversize slacks. At forty-seven, he was exactly twenty years Ruben's senior, but he still hadn't found a tailor.

Rooting through the fridge again, Ruben said, "You didn't happen to see another bottle of my—did you see another bottle of the—"

"We won't have a parade, you think? You don't think we'll—"

"We'll win," Ruben said, "it's not that. I could've sworn, though, that I'd brought another bottle."

"There's a drawer in the fridge, did you check? And why no parade, then, if we'll win? I want a parade if we win, I want a parade like this."

Ruben checked the drawer in the fridge, even though he'd already checked it several times. "It's not Armenian, a parade. A parade—it's so . . . *French*. Can you imagine us parading? High-stepping over piles of horse shit? No. Dancing, singing, yes. But trotting in costumes like kids in a school play? Can you imagine us? Turkey issuing an apology, Turkey paying reparations, ceding land, and Armenians on the streets? No, we'll be in our homes, in our halls and our churches, praising each other. These Frenchmen, my God. I don't care what they say the parade is for—if you have to perform like that, you're not free. Is there another drawer in here I'm not seeing?"

Varoujan said, "I think I've got the terminal memorized, every detail. I'll review again tonight, but I could use some fresh air. I can go for you, Ruben-jan, if you need more of—what was it you've been drinking?"

The man was a father and a husband, Ruben remembered, and it occurred to him for the first time since they'd arrived in Paris together three days earlier that all of Varoujan's deference and respect might have been an act. Probably Varoujan was seething—paired up with a kid his daughter's age. He probably thought Ruben was demented, what with the addiction to apple cider vinegar, what with the particular way the kid had been forced to re-earn the boss's trust. Turning on a brother like that. A cousin's cousin, but still. Varoujan had taken the hotel key off the nightstand and was heading for the door when Ruben stopped him. Possibly he would go to the police, Ruben thought. Maybe this was all a setup. Who was this man in slouching slacks? He hardly knew him.

"No," Ruben said, and he took the key from his partner's hand. "I'll go. What I need is hard to find. Go rest. Read the paper. Enjoy the parade."

For a short while, Varoujan feigned protest. Then, satisfied with his effort, he dragged the hems of his pants to the chaise longue, retrieved his paper, and went with it to the balcony.

Ruben knew the parade would go on until noon, and then the metro would be clogged all day with people crossing the city and loitering until the fireworks began at dusk. The choice—join the mobs in the torrid streets or else stay in the hotel room while Varoujan sauntered off suspiciously—was unpleasant but clear. Soon he was on the elevator, descending to the lobby, and in a flash of heat, he found himself among the people.

Over the chaos of laughter and whistling from the parade came the ringing of a distant bell—*om, om, om*—and it swelled as Ruben realized he was following it. Otherwise, it was almost impossible to tell in which direction he was going. The city swarmed with people, and every hat in the crowd lurched sideways like a thirsty tongue. It was mid-July, and the heat was just beginning to wear out its welcome. Ruben—who refused even to go out for a pack of cigarettes wearing anything less dignified than a suit—folded his jacket over his arm. A block later, he rolled up his shirtsleeves. The sheer number of people in the streets—he couldn't see over their heads—made him feel smaller than he'd felt in many years, and his smallness worked with the continuous ringing of the bell—*om, om, om*—to drive him off the boulevard and into a narrow, inconspicuous alleyway. There, alone, he caught his breath and regained his sense of size. He was sweating through his shirt and underwear, which clung to him like fearful children. He removed his shoes and peeled off his socks, which he rolled into tight balls that fit into the pockets of his folded jacket. Then he stepped barefoot back into his tasseled loafers. He'd get blisters, maybe, but the walk couldn't be much longer now. In fact, merging again into the crowd, he could make out, just off the sidewalk and manned by an Algerian wearing a thinning beard, an outdoor bodega selling his ointment.

In Paris, Ruben took pleasure in smoking special cigarettes he could find only there, Gauloises, and he put one in his mouth as he waited in the tangled cluster of buyers that passed for a line. He found a bottle of the stuff he'd come for and smoked two Gauloises before he made it to the Algerian with his makeshift register. As he paid, the bells struck again—*om, om, om*—and he saw, sandwiched between apartments along the Champs-Élysées, the engraved stone pediment and sea-foam spire of his church.

Not his, really, but theirs. The Armenian Apostolic Cathedral of Paris—how many times had he almost, but not quite, gone inside?

All those years ago, during his very first visit to Paris, he'd been invited to take a tour of the church. Mina had called ahead and arranged the whole thing. And although Ruben had agreed to go with her—had looked forward to it, in fact, holding secret beliefs that the church might transform them in some matrimonial and godly way—he failed to meet her in the lobby as they'd planned. Instead, he'd gone off with the men who'd invited him to follow them, and here he was, almost a decade later, still following them.

He stood in front of a black ornamental gate, waist-high, that opened onto a pathway made of stone. Ahead, between two mighty columns, an old oak door stood invitingly ajar. Ruben uncapped his fresh bottle of apple cider vinegar. He drank a swig and then let himself in.

With a heavy blow, the door closed behind him and shut out the raucous world. Here was a quiet place in a muted light, where even the few tourists escaping the parade seemed like penitents. Despite the shade, the heat felt thicker here, wetter, churning with the smell of driftwood. The scattered visitors craned their necks to marvel at the names of bishops engraved in the walls and at the chandeliers strung from the frescoed ceiling. The centerpiece descended on a wire from the tip of the cupola and cast alms of wheaten light over the narrow, extravagant rugs laid out along the aisle. There were no pews, only wooden chairs arranged in rows. Ruben took a seat in the back and started removing his shoes again. Disrespectful, probably, to be sockless in a place like this.

An old priest in a black hood and a purple cloak lingered at the altar, seemingly unaware of the visitors. He lit a tall candle planted in a trough of sand. Almost exclusively in pairs, the tourists came and went, until Ruben, socks and shoes back on, was alone with the candle-lighting priest. The bell had stopped ringing, and it was quiet—not *dead* quiet, but the other kind, the living quiet of green things at the surface of the sea. The living quiet of blood to the ears, of memories swarming and piling and competing to be remembered. How long had it been since he'd slept more than a few hours through? The priest lit a candle with a candle. Ruben crossed himself.

He'd come to Paris several days earlier from Athens, near where he'd lived for the past three years, after finding Avo. In 1980, they'd left the United States together and arrived in Greece to a small midnight audience. There were four men awaiting them in two idling cars outside the terminal, and they made up Hagop Hagopian's innermost circle: Surik, an arms negotiator; Hamik, the group's primary launderer; Zatik, an explosives engineer; and Martik, the man in charge of the place Avo was later taken to. Collectively, they were known throughout ASALA as the *chorse eekner*, the "Four Eeks"—Surik, Hamik, Zatik, and Martik. A rumor had spread that while every other ASALA loyalist around the world had been forced to slum it out in efficiencies and abandoned warehouses on the invisible dregs of cities, the Four Eeks had each been allotted a two-bedroom loft in the most luxurious high-rise in Palaio Faliro, a prosperous seaside suburb of Athens.

The rumor turned out to be only half true; for the sake of precaution, the Four Eeks in fact lived in separate buildings, only three of which could be called, with sunset-facing windows overlooking the indigo sheen of Phalerum Bay, luxurious. The inhabitants of these three apartments—Surik, Hamik, and Zatik—lived with their wives and small children, and even in the glowering din of the arrivals terminal at the airport, they seemed exuberantly tanned and happy. They didn't balk at the errand they were sent on that night, a kind of chauffeuring they hadn't been assigned since their early days with Hagopian in Aleppo. Instead, they seemed to take their participation as a sign of two things: Hagopian's dwindling trust in others to manage even the smallest business affairs, and the grave significance of the approaching pair.

As for the fourth Eek, Martik lived alone, separately, in the country. That night he waited in the driver's seat of one of the cars. He was the only one not to introduce himself to the two men he and the others had come for: the protégé, as Hagopian once called Ruben, and the traitor.

On the surface, only an idiot could mistake the two. The Four Eeks had been forewarned that the one who'd betrayed them in Los Angeles was enormous, and only one of the pair fit the bill, folding into the car like a dinner roll into a hungry mouth. Still, there was something upside down about the way the two men comported themselves: the big deserter wore a mundane upward bend in his thick eyebrow, as if he were being taken to a regular appointment. As he walked to the car, the thick fingers at the ends of his casually breezing arms seemed as relaxed as hanging ducks. Even as he slouched and scrunched in the passenger seat of Martik's car, a little glimmer reflected in his eyes in the window. According to Zatik, who kept his gun at the traitor's big bald head from the backseat, he was gawking like a tourist at the passing sights of town at midnight, the vacant canopied shops and the radiant churches, the balustrades of towering homes and the stone-still boats in the windless dock. He was the traitor, and yet there was in him a kind of innocence.

"We figured maybe we'd misunderstood Hagopian's message," Zatik told Ruben later. "You were the one who looked guilty!"

"Definitely," Surik said. "Ruben here was so little and nervous, shivering and wide-eyed like a raccoon caught in the garbage."

"Rolling his shoulders," Hamik said, "throwing glances around like darts."

Apparently, once he was in the car, Ruben had turned his

attention between Surik and Hamik so violently that his glasses fell off twice.

"You should be thanking every god that man ever invented," Hamik said, and laughed. "I don't know how we got it right, but you should thank us, too. That you weren't in the car with Martik. Can you imagine if we fucked that up? If we'd taken the traitor here to Palaio Faliro, eating baklava and drinking ouzo, telling stories, and meanwhile we'd sent our little protégé, Ruben, to that other place? Martik's place?"

When both passengers had been loaded, the two cars sped away—together at first. And for some distance, the red taillights of one car were visible to the other. South, south from the airport. And then, at a traffic signal, one car kept true. The other turned left.

"Thank whatever god you can find to thank," Hamik said again, "that you were in the right car."

The truth was, Ruben really did feel thankful. Thankful to God, yes, but also to Hagopian for trusting him again, for allowing him back into the fold, and not least of all to Surik, Hamik, and Zatik, who welcomed him into their homes like family.

Ruben swallowed another gulp from the bottle. At this rate, he'd have to stop by the bodega again on the way back to the hotel. Without it, the problems he'd been experiencing lately—burning ears, sweating palms, eyelids twitching, a tightening in his throat he could summon just by fearing it—would return. Cocaine and liquor—which had seemed to help the Eeks concentrate on their work—only made his problems worse, so he'd sworn off every chemical except cigarettes and this, a bottle of cooking juice he'd read about, secretly and ashamedly, in a dark corner of a library.

Now a light broke through the church. The door had come open, and—accompanied by the far-off sound of conversations in motion—a boy of maybe fifteen rushed in. He charged so quickly up the aisle that, almost tripping over the rug, he arrived at the altar just as the door came again to a close.

The boy was wearing a pageboy cap, which he kept adjusting as he spoke to the priest. The priest, who had begun a hymn, stopped singing to hear him. He whispered something to the boy, who disappeared behind the mural to a separate, invisible room. When he returned, the boy was wearing a red and white robe, and he'd lost the cap. Though not, Ruben noticed, the lines in his hair where the hat had rested.

The boy—less rushed now, but with the residue of panic in the halting way he approached Ruben—mentioned in French that the public hours for the church had come to an end.

"Give me five minutes," Ruben said in Armenian.

The boy looked over his own shoulder; the priest had disappeared into the invisible room. "You'll have to leave now, I'm sorry to say."

"You've already delayed him, haven't you? He had to light the candles himself like a choirboy."

The boy said, "The metro today, with the parade. I tried to explain."

"Do you have any family up there?" Ruben asked, pointing to the mural above the altar. Engraved there was a long list of names, Armenian clergymen lost between 1914 and 1918. The mural of God and Mary and the baby Christ encircled the names, as if committing them to memory.

"Only distant relatives," the boy said. "I hate to say it, but you really do have to leave now."

"Your robe is folded under in the front," Ruben said.

The boy fixed it. "You're welcome back tomorrow morning. At seven."

"Is heaven so strict? Tell the priest to kick me out himself."

The boy, exasperated, ran off and disappeared again behind the mural. A moment later, the priest emerged alone, almost as if the boy had transformed into him. The priest stepped slowly along the rugs down the aisle. When he arrived at the final row of chairs, he spoke in Armenian. "Tell me you at least made a donation at the front."

Ruben looked up at the chandeliers and around the church. Gold everywhere. Behind a glass case near the altar, a Bible encrusted with diamonds he could see sparkling from here.

"Looks like the church is doing fine without my pocket change," Ruben said.

"Whatever it takes to bring more people to the house of God."

Once, Ruben had tried to convince Avo to believe in God. They'd been very young. Avo had been reading his poems, and Ruben had told him to try reading the Bible for a change. The argument took off from there. Look at all the beautiful art made in the name of faith, Ruben had said. The architecture and the frescoes, the music and the sculptures, the book of poems in Avo's hands—he could thank God for all of it. Only through beauty could those artists communicate with God. But Avo had refused to believe that beauty was a means to an end. Beauty was the goal, he'd argued. Art was the end, and God was the first work of art.

"Tell me," Ruben said, "what do you say to people who claim that God is fiction?"

The priest sighed. "I tell them: Visiting hours are over, please leave a donation on the way out."

Ruben uncapped his apple cider vinegar and took a drink.

"Now you're breaking two rules," said the priest.

"You want some?"

The priest bent to see what it was and declined. Then he lifted his cloak a bit and sat in the chair beside Ruben. A lot of effort in that cloak.

"Am I keeping you from the Bastille Day parade?" Ruben said.

"So you're not French," the priest said. "I didn't think so, but now I know. We don't call it Bastille Day. Only tourists do. We don't celebrate the blood-soaked storming of the Bastille. Foreigners—especially Soviets and Americans, those bickering siblings—they think we do, but we don't."

"So what's the parade for?"

The priest told him that what was really being celebrated was the Fête de la Fédération, the fourteenth of July of the year *following* the prison storming. "This was in the year 1790, when political factions came together in unity, when the king became a constitutional monarch. A day without bloodshed, a day of reconciliation. Of course, peace wouldn't come until the end of the revolution, many years later—oh, I don't have to tell you. The French have a very famous history."

"Unlike us."

The priest sighed. "Unlike us."

It occurred to Ruben that he could have been a priest. He could have spent his days reprimanding his squire for failing to light candles before the end of open hours. He could have wrapped himself in his faith, could have turned his faith into a cloak to shroud the world beneath, could have blanketed the world in his belief, could have put his seriousness in service of the justice he believed was eternal, rather than the justice he hoped to bring about.

"I'd like to make a confession," he said.

The priest shook his arm until the sleeve of his purple cloak revealed an expensive watch. He said, "How big a confession are we talking?"

How big a confession would it take to explain what he'd done to the man from Moscow and dozens of others; that he had sent his cousin's cousin—his brother, really—to hell, just to regain the trust of a man whose true name he would never know; that he'd told his brother's love that she'd been pitied and fooled, ensuring that his brother died without her love in return, without her respect, without her even longing to say goodbye; that he couldn't sleep at night because of the heat in his ears, the ratcheting in his throat; that he couldn't stop imagining the untold agony he'd sent his brother to die in; that he couldn't stop remembering what the library book in Athens had told him about the sour taste on his lips, that another use for apple cider vinegar was to trap fruit flies at home. You were supposed to leave a few tablespoons of it in a wide-rimmed jar, stretch a sheet of plastic wrap over the top, and stab holes in the film using a fork. Flies could get in but not out. The same air holes that kept the flies alive had trapped them in the first place, and that's what his pain felt like, less a fire below than a film overhead. Was that too big a confession? That he suspected all of life to be like those holes in that film, all snare and grace at once?

"Too big," Ruben said, and stood to leave.

"To answer your earlier question," the priest said, "I tell unbelievers that I find it amusing. I simply find it amusing when a character calls his author fiction."

Outside, the parade was coming to an end, and the crowd blew apart like the heat in every direction. Ruben stopped by the bodega for a second bottle of his apple cider vinegar, but the Algerian's shop had closed in the time he'd been in church. As he started his journey back to the hotel, Ruben calculated the rations he could afford himself for the next day and a half, when he could return to Greece and buy more.

He wanted to believe what the priest had said, but he had a terrible sense that some men authored themselves.

After he'd found Avo outside a corner drugstore in Greensboro, North Carolina, and after he'd sent him to Martik's place to be erased, Ruben had spent three years establishing a routine in Greece with Surik, Hamik, and Zatik, a routine that had constituted something like a family life. At dawn every morning, a buzzer would announce their arrival, and Ruben would take the elevator down to join them on the street. They'd walk the dewy seaside paths to a small second-story restaurant called La Med. According to the list hammered like theses to the front door, the restaurant didn't open to the public for several hours, but the owner, a Greek-Armenian named Hayk, had already readied a table set for four. Ruben's first morning joining them, Hayk looked at him and nudged Surik in the shoulder. "Martik has been replaced?" And Surik said, "No, no. This is Ruben. He's only recently joined us. Martik will rejoin us soon, and then we'll be five." Relieved, Hayk went back to the unstaffed kitchen and brought, one by one, enormous bowls of steaming khash, the boiled bits of cows unused in other recipes.

After breakfast, they left La Med for Surik's loft, or Ruben's apartment, or wherever the kids and wives were strategically absent. From there, Ruben and the others spent long days smoking cigarettes, placing phone calls, laundering money at a jewelry shop on the boardwalk, driving to Athens and back to meet foreign buyers in bookshops, outdoor markets, cinemas, record stores—any place where they weren't waited on, where the meeting could end as abruptly and casually as a blown candle. They might return to the flat in Palaio Faliro, eat lunch—Ruben, still full from the khash, the exception—smoke cigarettes, smoke weed (Ruben again the exception), play records, extoll the Greeks for their culture and history, the only rivals to Armenian exceptionalism, praise their luck to be based in a country whose hatred for Turks allowed them to work more or less out in the open, smoke more cigarettes, drink ouzo, drink thin and yellow beer, eat dinner—Ruben the exception, no appetite, still, after that morning's hoof—and listen to Zatik explain the workings of a bomb he was designing, a bomb worthy of all his talents, a bomb he called "The Truth," a bomb he'd been designing for years, a story he told multiple times a week, no one with the heart to stop him. Or else they'd watch Hamik scribble math on a spiral-bound notebook the size of an encyclopedia, tallying up the day's sales, purchases, and trades negotiated by Surik, who ran his finger along his gums so slowly and purposefully as he listened to the others that Ruben kept expecting him to stop on a tooth as in a game of musical chairs and yank it clean out. They'd go back and forth from the living room to the balcony, enjoying the breeze and the view, until they'd grow restless and return inside. They called Ruben their little stoic—he didn't eat, he didn't drink anything but his vinegar, he didn't laugh, he didn't ask questions. No one could imagine him having sex.

Once, Surik brought a rolled-up tube of paper to Ruben's apartment and unfurled it to reveal a poster of Cher, the most famous Armenian in the world. The others got a laugh out of it and pasted it to Ruben's bedroom wall. Ruben didn't laugh, but he put his hands up in defeat. They must have been confused by Hagopian's giving Ruben a second chance—Ruben himself was—so he decided to leave the poster up as a sign of goodwill. He knew he was theirs, in a way. At a decent hour, they'd shuffle off for the night, each man in his own direction, and Ruben would lie in bed, finally hungry, beneath the image of Cher, and he would try again, and fail, to sleep. And then again the buzzer. And then again the khash.

Some nights, he woke from brief unmemorable dreams and imagined where his cousin's cousin had been taken. Where he himself had taken him.

Some nights, he took to his knees beside the bed and prayed. Not for forgiveness but for the courage to keep faithful. So that the sacrifices he'd made might be worth something in the end.

It was his job to communicate with ASALA affiliates in different cities around the world, and he spent most of his working days on the phone or at the desk, writing cryptically worded letters. Sometimes, during a break for coffee, or during a long, dull drive to the north of Athens for a small-arms trade, the conversation would turn to him, and in those moments, Ruben tried to keep his cigarette in his mouth so he could justify his mumbling.

"How come you don't have a girl?" Hamik sometimes asked. Or Zatik would say, "You can't live only for work, little man, you have to have family. I would be a psychopath if I didn't have my wife, my children, to come home to." Surik would laugh. "We can talk about a wife later, but at least tell us you're getting fucked every once in a while."

But Ruben had never slept with a woman. That is, unless you counted the nights when, kneeling at his bedside in prayer, he'd look up and catch the almost tropically humid gaze of Cher. She seemed to be judging him. For being a small man on his knees, begging for strength. In the photograph, she had her hair blown out in enormous black curls. He was twenty-five, twenty-six, twenty-seven years old. He'd never, not once, even so much as kissed a woman in a meaningful way.

"Are you not into women?" Surik once joked over breakfast, and Ruben threw his spoon into Surik's face, chipping a tooth. Martik put his hands on Ruben, but Surik laughed and told him to ease off. "So sensitive, Ruben-jan. Now I know where the line is for our little stoic. I was only joking, of course. How else can we get through all this struggle but to laugh every once in a while?"

"The Turks are laughing enough for all of us," Ruben said.

"Huh," Hamik said. "I can see why Hagop likes him."

"Okay," Zatik said, "but we've known him for a long time now, we've welcomed him into our family. We need to know one story about him, no? All we're asking is five minutes without the Turks. Okay, Ruben-jan? Tell us about the girl you gifted your virginity. Tell us about that lucky girl."

It was the word *lucky* that reminded him. He heard himself say, "She *was* lucky. She was the luckiest girl in Armenia." The men laughed, but he went on, explaining how she seemed able to control dice with her mind. He remembered the story Avo had told him, about their night on the roof. They were teenagers on the roof of the tallest building in Kirovakan. It was the first time either one of them had been touched. Ruben told the story word for word, except he replaced his brother's name with his own.

"And her name?" said Zatik.

"Her name," Ruben said, "was Mina."

Avo was dead, he knew. By sending him to Martik's place, Ruben himself had killed him.

But the act of telling his story, the act of imagining himself in Avo's skin, making love to Mina on a roof with a view, seemed to give him life again. He couldn't do that, not literally, but this was at least a gesture toward that miracle, the gesture of incorporation. Avo's story plaited naturally into his. A revival and a revision, a revisitation. It felt real. Leaving Mina, Ruben told the Four Eeks, was the only sacrifice he'd struggled to make. Much harder than turning in his traitor brother to Hagopian. He and Mina had plans to marry after he returned. He wanted her to know where he was, to visit him, but he was living underground, and he ran out of time.

She was married now, and he wanted to believe she was right to have stopped waiting for him. To fall in love with someone else. A paper shuffler by the name of Galust. Ruben wanted to believe that she was right to do what she did. But he was lying to himself. She was wrong to betray him, and she should feel hopelessly, irrevocably ashamed.

Surik, Hamik, and Zatik sat back. Looked at each other. Finally, Zatik scratched his beard and said, "Little stoic, the next time you tell that story, slow down during the sex part, and maybe speed up the rest?"

By May 1983, when Hagopian called with his plan for the Turkish Airlines terminal at Orly Airport, Ruben had all the contacts he needed in Paris to arrange Zatik's trip. Zatik had finally finished building The Truth, and Hagopian wanted the bomb for Orly. The boss believed this attack would be the turning point for the war against denialism. Zatik was adamant that he be in Paris to set off his beloved bomb himself, so he tried to arrange plans for his wife and children to be sent on vacation in mid-July, just in case they became implicated. But Zatik's wife didn't want to leave. She was in the middle of a book she was writing on parenting a child with Down syndrome. Not to mention, she continued, that she was in the middle of *parenting* a child with Down syndrome. Zatik couldn't budge her. He would have to stay in Greece.

"Ruben," he said one morning over khash. "You're going to be the one to do it."

Ruben knew better than to ask why. Surik and Hamik were in charge of the entire Greek operation, and Martik, who hardly came to breakfast anymore, didn't seem the traveling type. Ruben was the only one whose job could be done at a distance, so there was no choice to be made. Still, he reached into his coat pocket to retrieve his bottle of apple cider vinegar, holding his own wrist so the bottle didn't tremble as he drank from it.

Surik patted him on the knee. "You've done this before, Ruben-jan."

"Not like this."

"It's the same," Hamik offered gently, "only this time, a button instead of a trigger."

"It's not the same," Zatik said, indignant. "The Truth is my masterpiece. You can't just push a button. You have to know it, you have to study it, you have to love it. It has to be timed and done perfectly so that it actually goes off, and goes off when you want it to go off. In the air."

Passengers would die. Not ambassadors. Not representatives. Just—passengers. Ruben would be the one pulling it off. He scooped another spoonful of cow. "I don't know how I'll eat anything in Paris if I can't have this. Can Hayk come with me?"

"Poor Hayk," Hamik said. "Let's not implicate him even further. He's got a gun in that kitchen, and we don't want him to have to put it to use. He's been so good to us."

Ruben remembered the one missing Eek. He said, "I'll go to Paris. But I'd like to visit Martik's place before leaving."

Surik, Hamik, and Zatik went silent. They focused on their hooves. "His place isn't on the way," Surik said.

Zatik swallowed. "You don't have time, you have to study."

"And besides," Hamik said, laughing, "Martik doesn't treat his guests very well."

By the time Ruben returned to the hotel, Varoujan had finished the paper. "Let's go watch the fireworks tonight," he said, slapping a local page. "There's a bridge with a great view."

In the evening, having learned from the altar boy's mistake,

Ruben led his partner to the metro well before dusk. Crowds had already begun lining up along Pont de l'Alma, but the two of them were small enough to find space at the rail near the southern end. Waiting for the sun to set, they felt the depth of the crowd behind them grow. In Syria, Varoujan said, he'd once seen a man kiss a horse on the nose, nothing deviant but strange nonetheless, tender and—seeing as how he remembered it all these years later—somewhat moving. Sometimes, when he was bored, he liked to imagine what adventures that man and his horse had been through, what risks they'd taken together that had created such a bond. He liked to imagine them crossing rivers. Imagine them splitting their last apple, lost in the woods. When the sun finally dropped, when the darkness settled in around the famous tower and the lights along the bridge reflected in the river, when the first squeals of gunpowder sounded and the first bursts of color flowered in the sky, Varoujan was still talking about that man and his horse.

The explosions went off in the sky. Varoujan said something, and Ruben had to lean in and ask him to repeat himself.

"I know he wasn't really your brother," he said into Ruben's ear.

Confused, Ruben said, "Excuse me?"

"The traitor. He wasn't really your brother, right?"

Was the bridge collapsing? Ruben removed his bottle of apple cider vinegar from inside his coat. He sipped from it.

"I've heard conflicting reports," Varoujan said directly into his ear.

"Like what?" Ruben said. He pictured himself throwing the man off the bridge.

"There are rumors, is all. You don't have to worry. I understand. That kind of love is rare. Two people, you know. Or a man and his horse. I wish I had that. With a woman, of course, in my case."

But Varoujan had it all wrong. How could Ruben explain the texture of his love for Avo? Not the easy love it had been mistaken for, but something else, something holy and rutted, a deep recognition. On the bridge, he felt a sudden readiness to be done with ASALA, to go back to that church. But he also felt that his inability to quit was a kind of testament to his love for Avo. Quitting now would evaporate Avo's sacrifice, ironing flat the holy texture of their love.

But how could he explain?

"He wasn't my brother," Ruben said, "but he wasn't that, either. He was another myself."

All night the fireworks cracked, and Ruben was awake to hear them. Every now and then, he stirred from his bed to sip from his bottle, and the dark blue shadows falling over Varoujan in his bed, on the other side of the room, made it impossible to see if his partner was asleep. In fact, the lump in the other bed, covered by a thin summer sheet, could've been anyone. In the morning, Ruben washed his socks in the sink, showered, and dressed himself. He followed Varoujan to the lobby, where they checked out. Stepping into the backseat of the taxi to the airport, he squished in his wet socks.

Varoujan sat in the front passenger seat, and he wouldn't stop talking to the driver, another Algerian. Varoujan stretched in his seat and explained how he used to be a cabbie back in Syria, where he used to drive important men between meetings, used to pretend he was a horse-carriage driver in a story by an old Russian, used to imagine little ghosts of himself leaving the car with every passenger he dropped off, so that every stop left him a little less of himself. On and on he went, as if the Algerian were paying attention, as if the Algerian, whose father had been one of two hundred immigrants gunned down by the Parisian police in a massacre in October 1961, had asked a single question.

Still Varoujan went on, and Ruben sat quietly in the backseat with The Truth in a briefcase in his lap. He remembered how, outside the drugstore in Greensboro, North Carolina, Avo hadn't said a single word. Avo hadn't explained himself, hadn't defended his choice to tip off the professor, hadn't even asked to be allowed back home. The day had been bright and green but cool, and as they'd waited for a car outside the drugstore, prisms of color hovered in the wet trees.

And there was Avo, not saying a word. He didn't say, for example, "The beard suits you, Ruben-jan. You look older. More sophisticated. Still small, bro, but good."

Bright but cool. "It's sneezing weather," Avo didn't say. "Nothing at all like home."

The plan had been to take a motel near the airport and leave the next morning for Athens. But something caught Ruben's attention. Avo didn't ask what it was. He just followed Ruben's gaze to a park beside the precinct, where many pairs of men were playing chess. And backgammon. Ruben didn't say, "I haven't played in I don't know how long." He just started walking. And Avo followed.

At an oak table near the entry to the park, two black men were at the backgammon board, rolling dice. Both men were bundled in thick coats and scarves over their mouths. Gray eyebrows on one, playing ivory. A younger man on the other side, playing mahogany. Mittens cupping their dice.

Mittens hitting the timer. Pigeons mulling about their boots, looking for crumbs that had fallen there a long time ago.

The men played, and Ruben watched the way a magician inspected a trick being performed. "You in?" asked the gray man, the winner. And Ruben switched places with the younger man. The pigeons fluttered half-heartedly, making room. Everything was reset—the board and the clock, all that dwindling time recharged with just the punch of a mitten.

"How did you find me?" Avo didn't ask, but Ruben answered anyway.

"Hagopian wouldn't let me back until I found you," he said. The man across the board raised an eyebrow but kept playing.

"Two years," Ruben said, taking his turn. "Failing again and again. Until I met the most vulgar man. He led me to you."

Avo didn't say a word, but Ruben could feel he hadn't left.

"If you come with me, Hagopian will let us explain. You can go home." He could sense his brother stirring, getting ready to run. That was when he said, "Mina is married, Avo."

He didn't turn to see Avo's reaction, but he felt the sphere of his brother's heart expand and shrink, seeking another like a signal in the night. When Ruben was sure Avo wouldn't run, he added one more point to punish him for the past two years. "She knows," he said. "About Tigran, I mean. It's over, brother. I told her what you did."

His opponent played his turn. When his mitten came down, time was restored.

Ruben led Varoujan out of the cab and into the terminal gates, where they traded luggage. Varoujan took their bags to the Luxair check-in counter. They'd be boarding soon on their way to Luxembourg. Meanwhile, Ruben took his briefcase to the nearest restroom, where he locked himself into a stall, swallowed the last of his apple cider vinegar, and began his work.

Zatik had given him the instructions so many times that the twelve-volt lead acid battery at the center of the device had always seemed to him a purely mathematical object. But now, his hands trembling, his thoughts returning to what Avo hadn't said—not a word of righteousness, not a word in defense of mercy—the battery looked more like an organ in a vivisected body. There was a life in it, in the cylindrical remote detonator fitting into his palm like a vertebra. In the lining of the briefcase, the Eeks had stitched the names of victims of the genocide. In ink, Ruben had added the names of Yergat and Siranoush, and there seemed to be more life in this meticulously and lovingly built object of death than there was in the line of passengers at the gate.

Varoujan was waiting for him at the Luxair gate, a few hundred paces from the Turkish Airlines gate where Ruben dropped off The Truth.

"We should be boarding in no time," Varoujan said. "If all the bags were checked."

"I left mine in the gate," Ruben said.

Varoujan grabbed his shoulder. "You're kidding. It was supposed to go on the plane."

"Planes crash and burn all the time," Ruben said.

For the first time in years, he felt comfortable in his body. His skin was soft and matte, like it used to be when he was a child.

He said, "My way's more memorable."

Varoujan sat with his head in his hands. Then he rushed out of the gate area, on through the terminal, out to a taxi stand. He knew, just as Ruben knew, that their plane to Luxembourg wouldn't board on time.

16

Los Angeles, California, 1989

Wordlessly, Mina led me from the roof to her apartment and then closed the door behind us. The apartment—in the laced light of one curtained window at the front—bloomed into view. Floral portraits hung in gold-latticed frames on the walls, petaled patterns stretched between the fabric of an armchair and its matching couch, and even the carvings at the feet of the coffee table seemed to bring the whole room together like a trellis in a garden. Pink and yellow and eggshell frills skirted between the furniture and the carpet, and the oven in the kitchenette where we were standing was still warm with the day's baking, rich with the botanical smells of basil and thyme. When Mina dropped a large weight in my arms, I thought for a minute she'd given me a bouquet of dark roses. But the roses purred against my collarbone, and I saw that I was holding a cat, my cat, who'd grown black and long and slender. "Hold him," Mina said, "so if they're coming in to see us, they're seeing why you're here, for him, not for me."

"You were supposed to get married to him," I said.

"What?"

"The Brow Beater. You were the one he was telling me about, the girl back home he was going to marry."

Mina stood there in front of me, shaking her head slightly until she finally let out a sad laugh. Then she went to the kitchen and started cleaning. I hadn't noticed the mess: greasy sheets of tinfoil, flour-blasted cutting boards, dishes piled in the sink like a cairn. She flipped on the faucet, which hissed and hissed as she spoke.

"I'm feeling very stupid," she said. "I thought maybe you're coming here because you know where he is. But you don't."

"No," I said. "I don't."

"Then you're here to tell me what I'm already knowing?"

"No," I said. "You told me you had one half of his story, and that I had the other half, and that together we could find out what happened to him. You said that, right?"

"But you're not telling me anything new."

"I'm trying, Mina. I really am. Will you shut off the faucet? Will you listen to me? I didn't mean to come here. You asked for his life in America and I couldn't tell you before, but I can tell you now, because I didn't realize who you were. I didn't realize you were the one he talked about."

At last she cut the water. "Try, then. Tell me what you're trying to say."

I couldn't know where to begin, how to explain my friendship with the man she'd loved. My head was blitzed by small, seemingly meaningless details of our time together, like how The Brow Beater loved the smell of gasoline so much he splashed a little on his wrists every time we filled up the tank. We used to cook steaks on the engine of my old Catalina—unbolting the heat shield from the exhaust manifold where all the cylinders come together, hiking the steak right underneath the gasket—and the meat would come out seasoned with petrol. What else? He chewed like my brother, back to front. I'd tell him again and again how much he and Gil would've loved each other, and he'd shine—absolutely shine. He saved me in about five hundred fights I picked in bars and locker rooms around the country, and I saved him that once, during the debacle in Duluth. When my Catalina finally broke down, we picked out my Ranger together. It's half his—maybe that's what I should've told Mina. The truck in front of her apartment complex—half of it belonged to the man who loved her. I tried to teach him how to drive once, but he refused. I think he liked looking out the window too much. He collected arrowheads and subway tokens and all sorts of touristy crap, and when he took off, he left all of that in the truck, in that red fanny pack he used to carry his money in. And there was the real point of my story, the best forgetting I ever did, and maybe, if I started telling Mina the small surrounding memories, I'd get around to telling her the center.

But as long as I could remember, even before my life in the wrestling business, all my talking—my honest talking, that is—happened on the road. Maybe it was the enclosure of the car, intimate as any confessional booth I'd feared as a child. Or maybe it was the movement involved, the sense that, since we were heading from one place to another, there followed a human impulse to match that movement in other, less geographical ways. Maybe that movement, that invisible shift in a person, happens most naturally through honest conversation, and so on the road, we reveal things—I reveal things—we otherwise might've kept buried at home. I asked Mina, "Is there any way we can keep talking out in my truck?"

Mina just shook her head. From behind the sink, she looked at me, looked down at the dishes, and turned the faucet back on. There came again the hiss of the spray.

I could feel Smokey's ribs expanding, a life I'd arranged.

"You know," I said, "you really broke his heart, Mina."

"You should be going."

"You did that," I went on. "You broke him. You didn't, you know, marry him like he wanted, and he was out here all alone. I mean, did you ever think of that? He didn't know anybody out here. I was his only friend, you understand? I was here for him, but otherwise, he was all alone. Turn that water off, now, and tell me why you didn't marry him. What took you so long to get here? He waited for you for a long time, you know, years, and he never touched another woman, I swear to God, he was a good man, and he waited for you, and how come you failed him? Turn that water off and tell me why you failed to join him here. Why did you stay home and marry that old man instead? Why'd you do that to him? Tell me why he deserved that. Tell me why The Brow Beater deserved what you did to him. Shut off the water and tell me what happened. You tell me!"

The cat leaped out of my arms, and Mina jumped back, startled, cutting her finger on a knife she'd been scrubbing. I tried to help her run the blood off under the running water, but she held her wound and said, "Go—please, go."

"If we could just talk in my truck," I said, "we could talk the truth. I can tell you what I know, and you can explain your story to me."

Mina sucked the cut at the side of her finger. With her elbow, she knocked off the water. "Explaining a story is killing a story. Same thing. I'm not killing my story for a man like you, who is only talking the truth in his car. Goodbye, Mr. Krill. Go."

In all my life, I'd fought with only one other woman, and that hadn't gone much better.

According to almost everyone, my brother was killed in December 1950. His girlfriend back home, however, disbelieved the news. It was a surprising act of delusion from an otherwise bright, levelheaded kid. She was only seventeen, Joyce, but she was headed to UC Berkeley, and her voice had a tremor every time she steered the conversation toward something she cared about—geology, art, or politics—and the few times I saw her before Gil shipped out, she had, like a pilot's eject button, a book within reach, just in case the conversation bored her and she had to make a sudden escape. I was ready to write off her fantasy about Gil's survival of his own death as a kind of melodramatic performance of grief, but she didn't seem to be grieving. She seemed clear-eyed and precise, as if she had access to an entirely different set of facts.

After Gil's body came back, she went off to California but kept in touch with my parents, who for years had considered her a daughter of their own. It was in those letters, dating from the '50s, that I learned Joyce's point of view regarding Gil and the official story of his death.

By the time I got ahold of her old letters to my mother, I had already traded the fishing vessel for the road, wrestling the territories. This was in 1961—I'd come home briefly to help my father clear out my mother's things, and found the letters from Joyce. At first her letters simply proposed the idea that Gil hadn't died, that he was still alive and held captive, perhaps, someplace in South Asia, that there had been a mistake involving the body. Those ideas seemed to me desperate and sad but not at all concerning, a kind of hopeful fib she was laying over my mother like a shawl.

Then her language changed. After graduating from Berkeley in 1955, two years after the war had ended, her letters took on a new, more menacing tone. She had proof, she wrote to my mother, that the United States government had handed over a significant number of soldiers and sailors to the Communists in Korea as part of an arms deal against the Soviets, proof that Gil had essentially been traded like a chip at a casino, and that the United States government, in an effort to cover up their treasonous bargain, had sent home false remains.

My mother, who had always loved Gil better than me, took to believing her. She stopped cooking for my father, and when my father started cooking for her, she hardly ate a bite. She bought a book on Korean and spent most of her waking hours practicing in the dim light under the kitchen window. She had a cat she adored but let it go one day into the woods behind the barn. According to my father, the cat came back a few times, but my mother shooed it away in Korean. Her last years, all she wanted to do was travel to the peninsula, as if disentangling a conspiracy or negotiating with a Communist regime or raising the dead from their graves—as if every miracle were just a language you could learn from a book. She expanded her vocabulary, and she corresponded with Joyce, but she never did get to Korea.

I'd been on the road and hadn't kept in touch with Joyce, which allowed me to cut through any concern I might've felt for her mental health so that I could jump straight to my own bleeding anger at her manipulation of my dying mother's heart.

So when my schedule brought me to Tucson, where Joyce had gone after college, I looked her up. It was 1962, and I found her working behind the desk at a bookstore, shoeless and tanned, splitting a cigarette with a woman wearing a feather in her hair. Joyce saw me and burst into tears. "I thought you were him," she said.

"That's not ever going to happen," I said. I told her never again to lie about my brother. I told her what she'd done to my aging mother, lying to her about the death of her son, was evil. "You turned her grief into poison," I said. "You made his death last longer than death."

She was wearing those lapis lazuli earrings, blue as planets and flecked with gold. "And you're blameless?" she said. "You, who found an endless road so that you never had to stop leaving?"

The woman beside her took the cigarette. "Only two reasons people come in here," she said, and Joyce gave me my options: "So tell me, Terry—did you come here to confess something, or are you just shopping for a book?"

On my way out, I kicked a pile of new-age paperbacks. I left as though I'd never see Joyce again, but I must've known the truth. All we'd done was start a new angle.

When I got to my truck, I realized how late it was, how I'd only meant to spend an hour away from the jewelry store, but almost four hours had gone by. It was all right, I told myself. I'd sweep by to retrieve Fuji, apologize to a pair of women I'd never see again, and drive clear on through to Johnny Trumpet's bungalow. I was finished, I thought, with The Brow Beater.

In the back camper of my truck, I found that red fanny pack of his, filled with tchotchkes. I plucked it like a weed and headed back up to Mina's apartment one last time. When I opened the door, she was sitting among the floral furniture, bandaging her finger.

"I'm leaving," I said, "but here's his American memorabilia if you want it. Throw it out if you don't, because that's what I was going to do with it." I tossed the fanny pack onto the carpet beside her, and the zipper came loose, letting free some of The Brow Beater's cheap collectibles: a halved seashell, several mismatched dice, an arrowhead. Mina stood from her armchair. She knelt to the floor. She picked up one of the dice and then said something in her language.

The rest of the bag, she picked up and dumped out on the counter in the kitchenette. A couple dozen more dice came tumbling out, blue and red and green and white and black and clear. Mina said, "I'm not knowing how to drive, Mr. Krill. Can you take me somewhere?"

I could've told her I had just decided to be done with The Brow Beater. I explained that my cat was waiting for me, three hours late, at a jewelry store in Glendale, and that I was expected to be in the desert in the morning for work, gone from the city of freeways altogether and forever. But I was curious about the dice, and I thought taking Mina on the road might allow me to tell her what I'd come to tell her, which I couldn't tell her outside of the truck. I said, "All right, I'll take you, but I'm picking my cat up first, and we're leaving right now."

She told me to wait at the gas station around the corner. She said she had to cover for herself at home, tell her husband that she was off to buy more food or liquor for their friends on the roof. She put all of The Brow Beater's things back into the zipped bag and hid the thing in a cupboard beneath the sink.

I said, "If you're not at the gas station in ten minutes, I'm leaving without you."

Again I left the building and crossed the street to my truck. I looked up and saw the orange sun pressing through the gray skim of the sky like a kiss through a shower door. Way up above me, on the roof of Mina's building, I saw Shen looking down on me. I waved goodbye as I got into my truck, but he didn't wave back.

17

The Mediterranean, 1980–1983

Of the Four Eeks, Martik was the only one who lived alone, on the verge of Spata in a small house made of stone. The house stood in a fallow where a vintner once worked, and except for the northern wheatears searching for beetles where the grapevines once blossomed, Martik had no neighbors. Inside the house, there were no rooms but for the central space, which stretched just far enough to fit a toilet and sink near the south end and a slim bed near the oven. At the foot of the bed stood a table with a mismatched chair tucked underneath, and old farm equipment—a scythe, a shovel, and a spike aerator—leaned like kindling in one of the corners. When the oven was burning, every stone of the house glowed. That was Martik's favorite feature of the house, the way the stones glowed when the oven was burning.

Martik said so as he stoked the fire with the four spikes of the aerator, hurtling the smell of wood smoke into the glowing house like bees from a hive. He was speaking to his latest guest, who seemed to be listening and watching the flickering stones of the ceiling.

The bed was too small, Martik thought. The feet—bound together with galvanized cable at the ankles—slumped off the edge of the mattress and onto the small table at the foot of the bed. The wrists were tied, too, and although Martik had left the mouth uncovered, his guest seemed uninterested in speaking. So Martik let him go on listening.

"The man with the gun," Martik said, jabbing at the fire, "the man with the gun who left after the binding, his name was Zatik. He's an engineer from Aleppo. And I'm from Istanbul. I'm not as young as Zatik or as smart. It's okay, though, because these are facts."

He'd grown up confused about facts, he said, because he'd learned one set of facts from his family, and another set of facts at school. To be an Armenian in Turkey was to learn to carry a weight on your tongue. Make it heavy. Slow it down. There, it was a serious crime to say the wrong word. *Genocide*. Insulting Turkishness, right there in the constitution. Textbooks piled with alternative histories. A light tongue would call them lies. A light tongue would get a boy's parents taken away.

Martik went to his knees at the oven, turning the wood with the aerator spikes.

He'd left school and played football all day with the Turkish boys. They were kind enough to let him join, or else desperate enough for someone to play goaltender. They played fairly with him. But when they fought, when the knives came out, the worst insult they could think of was to tell a fellow Turk: *You must have a secret Armenian in your family tree*.

He listened to those insults from the chicken-wire netting of the football goal. He wanted to hate those Turkish boys, wanted to fight them. But he didn't. He couldn't, in the end, blame them. They didn't have the facts at home the way he did. They learned only what their teachers had been instructed to instruct them. In that way, Martik had always been a generous person. He would've been ignorant of the facts, too, if he'd been born a Turk. He would've imprisoned his parents, too.

But he very much enjoyed playing goaltender. He never cared to score a goal of his own. He would rather protect a game than win one. He would grow up the same way, not an activist but a preservationist. That was what had drawn him to this role with Hagop Hagopian's group. Not the ambition to change but the ambition to save.

"I get each of my guests to say out loud the facts," he said, still at the fire.

The facts: Ottoman Turks systematically murdered and disappeared a million and a half Armenians beginning in 1915, destroying monuments and robbing the dead of their estates and their land, and their descendants continue perfecting the crime of erasure by denying the atrocities ever took place.

In some ways, hearing the facts from his guests—especially his most difficult ones, his most unpersuadable—elated him. Each admission, regardless of motive, felt like saving a soul—not the raising of the dead but the release of the dead.

In other ways, however, the truth left Martik feeling small. Another, more discomfiting truth seemed to be lurking beneath the others: no one but the victims wanted to do anything with the facts. Alliances with Turkey were growing around the world, not shrinking, and even sympathetic governments were willing to ignore its denial for the right price.

Finally satisfied with the oven, Martik left the spiked end of the aerator in the fire and then stood. He dragged the mismatched chair from under the table, took a seat, and said, "Not that you don't know the facts already."

"I was told Hagop Hagopian was coming to meet me here," Avo finally said, "so I could explain."

"Explain?" Martik said. He wasn't used to having conversations with his guests, but then again, this one was different. All his previous guests had been deniers. Without exception, he got an apology out of all of them. He used the old means. The ones their people had used on his. Symmetrical, that way. Different, this guest. Bigger, yes. But also: This wasn't a denier. This was, without precedent, a fellow Armenian. "Explaining, I've found, is ineffective."

How much did his guest know, he asked, about methods of torture at the end of the Ottoman Empire? *Falaka*—foot whipping. *Tecrit*—isolation. Fingernail removal. Skin removal. Genital removal. Eye removal. Bodily revision, in a way. Bodily erasure.

Avo said, "Hagopian just wants to make sure I left the group, that's all. He just wants to make sure I have no plans to ruin what he's building. I'm just out, that's all. I'm just returning back to the life I had."

The stones glowed, and the old farm equipment—the scythe, the shovel—remained piled at a slant like kindling in one of the corners. Many guests had been tied down to that bed. All of them smaller than this. "Explaining is the opposite of exploring," Martik said. "Explaining doesn't get us anywhere."

It was easy to assume that a man who tortured was a man without rules. Lawless. But for Martik, the opposite was true. Nobody adored a rule the way Martik adored a rule. The guests sent to him had broken the biggest rule of them all—never erase a death—and they had done so a million times over. Any pain he delivered to them seemed fractional compared to the punishment they deserved. In this way, Martik's job became almost clerical in nature, and because dullness in the face of great pain was a balm against insanity, Martik adored rules.

"I made a friend in America," Avo said. "He'd never heard of the genocide, he knew nothing about Armenians. It was through our friendship that he learned to care. This isn't the way. My friend learned to care."

"Oh, don't be sentimental," Martik said, using the aerator again to jostle the crackling logs. "You especially should know caring isn't enough. That professor in Los Angeles? Did you know he received forty thousand dollars from an unknown contributor last year, just after speaking at an assembly of the Association of Turkish Americans? Did you also know that he has gone on to teach three hundred and twenty-eight students since the day you spared his life? These are facts."

The others—Martik got the truth out of them. Apologies and promises. They would return to Turkey, they said, and convince the government to acknowledge their crimes. Reparations. Land. Anything, anything at all. But Martik had to explain: there was no need for all that. The pain itself was the result he'd been after. Didn't they understand?

In the old days, there was one method called *tabutluk*—coffin. A narrow cell the size of a woman's body. Dark as the gaps between stars. Nothing but you and the room inside your skin.

The guest was explaining himself, but Martik ignored him. The bed was too small. After a blow to the guest's head, it had taken both Martik and Zatik to bind him to the mattress at the chest and the thighs. Zatik had placed a gun in Martik's jacket, just in case the binding didn't hold, though of course it would.

Still, this guest was different. Hagop had explained everything. The betrayal. The ways in which he'd put the whole project of justice at risk. The example Martik was to set.

Too big for *tabutluk*. Big bare feet on the table off the edge of the bed. Martik went and found the rattan cane hiding among the old farm equipment in the corner. Ninety centimeters long, two centimeters in diameter. He rolled it between his hands as if to start a fire. Listening to his guest go on and on. Explaining.

Other guests had begged not for death but for shoes. They had tried but been unable to explain the effects of having exposed soles for prolonged periods of time, even if Martik never raised the cane. They couldn't explain the visceral craving for shoes. All five senses—they wanted to eat shoes and smell shoes and touch them and see them and hold them to their ears like shells and listen.

With the others, Martik wanted to use as many of the old ways as possible. A combination of every evil his family had survived and remembered, he tried to explain.

In Istanbul during the genocide, they'd tortured Armenians in a building that now belonged to the campus of Istanbul University.

His guest, Martik realized, had gone quiet eight hours into his stay. Just lying there. An Armenian, like him. Quiet and exhausted of explanation. Martik tossed the cane aside and went to the oven instead.

Different, this one. Not a denier. Not a liar. Just a coward or a fool. A runner. A survivor. Hagopian would disagree. Make an example, he'd said. The group depends on loyalty.

Martik picked up the spiked aerator from the fire, its four prongs orange and searing. He carried the long hot edge of the side prong up to his guest's face, hovering it over the line of his one eyebrow. He told his guest not to move or else he'd lose more than that. He said, "Deny the genocide."

His guest, eyes open, didn't respond.

"Deny the genocide," Martik said. "Pretend you're a Turk. I can't do my job until you do."

His guest said something else instead, and he said it so softly, Martik had to bend forward so far to hear him, he could feel the heat of the spikes between their faces. What his guest was whispering was not a plea or a prayer, and it was not an explanation.

"I killed a man once," said his guest.

Martik waited for more.

"An Armenian. A kind of father to the woman I love. I killed him."

Martik, feeling the heat of the spikes in his eyes, asked how.

"I knocked him over into the water. He fell. Cracked his skull against a rock."

"You meant to kill him?"

"Don't be sentimental. You know intention isn't enough."

Martik, breathing in the white-hot iron.

One method for the Ottomans was to trap boys and girls in churches and then burn the churches. Some churches were made of stone, so the children inside were baked alive. Imagine the suffering, and then imagine forgetting the suffering.

Martik lifted the searing aerator.

"My parents were burned alive," said his guest. A full minute between sentences. His guest seemed half-conscious. "Are you going to kill me?"

"No," Martik said, "but leaving here can't cost you nothing." He lowered the fiery edge of the blade and pressed it squarely along the eyebrow. Afterward, a wound like a marbled loaf of bread began to rise.

The guest was too big for the bed but shaking just the way a small man would. "You died here," Martik said, cutting the galvanized cable, sure his guest would run to the sink before trying to attack him. "Do you understand me? You died here, all right? Don't forget it."

Freed from his ties, his guest fell from the bed like a book to the floor. His agony was loud. At the sink near the toilet, he cried under the running water.

When the quiet came, Martik kept his gun in his hand and left money on the table. He told his guest to go to the docks and leave Greece. Find a boat heading elsewhere, he said, and board it. "You're dead."

Waiting for the strength to stand and leave, his guest looked like another stone glowing in the wall.

His pain was thick and thickening but could not be touched, and his eyes seemed sewed shut because of the swelling, and for a long while, Avo lay in the fallow where the grapevines once blossomed, believing himself to be blind. Finally, a grated light flickered between his eyelashes, and in the spasms of semi-blindness, he rose and then staggered through the broken grass toward the burnished smells of the sea.

He'd been suffering for three hours by the time he got to the docks near Artemida, and by then the place seemed grayscale and workmanlike, filled with the sounds of cargo pulleys and screeching gulls and the stricken matchbooks of ferrymen on the wharf. Even the toothless doyens on the docks turned with a start at the sight of his arrival, face-singed and huge and jittering from pain. He looked to be considering wading headfirst into the sea to calm the burning over his eyes, but a pair of old fishermen met him at the shore to warn him against infection. Their questions went unanswered. For the cash in his pocket, Avo was shown to a cabin in the *Viking Viscount*, a cargo and passenger ferry serving several stops along the Grecian isles. The cabin smelled of fish and oil and contained two miniature beds, one of which he lay on. One of the old fishermen bandaged the burn across Avo's face using the skinned scales of tilapia. Because they were among only a handful of passengers onboard the *Viking Viscount* during the off-season, the cabin—including the doorless toilet—remained Avo's and the old fisherman's alone to use. Once a week, the old fisherman replaced the scales with a fresh sleeve of tilapia, speaking Greek except for the nonverbal hushing of his pain.

Avo spent six weeks in the cabin, recovering, eating what the old fisherman brought down for him, until he peeled away the last of the scales from his eyes. Glad for the silence but greedy for more, Avo spent every minute he could outside the cabin, away from those beds. He stood on the deck of the *Viking*, leaning against the rails and feeling the wet gray wind run through him like clouds through a peak. A memory of fish guts in Angel Hair's sea stories came to him, the silvery opposite of pain.

From Artemida to Piraeus to Milos to Crete to Kasos to Karpathos, the ferry moved as slowly as the islands it traveled, and Avo absorbed its pace. He stood for long stretches of time without so much as shifting his weight or shivering. He felt his pulse lower in tempo. He thought in long uninterrupted strings, imagining the open water or the overhanging coastlines from the points of view of ancient mariners, or else he imagined the lives in the ascending rows of seaside homes with their roofs the color of squashes. Five months at sea and counting. A new year—several drunk cargomen shattered their bottles of wine to celebrate—had begun.

When the ferry came to its stop in Sitia, while most of the ferrymen and all of the other passengers took to dry land for a meal or a tour, Avo chose to stay on the deck of the *Viking*, wind-chilled and wet but for the hairless, senseless ridge over his eyes.

Freezing cold. And when he remembered Martik's words—*You're dead*—he felt he really was. No one dared to ask about his role on the boat. The old fisherman had returned to shore long ago. Ghostlike, Avo thought, or as close as he'd been since his life in America, and the proximity lent him a kind of entryway to little memories he'd forgotten he remembered: the apricot pits he would suck in the pouch of his cheeks as a boy; the rooster tattooed on one of Angel Hair's feet, the pig tattooed on the other; the smell of lemons underneath Mina's fingernails when he kissed the ball of her palm. And when his mind turned to his parents, he remembered them more clearly than he ever had, too—quirks of personality, recurring jokes between them, habits of speech and behavior so vivid he found himself repeating them now: a run of the tongue along the front of his teeth like his father used to do mid-joke, or his mother's tiny shuffling dance with her shoulders as she cooked.

But what surprised him more than the images unearthing themselves in his mind was the sense that his parents were there beside him now, staring out at the port and the lapping waves and the city with its rows of squash-colored homes, admiring the ferrymen shepherding cranes and crates, watching the boat take leave again, letting the wind and spray stretch through them like clouds. There they were, his parents, not memories but objects, present in a way he might've found sentimental just a short while ago, just a year ago, and it seemed clear to him now that memory was powered by the same fuel that powered imagination, and that most people had only enough fuel for one of those engines. He wanted to be a man who split his fuel evenly, wanted to be a man who remembered and imagined in equal force. Once, he remembered, his imagination had powered a whole variety of lives, and as the *Viking Viscount* reached its final port on the island of Karpathos, Avo dreamed of returning to that time, returning to Mina.

In Karpathos, he was invited onto a small trading vessel called *The Wise Man*, which was headed to the southern Turkish city of Mersin. A tradesman onboard with a whittled crucifix hanging from his throat had overheard Avo offering his labor in exchange for free passage, and the tradesman asked in English if he was a

Christian. "There's a whole lot of pilgrims onboard, heading to the site at Tarsus," the man said. "I usually sail alone with the crew, but I've always got room for a pilgrim—even a pilgrim as big as our boat. Help me unload it on the other side, and you've got yourself a ride."

Without lying directly about his lack of faith, Avo answered that he was from Armenia, which had accepted Christianity before any other nation in the world.

The tradesman clapped his hands together and said, "An Armenian, huh? There's a man onboard who absolutely hates Armenians. He was dumped by an Armenian woman in Mersin five years ago and still won't shut up about it. He truly annoys me, that man, and he'd hate to have you onboard. So, please, come onboard."

The Wise Man traded in antiques, and the joke among the tradesmen was that the boat itself could be part of the collection. The boat was a schooner, Avo learned, and he was shown how to work the sails on both masts. The sails were gaff-rigged rather than Bermuda-rigged, and Avo nodded along, pretending to understand the difference. All he knew was that the sails were as stained and tattered as a child's bedsheet, complete with a few sloppily stitched and yellowed patches. Every step Avo took on deck was accompanied by a croak in the boards, and Avo crossed himself—in part to perform the Christian he was half-believed to be, and in part out of a genuine fear of falling through the boat to the water—as the sails caught the wind heading east.

As for their destination, Avo had never heard of Tarsus, though he pretended he'd always hoped to visit. The tradesman wearing the cross was pleased and spoke longingly of the place. He'd taken a handful of pilgrims to Tarsus over the years—and why not, since the birthplace of Saint Paul was just twenty-five kilometers north of the Turkish port at Mersin.

The trip lasted two nights, and on the second night, the tradesmen invited a few of the laborers, including Avo, to drink together in a small cabin beneath the deck. Several hours into the torrent of sea stories, a man in the corner of the cabin who hadn't said a word all night broke through the rest of the voices with the smell of black licorice on his breath, the result of a quart or more of ouzo. "She loved me, my ass!"

Across the cabin, Avo caught the eye of the man wearing the cross, who winked at him and laughed into the neck of his beer as if to say, "I tried to warn you."

"She was an artist," the drunk man said, and someone shouted, "We heard it already a thousand times before," and the drunk pressed on: "Not everyone! There's new ears—I see new ears!"

"Happy New Ears!" some joked together.

"A real artist," the man said over them, "a painter, a sculptor—you name it, she did it. And did it well. Made a lot of money on her art, I helped her sell it, too, and she said she loved me. My ass. This is years ago, before the socialists came into power, but there were still tensions out there, you know, and her gallery was ransacked. Burgled, vandalized, destroyed. Apparently, she'd been making too much money on her art. Those bastards did the same thing to some of our most beautiful churches—every saint in Greece had his face rubbed clean out with alcohol, ancient glass in the windows shattered with bricks. God'll forgive them, but I won't."

The man wearing the cross said, "I'm going to have a birthday before this story is over."

"I'm this Greek and she's this Armenian and we're in love, my ass, and she got to her gallery one day and saw the place destroyed, and she had to start all over. She was brought on by one of the churches to repair some of the frescoes, to sculpt new faces for the saints. That's where I met her. I'd volunteered to help clean up the mess. That's where we fell in—" he said, and began to sob.

No joke seemed right while the drunk man cried, but pity seemed wrong, too, and so for a quarter of a bottle, the men drank and smoked without speaking, hoping the crying would stop.

Finally, it did, and the heartbroken man continued his story. "We ended up living together, she and I. Working together—she made the most immaculate items. A pair of walnut chairs she sold as George the First editions. A small copper ballerina she sold to a Degas collector who couldn't tell the difference. I hesitate to even call them forgeries, they were so beautiful. Upgrades to the originals, I always thought. Furniture, books, entire decks of cards—she could make every blot of ink ring true. But then one day, she left Greece for Mersin, where we're headed, where I still go every six months or so to see her at the antiques dealers. When she left Athens, she said she had to get away from Greeks. But the real reason is obvious to me, so many years later: she'd never felt for me what I felt for her. She was a skilled forger, I knew, but I didn't know how skilled. She'd forged her love, I believe, and unlike with a desk or a chair, that's a sin."

All the men drank. When Avo spoke, the entire crew looked up from their bottles. Only a couple of them had heard his voice before. "She forges papers, bro? Passports, visas?"

The drunk man sniffled. "Who are you? What happened to your face? Have you been here this whole time?"

"He's an Armenian," said the man with the cross, egging the drunk on.

"Shit on Armenians," the drunk said, but there was no heart in it, and Avo let it go.

"She's in Mersin?" Avo said. "What's her name, bro?"

"Bro?" muttered the drunk.

"Her name is Kami," said the man wearing the cross. "We've heard this story so many times, I can take you to her shopfront with a blindfold on. I'll take you there when we land, if you'd like."

"Don't fall in love with her," said the drunk, and he seemed to want to say more, but soon he was crying again, and several men near him allowed him to dry his face on their shirtsleeves.

Then the party seemed over, and the men took to their own cabins. In the morning, they landed at Mersin.

Avo must have been the only Armenian in history who had gone to America to hide and to Turkey to seek. True, Mersin was a Mediterranean port city in the south, six hundred kilometers west of the Anatolian Armenia of the genocide years, but the fact remained that Avo was in Turkey. Although he didn't have time to taste the air for any signs of genetic nostalgia or trauma flitting through the wind, he did remember Yergat and Siranoush, the redheaded girl who survived an ambush of teenage angels, as he kept moving with the crew, unloading the furniture the tradesmen wanted to sell at the markets. Once the final dining room table had been transferred to the truck, Avo's job was done, and so was his life at sea.

Although the man with the cross had offered him free passage in exchange for his labor, he also folded a few bills into Avo's shirt pocket when he said goodbye, and Avo used the money to buy a gyro at an outdoor café on 5706 Sokak. He ate slowly. Across the way, in front of the shops lining the road, he saw a woman peeling an orange. She had long white hair, and almost every article of clothing she wore was made of brown leather. She was speaking to a man and digging her thumbnails into the flesh of the orange, pulling long, curled strands of skin to the ground as she spoke.

When she was through with the man—a customer, Avo realized—she kicked the discarded peels into a gutter in the road, swallowed the naked orange in several enormous bites, and pulled a bottle of water out of her back pocket to rinse her hands beneath. Then she turned and stepped into one of the shops.

Avo followed her inside. To his surprise, he found himself not in a shop but in a gallery, with framed art on the walls and odd mechanical installations roped off in the center of the space. There was no sight of the woman. At the very back, a set of stairs led him up into a book-lined studio apartment, and there she was, hanging her coat, studying him like a sculpture in need of restoration. When he asked in Armenian if her name was Kami, she said, "Were you born with that face, or is that what happened the last time you followed a woman into her bedroom?"

When Avo laughed, covering his face gingerly with both hands, Kami seemed to understand how long it had been since he'd laughed. She told him to wait for her downstairs.

One painting caught his attention so sharply, he couldn't believe he'd walked past it on the way in. It was a portrait, blue and green, of a woman in a long-sleeved dress holding a handkerchief to her face. With her other hand, she cradled the opposite elbow. A long nose cast a teal shadow down her face, which looked angry and solemn all at once. The woman bore such a strong resemblance to Mina, Avo realized he'd been covering his chin.

"You found the Avetisyan," Kami said, coming down the stairs. "Armenians are drawn to each other, I guess."

"Is it a forgery?"

"You know, you're just like that pig I was yelling at earlier. I stopped doing forgeries a long time ago. Everything I sell here is real."

He might've been intimidated by her, but before coming downstairs, she'd tied her white hair back in just the way Angel Hair used to do, and this other resemblance comforted Avo enough to say exactly what he'd come to say. He was returning to Armenia after a long time away, he told Kami. He'd be traveling east through Turkey and would need papers to cross the border back home. He'd heard she might be able to help.

Where had he come from, she might've asked, or how had he landed in Mersin, of all places?

But she didn't ask a thing. Whether due to a free artistic spirit, a cultural understanding, or a dangerous naïveté, Avo couldn't say. All he could do was marvel at the way Kami turned and started walking, waving over her shoulder for him to follow, and announced along the way to the telephone that the restoration shop could always use some muscle, what with all those heavy works of art coming and going, as long as the muscle was careful and precise. She added that the money wouldn't be much, but it was something, which he'd need if he wanted to make the trip across the country, and there was an apartment beside hers that was vacant, where he could stay for half the cost of what he'd pay elsewhere in the city, and really, she should be thanking him, what a godsend he was, what a favor *he* would be doing for *her.*

"And at the end," she said, "when you've earned them, I'll set you up with your papers."

Would he have agreed to the arrangement had he known he was to spend two years in Mersin? It was impossible to say. Like a gas, time seemed to take the shape of its container, and two years in Kami's gallery flitted by in less than a heartbeat compared to the two years he'd spent on the road with Angel Hair, or even the one day he'd spent strapped down in Martik's bed.

In many ways, the job was repetitive—loading and unloading trucks, reasoning with unruly artists and buyers—but he took pride in the combination of power and touch needed to move the art correctly, which reminded him of the way Angel Hair had taught him to handle men in the ring. He also admired Kami's restoration talents—he'd bring in a statue of a cat with a missing ear, and he'd send it off a few weeks later with every hair in place. Watching her at work enthralled him, the way she approached every medium differently, the aggressive way she stalked a statue, circling it before getting up or down to its level, or the coaxing way she put her face as close to a canvas as possible, peering into it for the miscellaneous adventures of a brushstroke. And he enjoyed making stupid small talk with her, little nothing jokes like pointing out a dancer in a painting, a man in slim yellow tights, and claiming that his father had the same pair back home. The jokes were meaningless except they caused her to laugh, and the air in the room seemed fresher for the fun, and the hands on the clock moved so fast sometimes he thought she'd turned them all forward as a prank, a way to get back at him for joking that he, too, used to have long gray hair, before he shaved his head bald, and maybe she should do the same.

The dealers he met were sophisticated people who wore glasses with colored frames. They were polite, if not kind, and happy to ask about his scar and nod solemnly when he answered that he'd rather talk about the art. He did enjoy learning about the art, though not much of it stuck, and of course all of it had to do with this peculiar friendship he'd forged with Kami, consensually temporary and therefore honest and headlong and impossible to explain.

The closest he'd ever come to this was with Angel Hair, only Avo had never told the truth about his plans to leave. One of the few silver linings of being found by Ruben, in fact, was that it had happened while Avo was separated from Angel Hair, and so Avo had never had to say goodbye.

Although Kami hadn't asked him a single question about his life when he'd first asked her for help, they felt practically transparent to each other in a few months' time. She told him the entire saga of the drunk Greek he'd met on *The Wise Man*, and Avo told her about the death of his parents, and he told stories about Angel Hair and his brother, Gil, and he went on and on about Mina, who was the reason he was returning home.

Once, while he helped Kami arrange the latest exhibit, she took a seat on the bottom step of the staircase and said, "You're still young, but I'm at the age now where I can't help considering the legacy I'll leave behind. It's indulgent and morbid and sentimental, but it's true! My mind obsesses over the question."

"You give artists a space," Avo ventured, and although Kami made an agreeable sound, she returned to work and let the conversation end there.

From then on, Avo wondered what the right answer might've been. He got sick during this time, missing Mina, whose legacy had always appeared clearly tied to his, and his to hers. A legacy was a group project, it seemed to Avo, and so he'd given Kami an answer that involved the only group he'd seen her associate with, her community of artists.

Maybe Kami understood the problem, too, because she began to talk almost exclusively about her mother, who was nearly eighty years old and living in an orange grove some twenty miles away. Despite the proximity, they hadn't spoken in many years.

"Maybe I'll go see her," Kami would say every other week or so.

When Kami asked if Avo had given any thought, despite his youth, to the question of his own legacy, Avo hesitated: he'd given the question thought, but the answer embarrassed him. Still, to his surprise, the impulse to lie was replaced by the impulse to restore, and rather than putting on a mask, he pulled out a version of himself he'd almost forgotten he once believed in.

"You know," he said, "I always wanted to be a poet."

"I think you'd be a great poet," Kami said.

"Yeah?"

"Well, you've traveled the world, haven't you, collecting material?"

Soon a collector brought his teenage son to the gallery, looking for "the poet." The boy, having published in a small literary journal at his school, asked Avo to read his work. Avo stared down at the kid, the first living poet he'd ever met, and said, "Sure, sure."

"I thought he could pick your brain," Kami explained to Avo later.

How else did the two years go so quickly? Painfully, sometimes: the shoulder he'd dislocated in Toledo—and again in Newark—tended to slip from its socket whenever he lifted a heavy piece of art. Jolts of strange electricity sometimes shot up his spine with no trigger at all, and he'd have to hold his head under a dark cover for ten minutes if he looked too directly into the lights strung up above a portrait.

Mostly, though, those years rushed comfortably by. Sometimes Kami would invite him to gallery openings with a group of friends, or else dinner or a movie, always in groups, and he became known around the community as the big young scarred poet. One acquaintance happened to know the culture editor of a local newsletter, and nearly demanded that Avo send her one of his poems for publication. He said he'd think on it. He wouldn't want to send something lying around in his journals. He would want to honor the generous offer with a new poem written specifically for the publication, and that would take time.

The next day, Kami purchased a notebook for him from the café across the street, inscribed with the message: "Thus begins your legacy."

One day, late in their friendship, Kami showed up outside the gallery with a pair of bicycles. Together they rode to the outskirts of the city. They parked their bikes by a grove of orange trees.

On foot he followed her down a dusty aisle between the trees. Hundreds of oranges were popping from their leaves like bright round bulbs. She pointed at one high in a tree and asked Avo to pluck it for her. Avo told her about Mina and the lemon tree near the ski lift back home, and Kami said, "These are oranges." She was not like a lover or an aunt or a sister or a cousin, but a friend, the holiest love there was in the world, and he reached and plucked one of the fruits. "This one? Are you sure?" The orange in question was ripe to blackening.

Kami took the orange and peeled it for them to share. Little triangles of meat on the unfurled rind.

"My mother lives there," Kami said, pointing to the house at the end of the rows. She didn't need him for the final walk to the door. He waited for her among the trees.

In the end, Kami gave him the papers she'd forged, and they embraced for a long time. It was funny. The story of his friendship with Kami seemed so disconnected from the moving stream of his life.

Even to himself. Her name would never come out of his mouth again, not even to his deepest love. And yet Kami was important. For many years before his friendship with her, Avo had been brutal and brutalized in return, and had considered loyalty a thing made entirely of stone. He had come to a different understanding by the end of his stay in Mersin. And if somehow he'd been able to return to Mina without it, he would've failed, unable to love her well.

18

Kirovakan, Soviet Armenia, 1983

Tomorrow, Mina decided, she would take the children to the ski lift. She could see the lift from here, the roof of her building, and even Araksya, two years old, had pointed out the rising chairs in the distance. Her daughter seemed older than that—sturdier and more talkative—and ready to enjoy great heights. Already she was pointing from the roof of the tallest building in Kirovakan toward the hills beyond the city and calling every little cliff in the distance Masis, which was the peak of Mount Ararat. Two years old. Mina squeezed her, said she loved her so much she would eat her.

The girl covered her mouth with both hands when she laughed. It was as though she had a limited supply of laughter and was trying to keep as much of it inside as possible. She did that with food, too, slowing down and savoring her last bites. It really was, Mina thought, as if her baby girl were old already and had learned somewhere to fear spending the last of anything. Like she was somehow heightened.

Mina didn't let her get too close to the roof's steel railing. She kept her in the center, in or near the chairs at the backgammon table. It was hard to get Araksya to focus for longer than a few dice rolls, but that was okay. Her breaks in attention gave them a chance to take strolls around the table to stretch their legs, to hold hands, to talk. They pointed at and named the places in the distance, the church, the train station, the city square, the mountains with their patches of snow. "There's a village there," Mina said, "where it rains almost every day. And you see the snow up above? There's the ski lift there." She mimed a skier, planting her feet and her imaginary poles, shifting her weight from one leg to the other, making whooshing sounds through her teeth. The girl covered her mouth with both hands and shook, absolutely shook.

Tomorrow, Mina decided, she would take her girl and her sister's children there. The snow was patchy, melting before its time. She would take them tonight, right now, if not for the recital. January, and the snow melting already in patches.

The miming wore her out, so she made a big show of feeling exhausted and plunked herself down in a chair.

"Talin," Araksya said.

"That's right, soon we're going to see Talin sing and play music. Are you excited to see your cousin onstage?"

Araksya nodded so hard her teeth clattered, and then she laughed and covered her mouth.

They should be getting back inside. Galust would be home soon from work, and they'd have only a little bit of time to eat before needing to leave for the recital. She hadn't even chopped the cabbage for the borscht. What could she throw together if it came to that? There was lavash, and hummus she'd made for Araksya and her mother-in-law in the afternoon. Eggplant and lemon. Simple. Galust could snack on that while he waited for the soup, she thought. No rush, then, to leave the roof just yet.

"Masis," Araksya said, pointing again to the northern mountains. Mina corrected Araksya by directing her finger to the west. "Masis is over there," she said, "far, far away. Masis is much, much bigger than our puny village hills. It used to be part of our country, but now the border has moved."

The girl looked to the western horizon, saw nothing, and then turned back to their puny village hills. She said, "But these are bigger."

Perspective, Mina thought. How does any parent teach it?

They took another handheld stroll and sat down again at the backgammon table. Araksya rolled the dice. Mina showed her how to move the checkers. One die for one checker, the other for another.

Araksya liked the dice more than the checkers. She rolled them repeatedly and knew to keep them on the board. "Wow!" Mina said from time to time. The girl covered her mouth with both hands.

January, and the snow melting already. Mina had bundled Araksya in a winter coat and scarf, but she herself felt warm in just a light sweater. Could she remember the last winter like this?

Wishfully, maybe, or—not at all.

Her sister claimed she couldn't remember *anything* of her life before children. Mina wouldn't go that far, but she was beginning to understand her sister's point of view. Her *perspective*. The truth was Mina remembered less and less about her life before Araksya. It hadn't vanished, not entirely. More like the way the snow was melting—not at once but in swaths.

For example, Tigran and his wife used to have her over for dinner. His wife was a beautiful cook who'd worked, in her youth, in the kitchen at the consulate in Yerevan. And yet Mina couldn't remember a single dish from those dinners. They all seemed to merge in her mind as one ongoing feast. She couldn't remember any specific conversation they enjoyed at the table, either, only the old joke Tigran liked to make at grace: "Thank you, Lord, for allowing an old ape like me to dine with geniuses."

Was it after one of those dinners that Tigran gave her Shirakatsi's journal? No, that must've happened in the daylight—she remembered shadows on the page. He'd taken her to the forests in the foothills, not far from the railroad tracks, and told her Byzantine and medieval treasures lay buried there.

With everyone else, she was constantly aware of her sloping chin, her beaklike nose. But not with Tigran. Genius, he used to call her, and she believed it. She believed, at least, that he believed it.

That day in the forest when he'd brought her the journal, he'd pulled it from inside his coat. Shirakatsi's proofs. Passed from master to star pupil for hundreds of years, went the story. And she was the first girl to thumb those pages. He had chosen her.

"Another gift to a girl with many," Tigran said. They walked in the shadows of tall pines and larches. Daylight, then. She was young and grateful. She was alone. Her music was foreign and illegal, and her sister—who used to love the album *Pet Sounds* so much she would hum the melody to "Wouldn't It Be Nice" and tell their parents she'd invented it—had thrown away her records before marrying a regional deputy of the Party. Mina was, she'd started to believe, a genius trapped—in Armenia, in girlhood. She stepped into the old man's coat and kissed him terribly on the mouth.

Then she started to remove, at the shoulder, her shirt.

"Oh," Tigran said, and with just a syllable, he exposed the falseness of her escape. She was so ashamed she started running. Only when she was out of breath did she stop and sit on a felled tree. She'd done something clumsy and melodramatic and whorish, and she was afraid he'd take back all the confidence he'd given her. She was afraid he'd take back the book and give it to the other top student, that dour kid she'd known but not known for all her life.

She wasn't crying. She was licking her thumb to turn the pages.

Was there anything more beautiful than an ancient stanza of math? She read those beautiful proofs over and again. Eventually, she heard Tigran rustling toward her.

"When I was young and crazy with impatience for love," he said, "I once kissed my sister like that." He sat next to her on the log.

"You did?"

"I was so mortified I packed my bags and moved to Moscow. I mean, I changed my whole life because of my shame. The next time I saw my sister was twenty years later, and when I went to embrace her, we just burst out laughing. Right in front of the whole family, dozens of them. We shook hands instead, laughing so hard our faces turned purple. Until the day she died, we shook hands to say hello, shook hands to say goodbye, and no one knew why that cracked us up so bad, but sure enough, they laughed, too." He pushed himself up from the log and wiped his hands clean. "That laughter became the signature memory I have of her, the texture of our love. If I'd known, I wouldn't have escaped to Moscow. I'd have liked to have those twenty years back. I'd have liked to have more of that experience, shaking hands and losing our breath with laughter."

He was so caring with her she almost forgot what she'd done. It was as though he'd given her the only type of forgetting she'd ever known to be an act of kindness. He was willing to forget her stupidity to remember her genius.

Now, watching her child roll dice, Mina felt as far from genius as a woman could be.

No wonder Avo had pitied her, she thought. No wonder he'd faked his affection for her, no wonder he'd left without saying goodbye. All those years of pity she'd mistaken for love. She covered her chin.

* * *

After the conversation with Ruben at the wedding, throwing away the American map proved insufficient. Like her sister before her, she threw away her records. She threw away books of poetry and photographs in thick stacks, and burned many hundreds of pages of her journals over the stove. She even burned the invitation to the tournament bearing the Eiffel Tower. One day, Galust had come home from work sniffing. "What's on fire?" he asked, and she told him she'd burned the pilaf.

All that was left after those fiery first months of her marriage was the gift she'd been given in the shadows of the larches. She sometimes fanned the golden edges, smelling the three-hundred-year-old paper. She followed the lines of math like faint tracings of fossils. Galust had asked her politely to stop leading the student backgammon club so they could work on starting a family, and it saddened her beyond comprehension that she no longer had a student to groom.

Unlike all the previous recipients of the journal, she would fail to pass it on. Instead, she was living a typical domestic life. The day she realized she was pregnant, she took Shirakatsi's proofs straight to the stove.

But in the kitchen, she must have lost track of time, studying the math before destroying it, and Galust—had he been home all along?—found her at the stove with her nose in the crease. He said, "My love, my bookish love, what's that you're reading?" His heels lifted from the floor so he could kiss her on the lips. But he missed, as he often did when they were standing, and kissed her, accidentally, directly on the chin.

Right then Mina lost it. She was laughing and sobbing all at once in that ugly authentic way she'd been taught so many times to bury. But Galust held her and joked that he didn't know her chin was so sensitive. He'd kiss her more gently next time, he said. He loved her. And the way he loved her—no bargain at all. She knew his deepest fear was that he'd missed his chance to be a father, and she savored the brief moment before she exorcised that fear with her news. He must've seen a change in her eyes. He said, "Never mind about the book, my love, it's none of my business as long as you're enjoying it."

That was when she told him. "You'll be a father soon," she said.

He folded over himself and touched his cheek to her stomach, and he held her hands. They danced like that, right there in the kitchen. Not like an arranged marriage but like lovers, like real lovers.

Something about the impending baby turned her secrets into burdens, and she let them free almost dispassionately. It was a few months into her pregnancy when she explained the journal she'd nearly incinerated.

Galust asked if he could hold it. Together they marveled at its age, its history, its value.

"Why destroy it?" Galust asked, and Mina said, "I know it's crazy, but I have this feeling that this book is my last piece of bad luck, and I just need to get rid of it before the baby comes."

Galust said, "I'll light the stove now."

It was the word *now* that changed her mind. The idea that a single moment was all a person needed to erase centuries seemed vulgar. Whatever pain that book had caused for her, she couldn't destroy it. Besides, there was always the dim hope that the painful could become useful. She said, "What if we sell it? Use the money for the baby. For the baby's whole life."

From his previous post, Galust knew a man who ran an illegal shop out of his home in Leninakan. The man bought and sold and traded with foreign dealers. Rugs and glassware, mostly. But art and antiques, too.

* * *

On the westward train the next day, Mina felt sick on the tracks. Galust gave her his hat to throw up in, which she did. They arrived in the unreasonably bright afternoon. Galust streaked his hat through a fountain, singing a little song to hide the nature of his chore.

Inside the merchant's home, the walls seemed built of framed paintings. Landscapes, mostly—mountains and rivers with horses at the banks. In the lone spot of plaster between frames, Mina could make out a small pale stain where a crucifix once hung. Truncated wooden columns studded the entryway, bearing antique figurines of bronze and silver. Quickly, they were greeted by a cat who ran the soft bones of his body along Mina's calves.

Galust's friend appeared. He had the biggest face she'd ever seen, and his jowls rumbled with every word he spoke. "If you see something you like," he joked, "tell me so I can hike up the price."

The cat followed them to the back of the house. The merchant pulled a curtain to reveal a rack of rugs. Mina knelt to stroke the cat, and by the time she stood again, the false front had dropped, and her husband was showing his friend the proofs.

The merchant fixed a loupe in his big eye socket and studied the ink. He left and returned with another book, perhaps as old. He studied both books under his loupe.

Finally, he looked up at Galust. He didn't bother to take out the eyepiece. Slamming a book shut in each hand like a pincer, he said, "You've been had."

"Is that so," Galust said, but Mina stepped on his toe until he let her do the talking. She said, "I'm not claiming it's an original Shirakatsi from the fifth century, only a copy made by a cleric in the seventeenth century. Even still, that would make the book rare and valuable. Priceless, even."

"Priceless and worthless are synonyms to me," the merchant muttered, recessing his head into his jowls to drop the loupe into his shirt pocket. "Fifth century, seventeenth century—both ancient history compared to this. The ink here is Turkish-made. Can't be much older than your dear old husband, I'm afraid."

The cat was at her feet again, and this time she kicked him. She must've seemed possessed, because Galust asked if she needed to borrow his hat again. She declined. She looked to the merchant once more and asked if he was sure. Could he—please, and closely this time—check the ink again?

The man pursed his big face. Maybe because the shop was otherwise empty, or maybe because he had an authentic affection for Galust from some unknown shared history, or maybe because he could see by Mina's appearance and by her husband's soaking hat how much farther than a train ride she'd traveled to hear the news, he agreed to look once more. He popped the loupe back into his eye and opened the book. He spent a much longer time checking, even going so far as to leave and return with other artifacts for comparison. A Bible. A map. What appeared to be a list or a poem. Finally, he said, "I'm sorry."

Oh, apologies, Mina thought. They mean so much to Armenians. But now that she was in possession of one, she didn't know what to do with it. The apology just sat there in front of her, old words in a forged book. She told him to keep it.

"Oh," she said, almost at the door. "You haven't seen a collection of old mismatched dice come through here, have you?"

But all the man had was another apology.

Back home, she was getting big. In the mornings, her sister brought Mina's nephew and niece to the apartment. Those angels took turns rubbing their aunt's swollen feet. Her sister made tea and assorted bread and salted cucumbers and cheese. Every morning. Eating and laughing. Mina with her foot massages, talking with the children about nothing but the future. Vahan was eleven and wanted to be a pilot. Talin was seven and wanted to be a singer. She sang. They applauded.

Mina would always love those mornings.

And by the time Araksya arrived, Mina was so enamored with her family that she hardly had the space in her heart to remember the forgery. But when a small crack opened up—at night, usually, waiting for the baby to fall asleep—when she remembered the fraudulence of the book, she wondered if Tigran had lied to her on purpose—had simply made the whole story up—or if he himself had been fooled. It seemed to her that if he'd known the book was fake, it would have made the gift even sweeter, in a way, a lie to help her believe in herself. Or was his encouragement just as fraudulent as the book? She didn't know what to feel. And the crack in her heart went on opening and soldering itself, no less painful every time, because she would never know the truth, which is the only thing that can pin a heart open or seal it off forever.

Once she got to thinking about Tigran, it was only a matter of synapses before she was stuck again with Avo. He had pretended to love her, and she couldn't imagine a crueler lie. She dreamed sad, silly dreams of taking his love to an appraiser's shop, watching his heart go under an appraiser's loupe. She wished she hadn't been so eager to believe, so young and crazy and impatient for love.

She wished, too, after all these years, that she wasn't still doubting her doubt. Short passing moments of the day when the clearest light in the world came through in her heart, when she knew as certainly as a thing can be known that Ruben—from envy or hate—had lied, and that Avo's love was real.

No matter, though. All in the past now. Now what she had were those glorious mornings, her nephew and niece on the rug with the baby, speaking about nothing at all except for the future.

Now her daughter was two years old but more heightened than that. On the roof in January, she rolled the dice. Red faces, white pips. How many of those mornings with her cousins would Araksya go on to remember? Many, Mina hoped. Let more of them come. Tonight they would go to Talin's recital, and just over there, in the snow-scattered pines and larches, just up in the mountains there, that's where the skiers go. Tomorrow, Mina decided, she would take the children to the lift.

"Are you ready to go inside?" she asked her daughter. Her husband would be home soon, and she hadn't chopped the cabbage. It pained her to think of him going hungry for even one minute.

19

Kirovakan, Soviet Armenia, 1983

One last time as the workday ended, before he rushed off to the recital his niece was due to give, Galust admired the pin in his lapel. Gold and rimmed in pearl, the pin brought the job at the census bureau a kind of ancillary beauty that—after logging names and numbers in meticulously sharpened graphite all day—made him feel important. A civic mechanic, Mina had called him once, where names and dates were the nuts and bolts of history, and his calling was to ratchet them into place.

The pin said as much. Every morning, descending the elevator from the top floor of the tallest building in Kirovakan, as he walked across the city square to the administration building, he could feel the eyes of the citizens fall upon his pin. There he goes, they seemed to say, our next Secretary of the Regional Committee!

One last look in the mirror, then, before the clock reached the hour when he could rush home for a quick dinner. Beside his reflection, on the desk, he saw his wife and daughter. The two-year-old with the same chin as Mina, so steep that the bottom lip seemed to hang off the end of her face. Like a beautiful fish, he thought, and that's what he called Araksya, his little *dzuk*.

He was thinking, Fish, fish, fish, as he packed his typewriter for the day. That was when the knock came at the door.

"Sorry," he called out, locking the door. He straightened his pin in a mirror. "The office is closed for the day. Back in the morning."

Technically, the office was open for five more minutes, a fact that painfully discredited Galust's pin. Earlier, he'd given himself permission for this one transgression, justifying it by remembering all the compliments his work had received since he was transferred to Kirovakan from Leninakan. In just five years, he'd whipped the city's census bureau into shape. He'd earned the pin that suggested his future promotion.

He held his breath, hoping the person at the door wouldn't insist. One word, and Galust knew he'd fold and stay late to work.

No response came. Galust counted silently to one hundred, just to be safe.

At the count of ninety, he picked up his typewriter, which folded neatly into a smart blue briefcase with golden clasps that brought out the pin on his lapel. Then he pressed his ear to the door, waited a beat, and poked his head out into the hall.

The coast seemed clear. Locking up, he left the office and then the building, which let out into the city square, just across from the old statue Mina despised so much, the statue of Sergey Kirov. Whenever she came to see Galust, she would always walk around the entire city square to avoid getting near it, and he never asked why. He didn't want to burden her with questions or imply that he didn't love every part of her, even her eccentricities.

Love. He was a man unafraid to do it. When he was transferred from Leninakan to Kirovakan, his colleagues joked that he—sentimental, unguarded—would fit right in. He laughed along with the jokes, but he never explained how he'd come to be so unabashedly romantic. He'd failed to love his first wife and had always regretted the young man he'd been with her. Every doctor in Armenia had checked her, and no one could pinpoint why she'd been unable to get pregnant. He was fine, according to the doctors, and the invisibility of his first wife's issue made the problem difficult to trust. Galust's mother—meaning well, he still believed—kept telling her that the problem was in her head, that if only she wanted the baby badly enough, then she'd be fixed, a bit of nonsense that turned his wife depressive and bitter. Galust found himself in the terrible position of sympathizing with both his wife and his mother, whose yearning for a grandchild seemed intensely personal. He defended one to the other with all of his heart, so that he ended up without the trust of either. The truth was he believed his first wife was not, as his mother claimed, "faking it," and yet also felt that her inability to get pregnant was somehow a warning from fate: they weren't meant to be together. All of this led to him not loving her as well as he could have loved her, picking on her eccentricities, and now, over a decade after her death, he remembered her and missed her and regretted the man he'd been when she was his wife. He was much older now, almost sixty, and worked hard to avoid his earlier mistakes, loving Mina as well as he was able to, as kindly and as gratefully as he actually felt, walking home from the office, picturing her with their little fish in her arms.

Halfway through the city square, Galust heard a man calling his name. "Mr. Avakian," the man said, "I was just knocking on your door."

Galust turned and had to raise his chin to see the man's face. He was monstrous—huge and baldheaded, with a nasty deformation above his eyes—and Galust clutched the pin at his lapel. "We'll be open again in the morning," he offered without stopping.

"Please listen for just a minute," the man said. Again Galust looked at him and saw that the deformation was actually a burn.

Otherwise he seemed respectable enough—clean-shaven in a desperate way, as though he'd just shaved for the first time in many months, with nicks along his throat.

"All right," Galust said. "What is it?"

"You used to be the census man in Leninakan, yeah? I spent my early childhood there. I'm wondering if you knew my family."

The pin in Galust's lapel twinkled. "I'm sure I did. I knew every name in that city. What's yours?"

"Gregoryan," the man said, and Galust instantly remembered the tragedy.

"Were you there, in the factory fire? Is that how you got your scar?" he asked.

"No, but my parents were there."

Galust apologized, though that didn't seem right. He offered the man a cigarette and kept him company as he smoked. That seemed better, but still not quite right, either. "In some ways," he finally said, "I miss Leninakan."

"Oh yeah?"

"Kirovakan is beautiful, don't get me wrong. But everyone here is very sensitive. In Leninakan, no one would get offended by anything. We'd laugh at everyone and everything, and then we'd drink together and keep laughing. At least that's how I remember it. Here, everyone's very polite."

"Polite's not bad."

"No, no. Don't get me wrong. In most ways, I'd rather be here. In the most important ways."

"Yeah?"

Galust lit a cigarette for himself and pointed its heat off into the distance. "You see that building over there—the tallest one in the city? Every evening, my wife and daughter and mother wait for me in there to get home from work."

"That's very sweet."

"Ah, it's this city. Gentle people. My wife turned me into a sap the day I met her. Then my baby girl arrived, and I've basically turned into pudding. You should've seen me in Leninakan. I was much tougher. I could drink anyone—even a man your size—under the table."

Gregoryan said, "You know, I haven't heard a joke from Leninakan in a long time. You know any good ones?"

Galust laughed before the punch line even came to him. He said, "You know how people from Aparan are notoriously stupid? Well, this man there returns to his office after lunch and asks his secretary, 'While I was out, did I get a phone call from a man with a mustache?' "

Gregoryan smiled, finishing his cigarette. "That's a good one."

Galust stomped his cigarette out, too, but found himself sticking around. "I've got a million more," he said.

"Let me buy you a drink," Gregoryan said, and Galust said, "One quick one, okay."

Mina zipped Araksya into her little coat. Galust wasn't home in time, and they'd skipped dinner, and all day the gray sky had teased rain, and if she waited another minute, she'd be late to the recital and caught in the worst of the storm.

"We need to leave now," Mina told her mother-in-law, tugging at the fingers of her gloves.

"I'm not leaving without my son," Galust's mother said. "And you, a woman arriving at an event without her husband—I've never heard of such a thing. I'll wait for him, I'll do what you should be doing. You go on, you go on without me. I'll wait for him here. God forbid I ever see a concert again before I die. I used to go to concerts every month. People knew me as the lady who went to concerts."

"This isn't a concert, Mom, it's just kids having fun."

"Not a concert? Look at your daughter's gown. I hate that shade of green, but you chose it anyway. It won't look nice on the stage."

"She's not going onstage, Mom. This is her cousin's recital. We'll just be in the audience."

"And watch, her father will run to join you straight from work and leave me here all by myself."

Mina apologized, but there was no heart in it. She took her daughter by the hand and led her down the elevator of the tallest building in Kirovakan, and as soon as they stepped out from under the awning, the rain broke free over the city. Mina lifted the hood of her daughter's coat, leading her by the hand between the battered domes of umbrellas rushing from the streets to the covered shelters in the city square. She watched her daughter admire the hazed and glowing world. Mina had always loved the city in the rain. City rain allowed a kind of rebounding vision, the way bats twisted echoes into shapes. Everything—the sloping roofs of Volgas and Ladas parked along the motorway, the eyelid awnings of butchers and cafés, the bouquets of streetlamps—appeared outlined in a colorless glow. Haloed, like her daughter in her hooded coat, as they climbed the steps of the recital hall.

Sometime between the first and second drink, Galust had invited Gregoryan home for dinner with his family, and between the second and third drink, Galust remembered the recital.

It came to him in the middle of a joke Gregoryan was telling, the panic. Maybe, he thought, he could blame his faulty memory on the unexpected visit. Gregoryan had thrown him off his routine. But what was his excuse a month ago, when, for the first time since receiving it, he'd forgotten to wear the pin in his lapel to work? Or two weeks ago, when it had happened again? Or just last week, when he'd taken a break to go to Mano's shop for a new carton of cigarettes? He'd smoked the same brand for forty years, but on the walk over to Mano's, he couldn't remember the name. He could picture the case—blue and white box with a yellow continent in the corner—but the name escaped him. He took it as a blessing that Mano had the case waiting for him, as usual. Galust didn't need to stand there in his embarrassment, trying to recall the brand as if reaching for an olive at the bottom of an empty jar. He'd thanked Mano and stared at the word splashed across the case. *Belomorkanal*. It hardly rang a bell. Three packs a week for forty years, and the name hardly rang a bell. In the office that day, he'd torn out a page and done the math: almost 125,000 cigarettes. The number astonished him almost as much as the fact of his forgetting. When he'd told Mina, she'd laughed, and so he'd laughed, too. But now he'd forgotten his niece's recital. Where would the forgetting stop? The terrorizing idea came to him that one day he'd forget the name of his little fish. Galust slapped money onto the table. His daughter—Araksya, Araksya, Araksya—was with her mother at the recital hall, and he was supposed to be there with them. He'd forgotten.

The two men ran together to the tallest building in Kirovakan to fetch Galust's mother.

"Who is he?" said his mother, dressed in a blue gown. "Why are you late? The recital started forty minutes ago! If I'd known you were bringing a guest, I'd have gone myself. I like to see concerts, you know. Something different for a change. I'll go put on my shoes."

"My niece is singing," Galust told Gregoryan.

"I can leave, no problem."

"Perfect," said Galust's mother.

"No, Mom. It'll be over soon, we're already late. I've asked my new friend to dinner, and we're still on for when we get back. He'll come with us to the recital, if he doesn't mind, and we'll all have dinner together after."

"And who will make the dinner? Not your wife, whose borscht is hardly edible."

"We'll go to Mano's on the way back and bring food home."

"And spend money when we already have perfectly good food here?"

"We'll plan during the walk, Mom. We need to leave now."

"I'm ready," she said. "I'm waiting for you!"

The theater was full. It was only a little amphitheater near the city square, but it was raised in sophistication by the number of people and the manner of dress in the audience—fathers and mothers and uncles and aunts and grandparents and cousins in fine suits and gowns, bearing flowers for the talent they called their own, standing and talking in large groups in the aisles or else craning their necks and turning in their seats arranged in rows. The whole enterprise seemed holier than the playful, childish exhibit Mina had anticipated, rather more like a christening than a show, and suddenly, she regretted her raincoat and the ugly simple dress she wore beneath it, and her lack of earrings, and her showing up alone, without her husband. She recognized some of the parents in the third row, including her sister, and smiled and waved hello from a distance and covered her chin.

Leading her daughter, Mina began her search for consecutive empty seats. She had to ask a whole family to move down the aisle to make room. She thanked them for this as if they'd pulled her from a lake of fire. Still, only three empty seats were in the row. She planted her daughter into one, took another herself, and draped her raincoat over the empty seat beside her to save it for Galust.

The chair would be wet when he arrived, but at least it would be a seat. Galust's mother could stand in the aisle.

The lights dimmed, and the last of the gossips took their seats. Twice she had to whisper—and then repeat, louder—an explanation that the seat next to hers was reserved for her husband, and she could feel the eyes of the people standing in the aisle staring at the wet coat draped over that chair as the notes of the first song ended and the first footfalls of choreography began, and she tried to focus her attention on the children on the stage, avoiding the eyes she could feel in the dark. She took to pretending to be Lot's wife, convincing herself that turning to look for Galust now would turn her to salt, and she watched the children dance, and she prayed for a delay before her niece appeared on the stage.

And then it came—a long wispy breath of music, a single note hovering in the air before collapsing into a trill—the melody her niece had been practicing for months. And the lights came up a little in the front, and the jeweled leaves on Talin's gown reflected blue light into the audience, and she held the duduk at her lips like a pipe, straightforward and parallel to the stage. She was alone up there. The melody was a child's melody, whole notes and half notes and one tricky part with quarter notes—played on a child's duduk, miniature in size, just half the apricot wood of a standard instrument. The pitch was higher, like a record sped up, and some of the notes came through the reed as purely as breathing. Then she sang. Talin was alone up there, shining. Blue light on the faces in the crowd, none of which belonged to her uncle, and she was alone up there and shining.

Cheers and whistles. Whistles and cheers. Mina blew kisses. *You didn't see Uncle Galust? He was just over in the aisle, taking pictures.* Blew kisses. Blew kisses.

Somewhere in the middle of a choreographed song about different species of birds living in the same tree, Mina felt a hand on her shoulder. She was reflexively ready again to explain that the seat was taken, but she saw that the hand belonged to her husband. Galust moved her raincoat and sat in its puddle. He leaned over and kissed her on the shoulder. He said, "Did I miss Talin?"

Their family's song. Mina took his hand. Squeezed. Yes, he'd missed it. He lowered his voice. "A man came to my office late."

Another squeeze. *Explain later.*

"He had a burn on his face. I felt terrible."

"Please," Mina whispered.

"See? He's just over there."

Her attention left the dancing children. There in the aisle—standing among a dozen strangers, among a dozen smaller people whose blooming lives advanced untethered from hers, whose love had never belonged to her and never would—there he was. He was. The blue light from the stage washed his face browless and bare, but there, smiling a blue smile, he was, and the split in their histories began to curl and splice, and the children sang in chorus from the stage, and she felt the muscles in her face mirroring his, signaling a blue smile of her own, and she knew all at once about the roundness of time.

"You know him?" Galust said.

Another squeeze. *Let the children finish their singing.*

And when they did, the children broke free from behind the curtain and spilled from the stage to their families in the crowd. Talin ran straight to her cousin, and Galust picked both girls up and began his loving lies. *I heard you, Talin-jan, you sang beautifully.* Mina picked at the blue leaves on her niece's gown, saying, "Angel, angel," and she saw that Avo was no longer where he'd been, standing in the aisle. In fact, he was nowhere at all to be found in the theater. Without explanation, she started toward the door, pressing herself through the small gaps between people. Outside, night had come on, and the rain had been brushed aside by a cool and feathered wind, and she wrapped herself in her own arms as she spotted him, thinner than she remembered, smoking at the curb, saying her name.

She went to him. She unwrapped herself from herself and went to him.

"You know each other?" Galust asked when he came outside, carrying their daughter.

Three

20

Los Angeles, California, 1989

Late Wednesday afternoon, staked out in my Ranger at a gas station near her apartment, I waited for the woman with the dice. I'd given her ten minutes to make her excuses and join me, and already ten minutes had passed. I kept checking the rearview mirror, hoping to see her turn the corner out of the neighborhood, red fanny pack tied around her waist like a championship belt. I kept waiting, as we'd say in the business, for the pop at the sound of her music.

Meanwhile, Fuji was likewise waiting for me. By now he'd been at that jewelry store long after I'd told him I'd be back to get him, and the image of his searching out the window just as I was searching in my rearview mirror, impatient and lonely, broke my heart. Back home, my business had been stripped away, and it occurred to me, as I waited for Mina, that Fuji and I would have to invent a new kind of life for ourselves when we returned.

For now, again and again, I checked my mirrors. Instead of finding Mina there, I found myself remembering the morning I'd tried to teach The Brow Beater to drive. I'd told him to adjust the mirrors for his height, and maybe that was the connection. Back then we were still driving the Catalina, hadn't traded it in for the truck.

We were someplace in Wyoming where cliques of wild horses flattened the grass to shining at the foot of the snowcapped Bighorns. We'd stopped for gas seven thousand feet above sea level, and I remember watching from the pump as The Brow Beater stayed in the warmth of the car, spinning between his fingers one of those arrowheads he collected.

Even the enormous mountains of his hometown were half as tall, he'd said. I left to use the gas station bathroom, and when I came back, I found him way up on a snowbank behind the pumps. It was March 1980, not long before he disappeared, and the sky was huge, and the patches of snow on the ground reflected the sun so strongly I could hardly see him up there. He was looking down on the city and dreaming about something, I can't say what. When he came down to use the bathroom, I stepped into his boot prints and climbed the snowbank right up to where he'd been standing.

Wasn't the world supposed to look smaller from way up high? But the sun was directly overhead, and nothing cast a shadow on the snow, and everything—the flickering bed of sagebrush, and the train tracks hollowing a path through them, and the mountains, and the metallic blasts of horse trailers behind cars on the highway, and a few strangers looking up at me from the gas station, shading their eyes with a hand as if saluting—*everything* was saturated by this flat golden tint, and all the world seemed made of the same stuff, and it stretched on from me to the snow slopes and beyond, and wasn't the world supposed to look smaller? No, the golden world seemed endless. Timeless, too. I imagined those early settlers, those colonizers, coming west for gold. I pictured a man who'd heard about the mines near South Pass, Wyoming, arriving too late, a man who'd come to this place for one reason, who'd abandoned his family and the woman he loved for something that no longer existed. I pictured that man alone and ashamed. Up on that snowbank over the golden everywhere, alone with the vast sameness of the world, I'd traveled through time to be there, sifting alongside the forlorn prospector. I was with him at his final flash of hope, a discovery of golden flakes in the reservoir behind the gas station that had long since gone dry, golden flakes no one else could see, because he simply had to see them. Maybe word got out—gold!—and others arrived in droves and huddled around his shimmering hands. How long did they rejoice before they realized the gold was fool's gold or—worse—imagined altogether? How long before they saw his cupped hands less as an offering and more as a begging? How long did they watch him strain the invisible stuff between his fingers before they understood he'd gone mad?

He'd abandoned his home on a trick of the heart, on a story he'd stopped believing. I wondered what condition a man like that could return home in.

When I got back to the car, I told The Brow Beater that, after almost two years in the passenger seat, it was time for him to learn to drive.

The Brow Beater squeezed into the driver's seat and cranked the rusting door shut. He hunched, elbows digging into his hips. I said, "Turn and check over your shoulder," but he couldn't afford the space. I watched him suck in his gut and almost dislocate something just to find the seat lever.

"You got it," I said, but The Brow Beater leaned on the door until it popped open and fell out.

"I can't, bro," he said, stretching his legs.

"You got it, big fella," I said. I buckled my seat belt. "We're not leaving till you learn."

"You just want me to drive, bro, so you can sleep."

Maybe I should've joked with him, said, "You're damn right—it's about time you carry your weight in this marriage," but we'd been on the road so long, and lately, he'd become distant and quiet, less curious about his new country, less willing to play along with ribs and jokes, less interested in making me feel like I had a responsibility to him, a responsibility to teach him something, to break him in. All he seemed to care about in those last months was his money, and I wanted him to think bigger than that. I got out of the Catalina and said, "I want you to learn because you need to learn, all right? Every American should know how to drive a car. You want to be an American, don't you? You should enjoy the open road in front of you with your hands on the steering wheel like free will itself, like a big circular shield against fate, you know? I want you to learn because you should want to by now. You've been here long enough, haven't you? You speak English good enough, you get paid good enough. You gotta understand. Out here, a car's not just a car. This isn't like where you're from, where the government issues every family a ball-and-chain Volga so you get to the meat-processing plant on time, okay? Out here, a car's a portal, you understand. A car is independence. A car is not having to spend your whole damn life waiting for someone else to join you. So do you want to be an American or not?"

He tried, but not for himself. I could tell he was trying for me. He stalled again and again, and the Catalina went from the gas station to the pharmacy, a quarter mile or so down the road, before he cut the engine.

"Okay, bro," he said. "I think I learned it. You drive again."

"Let's get on the highway," I said. "You're not driving if you don't have a little speed."

But The Brow Beater said, "I'm done, bro."

That was when I reached over and put both of my hands over his one hand on the wheel. It was like we were praying together, two nonbelievers in a Pontiac Catalina. I said, "This is just like Gil.

I took him out a few times in our dad's 1942 Buick Super, and he wanted to quit after a few stalls. He was only twelve, mind you. We got into a fight, and he punched me right in the forehead, and if you look close enough, you can still make out a little dent right there above my left eyebrow. He was a kid, but man, he had diamonds for knuckles. Only reason he learned to drive that day was because he had to take me to the hospital to get stitched up. Me, bleeding and writhing all over the passenger seat, Gil absolutely freaking, trying to time the clutch and keep blood off our dad's leather at the same time, stalling and screeching all the way to the hospital. So don't tell me you can't do it, big fella. *That* was a challenging driving lesson. You've got it easy. Wide-open roads, no speed limits this far out in the country. Gil would've killed in this setting. My brother would've peeled out of the gas station and—"

"Bro," Avo said, so quiet I couldn't ignore it. I had to lean in to pay attention. "Your brother is dead. I am not your brother, bro."

He shouldered the door open and let the wind hammer it shut. He went and sat with all his weight on the hood, right in front of me, and I could feel the back wheels almost lift off the ground.

Eventually, the gas station attendant knocked at my window and told me to go wait somewhere else. I was curious enough—about where Mina needed to be taken with those dice—to give her ten more minutes, but I knew I'd have to draw the line soon. For now, I pulled alongside the curb out back, near the alleyway between the gas station and the neighborhood. For ten more minutes, I told myself, I'd keep my eye on the mirrors. I'd always attributed my honest conversations in cars to the confined nature of the space, but it occurred to me now how impossible it was, surrounded by reflections, to ignore the fact that what was framed in the windshield one minute would soon be swallowed up in the mirrors.

I was still thinking about my admonition of The Brow Beater that morning in Wyoming, the way I'd wanted him so badly to want to become an American. I'd been sensitive to his growing ambivalence about America ever since a gig in Concrete, Oregon, where a crowd had chanted horrible racial epithets while he wrestled. This was during the Iran hostage crisis, and we were playing that angle—The Brow Beater as an anti-American Islamic so-and-so—so as far as I was concerned, we'd done a good job getting the crowd to react with serious energy. We'd played the angle in one form or another many times before, but this time, The Brow Beater got to the locker room and unlaced his boots in a different mood.

I let him cool off, and then in the car that night, I mentioned offhandedly that if the gimmick wasn't working for him, we could always change it up. I started telling him about all the gimmicks I might've tried myself if I hadn't gotten injured. An astronaut, a spy, a new-age healer, and my favorite, a doctor who assists in suicide. For that one, I had a finisher in mind: a sleeper hold called Painless Death. I must've gone on for an hour. Finally, I said, "It's wrestling, big fella. We're only limited by our creativity and how much we're willing to work."

Without the pretense of a segue, The Brow Beater started listing all the gimmicks we'd come across in our time together. Pretty soon it became clear to me what he was saying. For white wrestlers, he could name all sorts of heroes and villains with distinct personalities and motivations and goals. But the black wrestlers all had chains or grass skirts, and the Indians were noble savages and almost never portrayed by real Indians, and the Mexicans wore mariachi hats or masks, and the brown folks wore turbans and sheets and shoes with curled toes, and he listed all the hackneyed gimmicks of his own that even the smartest mark wouldn't remember. The Shah, The Ra, The Beast from the Middle East. Killer fucking Kebob.

I said, "Look, it's not perfect, but wrestling is an art form built on types. You are what you appear to be. Our job is to emphasize what's already obvious about us."

"Bro," he said. "Obvious to who?"

That's when I told The Brow Beater the truth about Joyce. I hadn't meant to—I'd never mentioned her name to anyone—but I started telling him about Joyce's letters to my mother, her inability to accept my brother's death, and the time I found her in that bookstore in Tucson, Arizona. Pretty soon I was telling him the rest of the story, and in the car, I couldn't help but tell him the whole truth, the full picture of the mess I'd made with her.

After spotting her in that bookstore, I told The Brow Beater, I tried to forget about Joyce altogether. But when Kennedy was shot, I thought of her. I was with three other wrestlers in a motel room in St. Cloud, Minnesota, watching the horror televised, and Joyce was the first person who came to mind. At the time, I thought maybe it was because Jackie Kennedy with her wide-set eyes had always slightly reminded me of Joyce, and now—after she'd lost her man so suddenly, so violently—the resemblance was etched in stone. But later, when the monks were self-immolating on the news in a motel room in Boulder, Colorado, or when King was gunned down on a gym television set on the verge of Tallahassee, when I found myself thinking at every televised tragedy first and solely of Joyce, I began to worry. I began to consider, late at night, the possibility that Joyce and her conspiracies—which had seemed to me like sad fantasies during the years when the country was awash in its white, postwar glow—now seemed less impossible. As the country rioted, as I watched black wrestlers get taunted with nooses in stands in the South (which I'd seen before but hadn't paid attention to), as I saw uniformed servicemen spat upon, as I watched footage of brown-water navy vessels blasting orange arcs of napalm into civilian villages, as I read John White's report on the purely fictitious events at Tonkin, as I saw man after man who stood up get shot down, I thought: Good God, my country could've done it. They could've traded Gil, just as Joyce had said. In those moments, the idea no longer felt like a conspiracy but a clue, a clear emblem of my country's madness.

During the absolute height of tension and division in those years, when civil war or martial law seemed imminent, when both the hateful and the hated resorted to the comfort of their groups, I returned to Tucson once more. I found Joyce in an adobe house with three towering cacti splintering the yard. It was 1974, and Joyce had done well for herself as a new-age healer. She saw me and said, "You've injured yourself." It was probably evident from the stiff way I turned my half-healed neck, but I was so relieved by the recognition of my pain that I went up and hugged her tenderly. She placed different stones to my neck, limestone and quartz. She was crazy—I knew that—but she seemed newly in control. She'd been high on everything, she told me, so nothing much lifted her anymore but the crystal-clear truth. Though her study of geology in college gave her business an air of scientific authenticity, I knew she was no healer. Still, she impressed me. She seemed brave and relentless, like a woman who'd built a well at a mirage and refused to stop pumping. And I wasn't in any position to judge, staging fights for a living. I didn't know what story I was telling myself about myself anymore, what story my country was telling me, what story the world was trying to tell, and whether I had a role at all to play in it. I was so low that year that I ended up staying with Joyce for seven months. She burned sage around me, kissed me on the neck, and didn't charge me a dime for rent. I was so grateful, I didn't mind when she brought up those old conspiracies about Gil. I didn't even balk when, one night halfway through my stay, she asked me into her bed. In fact, I was grateful.

We got married in a little ceremony at the adobe house. A pastor made the trip from the city, and a few members of Joyce's community gathered in the living room as he led our vows. We lived like that for almost a year, pretending to heal the sick and damaged, pretending to heal ourselves. Pretending so well that we forgot we were pretending. In the end, we even discussed exhuming my brother's body, just to prove the extent of our faithful performance. Maybe I would've carried on that way, grasping at distrust like a salve. I might've held my brother's bones and claimed they were not his. But wrestling came calling. An ailing bodybuilder arrived in the adobe house for a geotherapy session, and I found a new role to play, and I asked if he'd ever considered professional wrestling. Soon I'd dubbed him Mickey "Makeshift" Starr, and I saw money in him, and only Johnny Trumpet would take my phone calls. With Trumpet's help, which I told him I'd always owe him for, I stopped living my own gimmick in Tucson with Joyce. With Trumpet's help, I broke Makeshift into the business and took him on the road, and we drew real money and we drove real miles. I'd never told anyone about Joyce and me except The Brow Beater. Joyce, my brother's girl, was my ex-wife. I knew I'd never forgive myself for being with her, and I also knew I'd never forgive myself for leaving her. But I was amazed at the phenomenon I started to witness once I was gone—that as my confidence in my new role grew, so did my confidence in my country. They seemed to go hand in hand, those two, so as I transformed again from Terry Krill to Angel Hair, Nixon fell to his disgraceful end, and the war fell to its, and the country seemed to regain some hold on its larger vision. And when I told

The Brow Beater the truth—serving, as I was, as his liaison to the country—I felt that my old faith in my country was once again redeemable. My country and myself—The Brow Beater had helped me find that the more I believed in one, the more I cared to believe in the other, that we were each other's keepers.

But The Brow Beater didn't seem moved by my story, and soon we were fighting in Wyoming. Finally, I brushed him off as a cynic. Nothing he could've said would've changed my mind. I had worked too hard to rebuild my faith in my country. I couldn't let it dissolve again.

Finally, my wait was over. Someone was in the mirror, approaching. I got out of the truck and stretched my legs.

"Shen," I said, recognizing the man from Mina's rooftop. I didn't know his friends, two large buzzcuts in tailored suits.

"Buddy," Shen said. "What're you doing in Glendale, huh?"

"I told you," I said. "Cat business."

The three of them started speaking Armenian, a language I was beginning to think I should learn.

"Long trip for a cat," Shen said, kicking my Washington plate with his heel.

"It's a rental," I said, and when Shen translated, they all looked at the Ranger, camper shell rusting at the bolts.

"Try again," Shen said. "What are you doing with Mina? She has a bandage on her hand, we noticed. Are you trying to intimidate her?"

"God, no."

"Are you a police officer? Are you working with the police?"

"Do I look like a cop? Is there something you're doing in my country that warrants a police presence?"

"Your country," Shen said. "Huh. Well, you've been sitting at this gas station for half an hour, and you lied about the rental, so you'll understand why we don't believe you when you say you're just minding your own business in your own country."

"I'm just an old wrestler," I said.

This seemed to please Shen, and he translated for his friends. "Wrestling is very big in my country. I used to wrestle pretty good. Let's have a wrestling match."

I had to laugh. I said, "I'm a professional. I don't wrestle for free."

"Just this once."

"I'm sixty-two," I said. "I got a bad neck. Otherwise I would've loved to kick your ass."

"Your hair makes you look younger. Did you wrestle freestyle, folk-style, or Greco-Roman?"

"Shen, this has nothing to do with you."

"I'm just curious about your wrestling. Or is that a lie, too?"

"I wasn't that kind of wrestler," I said.

"Ohhh," Shen said, drawing it out. He turned to his friends. All I could make out was "Hulk Hogan."

"You're one of those American wrestlers," Shen said. "What's the word? Fake."

"Hold on, now," I said. "I don't know who told you that, but that's not true. Trust me. What I did was very real."

"But the fighting, though. It's fake."

Call it predetermined, I could've said. Call it entertainment. But not that.

"You seem to be an expert," I said. "You're acting tough with your friends, but who are you, really?"

The buzzcuts removed their jackets. I tightened my ponytail.

"Take it back," I said, "and I'll get in my truck and leave without a problem. But you've got to take back what you said about my livelihood. Understood?" I waited while Shen and the others corroborated their message. "Take it back, Shen. Take back what you said about my life."

He licked a corner of his lips and looked me square in the face. "Fake," he said.

I lunged.

21

Kirovakan, Soviet Armenia, 1983

"They were very good friends, growing up together," Galust told his mother over dinner, and she winked and said, "I bet they were."

The snark couldn't reach Mina, not with Avo back. There he really was, seated at one end of the long table in her home, directly across from her husband. She looked back and forth between them as between players across a backgammon board, and nothing—not her mother-in-law's snide commentary or Araksya's fussiness in her high chair—could trawl the joy from her. It was as though the pieces of her had all come home, and she could begin at last to bear them off.

"So what happened to your face?" her mother-in-law asked Avo.

"He moved here from Leninakan after the factory fire," Galust said.

"That was earlier," Avo said, "when I was a teenager."

"And you left because why?"

"He was traveling the world," Galust said.

"And you're back because the world is overrated?"

Mina said, "Let the man eat, he's skinnier than he was at fifteen."

"It's okay, I'm eating, I'm eating."

Araksya began to cry.

Avo said, "No, the world isn't overrated."

"Do you have a favorite place?" Galust asked.

"Excluding brothels," his mother said.

"Did you like America?" Galust asked.

"It's too big for yes or no, I think," Avo said. "Yes *and* no."

Galust said, "Our daughter is only two but can add and subtract already. Care to see?"

Araksya cried.

"One plus one," Galust tried, but Araksya wouldn't stop crying.

"I enjoyed a place called Carlsbad, New Mexico, very much."

"One plus one, baby."

"He's trying to tell you about America," Mina said.

"I'm listening and listening," her mother-in-law said, "but we haven't heard a single thing yet about the concert. We shouldn't just dust the concert under the rug because an old friend of hers arrived."

"One plus one, baby."

"Talin was nearly perfect up there," Galust's mother said. "But those blue sequins were a touch gaudy, I thought."

"She was perfect," Mina said, and she kissed her daughter's cheeks.

"Two," Araksya said.

"Two!" Galust cheered.

"Very impressive," Avo said.

"Little girl," Galust's mother said, "lift your chin and stick it out as far as you can when you speak, like we practiced."

Araksya fixed her posture.

The other day Mina had yelled at her mother-in-law, having caught her teaching Araksya to stick out her jaw. She covered her own chin while she yelled. Galust's mother had said, "I'm only trying to make her more beautiful. What's wrong with being more beautiful?" Mina hadn't responded to that but now she wished she had.

"I have an idea," Mina said now. She wanted to say, "Why don't Mom and Araksya go put on their diapers and get ready for bed?" But she left out the diapers and said, "Go to bed. We'll clean up out here."

Araksya, out of her chair, ran straight to her room. Galust's mother looked one last time at her son, at Avo, and then back at Mina. "I'm coming," she called to her granddaughter, and left the table.

"She's beautiful," Avo said.

"No argument there," Galust said, "but she's a bit too old for you." Everyone laughed a bit in that stalling way people tend to do in new groups. Finally, Galust sighed and said, "No, my daughter—yes. She's a gorgeous and brilliant little girl. She's my little fish."

A silence fell between them, and Mina said she'd open a bottle of vodka if the men were in the mood to drink. "I am, anyway," she said, getting up.

When she returned, they all three moved to the living room, where the lights were low and where Galust had put on his favorite record, a rendition of Khachaturian's *Spartacus* by the Vienna Philharmonic. A ballet, Mina remembered, pouring the drinks. Galust's first wife had been a ballerina, she knew. Mina poured four vodkas before realizing they were only three in the room. Discreetly, she downed the extra before joining the men.

"A drinking wife—boy, times have changed," Galust said, goading Avo for either sympathy or a laugh. He had never made mention of it before, Mina thought, and she realized they'd never had a male audience to perform their home life in front of. It was the least attractive she'd found him since their initial meeting, but she indulged him because she didn't want to be sour. She laughed and then said, "Belligerence: no longer just for men."

"Your parents," Avo said. "Still living in the building? First floor?"

"The whole family," Galust said. "Her sister, too, on floor number three."

"The Armenian dream," Avo said, raising his glass.

"It's been helpful, especially with the baby," Mina said.

Galust agreed. "But it's about time we start looking for a bigger place. In a few months, Araksya will need a room of her own."

"It's a beautiful name."

"It's my mother's name," Galust said while Mina sipped her vodka. "If it had been a boy, we would've named him after my father. Shaunt. He would have loved to be a grandfather, my dad. Heart issues all his life, though. I promised I'd name my first son for him, and it's the best promise I'll ever keep."

"Salut," Avo said. They raised glasses again. Galust got up to get the bottle, insisting that Mina stay seated.

"The best promise I'll ever keep—I knew a man who asked me that once," Galust said from the bookshelf at the end of the room. The shelf served as a stationary drinking cart. He was looking into the glasses he was filling, but it was clear he was talking to Avo. It was a story he'd never mentioned to Mina.

"He was a Russian I met in Leninakan. This was a long time ago, when I was your age. A boy, really. What, you're twenty-seven? I thought I was a man already then, too, but that should have been my first clue. Only boys think they're men already. Real men think they're still boys. I was thirty years old, married already, with six years under my belt at the Leninakan bureau. I thought I had my whole life laid out ahead of me like a map. We had a little problem with getting pregnant, but my wife was seeing medical doctors and witch doctors, too, and between the two of them, I figured a solution would be found sooner or later. She was at home that night with all her female relatives, undergoing some sort of women's magic, and so I steered clear. After work, I went to a place above the market where I'd heard alcohol was served. It was hot outside, and I craved a cold beer. The place was almost empty. Just a few drunks and the friend who kept serving them. I sat at a table in the corner, listening to the radio, enjoying the music and the cold beer."

"Sweetheart, please—tell the story, don't relive it."

"The details are important! I want you to feel the moisture on the outside of the bottle."

"The only moisture is our drool as we fall asleep."

"A wife who talks to her husband like this in front of another man. We're in different times, my friend."

Avo smiled. "Go on."

"So I'm in the bar, killing time, when a very old man walks in. I can tell right away that he's Russian—he had those beady Russian eyes but also enormous features otherwise, with hair as white as Siberia and a mustache that would make even Stalin say, 'It's a bit much.' Well, this old man sits next to me and asks if I speak Russian. I do, a bit—my father used to speak it around the house. This man wants to know if I've noticed an increase in the area's seismic activity, if I've felt the ground shaking more frequently than in the past. At this, I point to the drunks at the bar and say, 'They'll be so relieved to hear it's not just them.' And when he laughs, that's when I know the Russian is not a crazy person. That's how you can tell the sane from the insane—laughter. Crazy people don't laugh at jokes, you understand. Their laughter is either absent or totally uncalled for. I learned that as a boy, when there was a crazy man in my grandfather's village we used to—"

"Don't you dare start another story in the middle of the first one," Mina said. It wasn't beyond her that she was performing, too, a kind of cantankerous-wife routine, but the performance was fun, and she was slightly drunk, and she imagined she could be behaving much worse than this, demonstrating her wifehood to the boy she once was engaged to marry.

"Okay, so—I tell the Russian I haven't noticed anything shakier than usual, and he seems relieved. He explains that he's a geophysicist, one of a number of scientists who've been traveling between Moscow and Yerevan for decades, measuring what he called hydrocarbons in drill sites across the Araks and Octemberian basins. You're looking at me skeptically, love. I remember every word he said! My memory is my calling. Anyway, he and his team had been drilling sites for oil and natural gas, sites Moscow had identified as having 'exploration potential.' He said they'd been drilling since the 1930s, and despite oil fields in Azerbaijan and Georgia, they hadn't found anything yet in Armenia. It took two years to dig one well to two thousand meters, and dozens of these sites had wells as deep as five thousand meters. All, apparently, for nothing."

Avo stood up, insisting it was his turn to fill the glasses.

"I told the Russian there was no harm in that, no harm in looking, that the thrill of exploration was inherent in men, and a lot of other bullshit a kid who thinks he's a man might say out loud without shame. But the Russian said I was absolutely, one hundred percent wrong. There was a great, great deal of harm in all that digging, and if I hadn't felt it shaking beneath my feet yet, I would soon. He said he'd warned Gosplan early on about the excessive drilling. He projected massive earthquakes in the region as a result. But his warnings went ignored, the drilling continued, and he remained among those at the helm. Now, as he was nearing the end of his life, he said, he regretted his life's work. He'd promised he'd never stop searching for oil in Armenia, and he regretted keeping that promise. He said it was the worst promise he'd ever kept. He drank his beer, and it was as if an idea occurred to him mid-gulp, because beer almost came out of his nose when he asked me that question I started with: the best promise I'd ever kept. I remember I said something about my wedding vows, how my wife and I were struggling to get pregnant, but how I was keeping my promise to love her through health and sickness, good times and bad. And we'd had enough to drink by then that we started to joke about how our problems were more alike than they'd first appeared, drilling with no luck and all that. I see you looking at me, love—thinking, Okay, a fine story, Galust-jan, but where's the point? Well, a story isn't a pencil, love. It doesn't need a point to work. When my father was sick, and it looked like I would never be a father myself, I thought of that Russian, and I made a promise I had no business making. I swore that one day I would have a son and name him after my father. I was already in my mid-forties, and the chances were slim. I had no business making that promise. But I felt compelled to say it, and I believed it. And now I'm fiftysomething, I still believe it, and I intend to keep it. When it happens, it will be the best promise I've ever kept, because of how improbable it is, and because of how much luck and love it will take to come true. It will be like striking oil in Armenia."

The end had come for *Spartacus*. Mina went to the record player and put on a new album, one of the few British albums she'd kept after all these years. *Pink Moon*. She wondered if Avo recognized the music. She couldn't say. He seemed not to notice much of anything as he finished his drink. Finally, he said it was getting late, that he should be going. The last train to Leninakan would leave soon. He had a friend there, he explained, an old boss of his named Shorty who'd been transferred to the factory his parents once worked in.

He wanted to visit his uncle there, too, whom he hadn't seen since leaving all those years ago.

"How long will you be there, visiting him?" Mina said. She wanted to tell him not to bother visiting if it was only going to be a few measly hours.

Avo said, "Just to say hello, I think."

As if returning were an event only in the life of the returner.

"Not a bad idea to be where you started," Galust said. "I wish my Russian geophysicist was here, we could ask him if there's some sort of scientific reasoning for why it feels so right to be on the land where you originated."

They both stood up to shake hands and to say good night. Mina, however, remained seated. She sipped her vodka.

Just then her mother-in-law came in, dressed in a nightgown, complaining about the volume of the music. Then, before going to bed, she said, "I'll make a bed for the big man on the couch."

"I'm leaving, actually, but thank you."

"You're not leaving this late in the night. The neighbors will talk."

"Mom, he's going."

But she'd already gone to the closet and returned with blankets and sheets and pillows for the couch.

"It's too small for him to sleep there," Galust said.

Mina sipped her drink. She said, "Let him decide."

"I've slept on worse," Avo said. "This is too kind, really."

Galust said, "Your train is leaving in just a few minutes. I can drive you to the station right now, if you say so."

"He won't say so," his mother said, "but can't you see he'd prefer to leave in the morning?"

"We can't force him to stay if he doesn't want to stay," Galust said, reaching for his car key.

Avo crouched to examine the couch and then looked up to Mina. "If I'm not in the way."

And when Galust's mother kissed Mina good night, Mina braced herself for whatever pithy shot she was about to receive in her ear. But when she spoke, Galust's mother said only, "Good night, young girl."

He would take the train in the morning, then. He'd lie on a couch in the home that, in another life, could have been his. He'd lie and pretend to sleep, pretend to wake in the morning, eat breakfast beside the daughter who could have been his, the mathematically inclined little fish of a man twice his age, an old widower from the same city he'd come from himself, a man who seemed, genuinely, to understand his good luck in ending up with Mina, a man who seemed to understand how tenuous a hold he had on the fortunes of his life, including this long and comfortable couch that could've belonged to someone else instead. The music had finished an hour ago, and the vodka just after that, and the family in all its generations was asleep, and the lights were off. Avo covered his feet with one blanket and his chest with another. He waited in the dark for daylight and for the long-delayed goodbye he would give Mina and her family. Her family and nobody else's.

But he didn't have to wait for daylight to pretend to wake up, because at some point in the quiet night, Avo heard the patter of feet against the hardwood floor. A shadow approached the bookshelf bearing the liquor, and then the figure fixed a drink. Fixed two.

"Help me with the door," Mina said, carrying the drinks there. Avo removed his blankets and held the door open for her. Quietly, he followed her out and down the hallway, past the elevator to the stairwell. Up and out they went to the best view in the city, the rooftop of the tallest building in Kirovakan.

"We were both performing a little all night," Mina said, handing him one of the drinks. "I figured now we can be real."

The rain had cleared, and the lights of the city—dependent, Galust had mentioned during drinks, on hydrocarbons imported from Russia—glinted in all directions.

"Tell me what happened to your face," Mina said.

"You can imagine."

"I'm sorry. I want to be real with you," Mina said.

"You can be. You should."

"It's so strange to see you again. I didn't think I would."

"You have a good life."

"I do. I have a good life. I love my family. Galust loves me and treats me well. I'm very lucky."

"You always have been."

They looked out onto the city and drank.

"When I saw you at the theater," Mina said, but the end of the sentence never came.

"Mina."

"I didn't think I'd love my husband. I could respect him, I thought, and I could care for him. But he's been so good to me and to our child that I really do love him. And I would never hurt him."

"I wouldn't want you to."

"What I'm saying is, he's almost sixty. And he's been forgetting things lately. My parents think it's nothing, but my sister says her husband thinks it might be early signs of something more serious. So I've been worried about him lately, and then you showed up, and a decision was made right there inside of me as soon as I saw you in the theater. Do you understand, Avo? I want to be real with you. I know it's terrible, but can I be real with you?"

"You can be real."

"You left that party in this building, and I never thought I'd see you again."

"I was told I'd be able to send for you, but I had to protect you first."

"You said our year would come, and I waited as many years as I could."

"I was lied to. I couldn't put you in danger."

"I waited for you, and if you'll do the same for me now, if you'll wait for me, then maybe we can live a second life together, maybe we can—"

"After Galust—"

"Don't say it. I hate to think of it. It's terrible."

"And if he lives until a hundred?"

"We'll be seventy. And we'll start then."

Avo laughed. What was time, he thought. Just a gas, filling its container. And he could live with this container. With this container he could live.

"And in the meantime," Avo said, "I'll get my old job with Shorty in Leninakan? You and I will visit? We'll be friends?"

Mina said, "I want to be real with you." She knelt so she could set down her glass.

"I want that, too," Avo said. He held her by the arms. She had to stretch herself and pull him down by the neck to look into his eyes. His burn was terrible. A fat pouch over the eyes. She touched it softly, once, twice.

"Does it hurt?" she asked.

He couldn't even feel her touch on the scar. Instant, visible pain could fade. His other pain—invisible and slow and disbelieved—would grind him to his death.

"It hurts because they could've taken an eyebrow from someone who had two," he said, getting Mina to laugh. When she picked up her drink and went to stand by the railing, he saw the city behind her, all light and dark, pure as then and now. How lovely, once in a while, to see no blend, to feel the clear-cut difference.

"He's something of a hero in town," Mina said. "Ruben, I mean."

Avo drank, waiting for her to continue.

"Now that he's in prison, I mean, he's a hero. I swear, we only respect martyrs." She turned away from the city and looked up at him. "Did you hear me?"

"I heard you," Avo said. "I'm just— I didn't know he'd been arrested."

"In Paris. Avo, where have you been all this time?"

He struggled to begin. He said, "I made a friend in America, and a long time ago, he took me to this place in the desert. New Mexico."

"Isn't Mexico as 'new' as America?"

"I know, I know. Everything that makes sense in that country is terrible, and everything that's nonsense has a kind of grace to it. I think I'd like to go back one day. If I don't end up here or in Leninakan, I'll go back to work with my old friend." He told her his name.

"What was in New Mexico?" Mina asked.

"When I was there, we went down into these enormous caves, as far below the surface of the earth as a person can get. I wrote you a postcard from there."

"What did it say?"

"I had a plan. Saving money for a new passport, for new everything. I was going to come back. I wanted to let you know."

"You sent it from underground?"

Avo laughed. "In every way."

"Here's a question," Mina said, and she held one elbow in her opposite hand. "It might sound cold, but it's not."

"I won't take it that way."

She drank. "What else are you here for, Avo?"

"Else?"

Mina covered her chin and then took her elbow again. She said, "I get the sense that you're here for something else, too. There's no such thing as a new life and an old one, Avo-jan. You know that. Our lives aren't metaphors, halved or broken or split. Our lives are our lives, whole if they feel complete, whole if they feel incomplete. Why did you stay in America so long and not come straight here?"

"I couldn't."

"But you could now? Your obstacles hadn't changed, had they?"

"Mina."

"It sounds cold, but I don't mean it that way. I just feel there's something else. You keep avoiding it. Ask yourself. Either you're being incurious, Avo, or you're not being real. Can I give it a try?"

"Mina."

"And it might sound cold."

"I won't take it that way."

"Okay," Mina said. She swallowed another swig of her drink. "When you left, you chose Ruben over me. That's how I always saw it. Whether you think of it that way or not, I always saw you as someone who confused love for something you could only loan out to one person at a time. You could only love one of us completely, you thought, and so you made a choice. And although I never thought of love that way, I understood, and I never blamed you for making that choice. It hurt me, it ruined me for a while, but I never blamed you. Ruben was your brother, after all. I understood. But now—if I'm being real—I'm getting a little upset that you've come back all this way and you still won't have the decency to tell me why you're here. You won't tell me that you're back so you can shed your guilt. You won't tell me that you've come to see me happy in what you call my new life so you can twist that happiness into something you deserve credit for. Your choice, which you regretted, isn't regretful after all. Your choice led to all of this, my family, my baby, my happiness. And now you want me to thank you. To *thank* you. That's what I think you've come here for, if I'm being real. And I don't mean to be cold, but, well, Avo, here you go: Thank you. I'm so glad you left me without saying goodbye all those years ago. We were young and stupid and impatient for love, we didn't know what real love was, and you saved me from myself. Now I know better, and I wouldn't have been able to recognize real love without your fake love to compare it to. So, once again: Thank you, Avo-jan. Thank you."

The city careened into silence. In the dark hills, they both knew, the rain was coming.

"I know what's underneath all of this," Avo said. "I know the actual pain we're not talking about, and it has nothing to do with my leaving. Ruben told me. He told me that he told you the truth. The reason I couldn't face you when I left."

"What Ruben told me at my wedding was nothing. Confusing love for pity—I didn't need your pity then, and I don't need it now, Avo."

"Ruben probably didn't tell you the whole truth, then. That I didn't mean to—"

"Please, let's go back to—"

"I didn't mean to kill Tigran. It was an accident. Ruben probably left that part out, am I right?"

Mina didn't blink, didn't move a centimeter. And yet Avo could see that suddenly, she had changed. She was the same woman she'd always been, but different, as if she'd been stolen and replaced by an invisible horde of angels. A new, bullish glaze crossed her eyes, the eyes of a stranger.

"I only meant to injure him," Avo went on, hoping that more explanation might bring Mina back. "Ruben told me he told you all of this already, but I want to be clear. I only meant to break his hip or his leg, so he couldn't travel with you to Paris. I know that's not a pleasant thing to admit, either, but I was a kid, and now I want you to know the whole truth. Since we're being real, you know. I'm sure Ruben didn't mention the part where it was an accident, that I never meant for what happened to happen."

The way she sat. That was how he realized she hadn't known. That Ruben had lied to him.

Ruben had never told her about Tigran's death at all. He'd lied to Avo to keep him away. Only now did Mina find out, straight from Avo's own lips, and he knew by the way she sat. The way her legs buckled and folded, the way she planted herself right there in the middle of the roof in a puddle from yesterday's rain, the same rain it always was, soaked up and spilled, soaked up and spilled, again and again for all of time, the same rain they'd once lain in, playacting lovers, the same rain she sat in now, a woman who knew for the first time the truth.

Avo dropped beside her. His big legs too battered to fold. He lay flat on his back, like taking a pinfall after a finisher in the middle of the ring.

Ruben had never told her. Sitting up, she looked down at Avo splayed out on the roof. She hardly recognized him. The wide, hairless scar where his eyebrow once was. Underneath it, his eyes had changed. Who was this man who claimed to know her? Who was this man who had killed Tigran? What other lives had he stolen from her without her noticing? She could've gone to Paris with Tigran, she might've won that tournament of hers, she might've become someone, she might've been in photos clipped by girls from newspapers, she might have lived a life that amounted to the ambitions of her mentor, of herself, a wild life. Instead, this. She would not forgive Avo now. She would not brush aside his crime or hug him goodbye. She would only say, cool as glass, as if speaking to no one at all in particular, "You shouldn't be here."

One day Avo hoped to find the right words. The heart didn't break so much as fold in on itself, the heart a coward and a shelter all at once. He was lying beside her on his back, just the way Angel Hair had taught him. One, two—what could he possibly say to stop the count? Sitting above him, Mina seemed to be floating.

She was as cool as glass and out of reach.

He sat up on his knees. "You don't know what I've gone through to come back to you," he said. "I won't just leave like this. It was an accident. And I meant to tell you right away, but I couldn't imagine adding to your pain. You look like you don't believe me, but I'm being honest. I've come all this way through hiding and hell, and I can't just leave you again. I want you to say something to me. Talk to me. Tell me what you're feeling. Tell me what I can do or say, ask me anything and I'll explain."

Mina stood. She dried her hands against her pants and breathed so deep a breath that her back cracked. She said, "This isn't our year."

"I'm sorry," Avo said, and it occurred to him that he hadn't said it yet, that it was the most obvious little sentence in the world to say, and he'd ruined its meaning by waiting too long to say it. What an insufficient little sentence it was, *I'm sorry*, like a blanket too small to cover the feet. If only he could stretch it, draw out from it more yarn, more thread, his apology might have unspooled to become the one he'd been waiting to hear all his life without knowing it, an apology not for a specific crime but for the ambivalence of life itself, for the way life seemed to wander on whether the truth was buried or excavated, whether the dead were mourned or forgotten, whether villains went heroized or heroes went vilified, whether or not the objects of our love revealed themselves to be the source of all our anguish, whether or not justice was real as pain or love. *I'm sorry.*

Today, Mina thought, she would take the children to the ski lift. She left the roof and listened from bed for the sound of the train, arriving like a paling in the east.

22

Paris, France, 1983–1988

The day following the explosion at Orly, a heat wave swept over Paris. Ruben, alone in his hotel room, read the paper and then fanned himself with the news he'd made. Of the eight dead, only two were Turks. Fifty more in the terminal were injured. According to one witness quoted in the article, "The noise made less of an impression. It was the flames." Men on fire had hobbled through the airport, and now a heat wave was spreading over the city, and Ruben took off his glasses and fanned himself. There was a pounding at the door of his hotel room. His partner, Varoujan, had gone out early in the morning and had not come back. The door was coming unhinged. Ruben drank the last of his vinegar. He folded his glasses neatly into his shirt pocket. Then he went to the front door and greeted the police.

Word of his arrest—one of dozens in the wake of the bombing—reached every corner of the diaspora, and soon there wasn't an Armenian in the world who hadn't come to an opinion about Ruben Petrosian. A restaurateur in Watertown, Massachusetts, invented a cocktail in his honor called Twisted Justice (equal parts vodka and arak, with a twist of lemon), and a mural featuring the circular lenses of Ruben's glasses stretched across the facade of an Odessa bakery.

The vast majority, however, came to a different conclusion about Ruben and his crew. These Armenians, who previously were sympathetic to ASALA's cause, whose support of ambassadorial intimidation and even violence had been abstract but nonetheless real, revolted against the specificity of Ruben's crime. The two Turks who were killed were ordinary citizens. For most Armenians, this was unforgivable. Their great epic of justice had been debased into the petty anecdote of vengeance, and support for ASALA dwindled.

This new pressure forced ASALA itself into a split. Loyalists to Hagop Hagopian argued that the time for moralizing had long since come and gone, while a new faction led by a young American leftist named Monte Melkonian argued for a renewed focus. (Reading Melkonian's name in the paper one morning, Mina said out loud to her husband, "I met him once, on a train blocked by a mudslide.")

As it became clear that the diaspora had rejected Hagop Hagopian's ruthlessness, the only question remaining was which side of the line claimed Ruben Petrosian. He had committed the attack at Orly, after all, and was largely responsible for the carnage there. But keen readers of the news pointed to evidence suggesting that the bomb had been designed originally to detonate while the plane was in flight. Instead, the bomb had exploded early, while still at the gate, saving—as it were—nearly two hundred lives. Ruben Petrosian had either ruined the bomb accidentally, or he'd sabotaged the attack at the last moment. Both stories were plausible, and a debate among the diaspora ensued.

Whether Ruben himself had an answer for the question, no one knew. Reporters could not reach him behind the bars at Fleury-Mérogis.

As he awaited sentencing, his mother sent him a few platitudinous letters, empty but for the smell of rain. He didn't expect Mina or anyone else from Armenia to contact him in prison, but he did find himself longing for a note from Hagop Hagopian. No logistical risk had been too obstructive for Hagopian to take in the past, and yet not a single word of thanks or morale from the man for whom Ruben had sacrificed so much came to his cell in France. Because of this, he embraced the idea that he was forgotten even among the inmates, and it was in this place of self-pity and abandonment that he met the conspiracy-minded prisoner known only as the eccentric.

"They're hoarding the tobacco," the eccentric muttered in the mess hall. He soaked his bread in his water and refused anything more. The meat, he had decided, was contaminated with chemicals. The vegetables—pumped with estrogen. He dipped his bread and glared at the Algerians at the other end of the hall.

"You don't know what you're talking about," one of the other Christians at the table said in French. "Those zealots don't smoke shit. Death cult, the whole lot. Anything that reminds them of life is banned and scorned."

"They're not *smoking* the tobacco," the eccentric said. "They're hoarding it. Buying it and keeping it out of reach of everyone else."

"And why would they do a thing like that?"

The eccentric placed his wet bread in his mouth. Kept it in his lower lip. "No cigarettes, and everyone will be on edge, everyone will feel desperate. And just when we're at our least, that's when they'll strike."

"Ah, your so-called great conversion," the other Christian said to the rest of the table. "Our friend needs a conjugal visit, stat. All his semen is backed up in his brain."

All the Christians at the table laughed. Except for the eccentric, dipping his bread in his water. Except for Ruben, dipping his.

According to the article, witnesses at Orly had mistaken the explosion for the last of the Bastille Day fireworks. Only when they saw men and women on fire, sprinting through the terminal, did they realize their mistake.

In prison, Ruben tried to picture those passengers running through the terminal on fire, but he couldn't. Not exactly. He could envision only a specific couple—a man and a woman—caught in the flames. He could see them so clearly in his mind, holding each other in their individual agony, that he could name them.

When the eccentric was released, Ruben cried in his cell. He'd never spoken a word to the man, knew nothing of his origin or his crime, and yet mourned his loss like a friend. In that way, Ruben remembered the eccentric longingly, and the triggered memory of one or another of his conspiracies brought a feeling of reassurance and warmth. The Algerians were hoarding every shred of tobacco in the canteen, went the thinking, and the homosexuals were tampering with the faucets in the showers. Strands of the plague were splashing back from the toilets, and the visiting imam was recruiting terrorists. The bunk mattresses were washed in chemicals that dimmed the population's wits as they slept, and the Bibles made available to inmates were coated in contagions and lice.

The overarching theme of the conspiracies was the intended suppression of Christian values, and although Ruben hadn't believed in many of the eccentric's specific accusations, he did begin to find evidence supporting the general concern. When an inmate called Moreau was found with a weapon whittled from the back of an old canvas, for instance, and his paints and supplies were confiscated, Ruben blamed the confiscation not on the weapon-making but on the images of Christ and Mary adorning many of Moreau's portraits. When Muslim prayer mats were brought into what had once been called the chapel, Ruben privately worried over the so-called great conversion. Like all diatribes, spoken or left unsaid, Ruben's new thinking seemed directed more at himself than at others, an overeager bird fluffing its feathers in anticipation of a predator who, somewhere in the invisible distance, might at any moment appear. He began to tell some of his observations to the Christians at the table, going on in the way people explained dreams, undeterred by the blank faces of the audience, practicing a kind of upside-down curiosity: *this* must be the answer, so what might be the question?

Although some prisoners began to call him the "new eccentric," Ruben differed from the original eccentric in one significant way. Unlike the mysterious origins of the former eccentric, Ruben's reputation preceded him. Early in his stay, rumors had spread that he'd worked closely with Arafat, or that he'd been a gunman at Munich in 1972, when he was just a teenager. Although some of the prisoners would ask for details, Ruben had decided to say absolutely nothing about his past. He'd let his cohorts go on guessing, which, for a while, they did. He enjoyed it, the mysterious power that came with owning a mysterious history. But as the others' interest in him began to fade, as his silence and seriousness became the burden to companionship they had always been, as his obvious boredom with his lewd compatriots turned his bright mysteriousness into dull vagueness, he grew tempted to explain. Yes, he wanted to say, he'd been a leader in the attack at Orly; yes, he'd worked directly with Hagopian—who had worked directly with Arafat—on a number of occasions; yes, he'd even once been rumored to be a possible successor; yes, he'd been so loyal to the cause that he'd sent his own brother to hell.

But in the face of his budding urge to sell his details for a friendly face, he held his tongue. He tried to forget his past altogether, and to focus instead on what else, if anything, he might notice that was meant to go unnoticed. But of course the remembering continued.

Ruben had never asked Avo a single question on the subject of his parents. The Leninakan factory fire had been more a national tragedy than a personal one, and because it had been known by everyone, because he assumed Avo was reminded of it everywhere, avoidance seemed the more thoughtful approach to take.

Only once did Avo bring up the subject of his parents on his own. They were still young. This was not long after the day they'd spent listening to Yergat and his redheaded wife, Siranoush, up in the hills. Now Avo had led Ruben to a pond. To teach him how to swim.

A pond. A puddle. A small ravine filled with rainwater.

The afternoon was clear, which was rare, so it's improbable that they were alone. Families and children must have gathered in droves, but that's not how Ruben remembered it. He remembered being alone with Avo, just the two of them at the edge of that pond.

Avo removed his shirt and pants and fell with a great splash into the water. "Don't worry," Avo said, standing in the pond. Feet in the mud, water up to his neck. "Doesn't get deeper than this."

But water up to one boy's neck was water over another boy's head. "I can't swim," Ruben said. Did he say it? He must've said it.

Avo would teach him. One day they would go to the Black Sea together, but for now that ravine full of rainwater was the greatest ocean they'd ever seen.

Not long before, Siranoush had read their fates in a bowl of milk. Had accused one of them of being a phony.

Ruben shed his clothes and then waded toward his cousin. His brother. He did exactly as he was told. He submitted his back to the sun. He stretched his arms forward and his legs back and let Avo cradle him by the belly.

The day was clear. There must have been others around in droves. And yet they were alone. The water was cool and thick, the opposite of flame.

His left arm arched while his right arm pulled. Again and again, in cycles. He inhaled from the side and exhaled into the water. His feet went on pittering.

And just then, as Ruben took off from his brother's arms, it happened: Avo spoke for the first and only time about his parents.

Did Ruben know that Avo's mother had been the first female factory worker in Leninakan?

That his father had been the joke of the city for letting his wife work a man's job? Avo's father would join in on the laughter and say, "The only job that's exclusively a man's job is to wipe his own ass. And you know what? If she had that particular ambition, I'd let her have that job, too!" Even as a little girl, everyone told him, his mother had possessed the rarest, loveliest combination: a skeptical mind yet an open heart. Avo wanted to be like her.

Of course Avo couldn't have told him all this on the day at the pond. There must've been many people there. A rare day of cloudlessness. The water so nice. But how did Ruben learn these details? Where and when had he heard them?

Not until the day after Orly did he remember that he'd misremembered.

It was a year or so after the day he'd learned to swim. Late at night, he'd left his village for the long walk into the city. He didn't have a flashlight. He was equipped only with the memory of the path. He'd gone to talk with the statue of Kirov in the square. His oldest friend. They hadn't been alone together in years, not since Avo had arrived.

He sat beside Kirov and heard footfalls in the square. At that hour, he was afraid the steps belonged to a group of boys who would hurt him. He hid behind the statue.

The sound of laughter curled around the plinth. He heard the voices of Avo and Mina and looked quickly enough to see them hand in hand. Again Ruben ducked behind the statue and listened.

They sat at the other side of Kirov. They were whispering, but Ruben could hear every word.

"What do you remember," Mina said, "about your parents?"

It was the question Ruben had never asked. The question, he realized just then, he should've asked.

"My answer's kind of pathetic," Avo said.

"You don't have to answer if you don't want to."

"No, I do. Actually, I appreciate you asking."

"Why do you say pathetic?"

"I think it's a shame that my memory of their death is bigger than any memory I have of their life."

"But you were a kid."

"I had fifteen years with them, and I remember almost nothing except the fire."

"Almost nothing?"

And that was when Ruben heard the details he'd incorrectly remembered hearing at the pond.

"You know what caused the fire?" Avo said. "A spark from a boiler explosion. The boiler hadn't been checked in years. Afterward, inspectors said the boiler had been too weak for the pressure it was under."

Mina didn't say anything. She knew exactly when to speak and exactly when to listen. Maybe, Ruben thought, that was the source of her luck.

"You want to know a joke?" Mina finally said, and Avo laughed. "That wasn't the joke yet," Mina said, getting another laugh.

"Sure," Avo said. "Shoot."

"Three dogs are swimming in a lake . . ."

A joke, Ruben thought. At a time like that. She had his heart in her arms, cradled on the surface of a great depth, and she was using that time to make a joke.

The laughter changed. It was almost tearful, from Avo's core rather than from his face. But the laugh-cry seemed less like a split than a seal. They weren't halves coming together but two complete hearts colliding to create a third. Ruben, hidden, listened. It was a music more complex and stirring than any two reeds could muster.

The last of yesterday's fireworks—that's what the witnesses thought, hearing the explosion.

Not long after his eavesdropping, Ruben decided he would try it—what Mina had accomplished—at the Black Sea. He would ask Avo to open his heart about the death of his parents.

He would hear exactly the same answer, but it would be different, directed at him. He would try to create a new third heart with his brother. But at the beach, he delayed, and then came the matter with Tigran, and then Paris, where Hagop Hagopian offered him a different kind of fullness to join, and then, and then, and then.

The last of yesterday's fireworks. The flames from a decades-old factory fire. For years, the boiler had gone unchecked. Weakness under pressure. Forgotten and forgotten until it refused to be forgotten.

* * *

In the shower, Ruben used hardly any soap or water at all, just a slap on his head, slicking back his hair, which was receding badly at the corners of his forehead, and a few quick rinses of his pubic hair, so thick his penis, like a cashew in a salad, barely emerged from its leaves.

At the mess hall, the Christians at the table no longer welcomed his eccentricity, and Ruben sat alone near the guards. "Some of them aren't really Christians, I hope you understand," he told them, and the guards told him to shut up.

He did. He stopped speaking altogether, never so much as acknowledging a word his fellow prisoners said, even if he happened to be alone with one of them. Silence was an easier habit to adopt than he'd imagined, and he kept silent so well that he tricked himself into believing he enjoyed it, that he was gaining some unnamable force from choosing nothing all day but to remain quietly observant. The question of whether the old eccentric's conspiracies were true or insane began to seem beyond the point entirely. I'm the only one he would've trusted, Ruben thought, and his heart swelled. A sentence like that—it meant something to an abandoned person. No matter who said it or why. Or if.

The man with the long fingers had been from Moscow. After cleaning up the hotel room, Ruben had taken a cab from the hotel in Paris to the airport in order to return to his search in Los Angeles.

Hagopian himself had instructed him to do exactly that, but something had changed in the ASALA leader. The new angles in his face weren't the effect of age but of worry. Worry was not the emotion, Ruben thought, of a man whose true aim was to fix his people's past. Worry was an emotion for men consumed by their own personal fate. And that change in priorities worried Ruben—shouldn't he be above worry, too?—in loops.

And so, in the terminal, Ruben changed his flight to include a brief stop before moving on to Los Angeles. There was, he'd heard, a wedding back home.

He arrived in Kirovakan by taxi from the capital, and tipped the driver a month's salary, asking him to wait outside the church as long as it took him to return.

There she was, Mina, standing at the altar in her gown. Her posture—lurching her forehead to the shorter groom's, bracing the weight of the priest's relic, bearing a bouquet like the handle of a broadsword at her sternum—turned her into a classroom skeleton, all shoulder blades and elbows. And then she laughed, apropos of nothing, and he thought maybe he'd brought the smell of rain into the church, and she'd sniffed his arrival. Who was he to say if she was beautiful? She was a friend. A woman he'd always wished to be kind to. She was laughing. He was glad he'd come.

Hagopian had asked after her outside the jazz club in Paris—hadn't it occurred to Ruben that Avo might be in contact with the girl from the tournament, might in fact be hiding in her dress skirts? Ruben said it was unlikely, explaining what he'd learned in America and the trap he'd laid over there, which Avo was bound to fall into sooner rather than later. In a way, Hagopian seemed satisfied with that, but Ruben knew someone would be sent to check on Mina, just in case. So he had come to her wedding to check in on her himself.

After the ceremony, he watched her dance. He knew he needed to warn her against helping Avo, but he didn't know how. He couldn't tell her the truth, that he'd agreed to hunt down Avo, who'd gone missing in America. So he decided to tell her the most painful truth he could afford to tell her, the only way he could separate Mina and Avo for good without betraying Hagopian's trust. He watched her dance. He watched her recognize him. His heart levitated. She was running to him. He said a little prayer, asking for the courage to undo the lie they'd told her about Tigran's death, but the courage never came. He couldn't admit his role in that story, and so he couldn't admit Avo's role, either. Instead, at the last moment, he came up with a new lie that would stop Mina from ever harboring an ambition to see Avo again. Avo had pitied her, Ruben said. Avo had escaped as soon as he could manage to escape. Avo had never, not even briefly, loved her. He wouldn't even come back for her wedding.

Although early rumors had fellow inmates believing he'd been solely in charge of the Orly attack, the court in Créteil saw it differently. In their ruling on March 3, 1985—almost two years after the attack—his partner, Varoujan, was deemed to be the operation's chief planner. Ruben, they decided under public pressure, had been mostly a pawn who'd made the lifesaving decision to stop the explosive from detonating in midair. Although his last-minute subversion was only partially successful, an act of conscience like his warranted a lesser punishment. Whereas Varoujan was given a life sentence at a notoriously violent prison in the north, Ruben was given twenty years at Fleury-Mérogis.

"Negotiable, I think," the lawyer told him, but all Ruben could hear was the word *pawn* again and again in his inner ear. Tigran had told him once, and he should've listened: sometimes a man thinks he's the dice when he's really just a checker.

Month after month of silence, Ruben continued to shrink. He ate nothing but the bread he deemed safe, and although he craved meat and cigarettes, the canteen couldn't keep them in stock, thanks to the Algerians, who were hoarding the tobacco.

Then one day he saw a Christian smoking in the yard. He'd

just won the cigarette against an inmate in a makeshift game of backgammon. The dice—a paper wheel spun twice—beckoned him to watch. Ruben didn't break his oath of silence. He didn't speak. But—how did it happen?—he started to play.

Soon he was playing any chance he had. Hundreds of inmates challenged him. They played for canteen goods. Candy bars and cigarettes and the rare jar of Nutella—none of which Ruben would eat. Of course he won every game. He took the rewards of his victories and passed them along to the other Christians.

By 1987, four years after Orly and two into his sentence, Ruben couldn't remember the sound of his own voice. The other inmates, tired of losing, had stopped coming to play backgammon.

"Look at those clouds," the eccentric had said once, holding a towel over his nose and mouth in the yard. "Look at their edges, that hint of green surrounding them. Those aren't typical clouds. Those are chemical deposits. Cover your face, brother. They're trying to strip us of our senses. They're capable of it. They're capable of anything."

Ruben sat alone in the yard, spinning his paper dice with one hand, filtering his breath through a rag with the other.

The longer it had taken him to find Avo, the thinner and thinner wore the fabric of Hagopian's trust. How many extensions had he begged for from pay phones as he searched the piggish gutters of America? How many false leads had he followed from the six men who'd been arrested on Sperry Street? Two years, he spoke with bartenders and merchants, carnies and freaks. He looked into every shadow of that country, but because he was looking for only one thing, he saw absolutely nothing but Avo's absence.

"I want him safely returned back home," Hagopian assured

him. "I just need to speak with him before I feel confident he'll keep our names out of his mouth. That's all."

Did Ruben believe him? He couldn't now say. When he finally found Avo, he made the same assurance.

"You're going home," he said. "We're just stopping by Greece first, to clear the air. Then you're going home."

If, at Fleury-Mérogis, he'd begun as a rumor, he later became a ghost. His name was never written on any ledger. His name, his crime, his race—none of it was known beyond the desks of diplomats and wardens. In the ghost stories he read in the prison library, he discovered that haunting wasn't a returning so much as a remaining. He imagined returning home one day, or else imagined that he'd never really left, that he'd remained in Kirovakan all along, haunting the city square. What disgrace had he brought there? What hope? Had he hurt more people than he'd avenged? Not even Shirakatsi could do that math. The justice he was after involved too many invisible lives, too many ghosts. Ruben began to understand it as the fundamental obstacle of the Armenian cause. It was just too abstract of an ask for the world to say, "Yes, your ghosts are real. Your pain hasn't returned, it's remained."

And what about his hate? Not everyone was blessed enough to hate the living. Some people have nobody but ghosts to hate, and it's difficult to understand how that can make a man *different*.

Nobody can know all the places a man puts his ghost-hate. It either stays inside and rots him, or else it spews out directionless and cold. Ruben wanted to shake his younger self for hating the classmates who had bullied him in the square, wanted to tell that child how blessed he'd been to be able to look in the eyes of the ones who'd done him wrong. What a luxury it had been to hate the boys who kicked gravel into his teeth, who sent his glasses from his face. What a luxury it had been to see them cause his pain, to know they were responsible, to choose to curse them or fight them or spit in their eyes or run. To choose a vessel for his hate and move on.

Several years into his prison sentence, representatives of the nations of France and the Armenian Socialist Soviet Republic brokered a deal to extradite Ruben Petrosian, former member of the Armenian Secret Army for the Liberation of Armenia, under the condition that he be confined to the borders of the Armenian Socialist Soviet Republic for the remainder of his life.

Before returning to Armenia, he asked, could he stop in Greece one last time? When asked by the French authorities why, he told them the truth. After a while, they agreed.

On the morning of April 28, 1988, Ruben was set, in one way, free. In Palaio Faliro, the dawn raised pink whitecaps to the surface of the sea. He had several hours before he was to be extradited home, once and for all. He knew exactly how to spend his time.

23

Los Angeles, California, 1989

There I was, laid out under a wool blanket on a sofa printed with flowers, wearing several zipped sandwich bags of ice.

Way back in my wrestling days, in the moments after the botched piledriver that broke my neck, all I could move—I was told—were my eyelids and my lips, which kept smacking. It wasn't something I'd ever imagined my body capable of, shutting down like that, and for many years afterward, I dreamed of paralysis and woke with pins in my fingers and needles in my toes.

A long time had passed since those nightmares, but now I remembered them clearly. I stretched my legs and toes and my arms and fingers, relieved to find everything in order. Then I stirred on the furniture, this way and that, dropping one of the bags of ice. A cat—Smokey, I understood—pounced, pawing it across the carpet to the linoleum in the kitchen, where an old man picked it up.

"Galust," I said, but my jaw hurt too bad to keep talking. Mina's husband and I couldn't communicate that way, anyway, thanks to the language barrier. He set down the ice and then opened a pack of cigarettes, offering me one. For a while, we smoked without talking. Then he went to the kitchen and came back with two glasses and a bottle of brown liquor I recognized by smell to be cognac.

I was afraid to laugh because it hurt too bad, but I couldn't help it, and the pain of laughing wasn't so bad compared to the burning cigarette and liquor against the open cuts on my mouth.

After a smoke and a drink each, and going on round two, the same could be said of talking. It hurt to speak, and I knew Galust couldn't understand a word I was saying, but the pain seemed more intense in silence.

I said, "I'm a little out of practice, fighting. Fifteen years ago, I would've beat all three of those jabronis without pausing for a commercial break, you know?"

Galust spoke his language, and we both shrugged and laughed. I said, "I'm going to keep on talking, if that's all right."

I told him we were old, both in our sixties, and I said, "This country lost its mind in the sixties, so why not us, too?" He spoke next. I shrugged, he laughed. I said, "Your wife is a kid compared to us. Half our age. Mina—she's young, she's pretty. You—old and short and hairy, not so much. How did you get so lucky?"

Only when I'd said his wife's name did he react. The skin on his forehead tightened. Then he shrugged.

We laughed. We toasted.

For a while, Galust took his turn speaking, and I got to experience what he'd been experiencing. I listened for cognates—an old trick I remembered from the Mexican luchadores I worked with in the Southwest—but Galust's language bore absolutely no relation to mine, so there was nothing for me to grasp. I was left enjoying the swell of his sentences just for the sounds of them. It was like coming out of the symphony, marveling at the noise the band made tuning up.

By our third cigarettes, I was feeling good enough to try standing. My mouth and throat were dry with tobacco and blood, and I wanted water. After I did some miming, Galust showed me to the bathroom, where I swallowed palmfuls of water from the tap and checked the damage to my face. Half had swelled to pink and gloss, and my eye socket looked broken. Woozy and presumably concussed, I limped back to the living room, where the sound of a key wrestling the lock in the door sent Galust to check the peephole. He motioned for me to stay in the hallway, out of sight, and it occurred to me that he was protecting me. I hadn't realized how old I was until I'd seen that he and I were the same age. Then he opened the door, and I braced for Mina to see me and finish the job Shen and his friends had started. But when she came in with the kids and found me in her living room, broken and old, she just went to the sink and rinsed our cognac glasses. Then she said, "Is my husband forcing you to drink?"

The kids crowded me, wanting to know what had happened. I said, "I fell off the roof, thinking I could fly."

Mina must've told Galust to take the kids away, because soon he was ushering them outside. "You never showed up at the gas station," I said.

"Shen was telling me he'll follow if I go. Cause trouble."

"He did, anyway. With, I don't know, eight or nine of his friends."

Mina brought me a glass of water. She said, "Only two friends."

"Felt like more," I said.

But Mina knew the truth. Apparently, she spent her Sundays teaching backgammon to a group of old Armenians who played at the laundromat across from the gas station. They saw the fight, and stopped it, and called Mina for her English. When Mina got there, I was covered in blood and concussed. "I'm telling you I'm calling an ambulance," she said, "but you're saying, 'No insurance. No insurance.' So I'm taking you here instead."

"To Shen's building."

"He's meaning well. He's a good man."

"The best."

For the first time since I'd come to Los Angeles, Mina smiled. "I can see why you got along with Avo," she said.

I raised my glass of water, a salute, and then drank carefully around my wounds. "Shen's not going to come down here," I said, "and finish the job, is he?"

Mina assured me he wouldn't. "Almost all of us in this building are coming after the earthquake in Armenia. We lost everything. Shen is helping everyone make a new home. We're being careful not to lose anything else in the moving, you understand?"

I said I did, but I wasn't sure. "Well," I said, "I'll get out of your way, then." If I'd had a hat, I'd have tipped it. Instead, I left with a tiny, painful bow.

Outside, I was surprised to see how much time had passed. The sun was setting.

Slow-moving as I was, I hadn't reached the building's stairwell before Mina caught up with me out in the open-air hallway. She was holding that red fanny pack. She called up to the roof, where her husband had taken the children, and he called back down to us.

"I'm telling him we're going to the hospital," she said, strapping the bag around her waist just as I'd imagined. "But really, you're taking me somewhere else. Okay?"

It was dusk, and all the waking crickets of Glendale were chirping.

"All right," I said. "If you'll fill up my tank, let's go."

"Bro," The Brow Beater had told me in Wyoming, refusing to drive. "I am not your brother."

From there, everything broke down. On the outskirts of Omaha, the Catalina went first. We had to take a tow back to the city, where we split the price on my Ranger. I hadn't even signed the paperwork before The Brow Beater threw his things—a piece of luggage he'd finally bought for his ring gear, his red fanny pack—into the truck. We'd been splitting gas fees for years, but it was my car that needed replacing, so I was ready to buy the truck on my own. The Brow Beater insisted, though. Maybe he felt guilty for what he'd said back near Laramie.

I drove us east, and we went long stretches of the country without speaking at all. Here and there, The Brow Beater asked about Gil, trying to get me to open up again, but I was done talking about my brother. I said, "You know, I just don't remember that much about him anymore."

A few months before then, I'd started receiving letters in my P.O. box telling me to call Johnny Trumpet. He wanted to know why I kept skipping Kentucky. I told him it was just the way business had worked out, that I was sure we'd cross paths again soon.

"You still working with that big unibrowed kid? Avo, right?"

It wasn't like Johnny Trumpet to use a wrestler's real name, so I understood that his interest in The Brow Beater wasn't general. At the risk of being paranoid, I lied and said, "You know, he bounces around a lot nowadays, takes long stretches away from the road. He calls me last-minute if he wants to work a gig."

"Do me a favor, then," Johnny Trumpet said. "Let me know the next time you've got him booked a few days in advance. I'd like to come check him out, see his progress."

"Sure thing," I said.

That night in the motel room, while The Brow Beater slept, I opened his red bag to see if he was hiding something from me. But all I found were his money and his stupid collectibles.

Among the sky-rises glaring their gap-toothed windows against the twilit basin, I told Mina how strange I found it to have a woman in the passenger seat. The cognac and the cigarettes were still burning in me, and my face was broken, but I made the effort to speak. Traffic swept all around us on the freeway, but we were moving. Mina was telling me where to go, and I was free as I drove to notice every sun-popped blister of paint in the reflective lane-dashes clipping by, every little shadow of gravel. It was almost paralyzing, noticing so much passing so quickly, and it was during one of these flashing dashes that I realized I'd forgotten Fuji at the jeweler.

But by then we were already near our destination, far away, in Long Beach. Mina told me to pull into a metered spot outside a florist, where she bought a bouquet of white orchids. "We're almost there," she said, handing me the flowers.

"Thank you," I said jokingly, but it came out sincere. "They're beautiful."

The next time we got out of the car, we were in the parking lot of an assisted living facility called Home Again.

Inside, Mina asked the young woman at the front desk for the room number of a person whose name I didn't recognize, and we were led to the elevator and to the second floor. Everything there smelled severely of lemon-scented cleaners, and the laminated hallway floors gleamed and squeaked under our shoes. I followed Mina into room 242, where the first bed was empty, and where, on the other side of the opened partition, near the window, a second bed lay bent into a forty-degree angle. In it, a woman of immeasurable age was spooning Jell-O against her gums and glaring up at the television set.

Mina went to her. The old woman was balding in patches, and when she looked at me with an enormous, toothless grin, I excused myself to find a vase for the flowers.

Out in the hallway, I found a storage closet with some empty mason jars. I took one and filled it with water at a drinking fountain.

The flowers were a bit tall for the jar, so I went back down the elevator to the front desk and asked for a pair of scissors.

The young woman said, "I'm sorry, I'm new here. Are you a Home Again community member?"

I straightened my ponytail. I said, "You think I'm that old, huh?"

"Oh, no, I didn't mean— Well, it's just that, well, I can't give scissors to a Home Again community member. Safety precautions, right? I'm new here, so I just wanted to be extra cautious."

"I'm not going to stab a senior citizen," I said, "if that's what you're worried about."

"Oh, I know," the girl said. "The rule's in place because of self-harm, actually. With your injuries on your face and neck, well, I thought maybe— Well, I haven't seen it myself, but there have been instances of self-harm."

I lifted the jar of flowers high. I said, "I'm just looking for a stem trim, that's all."

"I hope you're not offended," she said. "I actually think your hair is great."

I thanked her, even as she insisted on cutting the flowers herself.

"I am not your brother," The Brow Beater had said, and the Catalina broke down on our way to the East Coast. We didn't speak more than a few words at a time. While he paid his half of the check at a diner near Atlanta, I found a phone booth outside and called Johnny Trumpet. I said, "Tell me why you're looking for The Brow Beater."

"I could bullshit you," he said, "but I won't. I got a guy looking for him. Little guy in glasses and a suit, seems important. I'd have said IRS or some shit, but then he offered money if I could lead him to your guy."

"Money? For Avo?"

"Illegal shit, sounds like. I don't think your giant's as green as we thought he was."

"Must be a mistake."

"Money's real either way. Look, I could've gone out of my way to find the kid, keep the money for myself. But I know you've got love for him, so I thought I'd let you decide whether or not to tip off the guy looking for him."

Through the large panes of the diner, I could see The Brow Beater paying his bill. He was shaking hands with the young man behind the register, making him laugh. Everywhere we went, people would stop and ask him how tall he was or if his eyebrow was painted on. And I used to bark at them to leave the big fella alone. But The Brow Beater never got tired of it. He always stopped. He always made people feel good. It was bad for kayfabe, and I told him to cut it out. But he enjoyed it, seeing people, being seen. In a few years' time, I have no doubt, he could've been great. He could've been an all-time great.

When I returned with the jar of flowers to the room, Mina was painting the old woman's fingernails. I placed the bouquet on the windowsill, and Mina said, "She's saying you're very handsome."

"Is that so?"

"She's not seeing a man in a long, long time."

"Or maybe the swelling and bleeding are improvements I should hang on to."

When I finally asked who the woman was, Mina told me she was the wife of a former backgammon instructor. I suppose I'd been expecting a closer tie than that, because Mina was quick to add that this woman—the widow of a man called Tigran—was like family, especially since the earthquake.

Maybe I was getting too comfortable. I said, "Did you lose anyone?"

Mina blew on the old woman's fingernails. "Everyone," she said. "Galust's mother, my mother, my father, my sister, her husband and children—everyone was living in the same building." Again she dried the polish with her breath. "The tallest building."

The TV was on, and for a long time, I kept my eyes on it. When I looked back at Mina, she'd finished painting the old woman's nails. The color of the nail polish was the same shade of red as the fanny pack around Mina's waist. I didn't realize it until Mina set the bag on the woman's lap.

Slowly, Mina removed every arrowhead and shell, every coin and token and stamp, and set them at the foot of the bed. Then she reached into the bag and removed, one by one, the collection of dice.

The old woman took each die in her palm. Dozens of them. Red and black and white and yellow, pips of every shade. Glass and ivory and jade. More than I'd ever cared to count, more than seemed possible to fit. They tumbled from the bag into her palms, out onto the blanket and then the floor, rattling and rattling until they stopped.

"I was making a promise to her," Mina said. "I would find them. But I couldn't. You had them."

The final wrestling match of The Brow Beater's career took place in front of twenty-two hundred fans in the Greensboro Coliseum Complex Exhibition Building in Greensboro, North Carolina, and ended at nine minutes and thirty-three seconds in a count-out victory over Ty "Bona Fide" Wilmington. The win came largely because of my opportune interference, choking Bona Fide out with my gimmicked halo just as the referee turned his back. Under a torrent of jeers and flying garbage, The Brow Beater lifted me onto his shoulders, and we celebrated all the way down the ramp to the curtain, behind which, after a final bluster of devilishness, we disappeared.

Afterward, the boys made themselves at home in the hotel bar, and I watched with a bit of surprise and a touch of pride as The Brow Beater held court at the center of the rail. I don't remember the jokes, but I remember the laughter, the sense I got that The Brow Beater wasn't the greenest guy in the room anymore. At one point, he saw me watching him from the other end of the bar, and he lifted his vodka, and I lifted my beer. Our hellos.

And our good nights—because pretty soon after that I was up in our hotel room, way before the party had ended, and lying in bed. Four or five hours must've passed before the door came unlocked and a column of light broke into the room. I lay on my side facing the other way, where The Brow Beater's enormous shadow stamped the wall.

"Bro," he whispered. "Bro."

But I went on pretending to sleep. All night, I pretended.

In the morning, he got up before me and started running the shower. Once I knew he was behind the curtain, I stepped into the bathroom and said, "Morning."

"You disappeared, bro," he said over the curtain, over the hiss of the water. "You good?"

"A little sick, I think. Stomach bug."

He turned off the water and wrapped himself in a towel. When he was dressed, I asked if he'd do me a favor and run over to pick up some medicine for me at the corner drugstore. "That way," I said, giving him some cash, "I can shower and be ready to hit the road again when you get back."

"Sure," he said in that way of his, that way that meant certainty. "Sure."

Soon he was gone. I tied back my hair. I knew there was someone waiting for him outside the corner drugstore and that I wouldn't see him again. I washed my face. I packed my suitcase. Only then did I see the red fanny pack beside his bed. Unzipping it, I expected to find all the money he'd saved in our two years on the road. But there was only about three hundred dollars in that bag of his, most of which was filled with the stupid talismans he'd collected, arrowheads and dice and key chains.

I left the money for the cleaning woman and went to the lobby to check out.

"And your friend?" said the man at the counter.

I'd snapped the red bag around my waist, and I couldn't pull the strap any tighter without ripping it in two. I said, "My brother, believe it or not. We don't look alike, but, well, in any case, he's already in the car, waiting for me."

On the way back to her apartment, Mina asked if I thought we'd ever find out what had happened to Avo. I told her no, I didn't think we would.

Here's what we did know: Avo returned to Mina in 1983 and told her what he'd gone through to get back home. Torture, hell.

"He went through all that?" I asked.

Yes. And still Mina turned him away.

"Why?" I asked.

There'd been a lie, she said, that revived a painful incident when they were younger, and she couldn't imagine circumstances changing enough that she'd want to forgive him. But then everything she couldn't imagine changing, changed. "I'm in a new country. My husband—his memory is being disappeared. My children are speaking a language I'm not so good using. I'm afraid I'm embarrassing them when I'm taking them to school, talking with other parents. And then in December, the earthquake in Armenia, and I'm feeling it right here, right here. Everything, everyone I left, gone. And so all I'm thinking is what happened to Avo. I'm at library, I'm at city hall, searching. I'm finding your name, and I'm coming to you for help. You're coming all the way here. But look at us. We're still not knowing. Was he there during earthquake? Is he buried in rubble? Or is he leaving the country as soon as I tell him to go? Is he alive? If we're not knowing, can we miss him?"

"We can miss him," I said. I had more to say, but I knew I couldn't speak another word without hurting. "Mina," I said, close to her in the cab of my truck. We were parked in front of her apartment, where her children were waiting. Stars were invisible but not the moon. "Mina," I said, and in the gray flood of its light, I asked for her forgiveness.

24

Kars, Turkey, 1983

On the train west from Kirovakan, the conductor waltzed from one car to another until he arrived at Avo's, humming a tune, checking tickets, making small talk, rambling about the histories of the cities they had left, the cities they were headed to, the places he wished they'd all return. When he arrived at Avo—crunched in a seat at the back of a car designated for luggage—the conductor's tune spun naturally into a whistle. He said, "Anyone ever ask how you got that scar?"

"You'd be the first," Avo said. He reached into the valise he'd taken from the shop in Mersin and emptied all its contents onto the empty seat beside him. He'd kept some Turkish money in Mersin, and the papers Kami had forged for him. He had a pen and a little spiral notebook he'd purchased at the train station, filled with a few mediocre but heartfelt poems. And the train ticket.

"Leaving Armenia, huh? All the way to Kars, huh? You know they'll have to check your papers at the border."

"I understand, yes. I was hoping to spend some time in Leninakan first. Will the train wait there for a while?"

"Just three quarters of an hour, I'm afraid."

"That'll be fine."

"You can't be a minute late, you understand? The train won't wait. You'll have to buy an entirely new ticket from there if you miss it."

"Sure. Sure."

"Good, I just want to be certain. I know how big men sometimes believe the rules will bend to suit them. But you seem to have the heart of a much smaller man. I mean that as a compliment."

"I'd like to be alone now, thanks."

"Certainly. Long journey ahead of you, seems like. Between us fellow Armenians, I must say I don't know why you'd go to Kars. Like a graveyard, that whole city. I once visited when I first started working this line. Never again will I get off this train in that place. A graveyard, the whole city. I swear, the people there pretend Armenians never existed. It's quite surreal. You can see that some of the building blocks of post offices and cafés are actually old headstones. Literally stolen from graveyards that no longer exist. I was eating a meal outside a café and I saw it—the faint etchings of an Armenian name and dates. Upside down. Those headstones are just rocks now. I pointed it out to my waiter, and he turned cold. Didn't even return with the check. I swear, the people are nice until you ask about those stones, those etchings in the stones. Then they shut off, like you're a phantom they've lost the ability to see or hear. Just shut off, that's what happened to me. I'll never step foot in that city again. A graveyard, the whole place. Much happier to be on this train. Can't move without me, so no one can tell me I don't exist. And yet you're going there. To Kars, huh?"

"Not for long," Avo said, feeling the need to explain. "From there I'm going farther west, and south. To Mersin. And then to America."

"Wow, quite the journey. I've heard it's beautiful. Mersin, I mean. The sea and the chapel for Saint Paul. And maybe the Turks there are more honest about the past than they are in Kars. I don't know. More openhearted?"

"Maybe."

"And America? I've heard stories, of course, but never been. Do you know it?"

Avo took back his ticket and repacked his valise. He was heading to Mersin for a last favor. His papers were only a diplomat's passport between Turkey and the USSR; in order to fly back to the U.S., he'd need one final forgery from Kami. He said, "Everything you've heard is true, everything you've heard is false."

At the stop in Leninakan, he'd planned to drop in on his old boss from the factory, but the shorter-than-expected delay on the rails didn't leave enough time to travel across the city and back. So instead of hailing a cab across town, Avo took the short walk down the steps from the train station, down Ghandilyan Street, which he remembered vaguely from his childhood except for the cemetery, which he remembered in great detail, just south of the train station.

Some of the graves were marked by monuments, enormous headstones engraved with the faces of their treasures and long paragraphs of achievements. But most of the graves were simple flat plaques in the ground, dark absences of grass, maybe the size of glossy magazines. Among these flat stones, in the shadows of marble angels and columns, lay his parents. How much of them? Not much. Charred bodies if bodies at all. He knelt at their headstones, at their names.

One night at a bar in Ypsilanti, Michigan, he'd broken up a fight. Max Ravage, a fellow wrestler who wore orange face and body paint, had refused to take off the paint before going to the bar. He'd become the butt of the locals' jokes. He never told Avo his real name, and had grown to believe, as his character did, that the orange paint on his body was the source of his strength. More likely sources—large quantities of cocaine and amphetamines, for instance—failed him that night in Ypsilanti, because as Avo went to help him, Max Ravage was being ravaged.

After the bar cleared out, Angel Hair met Avo at the bar, bought him a beer, and issued a warning. "That right there—when a guy loses sight of the line between his real life and the role he's playing—we call that *living the gimmick*. Most dangerous thing in the world, my friend, to become a mark for yourself. Don't let it be you."

After boarding the train again, Avo began writing a poem in his notebook. It would be a long poem, he thought, about all the gimmicks he'd tricked himself into living, and all the rest he couldn't wait to try.

It seemed impossible that the train would pick up momentum again, but it happened, slowly, heading southwest through the countryside toward the border. There, Avo felt another grinding trundle to a stop. Out the window, he could see parts of the machinery that made up the checkpoint: a barbed wire fence stretching into the horizon; a collection of military vehicles parked at different angles; a few green-capped patrolmen ambling along the tracks. Finally, two of the patrolmen, one led by a leashed dog, came through the train, checking papers.

Avo emptied his valise a second time, and the dog sniffed its contents.

The gendarmes—Avo couldn't help thinking of the patrolmen this way—took turns examining his documents. One of the gendarmes was old, and the other was young. They spoke in Turkish, which Avo had never learned. While the old one had his eyes on the papers, the young one seemed to be sizing Avo up as if estimating his vitals. He seemed nervous, this young, fat Turk, almost charmingly so, like the marks who waited in the parking lots for autographs. The Turk craned to look over the papers in his partner's hands. Avo caught a flash, beneath the jacket flap at the patrolman's hip, of his gun.

At last the old gendarme returned his papers and led the dog away. The young one lingered for an awkward beat, which no one but Avo seemed to notice. Then the gendarmes moved on to the next car, and Avo put away his things again, thanking Kami under his breath for the quality of her forgeries.

The train was set to start again, and all the sounds of life seemed caught in its gears. What a relief to hear them.

He slept the fifty kilometers to Kars, the end of the line. He could've—should've—switched trains, bought another ticket, kept going west without a pause. But the conductor's description of the city as an Armenian graveyard had sparked his curiosity. Plus, he could use the rest. He had a long journey ahead of him through eastern Turkey, through what used to be Armenia. From Mersin, he would return to America and live the rest of his life there. What was the harm in spending one night in the old, old country?

He found a small, cheap hotel. The Turkish clerk did his best to accommodate him despite the barriers in language. He even offered a few Armenian words, which Avo accepted as an act of kindness if not a kind of apology, the closest he'd ever get. He thanked the clerk and went to his room.

He showered. He opened a map on the bed. The size of the world, it just—amazes.

In the lobby, he asked the friendly clerk for a recommendation for dinner. He mimed a spoon and bowl, and the stranger laughed like an old friend.

From there he followed the hand-drawn map to an outdoor bistro called Kedi ve Köpek Kafe. The food was like Ruben's mother's cooking. The waiter must've pitied his scar, because he brought over extra desserts. Baklava, rolled into scrunched and honeyed tubes the way his mother had made it. Free of charge. Avo licked his fingers clean. He had hardly any money to spare, but he left a tip. It was the most American thing he'd done since leaving. It was practice for what he would become.

He imagined and savored Ruben's ire. Free money to a Turk. Payment to the indebted. Not the act of a real Armenian.

A stone building in the distance caught his attention, reminding him of the conductor's story. Avo went there and followed the perimeter of the building, looking for Armenian letters in the stones. He found some etchings here and there—nothing clear enough to read—except here, maybe, along this alley, this little gulf between buildings.

And just as he said the name of his brother—his cousin's cousin—Ruben himself materialized. No—it was someone who looked a bit like him, small and peering around the corner of the building made of stone. The man's leer was different than the passing stares of the earlier strangers in the street. Less curious. As if he had seen Avo before.

He had. Avo hadn't recognized him without the green cap or the dog on the leash. But the young Turk with the fat face certainly recognized him. He'd left the dog at the border and taken the train just after his final rounds. He'd followed the tall Armenian with suspicious papers from the train station to the hotel to the bistro to here, this deserted alleyway not five blocks from the young Turk's home in Kars.

"What are you doing?" he asked, but Avo didn't speak his language.

"Do you speak English?" Avo tried.

"It looks suspicious," the Turk continued, "rooting around in the dark."

"I don't understand. Do you speak Russian?"

"I'm placing you under arrest," the young Turk said, and removed and displayed his badge.

"I'm a visitor," Avo said, raising his hands. "I'm a visitor. I'm going back to my hotel now."

Behind him in the alley was a wall so high not even he could scale it. He kept his hands shown as he stepped slowly toward the Turk.

"Don't move any closer," the gendarme said. He pulled his jacket aside to show off his gun.

Avo stopped. He said, "I only came down this way to see the stones, bro. I heard there was history in the stones."

"You think you're a big man, you don't have to follow the rules. No respect for my country."

"I don't understand you."

"Your papers are forged. My superior bought it, but not me. He told me to go home. But I knew you'd be up to something suspicious. Inspecting the security of the buildings."

"Bro, I'm just going to move past you very slow, okay?"

"In the news all the time. You Armenians. I won't let you hurt my family, my country. I won't let that happen, you understand?"

Avo understood the word *Armenian* and the poisonous way it was said. There was no talking his way out of this.

"I'm going to sit down," he said. "I'm going to lie flat on the ground, so you can check and see, bro. I'm not armed."

But as soon as he went to bend over, his stomach exploded into pain. Crushing, the greatest he'd felt. There was no way to explain it other than to say it couldn't possibly have happened all at once. The pain was too vast. It must've been growing, that pain, for many years, for longer than he'd even been alive.

The young Turk took several quick steps closer before shooting again.

25

King County, Washington, 1989

It's November, and I'm home.

I'm expecting a visit today from the local chapter of the Audubon Society. I've agreed to turn the old breeding stables into a residential bird sanctuary, thanks to a compromise with the chapter's community engagement manager. Consultations happen today, with construction slated to begin next month. By the spring, we should be ready for all kinds of birds—thrushes and swallows and some I can't begin to name.

I never did make it to that bungalow of Johnny Trumpet's, though I got close. I took Mina home, where I confessed to her what I'd done to The Brow Beater. In the clearest English she'd ever spoken, she told me to leave. I did. I spent the night in my truck near the jewelry store, and climbed the stucco steps early Thursday morning to explain my disappearance to Valantin, to apologize, and to pick up Fuji. But as I talked to Valantin, her aunt took a seat near the window, rocking Fuji in her arms. She had her eyes closed under a square of sunlight falling through the pane, letting it warm her face, and Fuji was in the light, too. At one point, without opening her eyes, the old walnut pressed her lips against the top of Fuji's head, all fluff and lavender from the bath she'd given him. Fuji—my oldest. A companion through and through. He was loved, and he was warm in the old walnut's arms, and warm in the square of light, and I asked if she'd keep him and care for him, and she said, in her language, that she would.

From there I drove east into the desert for a hundred and fifty miles and parked on the side of the road in the shade of a brambling patch of Joshua trees. About half a mile down the road, I saw Johnny Trumpet's bungalow, its yellow deck like a blade on the horizon.

When I was in Tucson, living the gimmick with Joyce, holding on to a fiction that seemed to keep my brother alive but in actual fact degraded him again and again, Johnny Trumpet had taken my call. No one else in the business had been willing to give me another run as a manager. Only Johnny Trumpet believed in me enough to bring me back onboard. I would always be grateful to him for that, but I knew now that I didn't owe him more than gratitude.

So, after finally arriving at his bungalow, with hardly any time at all to spare, I put the truck in drive. I kept the wheels straight, heading even farther east.

At the jewelry store, Valantin had brought out a first-aid kit to patch up my face. As she rubbed hydrogen peroxide into my wounds, she caught me focusing on one jewelry case in particular. "Every time you've come in here," she said, "you've eyed those lapis lazuli earrings."

I told her they reminded me of a girl I used to know. "A girl I should've apologized to a long time ago."

"Have them," Valantin said, and when I asked if she was sure, she said, "A fair trade for the cat."

I left Johnny Trumpet's bungalow in the desert and drove with the earrings clutched to my heart all the way to Tucson. The adobe house looked just as I'd remembered it, rockscape in the yard and a hand-painted signboard ("Joyce's Geotherapy") pitched near the door.

She must've seen me in the window, because I didn't get to ring the bell. She came to meet me outside.

I gave her the earrings. She rolled them between her fingers and then tossed them into the rocks.

I said, "Business is that good, huh?"

"They're fakes. Whoever sold them to you ripped you right off."

"I deserve it, I suppose."

"What do you want, Terry?"

Now that she was older, I could see how beautiful she was. She was my sister. "You're the last one who knew him," I said. "That's all."

"Gilbert?" she said. "He's still around."

She invited me inside and made us tea. All evening we traded stories about Gil. I'd like to say we laughed so hard we cried and cried so hard we had to laugh, but the truth is we just remembered him, and that can be a quiet thing, too.

When she walked me out at the end of the night, she tiptoed barefoot along the rocks to retrieve the earrings. It took us twenty minutes to find them, but there they were, blue and silver as the dust between stars. She put them on as I was getting into the truck. Fake or not, they sure did shine her up.

In the end, I'm drawn back to one memory in particular, the time I followed The Brow Beater to the center of the earth. After a long stretch on the eastern seaboard, we'd looped back toward the Southwest. He was in the passenger seat, folded in on himself and breathing on his knees. Out the windows, we couldn't see a thing but the whole country ambling past, every plot of land a home that wasn't ours yet. After whole days spent flickering past hypnotizing rows of soybean and corn, we were kicking up dust in the desert. Countless acres of sediment and sagebrush surrounded us, and every now and then, a mesa lifted the horizon like a nail pried out of a floorboard. In the distance, a mountain range appeared in blue and gray arrowheads.

Arrowheads—I'd watched The Brow Beater reach into his red fanny pack to pay for a few of them at a roadside boutique in Santa Fe, New Mexico. A woman with hair that reached her shoes explained the whole crime of westward expansion in just under fourteen minutes. She gave him a good price on those arrowheads, told him loud enough so I could hear that she'd charged him less than she did the white folks who stopped by. A little tax she collected, penny by penny, that might in a trillion years make a dent in the debt that's owed.

This was just before the caverns in Carlsbad. The Brow Beater had read about them in a book. I veered off the highway and up a winding crest. From the parking lot, I followed him to the mouth of an enormous cave. "Finally," I said, "an entrance big enough for your giant ass."

Together we went in. We looked back out at the pinhole of light through which we'd come.

Then it was just darkness, and descending, descending. Strangely, ahead and below became synonymous. We made our way by the dim orange bulbs placed periodically along the railings. The path spiraled deeper. The air, cool and damp, pressed us along. Great formations reached like fingers from the ceiling and the floor, desperate to touch. The top fingers dripped, and the bottom fingers collected, and in that way, they spent eternity growing closer. Some ancient pairs touched tip to tip, and a few had spent so many lifetimes reaching that they'd become single luminous columns. We continued on, descending for what felt like forever and which, in a way, was. A bolted placard claimed that every step down the sloping path was a step backward in time. The thought was an unnerving and thrilling one. What secret origin story lay waiting for us at the bottom? The absurd idea occurred to me that my brother might be waiting for me at the bottom of the trail, that we'd reversed the arrow of time, that a person from my past had come back to meet me at this point in my journey, just as the stalagmites and stalactites did their dripping and reaching, that the people we called family could come from the other side to take us home again.

But when we arrived at the bottom, the truth seemed even more absurd than the fantasy I'd conjured up. The truth was that, at the center of the earth, there lived a little gift shop. I held a T-shirt against my chest, checking the size, and The Brow Beater rested against the commonest blue postal box. There was even a bathroom, which I used, and I came back wearing my new shirt. "You're not going to buy anything?" I said, and The Brow Beater ignored me. He was turning a squeaky rack of postcards. Eventually, he did buy one, along with a stamp. He scribbled an address with so much confidence, I figured it was his own home. The rest of the message he wrote mostly in that language I hadn't seen since the chalkboard at The Gutshot. I wrote a postcard, too, and we dropped our messages into the mailbox. Then we took an elevator up and out of the planet, and lingered near the parking lot until dusk, when, according to the image on the postcards we'd just purchased, something miraculous was scheduled to happen. Sure enough, as the sun began to set, a group of park rangers lined everybody up outside the big mouth of the main cavern. Just as the sun slipped behind the mountains, there came the bats. Countless thousands of them, shooting like streamers from the big mouth into the red and ocher sky. Worth a million miles crammed into a car too small, breathing on your knees. Worth surviving it all to see. "It's like art," The Brow Beater said, "but real."

Now it's November, and I'm done driving. Now I know they're not out there on the road, my brothers. Not on a fishing boat near the Greek or Aleutian islands, not among the marbled dust of an heirloom boutique on the southern coast of Turkey, not in the polylingual boroughs of American cities, not buried in the sea between Hungnam and Wonsan, or in the locker rooms of New York or Atlanta or the shunted scraps of the territories. I know that in order to find them, I'll have to go in. Into the bat-beaten caverns of the heart, into the endless drips and pools of history, into the pressing rib cage of the earth. Inside, I'll find them—right there in the center, present, waiting for me.

In the meantime, I'll wait for the birds and watch the news. Just now, the wall is coming down. The evil empire is fading. We who have believed all along in the story of our march will be vindicated. The future will be kind to us because we were right. We were free. We were not marks. There will be no fooling us now.

26

Kirovakan, Soviet Armenia, 1988–present

Just last spring in Kirovakan, during a silver hour of peace from the rain, a crowd of people filled the station. They wore their children on their shoulders, peering down the tracks. Birds bathed in the still pools between the crossties, their chirrups giving way to the thrumming din of a far-off, approaching thing. Stillness in the puddles gave way to quivers. The train was coming. Whistling like a reed. Hollering. The crowd hollered, too—some cheering, some hissing. They lifted what they'd brought—sweets in their hands, or baskets of fruit, or signs saying "SHAME," or signs saying "THANKS."

At the airport in Zvartnots an hour earlier, a delegation including his parents and the first secretary of Soviet Armenia himself, Karen Demirchyan, greeted him with an honorary pen. A gift for writing the truth, he said, in the pages of world history. Ruben gave the pen to his father. On the train, his mother asked after Avo, and Ruben buried himself in her neck, in her arms, like a boy. His father sat beside them, turning the pen in his hands.

Getting off the train, waving ceremoniously, stepping arm in arm with his parents, Ruben found it impossible to tell apart the faces in the crowd or their attitudes, which particular people were present at all. He fell into the car with the baskets of apples and pomegranates, a paper bag of homemade cards and sugar cookies and honeyed bars and the bottles of wine the driver loaded in the trunk and in their laps. And they went up and back and around the muddy road to the village, all sludge and muck, up and back to his childhood home, where the chickens were gone, and he slept and slept and slept.

It was impossible to say who'd been at the station and who hadn't. Ruben remembered it alternately as a crowd full of strangers and as an assembled collection of every person he'd ever known, living or dead. But as the weeks went on, as the gifts and curses sent to his home in the village began to arrive less and less frequently, as his dates in the city to meet with officials, to dine with people who called themselves old friends—Mr. V, one night, and a father of six who'd once kicked gravel into his face—came and went, as he ventured into the city square less often, finally only to collect the monthly stipend for his honorary position as Kirovakan cultural watchman, he was convinced that one person in particular had not been in attendance at his return. In fact, she seemed to be totally avoiding him.

Where was she, Mina? At first it seemed inevitable that they would speak, that she would invite him to dinner as everyone else had, that her husband would conduct some business with him at the census bureau. And yet she'd made no contact, none whatsoever, not even when Ruben thought he spotted her on the steps of the city hall, affixing a golden pin to her husband's lapel, when their eyes caught just the way they had at the wedding years earlier. But Mina—he wasn't sure if it was her—didn't wave hello. She turned and guided her husband into the bureau. He knew then they'd never speak again, that she was in denial that he'd returned at all, that he'd been erased in prison or elsewhere, stabbed to death or hanged, or simply lost to history and gone.

His monthly visits to the city square went on without ever seeing her again, and every now and then someone from his childhood would ask, "What about that big tall friend of yours," or, "Whatever happened to that brother of yours with the eyebrow," and Ruben started avoiding them, too, sending his father to the city square to collect his checks. Even up in the village, the neighbors began to avoid him, and the time he spent at home with his parents grew heavy and thick, and time felt less like an arrow than it had in the past and more like a block with depth and weight, and those in the village who spotted him feeding the goats or helping the dogs unbury bones began to whisper together about how ill he looked, how young and frail, like a little boy, tiny and weak and sometimes even curled in his mother's arms. Others disagreed. He looked elderly, they thought, infirm and shriveled but for his enormous eyes, which beamed from behind his glasses. No one could quite remember his real age. And when the fights raged on between his parents in the night, they roared through the village, and the father said his son was broken, and he blamed the mother's coddling, and the mother screamed and pointed to the father's drinking, and the neighbors shut their windows and cowered their heads into blankets and pillows until at last a child gathered her courage to shout, from a window near the dogs, "You're both to blame, now go to sleep!"

And so he was—asleep—when it happened. When God seized him by the shoulders and shook him awake. Twenty seconds on the morning of December 7, 1988. That's all it took. Twenty of the thickest seconds in history, when the devil rattled Armenia like dice in his hand, when every Brezhnev-era building from Leninakan to

Kirovakan crumbled as swiftly as old men in the sea, when fifty thousand people were killed or buried and lost, when the animals clambered over the ruins of villages and cities alike, when the graveyards split open like wounds, when the body parts of corpses new and old were scattered on sheets of slate and steel, when hell arrived again in Armenia—Ruben was asleep. He thought he was dreaming. Mother with the gash in her head.

Father bent over her, mud on his face and crying. Dreaming. Ruben wound down the path to join the digging. Mudslides trapping children, burying the old. He went on digging in that mud. All that sludge and muck, hoping and worrying that a hand might pull him under.

Broken. It was his father's word. *All that coddling and now he's broken*. Now the city was, too. There wasn't a building left standing unscathed. Not even the tallest.

The dice had rolled her way more often than not, and mosquitoes never bit her, and her arranged marriage had led to real love, but her building, the tallest in the city, had come down just like the rest.

He couldn't say if she'd survived or not, but he dreamed of pulling her out of the rubble, the lucky one. The farthest he could get, though, was the city square, and as his father fell deeper into his drunkenness, Ruben began to stay there, outdoors, near where the statue of Kirov in his defiance kept standing. Kirov's bronze head had split in half like an apple, but he had not fallen. Ruben began to sleep there even in the rain, and if his father died, he wouldn't know it, because Ruben hardly remembered him.

And who remembered him, Ruben Petrosian? Hero with a pen. Cultural watchman. No one. He was just another bum in the broken streets, another thing displaced and unrecognizable. Still, he hoped she might remember him, that if anyone could remember who he really was, it would be her, the lucky one.

One morning before sunrise, he gathered himself and combed down his rain-soaked beard, slicked back his grown-out hair, adjusted on his nose the frames without lenses, and he went there, to the rubble that used to be the tallest building in Kirovakan. A year had passed, and the mess was just as bad. He climbed up the stones like a pristine stairwell and imagined he was standing on the roof. Eventually, he thought, she would join him there. In the meantime, he leaned against a jutting wall and watched the sun rise through the slashing rain. All that devastation at once. The whole world as broken as he was. The sun rose and rose, nothing so glorious as the April dawn he'd witnessed in Palaio Faliro, in those narrow hours between prison and home. Who had taken the credit? The PLO, certainly, and Turkish agents, no doubt. The Israelis, in retaliation for Hagopian's early role in Munich. Even ASALA itself had been suspected, the final push for new leadership under Monte Melkonian. But Ruben knew the truth. It had been half past four in the morning. Early dawn. Hagopian was out on the street, a piece of luggage at his feet, waiting for a taxi. Ruben had broken into the khash restaurant and stolen old Hayk's gun from the kitchen. What had Ruben said to Hagopian before shooting? Something about his friend. The tall one. The giant. He had said his name and then shot and then run. The sunrise kissing the Mediterranean. Everybody took credit for killing Hagopian, so no one would know the truth. Ruben, standing over the ruins of Kirovakan, laughed. Nothing maniacal, just a brief, incredulous snort. He couldn't help it. It was funny. To know a fact of history that nobody else would ever know. It was funny.

As for what he'd say to the lucky one when she joined him on the tumbled roof, he had time. Maybe she had left the city, the country, before the earthquake. She had a child, maybe, and he envied her that—not because of her luck but because, although he'd seen the world, she'd made one of her own. He wanted to explain to her, wanted to tell her all of his memories so he could sort out which were true and which were fiction. Finally, he decided to leave the rubble and return again tomorrow, when he'd come up with someplace to start explaining, but tomorrow came and he didn't know how to explain himself then, either, and he slept under the statue of Kirov in the square.

Funny. If anyone wanted to know who'd killed Hagop Hagopian, all he had to do was witness the change in attitude of one little bespectacled man in Kirovakan. All his life, he'd been serious and stern and unwelcome to joy. But now he'd completely changed. He lived in the streets, but that didn't seem to bother him. He was endlessly, genuinely cheerful. He enjoyed tipping the empty frames of his glasses to people in the streets as a way to say hello, and he had loud, funny conversations with the broken statue of Kirov in the square, a habit that became a kind of ritual for the city, and people began to take their children to watch him with the statue, a kind of puppet show, a performance, with stories and jokes that seemed to arrive from the different corners of the world, cheerful anecdotes about what all nations had in common, and people would toss coins into a hat for him, or bring food and sweets to feed him, and even after the Soviets fell, when Armenia gained independence, when Kirovakan scrubbed itself of the name of that old Soviet guard and leveled the statue of him in bronze, even then, that little man with the glasses went on performing, speaking to the birds in the trees or the cats dipping their noses into the fountain for a drink. And when people asked him if he'd always lived out in the rain, or when people asked him for his name, he seemed perfectly unable to remember. The only person who might have reminded him had taken her family to live under the promise of a thousand points of light. And what would he have said to her, anyway? He was too happy to continue his eccentric strolls through the city, pretending to be in control of the lamps and the streetlights that zapped on and off at random, now that the natural gas and oil from Russia had been cut off, now that independence meant a landlocked homestead surrounded by ancient enemies. Long stretches of powerlessness came over the city, and winters were impossible, but oh God were they free. Free as that little man in his glasses, smiling and laughing and waltzing through the city, covering his head in a scarf, saying bits of nonsense to the birds and the lamps: Nothing phony about me, said the real one. Nothing real about me, said the fake.

Acknowledgments

For the gift of time, space, and money—or some lucky combination of the three—I'm grateful to the Zell Fellowship at the University of Michigan, the Ucross Foundation in Wyoming, and the Andreas Faculty Grant provided by Minnesota State University, Mankato. The grant allowed me to visit Armenia, where my beloved aunt, Madlena mokor, joined me as a guide and translator, and I'm forever thankful to her and to my new Armenian friends for their hospitality and generosity. Շնորհակալություն.

My agent, Julia Kardon, sharpened this novel beyond measure and cannot be outhustled. To be able to count on her belief and her tenacity is a boundless privilege. And to land at Harper is dream enough, but to score the extra luck of working alongside Mary Gaule seems cosmically unfair. Her support means more to me than she knows, and her work—editing this novel from the inside out, with empathy and artistry—shows on every page. To the rest of the team at Harper who helped to make this book real, especially the tireless copy editors and designers: thank you so much.

For my understanding of the historical fact of the Armenian Genocide and the global legacy of its denial, I'm indebted to a long list of scholars and writers, including Ronald Grigor Suny, Michael J. Arlen, Eugene Rogan, Meline Toumani, Carol Edgarian, Taner Akçam, and Peter Balakian. I'm also forever grateful to my extended family—the Kantzabedians, the Manukyans, the Aprahamians, the Lusparyans, the Sarkissians, the Artsrunis, and the Aminian Baghais—for the stories and the love.

Thank you to David Shoemaker, Thomas Hackett, and Tim Hornbaker for their lively and informative histories of professional wrestling, and to Kayfabe Commentaries and The Hannibal TV for their productions of shoot interviews with wrestlers from the territory days.

Endless thanks to all my teachers, colleagues, and students.

I owe so much to readers of this novel in its earliest stages. Brit Bennett: winning big at a craps table with you was nothing compared to the luck I've had in counting you as a friend and sister. Johannes Lichtman: your smarts and your jokes make me forget my distaste for phone calls. Thank you both for your mindful time.

Thank you to Derrick Austin, Ezra Carlsen, Dan Hornsby, Matt Robison, Jia Tolentino, and Maya West. What luck to call you brilliant writers my people.

Jenna Meacham, for all the years and all the art: thank you. Tim Longtin, for those long Michigan nights, which I miss dearly: thank you. Adam and Shelby Smith, your friendship sustains me all the way from the ocean. Andrew Daley and Andy Henderson, thank you both for watching wrestling, talking wrestling, and spearing me through a door that one time. Research!

My parents deserve more space for gratitude than this page will allow. I'll be thanking them for it all, always and always. Same goes for my sister, Madelein, who set the bar so high all my life. I'm lucky to be in her shadow.

Finally, thank you to Mairead Small Staid, my found one, and the countless trillion coincidences that led us together. You worked on this book as if it were your own, a fact I'll publicly emphasize if the reviews are bad. The truth is I couldn't have invented this story if I weren't in love with you. In that way it is—yours.

About the Author

Chris McCormick is the author of a collection of stories, *Desert Boys*, the recipient of the 2017 Stonewall Book Award. Born in 1987 and raised on the California side of the Mojave Desert, he now lives and teaches in Minnesota.